Praise for Delores Fossen

"The perfect blend of sexy cowboys, humor and romance will rein you in from the first line."
—*New York Times* bestselling author B.J. Daniels

"From the shocking opening paragraph on, Fossen's tale just keeps getting better."
—*RT Book Reviews* on *Sawyer*, 4½ stars, Top Pick

"*Rustling Up Trouble* is action packed, but it's the relationship and emotional drama (and the sexy hero) that will reel readers in."
—*RT Book Reviews*, 4½ stars

"While not lacking in action or intrigue, it's the romance of two unlikely people that soars."
—*RT Book Reviews* on *Maverick Sheriff*, 4 stars

DELORES FOSSEN

BLAME IT ON THE COWBOY

HQN™

HQN™

ISBN-13: 978-0-373-78963-4

Recycling programs for this product may not exist in your area.

Blame It on the Cowboy

CONTENTS

BLAME IT ON
THE COWBOY

CHAPTER ONE

Logan McCord hated two things: clowns and liars. Tonight, he saw both right in front of him on the antique desk in Langford's Interior Designs, and he knew his life had changed forever. He would *never* look at a red squeaky nose the same way again.

Ten minutes earlier

Logan glanced at the four signs and groaned.

Marry
Me?
You
Will

It was not the way he wanted to present this proposal to his future wife.

His younger brother, Riley, was carrying the You. His twin brother, Lucky, the Will. Riley's wife, Claire, the Marry. Lucky's girlfriend, Cassie, the Me?

"Unless I want this proposal to sound like Yoda, switch places," Logan insisted.

Since everyone but Logan had clearly had too much to drink in the precelebration prep for this occasion, he took them by the shoulders and one by one put them in the right places.

Lucky. Riley. Claire. Cassie.

"Will you marry me?" Logan double-checked. Then he checked again.

Logan wanted this to be perfect while still feeling a little spontaneous. Just the day before, his longtime girlfriend, Helene Langford, had told him he should be a little more whimsical.

Somewhat wild, even.

Logan was certain most people in their small hometown of Spring Hill, Texas, wouldn't consider him wild even when the expectations were lowered with that *somewhat*. That was his twin brother Lucky's specialty. Still, if Helene wanted something whimsical, then this marriage proposal should do it.

Helene was perfect for him. A savvy businesswoman, beautiful, smart, and her even temperament made her easy to get along with. She'd never once complained about his frequent seventy-hour workweeks, and he could count on one hand how many disagreements they'd had.

She was the only child of state senator Edwin Langford and a former Miss Texas beauty contestant. Her family loved him, and Logan was pretty sure his own family felt the same way about her.

"You got the ring?" Lucky whispered. Or rather, tried to whisper.

Yeah, his siblings, sibling-in-law and future sibling-in-law were buzzed on champagne, all in the name of celebrating the fact that he was finally going to pop the question to the woman he'd been dating all these years.

Logan double-checked the ring. The blue Tiffany box was in his jacket pocket. It was perfect, as well. A two-carat diamond—flawless like Helene—with a platinum setting. It would look just right on the hand of the woman who would eventually help him run Mc-Cord Cattle Brokers.

He took another bottle of chilled champagne from his car. This one he would share with his future bride right after she said yes, and he'd do that sharing without his family around. He wanted to get Helene alone, maybe show her just how spontaneous he could be by having sex with her on her pricey antique desk. The very one she had professionally polished every week.

"All right, no talking once we're inside," Logan reminded them. "No giggling, either," he warned Claire.

It was dark, after closing hours, and any chatter or giggling would immediately carry through the building and all the way to Helene's office in the back of her interior design business. He wouldn't have to worry about other customers, though, since it was Wednesday, the night that Helene used to catch up on paperwork.

Logan eased his key into the lock, turning it slowly so that Helene wouldn't be alerted to the clicking sound. He gave the sign crew one last stern look to keep quiet, and they all tiptoed toward the back. Well, they tiptoed as much as four drunk people could manage, but he wouldn't have to put up with their drunken giddiness much longer. Logan had already arranged for the town's only taxi driver to pick them up in fifteen minutes.

Leading the way, Logan headed to Helene's office. The door was already cracked so he pushed it open, motioning for the others to go ahead of him and get ready to spring into action. They did. Lucky. Riley. Claire. Cassie. All in the correct order, but what they didn't do was hold up their signs. That's because they froze.

All of them.

They stood there, signs frozen in their hands, too.

Logan's stomach went to his knees, and in the split second that followed, he tried to figure out what would have caused them to react like that.

Hell.

If Helene had been hurt, at least one of them would have rushed to check on her, but there was no rushing. Even though it was hard to wrap his mind around it, the freezing could mean they'd just walked in on Helene doing something bad.

Like maybe she was with another man.

She couldn't be, though. Helene had never given him any reason whatsoever not to trust her. Ditto for giving him any reason whatsoever to believe she was unhappy. Just an hour earlier she'd called Logan to tell him she loved him.

Riley looked back at Logan, shaking his head. "Uh, you don't want to see this," Riley insisted.

But Logan did. He had to see it. Because there was nothing in the room that was worse than what he was already imagining.

Or so he thought.

However, Logan was wrong. It was worse. *Much, much* worse.

CHAPTER TWO

LIARS AND CLOWNS. Logan had seen both tonight. The liar was a woman he thought loved him. Helene. And the clown, well, Logan wasn't sure he could process that image just yet.

Maybe after lots of booze, though.

He hadn't been drunk since his twenty-first birthday nearly thirteen years ago. But he was about to remedy that now. He motioned for the bartender to set him up with another pair of Glenlivet shots.

His phone buzzed again, indicating another call had just gone to voice mail. One of his siblings no doubt wanting to make sure he was all right. He wasn't. But talking to them about it wouldn't help, and Logan didn't want anyone he knew to see or hear him like this.

It was possible there'd be some slurring involved. Puking, too.

He'd never been sure what to call Helene. His long-time girlfriend? *Girlfriend* seemed too high school. So, he'd toyed with thinking of her as his future fiancée. Or in social situations—she was his business associate who often ran his marketing campaigns. But tonight Logan wasn't calling her any of those things. As far as he was concerned, he never wanted to think of her, her name or what to call her again.

Too bad that image of her was stuck in his head, but

that's where he was hoping generous amounts of single malt Scotch would help.

Even though Riley, Claire, Lucky and Cassie wouldn't breathe a word about this, it would still get around town. Logan wasn't sure how, but gossip seemed to defy the time-space continuum in Spring Hill. People would soon know, if they didn't already, and those same people would never look at him the same way again. It would hurt business.

Hell. It hurt *him*.

That's why he was here in this hotel bar in San Antonio. It was only thirty miles from Spring Hill, but tonight he hoped it'd be far enough away that no one he knew would see him get drunk. Then he could stagger to his room and puke in peace. Not that he was looking forward to the puking part, but it would give him something else to think about other than *her*.

It was his first time in this hotel, though he stayed in San Antonio often on business. Logan hadn't wanted to risk running into anyone he knew, and he certainly wouldn't at this trendy "boutique" place. Not with a name like the Purple Cactus and its vegan restaurant.

If the staff found out he was a cattle broker, he might be booted out. Or forced to eat tofu. That's the reason Logan had used cash when he checked in. No sense risking someone recognizing his name from his credit card.

The clerk had seemed skeptical when Logan had told him that his ID and credit cards had been stolen and that's why he couldn't produce anything with his name on it. Of course, when Logan had slipped the guy an extra hundred dollar bill, it had caused that doubt to disappear.

"Drinking your troubles away?" a woman asked.

"Trying."

Though he wasn't drunk enough that he couldn't see what was waiting for him at the end of this. A hangover, a missed 8:00 a.m. meeting, his family worried about him—the puking—and it wouldn't fix anything other than to give him a couple hours of mind-numbing solace.

At the moment, though, mind-numbing solace even if it was temporary seemed like a good trade-off.

"Me, too," she said. "Drinking my troubles away."

Judging from the sultry tone in her voice, Logan first thought she might be a prostitute, but then he got a look at her.

Nope. Not a pro.

Or if she was, she'd done nothing to market herself as such. No low-cut dress to show her cleavage. She had on a T-shirt with cartoon turtles on the front, a baggy white skirt and flip-flops. It looked as if she'd grabbed the first items of clothing she could find off a very cluttered floor of her very cluttered apartment.

Logan wasn't into clutter.

And he'd thought Helene wasn't, either. He'd been wrong about that, too. That antique desk of hers had been plenty cluttered with a clown's bare ass.

"Mind if I join you?" Miss Turtle-shirt said. "I'm having sort of a going-away party."

She waited until Logan mumbled, "Suit yourself," and she slid onto the purple bar stool next to him.

She smelled like limes.

Her hair was varying shades of pink and looked as if it'd been cut with a weed whacker. It was already messy, but apparently it wasn't messy enough for her because she dragged her hand through it, pushing it away from her face.

"Tequila, top shelf. Four shots and a bowl of lime slices," she told the bartender.

Apparently, he wasn't the only person in San Antonio with plans to get shit-faced tonight. And it explained the lime scent. These clearly weren't her first shots of the night.

"Do me a favor, though," she said to Logan after he downed his next drink. "Don't ask my name, or anything personal about me, and I'll do the same for you."

Logan had probably never agreed to anything so fast in all his life. For one thing he really didn't want to spend time talking with this woman, and he especially didn't want to talk about what'd happened.

"If you feel the need to call me something, go with Julia," she added.

The name definitely wasn't a fit. He was expecting something more like Apple or Sunshine. Still, he didn't care what she called herself. Didn't care what her real name was, either, and he cared even less after his next shot of Glenlivet.

"So, you're a cowboy, huh?" she asked.

The mind-numbing hadn't kicked in yet, but the orneriness had. "That's personal."

She shrugged. "Not really. You're wearing a cowboy hat, cowboy boots and jeans. It was more of an observation than a question."

"The clothes could be fashion statements," he pointed out.

"Julia" shook her head, downed the first shot of tequila, sucked on a lime slice. Made a face and shuddered. "You're not the kind of man to make fashion statements."

If he hadn't had a little buzz going on, he might have been insulted by that. "Unlike you?"

She glanced down at her clothes as if seeing them for the first time. Or maybe she was just trying to focus because the tequila had already gone to her head. "This was the first thing I grabbed off my floor."

Bingo. If that was her first grab, there was no telling how bad the outfits were beneath it.

Julia tossed back her second shot. "Have you ever found out something that changed your whole life?" she asked.

"Yeah." About four hours ago.

"Me, too. Without giving specifics, because that would be personal, did it make you feel as if fate were taking a leak on your head?"

"Four leaks," he grumbled. Logan finished off his next shot.

Julia made a sound of agreement. "I would compare yours with mine, and I'd win, but I don't want to go there. Instead, let's play a drinking game."

"Let's not," he argued. "And in a fate-pissing comparison, I don't think you'd win."

Julia made a sound of disagreement. Had another shot. Grimaced and shuddered again. "So, the game is a word association," she continued as if he'd agreed. "I say a word, you say the first thing that comes to mind. We take turns until we're too drunk to understand what the other one is saying."

Until she'd added that last part, Logan had been about to get up and move to a different spot. But hell, he was getting drunk, anyway, and at least this way he'd

have some company. Company he'd never see again.
Company he might not even be able to speak to if the
slurring went up a notch.

"Dream?" she threw out there.

"Family." That earned him a sound of approval from
her, and she motioned for him to take his turn. "Surprise?"

"Shitty," Julia said without hesitation.

Now it was Logan who made a grunt of approval.
Surprises could indeed be shit-related. The one he'd
gotten tonight certainly had been.

Her: "Tattoos?"

Him: "None." Then, "You?"

Her: "Two." Then, "Bucket list?"

Him: "That's two words." The orneriness was still
there despite the buzz.

Her: "Just bucket, then?"

Too late. Logan's fuzzy mind was already fixed on
the bucket list. He had one all right. Or rather, he'd
had one. A life with Helene that included all the trim-
mings, and this stupid game was a reminder that the
Glenlivet wasn't working nearly fast enough. So, he
had another shot.

Julia had one, as well. "Sex?" she said.

Logan shook his head. "I don't want to play this
game anymore."

When she didn't respond, Logan looked at her. Their
eyes met. Eyes that were already slightly unfocused.

Julia took the paper sleeve with her room key from
her pocket. Except there were two keys, and she slid
one Logan's way.

"It's not the game," she explained. "I'm offering you

sex with me. No names. No strings attached. Just one night, and we'll never tell another soul about it."

She finished off her last tequila shot, shuddered and stood. "Are you game?"

No way, and Logan would have probably said that if she hadn't leaned in and kissed him.

Maybe it was the weird combination of her tequila and his Scotch, or maybe it was because he was already drunker than he thought, but Logan felt himself moving right into that kiss.

LOGAN DREAMED, AND it wasn't about the great sex he'd just had. It was another dream that wasn't so pleasant. The night of his parents' car accident. Some dreams were a mishmash of reality and stuff that didn't make sense. But this dream always got it right.

Not a good thing.

It was like being trapped on a well-oiled hamster wheel, seeing the same thing come up over and over again and not being able to do a thing to stop it.

The dream rain felt and sounded so real. Just like that night. It was coming down so hard that the moment his truck wipers swished it away, the drops covered the windshield again. That's why it'd taken him so long to see the lights, and Logan was practically right on the scene of the wreck before he could fully brake. He went into a skid, costing him precious seconds. If he'd had those seconds, he could have called the ambulance sooner.

He could have saved them.

But he hadn't then. And he didn't now in the dream.

Logan chased away the images, and with his head still groggy, he did what he always did after the nightmare. He rewrote it. He got to his parents and stopped them from dying.

Every time except when it had really mattered, Logan saved them.

LOGAN WISHED HE could shoot out the sun. It was creating lines of light on each side of the curtains, and those lines were somehow managing to stab through his closed eyelids. That was probably because every nerve in his head and especially his eyelids were screaming at him, and anything—including the earth's rotation—added to his pain.

He wanted to ask himself: *What the hell have you done?*

But he knew. He'd had sex with a woman he didn't know. A woman who wore turtle T-shirts and had tattoos. He'd learned one of the tattoos, a rose, was on Julia's right breast. The other was on her lower stomach. Those were the things Logan could actually remember.

That, and the sex.

Not mind-numbing but rather more mind-blowing. Julia clearly didn't have any trouble being wild and spontaneous in bed. It was as if she'd just studied a sex manual and wanted to try every position. Thankfully, despite the Scotch, Logan had been able to keep up—literally.

Not so much now, though.

If the fire alarm had gone off and the flames had been burning his ass, he wasn't sure he would be able to move. Julia didn't have that problem, though. He felt the mattress shift when she got up. Since it was possible she was about to rob him, Logan figured he should at least see if she was going after his wallet, wherever the heck it was. But if she robbed him, he deserved it. His life was on the fast track to hell, and he'd been the one to put it in the handbasket.

At least he hadn't been so drunk that he'd forgotten to use condoms. Condoms that Julia had provided, so obviously she'd been ready for this sort of thing.

Julia made a soft sound of discomfort. He hoped it wasn't from the rough sex because he got a sudden flash of himself tying her hands to the bedposts with the sheets. It'd been Julia's idea.

And it'd been a darn good one.

Ditto for her idea of tying him up, too. He wasn't one to add some kink to sex, but for a little while it had gotten his mind off Helene and what he'd seen in her office.

Clearly, he hadn't known Helene at all.

Logan heard some more stirring around, and this time the movement was very close to him. Just in case Julia turned out to be a serial killer, he decided to risk opening one eye. And he nearly jolted at the big green eyeball staring back at him. Except it wasn't a human eye. It was on her turtle shirt.

If Julia felt the jolt or saw his one-eyed opening, she didn't say anything about it. She gave him a chaste kiss on the cheek, moved away, turning her back to him, and Logan watched as she stooped down and picked up his jacket. So, not a serial killer but rather just a thief, after all. But she didn't take anything out.

She put something *in* the pocket.

Logan couldn't tell what it was exactly. Maybe her number. Which he would toss first chance he got. But if so, he couldn't figure out why she just hadn't left it on the bed.

Julia picked up her purse, hooking it over her shoulder, and without even glancing back at him, she walked out the door. Strange, since this was her room. Maybe she was headed out to get them some coffee. If so, that was his cue to dress and get the devil out of there before she came back.

Easier said than done.

His hair hurt.

He could feel every strand of it on his head. His eyelashes, too. Still, Logan forced himself from the bed, only to realize the soles of his feet hurt, as well. It was hard not to identify something on him that didn't hurt so he quit naming parts and put on his boxers and jeans. Then he had a look at what Julia had put in his pocket next to the box with the engagement ring.

A gold watch.

Not a modern one. It was old with a snap-up top that had a crest design on it. The initials BWS had been engraved in the center of the crest.

The inside looked just as expensive as the gold case except for the fact that the watch face crystal inside was shattered. Even though he knew little about antiques, Logan figured it was worth at least a couple hundred dollars.

So why had Julia put it in his pocket?

Since he was a skeptic, his first thought was that she might be trying to set him up, to make it look as if he'd robbed her. But Logan couldn't imagine why anyone would do that unless she was planning to try to blackmail him with it.

He dropped the watch on the bed and finished dressing, all the while staring at it. He cleared out some of the cotton in his brain and grabbed the hotel phone to call the front desk. Someone answered on the first ring.

"I'm in room…" Logan had to check the phone. "Two-sixteen, and I need to know…" He had to stop again and think. "I need to know if Julia is there in the lobby. She left something in the room."

"No, sir. I'm afraid you just missed her. But checkout isn't until noon, and she said her guest might be staying past then so she paid for an extra day."

"Uh, could you tell me how to spell Julia's last name? I need to leave her a note in case she comes back."

"Oh, she said she wouldn't be coming back, that this was her goodbye party. And as for how to spell her name, well, it's Child, just like it sounds."

Julia Child?

Right. Obviously, the clerk wasn't old enough or enough of a foodie to recognize the name of the famous chef.

"I don't suppose she paid with a credit card?" Logan asked.

"No. She paid in cash and then left a prepaid credit card for the second night."

Of course. "What about an address?" Logan kept trying.

"I'm really not supposed to give that out—"

"She left something very expensive in the room, and I know she'll want it back."

The guy hemmed and hawed a little, but he finally rattled off, "221B Baker Street, London, England."

That was Sherlock Holmes's address.

Logan groaned, cursed. He didn't bother asking for a phone number because the one she left was probably for Hogwarts. He hung up and hurried to the window, hoping he could catch a glimpse of her getting into a car. Not that he intended to follow her or anything, but if she was going to blackmail him, he wanted to know as much about her as possible.

No sign of her, but Logan got a flash of something else. A memory.

Shit.

They'd taken pictures.

Or at least Julia had with the camera on her phone. He remembered nude selfies of them from the waist up. At least he hoped it was from the waist up.

Yeah, that trip to hell in a handbasket was moving even faster right now.

Logan threw on the rest of his clothes, already trying to figure out how to do damage control. He was the CEO of a multimillion-dollar company. He was the face that people put with the family business, and before last night he'd never done a thing to tarnish the image of McCord Cattle Brokers.

He couldn't say that any longer.

He was in such a hurry to rush out the door that he nearly missed the note on the desk. Maybe it was the start of the blackmail. He snatched it up, steeling himself for the worst. But if this was blackmail, then Julia sure had a funny sense of humor.

"Goodbye, hot cowboy," she'd written. "Thanks for the sweet send-off. Don't worry. What happens in San Antonio stays in San Antonio. I'll take this to the grave."

CHAPTER THREE

HAVING ONE FOOT in the grave was not a laughing matter, though Reese Stephens tried to make it one.

So, as the final thing on her bucket list she'd bought every joke book she could find on death, dying and other morbid things. It wasn't helping, but it wasn't hurting, either. At this point, that was as good as it was going to get for her.

She added the joke books to the stack of sex manuals she'd purchased. Donating both to the same place might be a problem so Reese decided she'd just leave them all in a stack in the corner of her apartment.

"You're sure you want to get rid of these?" Todd, her neighbor, asked. He had a box of vinyl albums under one arm and a pink stuffed elephant under the other.

Since Reese had bought the vinyls just the month before at a garage sale, it wouldn't be a great sentimental loss. She could say that about everything in her apartment, though.

Now that the watch was gone.

Reese hadn't intended to leave it with the cowboy, but it'd just felt right at the time, as if it were something he would appreciate.

As for the elephant, she'd found it by the Dumpster and couldn't stand the thought of it having the stuffing crushed out of it so Reese had given it a temporary home. Temporary was the norm for her, too, and she made a habit of not staying in one place for long.

"Take them," Reese assured Todd. "I won't be able to bring anything with me to Cambodia."

Reese wasn't sure why the lie about Cambodia had rolled so easily off her tongue, but it did now just as it had the first time she'd told it. So had the other lies needed to support that one because as she'd quickly learned one solo lie just led to more questions.

Questions she didn't want to answer.

As the story now went, she was moving to Cambodia to do a reality show about jungle cooking. She wouldn't be able to communicate with anyone for at least a year, and after that, the producers of the show were sending her to Vietnam. It was surprising that everyone believed her. Of course, everyone wasn't close to her. That was her fault.

In my next life I need to make more friends. And not move every few months.

But with mental memos like that came the depression. She wouldn't cry. She'd already wasted too many tears on something she couldn't change. Though if there was more time, she would have run to the store for some books on coping with grief.

"Knock, knock," someone called out from the open door. "Food pimp has arrived." Jimena Martinelli wiggled her away around a departing Todd, ignoring both the elephant and the heated look Todd gave her.

Jimena was the worst chef Reese had ever worked with, but she was also Reese's only friend. In every way that counted, she was like a sister.

The genetic product of an Irish-Mexican mother and Korean-Italian father, even in a blended city like San

Antonio, Jimena stood out partly because she was stunning. Also partly because she drank like a fish, cursed like a sailor and ate like a pig. Her motto was *If it's not fun, don't fucking do it*, and she literally had those words tattooed on her back.

Reese had first met her when they were sixteen, homeless and trying to scrape by. At various times they'd been roommates. Other times Jimena had stayed behind to be with a boyfriend or a job she particularly liked when Reese had felt those restless stirrings to move. But eventually Jimena had felt similar stirrings—or else had gotten dumped—and had caught up with Reese.

Jimena was also the only person other than Reese's doctor who knew her diagnosis. The sole reason Reese had told her was so there'd be someone to tie up any loose ends in case the last-ditch treatment failed.

Which it almost certainly would.

A 2 percent chance pretty much spelled *failure*.

"I brought the good stuff," Jimena announced. She breezed toward Reese and sat down on the floor beside her despite the fact Jimena was wearing shorts so tight that the movement alone could have given her an orgasm.

Jimena didn't ask what most people would have asked: *How are you feeling?* Nor did she give Reese any sad sympathetic looks. That was the reason Reese had told her. Jimena perhaps wanted to know, but asking Reese about her death diagnosis wasn't *fun*, therefore it wasn't something Jimena was going to do. And that was fine.

Especially since Reese wasn't sure how she felt, anyway. She'd been drinking too much, eating too much, and she'd had a headache since this whole ordeal had begun. Of course, she wasn't sure how much was because of the tumor, which she'd named Myrtle, or if the overindulgence was playing into this. Reese suspected both.

"Milk Duds," Jimena said, taking out the first item from the bag. There were at least a dozen boxes of them. "Cheetos." Three family-size bags. "Not that reduced-fat shit, either. These are orange and greasy." She pulled out powdered doughnuts next. "Oh, and Diet Dr. Pepper. The store clerk said, 'Why bother?' when he saw it was diet, but I told him I try to cut calories here and there."

Reese wished that all those food items, either separately or collectively, would have turned her stomach. After all, she was a chef with supposedly refined tastes, but she was a shallow foodie.

"I've already eaten so much my jeans are too tight," Reese told her while she was opening the Milk Duds. "At this rate, I won't be able to fit in my coffin."

Jimena started in on the Cheetos as if this were the most normal conversation in the world. "You said you wanted to be cremated, anyway."

"I might not fit into my urn," Reese amended.

"Then I'll make sure you have two urns. Eat up. You can't be miserable while eating junk food."

Well, you could be until the sugar high kicked in, but that would no doubt happen soon.

"Making any more progress with the bucket list?" Jimena asked, taking the notepad that Reese had placed next to her.

Number one was "give away stuff."

Now that the vinyls and elephant were gone, Reese could check that off. The only things left were the blow-up mattress she used for a bed, the books, her clothes, a box of baking soda in the fridge and a three-month-old tin of caramel popcorn that was now glued together from the humidity. She would toss it, of course, but Reese had wanted to look at the cute puppies on the tin a few more times.

Oh, and there was the backpack.

She'd named it Tootsie Roll because of the color and because it frequently contained some of the candies.

Reese tipped her head to it, the only other item in the living room. "Everything in there goes to you," she told Jimena.

Jimena looked at the worn hiker's backpack as if it might contain gold bullion. Then snakes. "You're sure?" she asked.

"Positive."

Jimena was taking care of her death wishes so it seemed only natural to give her the things Reese had carried with her from move to move. Most of the stuff in the backpack would just disappoint her friend, but there was a nice pair of Shun knives Jimena might like if she ever learned how to do food prep.

"Number two," Jimena read from the list. "'Quit job.' Well, we know that's done after what you said to Chef Dante. I heard the part about you saying you wished someone would crush his balls with a rusty garlic press."

Yes, Reese had said that. And Dante had deserved it and worse. That was the first thing she'd checked off the list, and Reese had done it the day after she'd gotten the diagnosis. Not that she'd heard much of the actual diagnosis after Dr. Gutzman had said the words that'd changed her life.

Inoperable brain tumor. Vascularization. Radiation treatments.

She'd gone in for tests for a sinus infection and had come out with a death sentence.

Those 2 percent odds were the best she had even with intense radiation treatments, and the doctor estimated she had less than a month to live. He'd also explained in nauseating detail what the radiation treatments (the ones that stood almost no chance of working) would do to her body.

Still, Reese would have them, starting tomorrow morning, because an almost chance was the only chance she had. However, she'd wanted this time to get her life in order while she still had the mind to do it.

"Number three," Jimena continued to read. "'Donate money to charity.' You finished that?" she asked, stuffing eight puffy Cheetos into her mouth at once.

Reese nodded. "It's all done. I kept just enough for me to live on…" Or rather, die on. She didn't have much, but she had tried to figure out where it would do the most good. "I divided it between Save the Whales, a local culinary academy and a fund for cosmetology scholarships at a beauty school."

Because on one of her find-the-best-tequila quests, Reese had decided the world needed more beauty, good food and whale protection.

Number four was "find the best tequila."

She'd checked that off only because they'd all started to taste the same.

Number five was dye her hair pink, and number six was eat whatever she wanted and in any amount she wanted. Reese wasn't sure exactly how much weight she'd gained, but she had been forced to wear a T-shirt and a skirt with an elastic waist.

And yet she'd still managed to accomplish number seven.

Have sex with a hot cowboy.

"It's ticked off," Jimena said, looking at number seven. "You actually went through with it? You didn't chicken out?"

Reese nodded. No chickening for her.

"Any, well, you know, bad memories?" Jimena asked. "And sorry if I'm bringing up bad memories just by asking if it brought up bad memories. Because you know the last thing I want is for you to remember the bad shit."

Despite the semirambling apology, Reese knew what Jimena meant and dismissed it. "No bad memories." It was true. There hadn't been, but the bad memories always felt just a heartbeat away. Because they were. "It was nice. *He* was nice."

Jimena smiled, and yes, she did it with that mouthful of chewed-up Cheetos. "So, how nice is nice? Tell me all about it."

"It was good." Reese wouldn't do the tell-all, though. The cowboy was the bright spot in all of this, and the last thing on her bucket list she'd gotten around to doing.

Jimena stared at her. "That's it? *Good?* If you checked it off, it must have been better than just good, or you'd be looking for another one."

It was more than just good, but even if it hadn't been, Reese wouldn't have looked for another one. No time. After the radiation treatments started tomorrow, she'd be too sick and tired to pick up a cowboy in a hotel bar.

"He was hot," Reese settled for saying, and she

showed Jimena the picture she had taken on her phone. Definitely not an Instagram-worthy shot, but Reese had wanted something to look at after she left him.

Jimena squealed. "Yeah, he's hot. Like on a scale of one to ten—he's like a six-hundred kind of hot."

She made a hmm-ing sound, looked at Reese, and even though Jimena didn't say it, she was no doubt thinking how the heck had Reese managed to get him into bed. He was a six hundred, and Reese was a six on a really good day.

Last night hadn't been a really good day.

Jimena took the phone, studied the picture. "You know, he looks kinda familiar. Is he an actor or somebody famous?"

Reese had another look for herself. He didn't look familiar to her, but he was special. He'd given her the best sex of her life. Right in the nick of time, too, since he would be her last lover.

"Are you going to try to see him again?" Jimena asked.

"No. I don't even know his name. Besides, this morning I found an engagement ring box in his pocket so I think last night for him must have been a sow-your-wild-oats kind of thing."

"Ewww." She jabbed the button to close the photo. "Then he's a hot asshole cowboy."

Yes, he was, if that's what had happened. "But it's possible his girlfriend turned him down. I figure there's a reason he was drinking all that Scotch, and he seemed almost as miserable as I was."

At least, that's how Reese was choosing to see it.

"And the watch?" Jimena pressed.

"The cowboy has it."

However, if Reese had seen that ring the night before, she wouldn't have landed in bed with him or given him the watch. Which meant, of course, that she'd given her most prized possession to a potential hot a-hole, but since this was her fantasy, she preferred to believe that he would treasure it as a reminder of their one incredible night together.

"Good." Jimena made a shivery, ick sound. And Reese knew why. Jimena had this aversion to antiques or rather what she called "old shit previously owned by dead people." That's the reason Reese hadn't given the watch to her one and only friend.

"So, what's left?" Jimena said, looking at the bucket list again.

"Nothing."

And no, Reese wasn't counting throwing away the popcorn glue. Since she'd traveled all over the world, there weren't any places left that she really wanted to see. Besides, she'd learned about four moves ago somewhere around Tulsa that, like tequila, places were really all just the same.

So, there it was—everything important ticked off her bucket list.

For the past week there'd been times when it felt as if a meaty fist had clamped on to her heart to give it a squeeze. That fist was doing a lot of squeezing now.

"I started my own bucket list of sorts," Jimena said. "I've decided to sleep my way through the alphabet so last night I had sex with that busboy named Aaron."

Most people put travel and such on their bucket lists, but this was so Jimena. She didn't have any filters when it came to sex and saw it more as a recreational sport. Unlike Reese. Sex for her was more like forbidden fruit.

It meant tearing down barriers, letting someone into her life, and while it had been an amazing night with the cowboy, part of that amazement was that he hadn't known who she really was.

Not exactly a pleasant reminder.

Reese stood to excuse herself so she could go lie down on the air mattress. Jimena wouldn't even question it, thank God, but before Reese could say anything, she heard the movement in the still-open doorway.

"All the stuff is gone," Reese said, figuring this was just another neighbor responding to her "free stuff" sign that she had taped on the side of the apartment complex's mailboxes.

But it wasn't a neighbor.

It was Dr. Gutzman.

Since Reese had never seen the stocky gray-haired man outside his office and never dressed in anything but a white coat, it took her a moment to realize who he was. Another moment for her to think the worst.

"Did you come to tell me there'll be no radiation, after all?" Reese managed to ask.

He opened his mouth, closed it. Then nodded. "You won't be having radiation," he confirmed.

As much as Reese was dreading the treatments—and she was indeed dreading them—they'd been the tiny sliver of hope. Her 2 percent chance of survival. Of course, she hadn't truly embraced that sliver, but now Dr. Gutzman had just taken it away.

"I'd rather not die in a hospital," Reese volunteered.

Jimena stood and took hold of her hand. Reese could feel the bits of sticky Cheetos on her friend's fingers.

The doctor nodded, came in and eased the door shut.

He glanced around the nearly empty room and frowned. Perhaps because of the junk-food stash.

"You're not going to die in a hospital," he said. "At least, not in the next week or so from an inoperable brain tumor."

Reese was still on the page of thinking the worst. "Does that mean I'm going to die even sooner?"

He huffed, glanced around as if this were the last place he wanted to be. "There was a glitch with the new electronic records system. Your images got mixed up with another patient. When I realized the mistake, I had a look at yours, and other than an enlarged left sinus cavity, you're fine."

Reese couldn't speak. She just stared at him, waiting for the other shoe to drop. The doctor didn't look like a prankster, but maybe this was his idea of a really bad joke.

"Did you hear me?" he asked.

She had. Every word. And Reese was desperately trying to process something that just wasn't processing in her mind.

"So, there's really nothing wrong with her?" Jimena asked.

"Nothing. She's as healthy as a horse."

Reese hadn't been around too many horses to know if they were especially healthy or not, but she would take the doc's news as gospel.

Right after she threw up, that is.

God, she was going to live.

LOGAN SLAMMED DOWN the phone. Jason Murdock, his friend and the rancher Logan had been buying stock from for years, had just given Logan a much-too-sweet deal on some Angus.

Hell.

Much more of this and Logan was going to beat the crap out of somebody. Especially the next person who was overly nice to him or gave him a sweet deal on anything.

For the past three months since the mess with Helene, nearly everybody who called or came into the office was walking on sonofabitching eggshells around him, and it not only pissed him off, it was disrespectful.

He'd run McCord Cattle Brokers since he was nineteen, since his folks had been killed in a car crash, and he'd run it well. In those early years people had questioned his ability to handle a company this size.

Silently questioned it, anyway.

But Logan had built the image and reputation he needed to make sure those questions were never spoken aloud. He'd done that through ball-busting business practices where nobody but nobody walked on eggshells. Yet, here they were all still doing just that. After three months.

Not just his family, either.

He'd halfway expected it from Riley, Claire, Lucky and Cassie because they'd been at the scene of what Lucky was calling the great proposal fuckup. Logan expected it, too, from his assistant, Greg Larkin, since he was the sort who remembered birthdays and such shit.

But everybody in Spring Hill who'd had a reason to come to Logan's office door had looked at him with those sad puppy-dog eyes. He could only imagine how bad it was when those puppy-eyed people weren't right in front of him. All the behind-the-hand whispers were no doubt mumbles about poor, pitiful Logan and what Helene had done to him.

Logan tried to make a note on the business contract he was reading and cursed when his pen didn't work. He yanked open his desk drawer with enough force to rip it from its runners, and got another reminder he didn't want.

That blasted gold watch.

Why he still had it, Logan didn't know, but every time he saw it he remembered his night with Julia. Or whatever the hell her name was. She should have been nothing but a distant memory now and soon would be once he found her and returned the blasted watch. Until then, he moved it to his bottom drawer next to the bottle of Glenlivet he kept there.

Of course, if it hadn't been for the Glenlivet, he probably wouldn't have slept with Julia and wouldn't have had the watch in the first place.

Logan moved it to the bottom drawer on the other side.

Damn it all to hell!

The engagement ring was still there, too. The bottom drawers of his desk were metaphorical land mines, and this time he made a note. Two of them.

Get rid of the ring.

Find Julia and have someone return the watch.

Logan didn't want the ring around because he was over Helene. And as for the watch—he didn't want it around in case there was something to the blackmail/extortion theory he'd had about her. Even though it had been three months since their encounter, that didn't mean she wasn't out there plotting some way to do something he wasn't going to like. That's why he'd hired a private investigator to find her, but so far the PI had come up empty.

"Don't," Logan barked when Lucky appeared in the doorway of his office.

He hadn't heard his brother coming up the hall, but since Lucky was wearing his good jeans and a jacket, it probably meant he was there for a meeting. Lucky certainly wouldn't have dressed up just to check on him.

"Don't interrupt you, or don't draw my next breath?" Lucky asked. He bracketed his hands on the office door, cocked his head to the side.

"Both if you're here to talk about anything that doesn't involve a cow, bull or a horse."

"How about bullshit?"

Logan looked up from the contract to see if Lucky was serious. He appeared to be. Just in case, Logan decided to clarify. "Bullshit that's not specifically related to anything that involves my ex?"

"Well, unless Helene has started secretly pooping in the pastures, it doesn't," Lucky confirmed.

Logan was almost afraid to motion for Lucky to continue, but he finally did. Curiosity was a sick thing sometimes.

"You haven't been to the house, well, in a couple of months," Lucky went on, "but I had thirty bulls delivered to those pastures and corrals we talked about using."

So, definitely not a Helene problem. And Logan knew which pastures and corrals Lucky meant. The pastures were on the east side of the house, and with the right mixture of grasses for the young bulls they'd bought so they could be trained for the rodeo.

"The wind must have shifted or something because,

this morning, all you could smell was bullshit in the house. Everybody's complaining, even Mia," Lucky added.

A first for Mia. To the best of Logan's knowledge, the four-year-old girl never complained about anything. Unlike her thirteen-year-old sister, Mackenzie. Lucky and Cassie had guardianship of the pair, but the girls were yin and yang. If Mia was complaining, Logan didn't want to know how much Mackenzie was carrying on. Or the longtime housekeepers, Della and Stella, who also lived at the ranch.

"You're sure it's bullshit and not cat shit?" Logan asked. Because along with inheriting guardianship of the girls, Lucky and Cassie had also inherited six cats. Five of those cats were now at the ranch.

Lucky shook his head. "Definitely bullshit, and I should know because I'm a bullshit connoisseur."

Since Lucky had been riding rodeo bulls for more than a decade, that did indeed make him an expert. Not just on the crap but the bulls themselves.

"That means I'm going to need to move them," Lucky went on, "and I was thinking about the back pastures. But Rico said you were planning on putting some horses back there."

He was. Or rather, Riley was since he was in charge of the new cutting horse program that they'd started. And Riley and Logan had indeed discussed that with Rico Callahan, one of their top ranch hands.

Logan sat there, debating on which would smell worse—horseshit or bullshit. It was a toss-up. "Move the bulls to the back pastures," Logan finally said. "When the horses arrive, I'll have Riley split them in the other pastures for the time being."

It was a temporary fix since Riley would eventually

want the cutting horses together so they'd be easier to train, and that meant they needed to prep one of the other two pastures they weren't using. The problem at the McCord Ranch wasn't enough land—there was plenty of that—but with their operation expanding, they needed someone who could manage the ranch grounds themselves. Someone more than just the hands.

"Hire whoever you need to fix this," Logan told his brother.

Whenever he was talking to Lucky, his twin, Logan always tried to tone down his voice. After all, Lucky could have been co-CEO, but in his will, their father had named only Logan. Logan supposed he felt guilty about that, but then until recently Lucky had shown zero interest in being part of McCord Cattle Brokers. Since it was something Logan had always wanted—all of his siblings helping him with the family business—he didn't want to push any of Lucky's buttons that might be waiting to be pushed.

Lucky mumbled that he would hire someone and checked his watch. "Say, it's lunchtime. Wanna go over to the Fork and Spoon and grab something to eat?"

Logan figured that was Lucky's plan all along, to get him out of the office because Lucky could have just called with the bullshit problem. Lucky did have an office just up the hall, but he rarely used it. He wasn't a behind-the-desk kind of guy. Plus, he still had his own rodeo promotion company to run. What with raising two kids and being in a fairly new relationship, Lucky didn't have a lot of free time.

Which meant this was a coddling attempt on Lucky's part.

"No." Lucky held up his hands in defense as if he

knew what Logan was thinking. Maybe he did. Logan had never experienced that twin telepathy thing, but it was possible Lucky did. Of course, telepathy wasn't needed since Lucky had seen what Helene had done.

"You're not here to check on me?" Logan clarified.

Lucky shook his head. "Della's on a health kick and is making baked chicken and salad for lunch. I want a mystery-meat grease burger and soggy fries from the Fork and Spoon."

Logan gestured for him to go for it.

Lucky huffed. "The waitresses," he said.

And Logan got it then. Not from telepathy, either. But Lucky had a reputation as a player, and despite the fact that he was now involved with Cassie, the waitresses and some other women in town seemed to enjoy testing Lucky's commitment to Cassie. His brother must want that burger pretty bad to go through another round of that.

"I'm not running interference for you with women," Logan warned him.

"No need. They'll be feeling so sorry for you that they'll leave me the heck alone. The last time I was in there, Sissy Lee spilled ice tea on my crotch and proceeded to wipe it off. Really hard and fast. I think she was trying her damnedest to give me a hand job."

If that had come from any other man, Logan would have considered it an exaggeration, but women did stuff like that to Lucky all the time, and it'd started around the time they hit puberty. Logan didn't get it. Lucky and he were identical, but if you put them in the middle of a bunch of horny women, 90 percent of them would go after Lucky first.

"You won't run into Helene," Lucky continued. "She hasn't come back to town since everything happened."

Yeah, Greg had mentioned that, but when his assistant had tried to give him more details, Logan had told him to get his butt back to work. He didn't need details about anything that involved Helene.

"I don't suppose you've heard from her?" Lucky asked.

Logan managed to stave off a scowl. "No. And I don't expect she'll call because I doubt she'll want to explain what was going on in her office that night."

"Oh, I'm pretty sure I know what was going on."

Yes. Logan was sure of that, too. Helene had been fucking a clown.

In hindsight, it was sort of surreal, like a perfect storm of Logan's nightmares. Well, it would have been if he'd had nightmares about Helene being unfaithful. He hadn't because it hadn't even been on his radar. But the clown nightmares? He'd had plenty of those since he was nine years old and had sneaked a copy of Stephen King's *It* from his dad's office.

"Still no idea who the clown was?" Lucky went on.

This time Logan did give him a scowl and no answer. Because no, he didn't have a clue. Nor did he want to know.

Once you saw your girlfriend screwing a clown, it didn't matter who was wearing those big floppy shoes and was behind the white face, red lips and red squeaky nose.

"So, what do you say about having a burger with me?" Lucky pressed when Logan didn't budge, answer or quit scowling. "I want to talk to you on the walk over.

Nothing else about Helene, I promise. This is something else. Something personal."

Since the Fork and Spoon Café was only a block and a half up from the McCord building, it would be a short conversation, but he wasn't sure Lucky was going to give up on this. Besides, Logan wanted a grease burger now, too.

Logan slipped on his cowboy hat, grabbed his phone and headed out. "Don't make a big deal about this," he warned Lucky, and then gave the same warning to Greg when they walked past his desk.

The lanky assistant jumped to his feet as if trying to contain his excitement. Maybe because it was the first time Logan had left the building in more than a week. Easy to stay under the roof of the converted Victorian house when he had a studio apartment on the third floor. It was even easier now that he was having his groceries delivered. The only time he left was for a business meeting out of town.

"Not a word," Logan added to Greg because Logan thought he needed to say something to wipe that gleeful look off his face. And Logan tried not to look too displeased that the guy was wearing a purple suit. Yes, purple. "And do the paperwork to finalize the sale of those cows I just bought from Jason Murdock."

Greg nodded, too eagerly, and Logan was sure he was still eager-ing when Lucky and he walked out the front door.

Logan immediately had to pull down the brim of his cowboy hat to shield his eyes. He'd gone too long without sunshine, and it would continue. The less contact he had with people right now, the better. In a couple more months when the gossip died down, he'd try to get back to normal.

After he learned what normal would be for him, that is.

"Two things," Lucky said as they walked. "How are you? And before you blast me, Della put me up to it. She and Stella are worried about you. I'm not. Because I know if your head was still messed up, you'd tell me."

No, he wouldn't. Logan wouldn't tell anyone, but he was semipleased that Lucky would think that. Or maybe Lucky knew it and was playing a mind game to get him to talk.

"I'm fine," Logan assured him.

That wasn't even close to the truth. He'd had two migraines in six days, and it felt as if another one might be tapping on his shoulder. He wasn't sleeping well, and when he did, he kept dreaming about what he'd seen in Helene's office. Part of him wished he'd asked her for an explanation. *Any* explanation. But then again, what was she going to say? Nothing that would have helped Logan understand, that's for sure.

"By the way, I've never told you this, but before we walked in on Helene, I didn't know what she was up to," Logan said to Lucky. "I had no idea she could, or would, cheat on me."

"Yeah, I figured that out. I read somewhere that repressed people do all sorts of weird sexual things."

Logan waved off anything else Lucky might have added because two women were walking toward them. Misty Reagan and Sandra Morrelli. He definitely didn't want them to hear anything he had to say about Helene so Logan put on his best smile, tipped his hat in greeting and then proceeded to talk to Lucky about those cows he'd just bought. Lucky cooperated, of course, but the conversation must have looked intense enough for the ladies not to issue more than smiles and greetings of their own.

Two bullets dodged.

"What'd you want to talk to me about?" Logan asked.

When Lucky hesitated, Logan thought he knew where this was going. "You want to make things official with Cassie and ask her to marry you, and you're hoping I'm okay with it. I am. You two should be together."

"Thanks for that."

It wasn't a grand gesture. Logan had never believed in the misery-loves-company notion. Besides, he was getting daily calls from Stella about how she didn't think it was a good idea for Cassie and Lucky to be *living in sin*, that it wasn't setting a good example for Mia and Mackenzie.

"When will you pop the question?" Logan asked.

"As soon as I get the ring."

Logan thought of the one in his drawer, the one that no one in his family had seen, and he considered offering it to Lucky. But then maybe it was jinxed or something.

Hell, maybe *he* was jinxed.

"Along with marrying Cassie," Lucky continued, "we've started paperwork to adopt the girls. Surprised?"

"Not in the least." But just three months ago, he would have been. However, Logan had no doubts now. None. Because his brother was in love, and Logan was completely happy for him.

They were still a few yards away from the Fork and Spoon when Logan got a whiff of the burger that brought in lunchtime diners. Today was no different.

Because of the glass front on the café, it was easy to see that the place was packed.

Crap.

He nearly turned around, but Lucky took hold of his arm and maneuvered him inside. The chatter stopped immediately, and the place went silent as a tomb. He should have just ordered takeout and had Greg pick it up.

"They need to see you out and about," Lucky whispered to him. "And it won't be long before they'll have something else to gossip about."

Logan wasn't betting on that. Despite three months passing, Helene was still the most tongue-wagging topic with Logan coming in a close second. The speculation about what he'd seen in Helene's office had probably reached levels of absurdity times ten.

"Hey, maybe I can start a rumor that I knocked up Cassie?" Lucky suggested.

Logan appreciated that, but he thought the offer might have something to do with Sissy Lee Culpepper, who was sauntering over to them. The busty blonde in the skintight Pepto Bismol–pink uniform eyed Lucky. Then she eyed his crotch. She then did the same to Logan and smiled, maybe because she remembered he was the lone McCord male left on the market.

"The only thing open is the counter," she said, "but I can shoo away someone from a booth if you like."

"The counter's fine," Logan insisted. "Could you get us two burger plates and make it fast? We're in a hurry."

"I want a root beer float with mine," Lucky added.

"Sure thing, sweetie."

Sissy Lee called everyone sweetie, honey or darling

so it wasn't exactly a term of endearment. More like a ploy to get a bigger tip.

"And for what it's worth," Sissy Lee said, "I think Helene is lower than hoof grit."

That got some mumbled agreements from the other diners. Logan hoped that the conversation would end if he gave a noncommittal nod.

It didn't.

"I got a name for a woman like that," Sissy Lee added in a whisper. "Hick-dead."

Logan wasn't sure if she was attempting pig Latin and was really calling Helene a dickhead. And he wasn't interested in trying to figure it out. He gave Sissy Lee another noncommittal nod. But it was Lucky's wink and smile that got the waitress moving. She added a wink of her own, and using her best femme fatale hip swish, she walked away.

Logan took the stool at the far end of the counter. Not ideal since the grill was just on the other side of a partial wall, and the smoke from the sizzling burgers came right at them.

"Other than a knocking-up rumor," Lucky continued, "you could give them something new to talk about by going on a date."

Logan gave him a blank stare. "There are no eligible women in town that you haven't slept with already. I don't need that kind of gossip. Or that kind of woman."

Lucky shrugged, made a sound as if that were possibly true. "There are always those dating sites."

He'd rather personally shovel every bit of bullshit from the pasture, one cow patty at a time. "No thanks."

"Then what about—"

"No. Thanks," Logan said a little louder than he intended.

It got people's attention. Not that their attention had strayed too far from him, anyway. He could practically feel the sympathy pouring over him.

"Suit yourself, but I was going to say you should ask her out." Lucky tipped his head to the fry cook. "She's new in town, and I haven't slept with her."

Logan looked up, at the veil of greasy-scented gray smoke that was between them and the cook. And his stomach dropped to his kneecaps.

Maybe Lucky hadn't slept with her, but Logan sure had.

Julia Child was in the process of flipping a burger.

CHAPTER FOUR

OH, GOD. THERE wasn't just one cowboy but two. And they didn't just look alike. They were identical.

Now what?

Reese tried not to react, tried not to give in to the gasp that was inching its way from her throat toward her mouth. But mercy, this was gasp-worthy.

She'd come to Spring Hill hoping to find the hot cowboy she had slept with and get her grandfather's watch back. And she'd wanted to do it without attracting any attention to herself—or to him. Especially since he might be engaged or even married by now. She definitely hadn't wanted to intrude on his life, not after that promise she'd given him.

What happens in San Antonio stays in San Antonio. I'll take this to the grave.

Reese had made that promise when she thought the grave was imminent, and she'd wanted to finish that idiotic bucket list. Well, she had finished it, but now she was in the process of undoing it.

But how did she undo this without admitting that she didn't even know which one she'd bedded? And here she had thought this might be the easiest thing left on her undoing quest.

She had finally lost the weight that she'd put on from her carb and sugar binges and had gotten her money back from the canceled cremation. She'd gone through with the charity donations, though, because it hadn't seemed fair to screw them over just because Myrtle the tumor had turned out to be all just a computer glitch.

That left the cowboy and the watch.

"Uh, you're sorta burning those burgers, sweetie," Sissy Lee said, giving Reese a nudge with her elbow.

Reese forced herself out of her panicking trance and looked down at what had been two one-third of a pound patties of prime Angus beef. They now resembled squashed cow dung.

"Sorry," Reese mumbled, and she pushed those aside, scraped down the grill and added two fresh burgers.

She didn't know the owner, Bert Starkley, that well, but it was possible he'd take them out of her pay. That was minor now compared to the fact that everyone in the café was looking at her and the stenchy smoke she'd created.

"No worries," Sissy Lee assured her. The woman got busy making an ice cream float. "Bert'll just give them to his dogs. But you should make the next ones medium rare since that's how Logan and Lucky like 'em."

Logan and Lucky.

So, those were their names, and since it was obvious that Sissy Lee knew them, Reese would be able to pump her for information.

The only other thing Reese knew was what she'd learned from the hotel clerk after she'd hurried back there to find the cowboy. The clerk couldn't give her the cowboy's name, but he'd said that he saw him driving a truck with a business sign on the side, and the only thing he could remember about the sign was that it had Spring "something or other," Texas, on it.

There were a lot of Spring "something or others" in Texas, Reese had learned, and that's why it had taken her all this time to track him down. Her search had left her a little low on money so she'd stayed around and started the job at the café.

While keeping a close eye on the burgers, Reese risked glancing up at the pair. The one at the far end of the counter glanced at her at the same time. Or maybe he, too, was just looking at the smoke because he gave no indication whatsoever that he knew her. It was possible he couldn't even see her, though. Added to that, her hair was back to its natural color now—dark brown. And the final factor affecting this? He could have been too drunk to remember much of anything.

"Lucky and Logan?" Reese said to Sissy Lee. "Twins, obviously."

Sissy Lee chuckled. Not just any ordinary chuckle. "Yeah, all the women in Spring Hill have fantasies about a threesome with those two."

Reese didn't know about a threesome, but her twosome had been pretty amazing.

"You know them well?" Reese asked, fishing while frying. She added some sliced onion to the grill, swirled it around in the grease runoff from the burger—an artery-clogging topping that Bert had told her his customers loved.

"Of course. Everybody does. They're the McCords. And they've got a brother, Riley. He's taken, though. Actually, Lucky, the one on the left, is maybe taken, too. Everybody in town figures he'll be popping the question to his girlfriend soon."

"Oh?" Reese had hoped her noncommittal response would keep Sissy Lee talking, but when it didn't work,

Reese had to come out and ask. "What about Logan? Is he involved with anyone?"

"Was," Sissy Lee said, lowering her voice and speaking behind her hand. "I'll tell you all about it later," she added just as another customer came in.

"Carry those burgers out to Lucky and Logan when you're done, will you?" Sissy Lee scooped up some fresh fries and put them on the sides of the plates. "I'll give Lucky his float and take care of Daniel."

Judging from the dreamy way Sissy Lee said Daniel's name, he was a juicy catch. But then Sissy Lee seemed to feel that way about every single guy who came into the café.

Reese finished the burgers, drowning them in the fried onions and thick slabs of American cheese—again as Bert had instructed. Her waitressing skills were a little rusty, but she balanced the plates, along with two glasses of ice water, and made her way to the counter. She set down the food and drinks, thinking it might be a good idea to make a quick exit and watch the Mc-Cords from the kitchen.

That didn't happen.

"You're new here," the one on the left said. He flashed her a smile that could have melted heavy-duty aluminum foil. He still didn't show any signs of recognition. "I'm Lucky McCord." He hitched his thumb to his brother. "This is Logan."

No melting smile from him. No sign of recognition, either. She should have asked Sissy Lee if the third brother was their triplet.

"And you are?" Lucky asked.

"Reese Stephens," she said.

Still no signs that they knew who she was, but then

she'd used an alias for the hotel. Julia Child. She looked to see if either of them had caught onto the lame joke of her using a superchef's name when she was nothing but a glorified fry cook. But nada.

Logan checked his watch. "I just remembered a meeting I have in Bulverde," he said, standing.

Lucky had just taken a big sip of the float, and he had to swallow first before he could respond. "What meeting?"

"With that seller. Could you please box this up?" he asked Reese after sparing her a glance. "I'll have my assistant come by and pick it up later." Logan dropped two twenties on the counter and walked out. Not in a hurry exactly but not a man who was dawdling, either.

"It's not you," Lucky said, watching his brother leave. "Logan's had it rough lately. I'm sure you've heard." His gaze drifted to Sissy Lee, who had practically put herself body to body with Daniel.

"I only arrived in town yesterday," Reese said. "I haven't had a chance to hear any gossip."

"Trust me, that's plenty of time. Six seconds is enough time." He paused, tilted his head to the side and looked at her. "Say, do I know you from somewhere?"

Reese pretended to study him, too, though she knew every detail because she'd studied the selfie on her phone. Often. Dark brown hair, cool blue eyes, a face not too chiseled. But it was also a face that was a lot more relaxed than the one on her phone.

"I think I saw you driving around town," she finally said. "Were you in a truck with some kind of sign on the side?"

He nodded, tackled a couple of his fries after he

dragged them through some ketchup. "McCord Cattle Brokers, the family business."

Reese needed a bit more than that. "And it had Spring Hill, Texas, on the sign?"

Another nod just as he took a bite of the burger.

So, it was Lucky she'd slept with, and since Sissy Lee had already said he would likely get engaged soon, then Reese needed to figure out how to get the watch without messing things up for him. She definitely wouldn't ask about it here. There were at least six customers seemingly hanging on their every word.

"The trucks were Logan's idea," Lucky added a moment later. "Good advertising, he said. That's why we all drive one. Even our housekeepers do."

All? Well, heck. That put her back to square one.

"Man, this burger's good. I think you're the best cook Bert's ever hired."

"Thanks," she mumbled.

Since it was obvious he was interested in eating his lunch and because she didn't want to pique his attention, Reese took Logan's plate back to the kitchen to box it. She'd barely gotten started, though, when Sissy Lee put in another hamburger order.

"Daniel likes his burger still mooing," Sissy Lee added.

Sissy Lee took over the boxing duties while Reese got started. "I didn't figure Logan would stay too long." She shook her head. "It's the first time he's come over for lunch since Helene, that hick-dead girlfriend of his, messed him up."

As gossip went, that was fairly lacking. "How'd she mess him up?"

"Well, that's just it. We're not really sure. The only

person who got a glimpse of it was Walter Meekins, the taxi driver. Logan had called him to drive Riley, Claire, Lucky and Cassie back home after Logan proposed to his girlfriend."

Reese didn't have a clue who Claire and Cassie were, but she didn't want to interrupt Sissy Lee. It wouldn't take that long to cook a rare burger, and then Sissy Lee would go back out to flirt with the customers.

"Anyway, Walter didn't see exactly what happened when Logan and the others went into Helene's office," Sissy Lee explained, "but he said he saw this clown running out the back."

"A clown. You mean like something in a circus? Or a horror novel?" Because Reese wasn't sure if Sissy Lee meant that word in a general sense.

"Circus or rodeo kind of clown," Sissy Lee verified. "Walter said when Logan came out he looked like he'd seen a ghost. He's never been the same since."

Lucky had been so sure that the gossips had filled Reese in by now, but obviously the townsfolk didn't know as much as the McCords thought they did.

"Of course, we don't know who the clown was," Sissy Lee went on. "I thought it was Brian, the guy who worked for Helene, but it turns out that he's gay. Of course, I guess he could actually be bi or else—"

"How long ago did that clown stuff happen to Logan?" Reese interrupted.

Sissy Lee shrugged. "This past summer."

That fit with Reese's timeline of her one-night stand three months ago. Maybe.

Sissy Lee put Logan's boxed burger meal aside, and while Reese dished up Daniel's plate, she got an idea.

"Where do the McCords live? Because I'll have a break soon, and I can drop that off to him."

"It's that big house on the edge of town. Can't miss it. Except Logan doesn't spend much time there anymore. You know that Victorian building just up the street? Well, that's his office, and he has a loft apartment there."

Reese had noticed the house. In fact, she was in the Bluebonnet Inn on the same block. She checked the time—still an hour before her break, but maybe Logan's assistant wouldn't come for the burger before then.

Because Reese wanted to get inside that building. She had some spying to do.

"REESE STEPHENS." Logan repeated her name under his breath as he read the initial report the private investigator had just sent him.

There wasn't much info yet, but then when Logan had called the PI the day before, the man had said it might take a while, that the woman wasn't showing up in his usual search engines.

There had to be a reason for that.

Logan didn't know what game she was playing, but she was up to something. No doubt about it. After all, she had that photo of him on her phone, so even if she'd been too drunk to remember, she would have seen it later and then recognized him at the café. Of course, there was the possibility that she hadn't known whether it was Lucky or him who'd gotten into that hotel bed with her, but there was still no reason for her not to fess up.

No good reason, anyway.

So, why was she here in Spring Hill? The private

investigator's initial report certainly didn't help with that. Her name was Reese Violet Stephens. She was twenty-nine, single. She'd attended culinary school in New Orleans and worked as a cook or chef at various restaurants all over the US. However, she'd never stayed at any of them for more than a couple of months. No criminal record—under that name, anyway.

And that was it.

She had no social media accounts, no driver's license, no paper trail that people usually left. That only made Logan even more suspicious. The PI, too, and that's why he was digging deeper. Hopefully, that digging wouldn't take too long.

Logan parked in the circular drive in front of his family's home, and he hadn't even stepped from his truck before he got a whiff of what Lucky and he had discussed the day before.

The manure.

Yeah, it was a problem all right. The bulls had already been moved, but it might take a while for the stench to clear out.

He was about to head up the steps to the porch when his phone buzzed, and after Logan saw the name on the screen, he knew it was a call he had to take.

Bert Starkley, the owner of the Fork and Spoon Café.

Logan had called him the night before, but Bert hadn't answered so Logan had left him a voice mail. Nothing specific and Logan had to make sure he didn't say anything to Reese's employer that would make the man suspicious. Or make Bert think Logan was interested in her. The last thing Logan needed was more gossip about him and a woman. Especially a woman who was almost certainly bad news.

Later, he'd curse himself again for that one-night stand, but now he needed to find out anything he could about her.

"Logan?" Bert said when he answered. "Is everything okay?"

It was a valid question, considering that Logan had never before called the man. "Everything's fine." And he chose his next words carefully. "I was at the café yesterday for lunch—"

"Yep, I heard. Sissy Lee," Bert added as if that explained everything. Which it did. The waitress had no doubt blabbed to everyone that Logan had left the café in a hurry.

"I had to leave for a meeting," Logan lied. He hated liars, but this little white one was necessary. Even if Bert didn't totally believe that lie, maybe he'd still repeat it to diffuse some of Sissy Lee's gossip. And he didn't have to think hard to imagine what that gossip might entail. It almost certainly hinged on Helene.

"Sissy Lee mentioned the meeting, too," Bert verified. "How can I help you? Is this about the catering job?"

Logan frowned. "What catering job?"

"Something Della wanted us to do for her."

This was the first Logan was hearing about it, but then he was too busy to get involved with the daily workings of the house. "No. I was calling about your new cook." Logan left it at that, to see what Bert would volunteer about her.

But nothing.

Clearly, Bert was waiting to see what Logan would volunteer.

"Renee?" Logan finally said. "Is that her name?"

"Reese." Again, that was it. Hell, Bert wasn't cooperating with this at all.

"She looked familiar," Logan continued. "I just wondered how you'd found her?"

"She came into the café, asked about the help-wanted sign that I had in the window. I gave her a trial run to see if she could cook. She can, by the way. I hope you enjoyed that burger she fixed."

He hadn't. Logan hadn't eaten a bite of it, so rather than lie again, he just made a sound of approval. "Reese dropped it off at my office after I had to leave. I wasn't there, but she left it with Greg."

Considering Logan had told Reese that Greg would be picking it up in the first place, he was even more suspicious that the woman had personally delivered it.

"You probably heard that Maggie's got to have some surgery," Bert added a moment later.

Maggie, Bert's wife, and yes, Logan had heard. *Female problems*, which was the only thing Logan had listened to after hearing those two words. "I hope Maggie will be okay," Logan said.

"Oh, she will be. Female problems," Bert repeated. "But it means I'll be out of the kitchen for a while. Reese said she'd have no trouble pulling double shifts for me."

Logan was even more leery. Why was she being so accommodating? Of course, the obvious reason might be that with double shifts she would be earning double pay, but Logan wasn't ready to cut her that kind of slack just yet.

"So, Reese had references when you hired her?" Logan pressed.

"Oh, I get it now. You're wanting to make sure she's experienced enough to do the catering job for Della?"

No, that wasn't it at all. "Is she qualified? What did her previous employers have to say about her?"

"Didn't check them out after I tasted a couple of things she cooked for me. The woman bakes, too. Melt in your mouth pies and cakes. She did this lemon thingy that had all the customers going on about it." Bert paused. "But if you're worried about her, I can check her references. Are you, uh, worried about her?"

The question was reasonable, but Logan heard something in Bert's tone. He'd used the word *worried* but what he really meant was *interested*. Hell's bells. Bert thought Logan was looking to hit on Reese.

"I just want to make sure Reese is the right person for the catering job," Logan clarified, though he was dead certain that wouldn't quell any of Bert's *interested* suspicions since Logan hadn't even known about the catering job before this phone call. "If you could follow through on her references, I'd appreciate it."

"Sure. I'll get back to you."

Logan ended the call, ready to go inside, but once again his phone buzzed. Good grief. At this rate, he'd never get in the house, but again it was a call he needed to take.

Jason Murdock's name was on the screen.

Logan and he had been friends since high school, and when Jason had taken over running his uncle's large ranch about thirty miles from Spring Hill, it made sense for them to do business together. Jason had cows to sell, and Logan needed to buy huge herds so he could resell in smaller groups and make a profit.

But there was a problem with Jason.

"If you're going to give me another pity deal," Logan said when he answered, "then I don't want it."

"Good. Because you're not getting pity from me. I don't do pity deals, pity fucks or pity anything else. I needed to unload those cows because I didn't have the room for them."

Logan wanted to believe him, but their friendship might have caused Jason to bend his no-pitying rule.

"I'm calling about Helene," Jason said a moment later. "And yeah, you can hang up if you want, but her mother, Mary, called me this morning. She was boo-hooing all over the place. She wanted me to try to talk you into seeing Helene."

"No." Logan didn't have to think about that, either. "Why would Mary call you?"

"Because she figured you'd just hang up on her. Let's face it, Logan, you're not exactly the forgiving sort."

He wasn't, and Logan liked that just fine. "Why did Mary want me to see Helene?" Logan asked.

"Hell if I know. And she wouldn't say. She just said it was important." Jason paused. "You know if you ever want to talk about what happened that night with Helene, all you have to do is call me."

"Thanks but no thanks." Logan had enough of those images in his head without reliving them through conversation.

Clowns and liars.

"If Mary calls back," Logan told his friend, "have her call me directly." Not that he especially wanted to talk to his ex's mom, but he also didn't want her pulling Jason into this.

Logan ended the call and went inside to ask Della about this catering issue. However, the moment he opened the door, he realized he might not be able to make a beeline for the kitchen as he'd planned. That's because Lucky and Cassie were down on their knees in the foyer. At first Logan thought he'd walked in on something sexual—always a possibility where his twin was concerned—but then he saw that this was something much more intimate.

Lucky was proposing.

He was in the process of slipping an engagement ring on Cassie's finger, and Cassie had tears in her eyes. Judging from her smile, they were tears of a happy variety.

"Crap," Lucky grumbled. "Sorry. I didn't want you to see this," he added to Logan.

Perhaps because Lucky thought it would bring back bad memories of Logan's own botched proposal. It did, but that didn't mean he wasn't happy for Lucky and Cassie. They were suited for each other, though that wasn't apparent to them when Cassie had come back into Lucky's life almost four months ago.

"I didn't like Lucky being on his knees alone," Cassie said, getting to her feet. "I said yes."

She held out the ring for Logan to see. Since he still hadn't closed the door, the sunlight caught the diamond just right, causing it to glint into his eyes.

It was their mother's ring.

Of course, Logan had always known that it was Lucky's to use if he wanted. Despite their mother only being in her forties when she'd been killed, she had made it a habit of saying which jewelry she would leave for each child. The engagement ring she'd wanted for Lucky. The wedding band for their kid sister, Anna. Logan had gotten her pearl necklace and Riley a gold bracelet.

Precious mementos.

But to Logan the most precious thing was his father's pocketknife. That meant as much to him as the engagement ring had meant to Lucky.

Logan gave Cassie a kiss on the cheek and his brother a hug. "Congrats to both of you. It's about time you made it official." He tried to keep his tone light, and he did mean the congrats. Still, that didn't help with the sudden lump in his throat.

"I'm going to tell Della and Stella," Cassie said, glancing at Logan.

She hurried away, probably because she sensed Logan needed some time with his brother. Or time alone. But while Logan would take that time alone, later, for now he needed to do a little business with Lucky.

"I won't keep you," Logan assured him. "I figure Cassie and you will want to celebrate before the girls get home from school." And by celebrate, he meant they'd want to have sex. "I just wanted to make sure the bull situation had been fixed before I leave for Dallas."

The Dallas trip was legit. Logan was on a 3:00 p.m. flight and would be gone at least a couple of days, but considering he was slammed with work and getting ready for several magazine interviews, he was BS-ing about asking about the BS.

Lucky's flat look told Logan he wasn't buying the reason for this visit. "All right, what's wrong with you?"

Logan hated to play the scorned-lover card, but he would this time. "You know what's wrong with me. That doesn't mean I'm not happy for Cassie and you. I am."

Lucky's flat look continued. "Does this have anything to do with the new cook at the Fork and Spoon?"

Either twin telepathy again or a good guess was in play here. "Why do you ask?" Logan settled for saying.

"Because of the way you lit out of there like your balls were on fire. But maybe they were on fire because of the lie you told her. You didn't have a meeting."

"But I did." One that Logan scheduled as soon as he left the café.

Lucky clearly knew he was semilying, again, but Logan didn't intend to let him in on anything. If Reese had meant "what happens in San Antonio stays in San Antonio," then maybe she had a good reason for not wanting the one-nighter spilled, either.

Of course, that good reason might have something to do with blackmail, but for now Logan would use that possibility to his advantage. Besides, he didn't want Lucky or anyone else to know he'd done something so stupid as to sleep with a woman he didn't know.

Lucky kept staring at him. "Reese and I chatted after you left," his brother tossed out there. And he watched, no doubt to see how Logan would respond.

Logan merely shrugged. At least he hoped that was the only thing his body was doing. "Let me guess—she flirted with you?" Easy guess because most women flirted with Lucky.

"No flirting. She asked about our trucks, said she thought she'd seen me driving one."

Logan's stomach tightened. He'd driven one of the company trucks to that San Antonio hotel, and if Reese had gotten a glimpse of it, then that could explain how she'd found him. Of course, he'd been on the cover of several Texas magazines, too, so perhaps that's how she had made the connection.

"You're not going to tell me what this is really about, are you?" Lucky asked.

Finally a question where Logan wouldn't have to lie. "No. I need to talk to Della," he said, heading for the kitchen.

Logan didn't have to ask if that's where Della was. He followed the scent of something cinnamon-y to the kitchen and found her taking some fresh bread from the oven. Perhaps an attempt to cover up the bull crap outside, and if so, it was working.

"Well, this is a surprise," Della said. It managed to sound like a greeting and a scolding all at once. A scolding because it'd been a while since he'd been home. "Great news about Lucky and Cassie, huh? She went to the garden to find Stella to tell her. You okay with this?"

"Of course."

"Okay with the ring, too?" Della pressed.

"Of course." Logan moved closer and thanked her when Della cut off a piece of the hot bread for him.

"So, was it lucky timing that you were here for the proposal?" Della continued.

Logan took a second, bobbling the hot bread in his hand and blowing on it. "Bert mentioned you were having something catered? Are you doing that for Lucky and Cassie?"

"For Mia. It's her fifth birthday in two weeks, and she wanted a fairy-princess tea party. I thought I'd have Reese do it."

Reese?

So, they were on a first-name basis. Logan wanted to ask how that'd happened, but Della had an even better radar than Lucky. Logan definitely didn't want her thinking there was something going on between Reese and him.

"She's got experience doing kids' parties?" Logan asked.

"Don't know about that, but everybody in town is talking about what a good cook she is. She made these lemon thingies that folks are going on about."

"Yeah, I heard. But does she have experience doing kids' parties?" he repeated.

"Don't know, but she's obviously got experience baking. I'm having her do a cake and make some party food. She'll be kinda busy what with Maggie's *female problems*." Della whispered those last two words as if it were some kind of secret. It wasn't. Then she paused, nibbled on a piece of the cinnamon bread. "So, any word from Helene?"

Logan had expected the third degree about his own well-being. Not that, though. "No. I won't hear from her, either." He waited, figuring there was more.

There was.

"Her mother, Mary, called me," Della continued. "We've gotten to know each other over the years because of coordinating Helene's schedule for family events and such. Anyway, I thought you should know that Helene had some kind of mental breakdown. She's in a hospital in Houston."

Suddenly, the bread didn't taste as sweet as it had a few seconds ago. Logan let the news sink in, and he was thankful that it wasn't the heart-crushing blow it would have been just three months ago. Still, he wasn't immune to the news because Helene had been in his life a long time.

"You want to know any other details?" Della asked.

Thankfully, Logan didn't have to make a decision about that because his phone buzzed, and he saw the new text from the PI. The subject was Reese Stephens aka Reese Stephenson.

So, that explained why the PI had found so little on her during his initial search. Stephenson was her real name. But clearly the PI had learned something else.

"I need to read this," Logan said to Della, and he went out onto the back porch.

Reese's age hadn't changed from the original report. Ditto for her going to culinary school and moving around. But there was a whole lot more to the woman he'd bedded in that hotel.

Logan read through the text, and once he got his jaw unclenched, he actually managed to say something.

"Shit."

CHAPTER FIVE

REESE HADN'T COUNTED on being able to make this trip to the McCord Ranch so soon after seeing the twins, but she was thankful that their housekeeper Della had called and asked her to come over and discuss the party plans. It was the perfect excuse for Reese to get the information she needed about Logan and Lucky.

Well, hopefully it was.

Considering that everyone in town was talking about Logan's fast exit from the café, it was possible that Della was going to try to pump Reese for info while Reese was pumping the woman. Either way, if this didn't work, Reese was just going to have to come clean and admit that she did something so sleazy as have sex with a man she didn't know. Then she could get back the watch and put this whole mess behind her.

Even if Reese's body wasn't letting her forget it.

Her body didn't have a say in this, though. She'd learned the hard way that lust often drove really bad decisions, and it was obvious that sleeping with either of the McCord twins was a bad decision she couldn't repeat.

Reese followed the crude map that Sissy Lee had made for her. It wasn't that long of a walk, less than a half mile, and the house was so big that she could see it long before she got to it. Judging from the sheer size of it and the land surrounding it, the McCords were rich. Of course, she'd already guessed that, but this was rich-rich, and that meant either Lucky or Logan might be especially concerned about having spent the night with someone like her. If so, that could work in her favor because they could be eager to get rid of her.

Part of her wished that wasn't the case, though.

If this had been just another ordinary town, Reese might have considered staying on longer than three months. The pay was decent, and Bert was a good boss. Shortly after he'd hired her, he'd even helped her find a place to live, temporarily. No way could Reese have managed to swing a stay at the Bluebonnet Inn on a daily basis, but Bert had talked the owner of the inn into renting her the converted attic apartment there. It wasn't much, but then she'd never needed much, and this morning she'd learned it had a special view.

Of the McCord Cattle Brokers' building.

She'd yet to see Logan or Lucky come and go, but from everything she'd heard, Logan only left for business trips, and Lucky was only there when he couldn't avoid it. Or when he was checking on his twin. The buzz was that Lucky was still worried about Logan. Everyone in town was.

Logan was Spring Hill's rock star.

And no one she'd encountered so far was taking his ex's side in the breakup. The general consensus was that Helene should be burned at the stake for breaking poor Logan's heart.

Reese walked up the circular drive, and as she neared the house, she caught the scent of poop. She hoped that wasn't some kind of bad omen.

She made her way up the porch, but the door opened

before she could even ring the bell. The outside of the house was so, well, pastoral looking, but that didn't apply to the inside. The tall brunette woman in the doorway looked frazzled. With good reason. There were cats—lots of them—darting around.

Two small children, as well.

There were shouts of laughter. Plain out shouting, too, from a teenage girl on the stairs who apparently wasn't happy about her sister using her makeup on one of the cats. Reese quickly spotted which cat. It was all white except for pink blush on its cheeks.

"I'm Reese—"

"Yes, I know. Della's expecting you. No school today," the woman said as if that explained everything. "I'm Cassie Weatherall. Please come in."

Cassie as in Lucky's soon-to-be fiancée. Reese recognized her from some TV talk shows, the sort where the host and his or her guests attempted to solve some huge problem in the span of an hour. Minus the commercials, of course. There were usually shouts and paternity test results involved.

Cassie looked around outside before she shut the door. "Where's your car?"

"I don't have one. I walked."

She shook her head. "If you need to come out here again, just call the house, and someone can come and get you. Mia, don't touch Mackenzie's makeup again," Cassie warned the younger girl without even pausing to take a breath.

"Sorry," the little girl said as she flew past them. A little boy was chasing her with what appeared to be a magic wand and a chocolate-chip cookie.

The meager apology was apparently enough to get

the teenager to whirl around and disappear into the hall off the top of the stairs.

"This way," Cassie said after she shouted for the children to settle down.

Cassie might look like the prim and proper therapist, but her shout was all mom. According to the gossip Reese had heard at the diner, Cassie had fallen right into that role. Had fallen into the role of being a McCord, too. Cassie had given up her job as a celebrity therapist and had opened an office in Spring Hill. Considering the divorce rate was almost nil, the crime rate as well, it was possible she wouldn't get a lot of business. Then again, there could be a lot of skeletons jangling in closets.

Reese didn't mean to dodge Cassie's gaze, but she couldn't quite look the woman in the eye. She had no idea if Lucky had actually cheated on Cassie, but if so, it was a little stomach-turning to think that Reese could have been the other woman.

Cassie led Reese to the back of the sprawling house to an equally sprawling kitchen where a woman with pinned-up gray hair was at the stove.

"You're here," Della said, smiling.

But she wasn't alone in the kitchen, and the person at the table definitely wasn't smiling. Even though Reese couldn't be certain, she thought this might be Logan.

"You're late," the man said.

Yes, Logan.

The brusque tone caused Reese to freeze. Not Della, though. The woman popped him on the shoulder with a wooden spoon. "What kind of welcome is that?" Della scolded him.

Reese suspected Della was one of the few people on

the planet who could get away with that question. Or
the spoon pop.

Cassie shot Logan a glare. "Reese had to walk here,"
Cassie informed him.

Logan didn't look exactly pleased with that explanation or the spoon popping. Or with Reese.

"Logan's mad because I said I wasn't going to ask
you for references," Della explained.

Oh.

Well, that told her loads. He was suspicious of her.
Unless Logan was this careful about everyone who
crossed paths with his family.

"We need to talk," Logan told her, and he took hold
of Reese's arm.

"She's here to go over the party," Della protested, but
she might as well have been talking to the air because
Logan didn't listen. And he was out of spoon range now.

Reese didn't put up any resistance whatsoever. She'd
come here hoping to have a private word with either
Logan or Lucky, and she was apparently going to get
it. Though it still didn't mean he was the one she'd
slept with. This little chat could be a warning for her to
stay away from his brother. Or away from his family's
kitchen if he was truly concerned about her references.

Logan led her to the side of the house to a sunroom
that overlooked one of the white-fenced pastures. Reese
hadn't smelled the poop in the main part of the house,
but she certainly did back here.

"Yeah, we're working on that," he grumbled.

Until he said that, Reese hadn't even been aware she
was making a face. That's because she was focused on
the face Logan was making at her. Sissy Lee had said
Lucky had a panty-dropping smile, but Logan must have

missed out on that particular genetic trait. His abilities seemed more geared toward intimidation tactics.

"What kind of game are you playing, huh?" Logan demanded.

Since that could cover a lot of territory, Reese went with a question of her own. "What kind of game do you think I'm playing?"

Man, he was the rock star of glares, too. "What happens in San Antonio stays in San Antonio?" he tossed at her.

Bingo. So, he was the one. Part of her was relieved that he was the hot cowboy and not Lucky. At least this way Cassie wouldn't be hurt.

"How did you find me?" he snapped.

"Your truck."

He nodded as if no further explanation was necessary. Reese braced herself for the questions that would almost certainly follow.

Or not.

Logan inched toward her, and it didn't appear he had question-asking on his mind. He moved close enough that Reese caught his scent. Very familiar. And as it done that night in the hotel bar, his scent slid right through her. Pretty amazing considering it wasn't any particular scent and managed to completely erase the bull-poop odor.

For a moment, she thought he was going to kiss her. He moved in as if he might just do that despite the steely look in his eyes. And for a moment it might have seemed to him as if he were going to kiss her, too. His gaze dropped to her mouth before he snapped it away and met her eye to eye.

"I ran a background check on you," he threw out there.

Of course he had. Reese wondered why she hadn't considered it sooner. Oh, mercy. Not this, not now. Had Logan learned what had happened? She hoped not. She hated the thought of anyone knowing how stupid she'd been.

"Are you here to run some kind of con?" Logan added, and his glare didn't ease up one bit.

So, he'd found out about that part of her past. He didn't know about Spenser. Because if Logan knew that, he would have brought it up first.

"I'm not here to con you." Reese was certain he wouldn't believe her, though. And he didn't.

Logan opened his mouth, no doubt to demand that she leave and never come back, but before he could say a word, someone yelled out, "No!" and it was followed by a loud cry.

Logan scrambled around her, running toward the sound of that cry, and when Reese caught up with him, she saw the little girl, Mia, on the floor at the bottom of the stairs. She was sobbing and holding her arm.

"Mia was chasing the cat on the stairs and fell," Cassie explained.

Cassie wasn't sobbing exactly, but she was crying. And looking very much like a concerned mom. So was the teenager who was coming down the steps to her sister's aid. And the little boy she'd seen playing with Mia earlier. He also had tears in his eyes. Heck, so did Reese, she realized.

"I think it's broked," Mia said through the sobs.

Logan was the only one not in the crying/panic mode. He eased Mia into his arms and started toward the door. "Cassie and I'll take her to the ER. Someone call Lucky and have him meet us there."

"Do you need me to go with you?" Reese asked him.

"No, stay here and finish your *chat* with Della."

Della took out her phone, and Cassie hurried to open the door. Logan followed Cassie out but not before looking back at Reese.

"This isn't over," Logan warned her.

REESE DREAMED ABOUT LOGAN. And tonight it was just as good as the real thing had been.

The kiss in the hotel bar especially.

Until that kiss Reese hadn't been sure she could even go through with the last item on her bucket list, but that kiss had pretty much put to bed any doubts she'd had. And it had just been the start.

Logan had initiated the second kiss, in the elevator as they'd headed up to the room. In fact, the kiss had gotten so scalding hot that his hand had ended up under her top, his leg between hers, and there was a whole lot of pressure from his body pressing hers against the elevator door.

That'd been incredible until the door opened, and they'd tumbled out into the hall and landed on their butts.

The clumsiness hadn't stopped there. Nope. They had been so busy kissing and grappling at each other that they'd banged into the wall outside her room, once with such precision that they'd nearly had accidental sex in the hall.

Even now in the dream, Reese could still feel that hunger. Hunger she hadn't even known was there. And there were sounds that had never been in the dream before, either. Knocking sounds. It was almost as if Logan and she were having sex against the wall, after all.

Or not.

Because the dream changed. Not to sex with Logan but to another part of her life. One she didn't want to remember. But she did.

Spenser.

It was hard to hide from memories in a dream because they chased you down, chewed you up, and there was nothing she could do to stop it.

But the sound stopped it. And the sound wasn't part of the dream this time. Definitely not Logan. That became clear when she heard someone call out her name. Her real name. Logan had only called her Julia that night. And whoever was calling out her name now was also knocking on her door.

Jimena.

For a moment, Reese thought her friend might be part of the dream, as well. She staggered out of bed and went to the door, checking the time along the way. It was close to midnight.

And it was Jimena, all right.

"Food pimp," Jimena said, holding up several large grocery bags. She came in, looked around. Not that she had to look far to take it all in. It was only about two hundred feet of space for the kitchen, bed, sitting area and bathroom.

"Uh, what are you doing here?" Reese asked.

Not that she wasn't happy to see her, but when Jimena had dropped Reese off in Spring Hill four days ago, Jimena had said she was heading back to Houston to see some old friends. When they'd spoken on the phone earlier that morning, Jimena hadn't mentioned anything about a visit.

"I'm here to help you." Jimena handed her the bags of groceries, which Reese was certain contained nothing but junk food. She closed the door, took Reese by the hand and led her to the window.

"See that guy?" Jimena asked.

There were streetlights, but it still took Reese several moments to pick through the night and see the man in the back parking lot of the McCord building. Definitely not Lucky or Logan.

"Who is he?" Reese wanted to know.

"Some guy I met at a bar in San Antonio. His name is Elrond—you know like in *Lord of the Rings*? His dad was a huge fan. I know, I violated my bucket rule of making my way through the alphabet. I was up to the *I*'s, but all the *I*-guys I met didn't do anything for me. Anyway, Elrond's a great kisser, but he's got something even better in his jeans."

Reese groaned. She was so not in the mood for one of Jimena's sex spill-alls. "I have the breakfast shift at the café. I have to be at work in six hours."

"Well, this shouldn't take long at all." She pointed to Elrond again. "He's got a key to the McCord building."

Instant suspicion.

Of course Reese had told Jimena about her Lucky/Logan dilemma, but she certainly hadn't expected Jimena to do anything about it. Especially anything illegal.

"Did he steal the key?" Reese asked.

"No. He was doing some renovations for the McCords a while back and forgot to return the key. I figured you could use it to look for the watch while no one's there."

Reese was still skeptical. "And how do you know no one is there? Logan has an apartment on the top floor."

Jimena smiled. "He's not there tonight. Don't you ever listen to gossip? The clerk at the gas station said Logan was in Dallas for a meeting and won't be back until tomorrow."

It was the first Reese was hearing of this—and yes, she did listen to gossip. Hard not to hear it in a town this small. But she hadn't been especially listening for gossip about Logan but rather Mia. It turned out that the little girl's arm wasn't broken, after all, just sprained and bruised.

"You said you were anxious to get the watch and then leave town," Jimena reminded her. "So, here's your chance. Say, what made you so eager to leave, anyway?"

"Logan. He ran a background check on me."

Jimena gasped. A reaction that Reese had had herself. Her past had a nasty way of coming back to haunt her. Usually she could outrun it, but this time it'd caught up with her.

"Did Logan tell your boss?" Jimena asked.

"Not yet. But he will." If it hadn't been for taking Mia to the ER and then this trip to Dallas, Logan probably would have already done it.

That meant tonight might be her last chance to find that watch. Bert probably wouldn't fire her on the spot, but that was only because of his wife's surgery. He needed her for both the breakfast and lunch shifts, but he would give Reese her walking papers as soon as he could find someone else. Or heck, maybe he would just close the café for a while.

"I don't even know if the watch is in the McCord building," Reese admitted.

"Elrond said Logan lives there, like all the time. Where else would he have put it?"

Maybe in the trash, but that tightened her stomach just thinking about it.

"If you find it, you won't even have to do the breakfast shift," Jimena said. "You can grab Tootsie Roll and ride back with me to San Antonio."

It was past being tempting, and it wasn't as if she had a ton of options. Now that Logan knew who she was, he might never give her back the watch because he might think she'd stolen it.

"You're sure you can trust Elrond?" Reese asked.

"The man gives multiple orgasms. Of course I can trust him."

There was no correlation to that, none, but Reese decided she had no choice but to risk it. She put the grocery bags on the counter, pulled on her jeans and a T-shirt and followed Jimena out to the stairs and then out of the Bluebonnet. They didn't walk on Main Street but rather on the street behind the inn. Probably because Jimena wanted to make sure they weren't seen.

Reese only hoped she didn't regret this, but she already had a bad feeling about it.

When they made it to Elrond, he kissed Jimena, and they started in on a make-out session while he handed Reese the key. His aim wobbled, because he had his eyes closed while kissing, and Reese finally just snagged them. Part of her almost hoped the key didn't work, that Logan had changed the locks.

But it worked just fine.

She slipped into the back door, the AC immediately

spilling over her. The floors were marble, all shiny and cool, and even the walls had some kind of slick finish to them. The bottom floor was dark except for the base lighting around a copper and bronze sculpture of a longhorn. It was large enough to have been a real cow, and Reese dodged the lethal-looking horns as she made her way around it.

She also had to fight back a scream when something went zipping past her. Sheez. It was possibly a raccoon.

Or a very small, hyped-up guard dog.

It shot out of the reception area and disappeared. No growling sounds. No clawing sounds, either, so she hoped it wasn't coming back for her.

Since she wasn't sure how much time she had, Reese went straight to the hall. There were a series of offices, thank goodness with nameplates on the outside. Logan's was all the way at the end.

And locked.

She tried the key, but it didn't work. Sadly, she knew how to pick a lock, but she hadn't brought the old tools of an old trade with her. Elrond probably had something that would work, but judging from the way Jimena and he had gone after each other, he probably had her on the backseat by now for another round of those multiple orgasms.

Instead, Reese went up the stairs. There were more offices here on the second floor, each door indicating the name of another person who worked for Logan and his brothers. She doubted he'd put a watch in any of these offices so she went up the final flight of stairs to the third floor.

There were double doors, wide-open, so she stepped inside.

Whoa.

Unlike her place at the Bluebonnet Inn, this loft was huge. It sprawled over the entire third floor. There were no overhead lights on, but thankfully there was enough illumination coming from the appliances in the kitchen area that she could see well enough.

And what she could see was a mess.

There were gouges in the walls as if someone had punched it multiple times. No, correction. Someone had thrown stuff at it because some of that stuff was still on the polished hardwood floors. Broken sculptures—including what appeared to be a porcelain breast of a woman. Books. Glass. Feathers. Even the remnants of a coffee table.

Had someone vandalized the place? Robbed it?

That caused her to mumble a couple of "Oh, Gods." Because that might mean this was some kind of setup. Maybe Elrond had willingly given her the keys so she could take the blame for this.

Reese turned to run out, but she caught the movement from the corner of her eye. In case the burglar was still there, she picked up the first thing she could grab off the floor. The porcelain breast. Hardly a serious weapon, but she could hurl it at the person if he attacked, and the nipple might put out an eye.

But he didn't attack.

He stepped from the shadows. Slowly. As if he had all the time in the world.

It was Logan.

And he was naked.

No, not naked. He was wearing boxers, but she had focused on the naked parts because they were more noticeable. He was sipping a drink, also slowly.

"Reese," he said, his voice low and slightly dangerous.

Or maybe that was confusion in his tone because of the porcelain nippled boob she had aimed at him.

"You didn't take this to the grave very long, did you?" Logan asked, and had another sip of his drink, clearly waiting for her answer.

CHAPTER SIX

LOGAN WASN'T SURPRISED to see Reese. In fact, he'd anticipated it. In hindsight, though, he should have coupled his anticipation with a pair of pants. Greeting a burglar in his boxers just wasn't very intimidating.

Reese noticed the boxers, all right. Her gaze slid over him, and even though he couldn't see her eyes that well in the darkness, he thought maybe she was remembering the night in the hotel.

Logan certainly was.

In fact, when he'd dozed off earlier, he'd dreamed about it.

"Should I offer you a drink or call the cops?" he asked. The second one wasn't really an option, of course. No way did he want to have to explain this to anyone. But Reese didn't know that.

"You want the cops to find out you slept with me?" Reese tossed right back at him.

So she did know it was a bluff. She probably thought that made this a stalemate. It didn't. Because Logan had something Reese wanted, and it didn't have anything to do with the part of his body she was gawking at.

To stop the gawking, Logan took his jeans from the bed and pulled them on. She looked away when he did that. Maybe because she realized she'd been gawking, but her attention landed on the porcelain tit she was holding. She eased it back onto the floor with the rest of the broken clutter.

It wasn't just any old porcelain tit, though. It'd been a "special" gift from Helene. Molded porcelain bookends of her breasts. An inside joke between the two of them. But one of the bookends had gone missing before she'd been able to give the set to him so Logan had instead used it as a decorative figurine.

Logan also took his dad's knife from the nightstand and slipped it in his pocket. Not because he thought he might need it to get Reese out of there but because he didn't want to risk her stealing it.

"By the way," she said. "There's a raccoon or weird dog running around downstairs."

"Cat," he corrected. "A couple of months ago my brother brought three cats here to stay temporarily. He moved the other two, but no one's been able to catch that one."

He could understand, though, how she'd mistaken it for a raccoon because it did look like one. And Reese suddenly looked a little horrified.

"Months?" she questioned. "Please tell me someone's feeding it."

He nodded, not that he wanted to have a conversation about the feline he'd dubbed Crazy Cat. "My assistant, Greg, leaves out food and changes the litter box."

Though Greg had yet to see the cat. In fact, to the best of Logan's knowledge, only he and now Reese had actually seen it since it had been brought to the building.

And this wasn't at all what he wanted to discuss or think about.

"Redecorating?" she asked. She didn't sound concerned that she'd just been caught breaking and entering. But she did look nervous. Reese was rubbing her hands along the sides of her jeans.

"More or less."

Definitely less. The items were all things Helene had given him, and for some reason it gave him pleasure to smash them to bits. And then look at the bits. Strange because usually he couldn't stand clutter or anything out of place, but he had no desire whatsoever to clean up this mess. In fact, he was enjoying watching the fine layers of dust build up with each passing week.

Reese stayed quiet a moment while she studied him. "It really was you with me in San Antonio. After I left your house, I considered the possibility that maybe you were trying to cover for your brother, and that perhaps he'd told you what the note I left in the hotel room said. You could have done that so his girlfriend wouldn't be hurt. But it really was you. I can see it now."

It did sting a little that she hadn't been able to see it right off. He might look like Lucky, but they didn't act anything alike. Of course, he hadn't been acting like himself at that hotel, either.

"Julia Child," he said to remind her that she had been the one to set the rules for that night.

Reese nodded, pushed her hair from her face. "Hot no-name cowboy."

He waited to see if she was going to explain any of what'd happened that night. Apparently not.

"I came for the watch," she said.

Yes, he'd figured that out. But what he hadn't figured out was why. "Was it part of some con?"

Now, most people would have looked shocked and asked, What con? Or seemed outraged at such a suggestion. But because he'd run that background check on her and because she'd just broken into his place, Reese probably knew outrage and surprise would seem as genuine as the name she'd given him in that bar.

"I'd like to have that drink now," she said.

Reese sank down onto one of the chairs in the sitting area. The stuffing was coming out of it, and it was covered with feathers from the throw pillows he'd gutted. Since it was copper colored, it looked like a huge molting chicken.

The drink offer hadn't been genuine, but since Logan needed a refill, he flipped on the lamp and poured them each a glass. He handed it to her and then backed away. Even though he had on jeans now, he was still shirtless, and he was remembering the heated look she'd given him earlier.

A look he'd probably given her, too.

He didn't understand why his body was attracted to this con woman, and he didn't care. The attraction wasn't going to play into this.

"How did you get into the building?" he asked. "Did you pick the lock?"

"Key." She fished through her jeans pocket, came up with a key and dropped it on the small table next to the chair. "And don't ask how I got it."

"How'd you get it?"

She tossed back the shot and made a face just as she'd done after the tequila shots in the bar. "Found it. And no, I didn't steal it. Nor did I steal anything once I was inside." Reese paused. "You found out about my parents."

"Yes," he settled for saying. Logan didn't add more. He wanted to see what spin she would put on this.

But there was no spin. She waited him out, and

Logan decided he'd already spent too much time on Reese.

"Your parents, Marty and Vickie, are con artists. Your father died in prison a few years ago, but both have multiple arrests for pulling various scams. Scams in some cases where they used you."

The PI had provided Logan with only one such case, but he figured there were more. In the one the that PI had learned about, Reese had distracted a store owner, claiming she fell and was hurt, while her parents stole items.

"That incident with Mia must have brought back some memories for you," he snapped. "Of course, the difference is she wasn't faking. So, what else did you fake? Did you pretend to be attracted to me—"

She came off the chair so fast that Logan didn't have time to react. Reese took hold of him, jerked him to her and kissed him. It wasn't the first time he'd been forced-kissed. It had happened one other time when he was a stupid teenager and had pretended to be Lucky so he could break up with a girl who was giving him some trouble.

That kiss was nothing like this one.

For one thing, there was some anger involved here. Not on his part. Logan was still trapped between surprise and "what the hell is she doing?" stage. Reese, though, was obviously trying to make a statement, and that statement was that she could make him feel the kiss in every inch of his body.

Every. Inch.

And she succeeded.

By the time she let go of him, Logan had moved on to the next stage. A hard-on. But since his dick had already caused him to make a bad decision by sleeping with her in the first place, Logan ignored the ache in his groin and stepped back.

"That's why I slept with you," she growled. "It didn't have anything to do with who I am, your bank account, your ranch or your dusty stuff." Reese flung her hand at the damaged items again.

The kiss obviously hadn't affected her the same way it had affected him. Or so he thought. But then Logan heard her uneven breathing, saw the flush in her cheeks. Saw her glance at his hard-on. A long glance. That caused her breathing to become even more ragged.

It didn't mean anything, of course.

So what if they were attracted to each other? It didn't mean he was going to act on it. However, he was going to act on something else—getting her out of his life and away from his dick.

"For the record, I haven't seen my mother in over two years," she finally said, sinking back down onto the chair. "I really am a chef. Went to culinary school. And I wasn't running a con on you."

"Really?" He couldn't have possibly sounded more skeptical.

"Really." And she couldn't have possibly sounded more pissed off. "What else did your spies dig up on me?"

Nothing. But clearly they'd missed something. Something that Logan would have them dig even deeper to find.

"Aren't your con-artist parents enough dirt?" he asked her.

She stayed quiet again for several moments, but Logan

thought she might be relieved. Yeah, there was definitely something else to learn about Reese Stephenson.

"I've done everything I can to distance myself from my parents and the things they did," she finally said. "I never stay in one place for too long because I don't want my mother to find me."

"Then that should fit right into my plans." He nearly brought up that he didn't know what her plan had been, but he decided it wasn't wise to risk another kiss. There were condoms in the loft, and he didn't want that hard part of his body suggesting sex.

"What plans?" she asked.

"For you to leave." He heard the words. The tone. It was probably a tone he used daily to someone involved in his business deals. But it did sound a little Old West, as if he were running her out of town.

Which he sort of was.

"I can't leave," she said on a heavy sigh. "Maggie's got female problems. Her uterus collapsed—"

Logan groaned. "I don't want to hear that. I know you're pulling shifts for Bert, but once that's done, there'll be no reason for you to stay."

"No reason other than that watch."

Logan took the laptop from the floor next to where he'd been sitting and showed her the screen. Footage from the security cameras. "Less than ten minutes ago, I saw you try the door to my office. Were you trying to take something more than the watch?"

She glanced at the screen, then at him. "If you have a security system, why didn't it go off when I came in the building?"

"Because I didn't arm it. I figured you'd come eventually, and I wanted to see what you were going to do."

"The watch," she repeated.

And maybe it only was, but Logan needed more. "If the watch means so much to you, why did you put it in my pocket?"

"I nearly didn't. After I saw the engagement ring."

Yes, that would have been a shock. Well, maybe. If it was a con, then nothing should have shocked her. If he was merely her no-names-allowed one-night stand, then she probably thought he was a sleazebag.

"An asshole," Reese corrected as if she'd known what he was thinking. "But then I didn't ask about your relationship status, and you didn't ask about mine."

"Glenlivet," he said.

"Tequila," she countered.

That was the problem with too much alcohol. It dulled people's minds so they didn't ask the right questions. Well, he was asking them now.

"Why give me the watch?" he pressed. "Was it because it was stolen and you didn't want to get caught with it."

Her eyes narrowed. "Don't make me kiss you again."

His body rather liked that threat. Thankfully, his face scowled instead, as though trying to discourage a reaction. "I thought maybe you were setting me up. Giving me stolen goods that you could use to blackmail me with later."

She looked at him as if he'd sprouted an extra nose. "It belonged to my grandfather."

Logan wasn't sure how to respond to that. "If that's true, then why the hell would you give it to me?"

"I thought I was dying, okay!"

Of all the things that Logan had thought she might

say, that wasn't one of them. As cons went, it was darn original.

"I had a bucket list," she added a moment later.

Logan thought about that a second. "And I was on it?"

"Not you specifically, but it was always a fantasy of mine to be with a hot Texas cowboy."

It was a little disarming, and flattering, to think he'd been her fantasy. Well, if he believed her, that is. He didn't.

"If it was so special, why couldn't you tell me apart from my brother when you got to town?" he asked. "Most people can."

"Tequila," Reese repeated. "Trust me, I can tell you apart now. Lucky actually seems like a nice guy. He smiles. And he doesn't bark and growl at people."

Logan hadn't put much stock in the flattering fantasy, but that stung a little. Because it was true. Lucky was a nice guy, and everybody, especially women, loved him. Women had come on to Logan before, even while half-drunk in bars, but it was a rare occurrence. For Lucky, it was an hourly thing.

"I'm the kind of man I need to be to run this business," Logan said, though he wasn't sure why he felt the need to explain himself to her.

"Right. Let me guess. When your folks died, you took it on yourself because you're the oldest. By two or three minutes at most. Or maybe your father—because you were probably closer to him than your mother—asked you to take care of things. And you did. You've devoted your life to taking care of things."

Since that was an eerily accurate summary, Logan just shrugged.

"I'm also guessing that knife you put in your pocket belonged to your father, and you value it so much that you didn't want to risk me stealing it," she continued. "Or maybe you just like keeping it close."

Both. But Logan didn't confirm it. "What does that have to do with anything?"

"Nothing. But you're the one who brought up the kind of man you are."

So he had. "Well, I know what kind of woman you are. I just don't know why you felt the need to tick me off your bucket list that night."

Reese took a deep breath. "I thought I had an inoperable brain tumor and was supposed to start radiation treatments two days after we met. But it turned out to be a mistake. The hospital mixed up my records with someone else. Shannon Satterfield. She did die, by the way."

With any good con, the devil was in the details, and Reese was certainly providing the details. Logan needed to find the devil in them now.

"So, that's why I was in that hotel bar," Reese continued. "And you were there because of Helene."

Reese didn't need any big deduction skills to know that. It was all over town, but no one other than his immediate family had seen exactly what had gone on in Helene's office. In hindsight, Logan supposed plenty would have found it funny, but Logan didn't have that kind of fun meter.

"I'm sorry," Reese said. "I've been cheated on before, and I know it sucks."

He was betting she'd never walked in on her boyfriend having sex with a clown.

She stood, faced him. "Look, just give me back the

watch, and I'll leave town as soon as Maggie's uterus is well enough for Bert to return to work."

Most men would have just given her back the watch then and there and made sure she kept her promise to leave town, but Logan wasn't most men.

"Here's how this will work," he said. "You'll do the shifts you promised Bert, then leave. Once you're out of town, you'll call me, and I'll drive to wherever you are and give you the watch. That way, I know you won't stay here and run a scam."

Oh, that did not set well with her. "Fine," she grumbled, and Reese headed for the door. She made it a whole couple of steps before she whirled back around.

She was going to kiss him again. Logan just knew it. And all so she could prove some stupid point that didn't need proving—that they were attracted to each other.

So, he did something about that.

He latched onto the back of her neck, hauled her to him and kissed her before she could kiss him. As ideas went, it was a truly bad one. Because he got a jolt of a reminder of her taste. Another jolt that his hard-on could apparently get harder, after all.

Logan kissed her, deepening it, pressing her against him. And he got another reminder: that he was playing with fire.

The problem with that was the fire was playing right back.

CHAPTER SEVEN

LOGAN FORCED HIMSELF to listen to what was going on in the meeting. Like most of his meetings, this one was important, but he just couldn't seem to process the big picture as he normally could. Too many nonbusiness thoughts.

Many of those thoughts involved Reese.

Because it'd been a week since their kissing session in his loft, Logan had figured this fire for her would have cooled. Or at least Maggie would have healed so that Bert could take over his shifts and Reese could leave town. But apparently Maggie had a uterus that didn't want to cooperate because Reese was still at the Fork and Spoon, and Logan was still trying to get her out of his head.

"Well?" someone said, and since that seemed to be directed at him, Logan looked up to find everyone staring at him.

Lucky, Jason, Riley and Greg. It was Jason who'd issued the "Well?" but Logan didn't have a clue what he was supposed to say. That's because other than that one word he hadn't heard the conversation for the last three minutes.

Possibly five.

"Say, Greg, could you get us some coffee?" Lucky asked the assistant. "I think we could all use a break."

Lucky was clearly looking out for him, probably because he thought Logan was slipping into a depression or something. He wasn't. But Logan didn't intend to tell his brother or anyone else that what was slipping was his sanity. Because he was obviously a fool to be spending this much mental energy thinking about a woman like Reese.

Greg scurried out in that twitchy way he had about him, and that's when Logan noticed Greg had a big red zipper running down the back of his yellow jacket. Probably some kind of fashion statement, but Logan wasn't even going to attempt to figure out what that statement was.

"Doesn't that guy own any normal clothes?" Jason mumbled.

"Apparently not," Logan answered, and his brothers made sounds of agreement.

"You should get a cowboy in here," Jason suggested. "At least one to man the front desk."

Logan huffed. "I tried that once. Let's just say I need slightly better people skills than the cowboy I hired. Greg's good at everything but clothing choices." He paused. "So, what did I miss?"

"You signed over your bank account to us," Riley joked. And he stared at Logan, apparently waiting for some kind of explanation as to why he'd tuned out.

"Headache," Logan said, tapping his temple. Not exactly a lie. He'd battled a migraine just the day before, and he still had traces of it.

Even though he'd never talked about his headaches to anyone but Lucky, Riley and Jason didn't seem surprised, which meant maybe Logan hadn't been as good at masking the pain as he'd thought. He certainly hadn't been good at masking his distraction.

"What's the bottom line here?" Logan asked Jason so he could get back on track and finish this.

To get the blood circulating better, Logan stood from the large oval desk in the meeting room and went to the window. Since this particular room was on the second floor, he had a bird's-eye view of Main Street. And, if he craned his neck just a little, of the Fork and Spoon. If he craned his neck in the other direction, he could see the Bluebonnet Inn where Reese was staying.

"Well?" Lucky asked again.

Apparently, with all that craning, Logan had missed the bottom line.

"Sorry, Jason, but I think we should put off buying the bulls," Lucky said, saving Logan's butt. Logan would thank him for it later. "The price is decent. Not great, mind you. You could do better, but we're heavily stocked at the moment."

Logan nodded and returned to the desk. "Can you hold off another month so we can reassess?" he asked Jason.

Jason flexed his eyebrows, huffed, signs that he didn't want to hold off, but he would. Maybe in a month Logan would have his head back on straight. Except he hoped it didn't take that long.

Greg came back in, scurrying still. The man moved like a cartoon character who drank an hourly six-pack of Red Bull, and he deposited a tray with coffee on the center of the table.

"Thanks," Logan said. "The meeting's done, but could you arrange a cleaning crew to go to my loft and remove everything but the appliances, my desk and my clothes? I also want them to patch up the holes in the wall."

The four men looked at him as if he'd lost his mind. He hadn't. This was the next step to regaining it.

"Anything else?" Greg asked.

"Call Henderson's and see if they can deliver new furniture as soon as the cleaning crew is done."

"Uh, what kind of furniture?" Greg asked.

Since this had always been Helene's domain, Logan didn't have a clue. "You decide."

Despite Greg's questionable taste in clothes, it wouldn't matter. Henderson's was the only furniture store in town, and they didn't have a purple or yellow piece of anything. Whatever Greg picked out would be boring and tasteful.

Greg jotted that down, hurried out. Riley and Lucky mumbled something about getting back to work, leaving Jason and Logan alone. Jason shut the door.

"Trying to rid yourself of Helene?" Jason asked.

"Yes," he admitted. Rid himself of the pieces of her, anyway, since he'd bashed most of the things she'd put in his loft.

Like a moth to a flame, Logan went to the window again and started more neck craning. He'd quit asking himself why he was doing it. "Della said Helene had a breakdown."

"I heard that," Jason admitted, then joined Logan at the window. "Do you still love her?"

"No." Logan didn't even have to think about that.

Jason shook his head, blew out a deep breath. "You two were together a long time. You're sure you just want to throw that all away?"

That was possibly the only question that could have

pulled Logan's attention away from the window. His friend, who was about to cross a line he shouldn't.

"You think I should forgive her?" Logan asked, already knowing that wasn't going to happen.

Jason nodded. "Not for her sake but for yours. Clearing out your loft is a good start. You need to do things like that to get your life back on track. But forgiving Helene is part of that, too." He paused again. "Did you ever really love her?"

Yep, that line had just been crossed, and Logan would have told Jason that if he hadn't looked back out the window and seen something that caught his attention. Reese, coming out of the Bluebonnet Inn. Since it was ten fifteen in the morning, she was no doubt on her way to the café to get ready for the lunch shift.

Logan was suddenly in the mood for a burger.

Which he'd resist, of course.

It was one thing to spy on her, just to make sure she wasn't up to something, but there was no reason for him to spy on her face-to-face. Or eat what she cooked.

Reese glanced around, something he'd noticed that she usually did. It was as if she expected someone or something to jump out at her. Probably something she'd learned from her con-artist past. But she didn't just look around. She also looked up.

Logan stepped back a little because she glanced up at the McCord building. Not at this particular window exactly. She seemed to be glancing at his loft. Reese might have done that because she expected him to be watching her.

Which he was.

He'd warned her that he would be keeping an eye on her. Despite that scalding kiss a week earlier, he had let her know that he still didn't trust her. That made him seem a little off-balanced because why would he kiss a woman he didn't trust? The bigger question, though, was why did he want to kiss her again?

He wouldn't. No way. And he wanted to believe that. Man, did he.

The best thing would be for Maggie to get better so Bert could return to his regular hours. Then he could give Reese the watch and send her on her way. That was the way to ensure there were no more kisses.

"Sorry," Jason said. "I just stepped in shit with that question about Helene. I'll take it back."

Good. Because Logan had no intention of dignifying it with an answer.

"That's the new cook at the Fork and Spoon," Jason remarked. "Have you had one of those lemon thingies she makes?"

"No." But Logan was starting to think he was missing out on something amazing since people brought it up all the time.

"It just sort of melts in your mouth," Jason went on. "She's attractive, isn't she? You know, in a hot unmade-bed kind of way? I know she's not my usual type, definitely nowhere near your type, either, but I was thinking about asking her out for a drink."

Jason was certainly stepping in a lot of shit today, and Logan was about to tell him that it was time for him to leave, but he saw something that grabbed his attention even more than Reese had.

The man following her.

The guy appeared to be in his late forties, thinning ginger hair, skinny, with a face like a rooster. He stepped out from the alley by the hardware store and fell in step behind her.

"You recognize that guy?" Jason asked, following Logan's gaze.

"No."

Reese kept on walking, but when she reached the Lookie Here Thrift Shop, she must have seen the guy's reflection in the storefront windows. She stopped, turned and faced him. Judging from her body language, she certainly recognized him. Logan wished he had binoculars because it was hard to see her expression, but he thought he saw her shoulders go stiff.

So did the man's.

They stood there, staring at each other, reminding Logan of two Old West gunslingers about to draw on each other. They stayed that way for several tense moments before the man reached out and slammed Reese against the door of the Lookie Here.

REESE'S HEAD WAS in the clouds. Or rather her eyeballs were on the window of the McCord building, and that's why she had no idea how long the man had been following her. But after seeing his reflection, she had no doubts that he was indeed following her.

Chucky Dayton.

She so didn't have time for this now. Reese spun around, stopping him in his tracks. He was scowling, but then she'd never seen Chucky without a scowl. She wasn't sure if his face had frozen that way in some kind of weird tic or if he saved those craggy scowls just for her.

"Reese." He said her name as if she were a persistent toenail fungus. "You know how long it took me to find you?"

"I'm guessing here…but about eight months."

Except it wasn't really a guess. He'd found her in Abilene, threatened her, scowled at her and generally made her life miserable until she'd left. Then again, she'd been planning on leaving Abilene that week, anyway. Chucky's arrival had just sped things up a bit.

"Eight months, three days," he corrected as if she'd just made a huge error in her time calculations. "I guess you didn't think I'd find you."

"No. I knew you would. You usually do." It just surprised her that it always took so long. She only used two names—Reese Stephens and Reese Stephenson. A three-year-old with a couple of minutes of internet access probably could have found her.

"And I'll keep on finding you," Chucky snarled, "until you give me what you owe me."

"What my parents owe you," she reminded him.

He didn't listen to that. Chucky never did. And it wasn't as if she could blame him for being angry.

Her parents had indeed conned him out of some money. How much exactly she wasn't sure. The first time Chucky had confronted her five years ago, the amount had been five grand. It had increased each time they met so either Chucky was into embellishment, had a bad memory or he continued to be conned by her mother so the amount was going up.

"You're their daughter," he argued. "And since I can't find your mother, that means you owe me. I want my eighteen thousand dollars, and I want it now."

Reese didn't have anywhere near that kind of money, especially after those charity donations she'd made, but even if she had the cash, she wouldn't have given it to Chucky to settle her parents' debt.

"You're not getting a dime from me," she told him. Maybe she should record that promise because she ended up saying the exact thing to him each time. "I don't clean up my parents' messes anymore."

Chucky wobbled his head, possibly trying to look indignant. He probably didn't know it made him look even more like a chicken than usual. "I can make things real bad for you here."

And then he made a mistake.

A big one.

He caught onto Reese and pushed her against the Lookie Here. Chucky didn't put much muscle behind it, probably because he didn't have much of it in his wormy body. But the slight push brought all the memories ramming into her. Just like that, Reese's breath vanished, and her heart was in her throat.

This wasn't Spenser, she reminded herself. And she repeated it like a stupid mantra.

Chucky's push didn't just get Reese's attention. It also got the store owner's attention, and Gemma Craft, who was Bert's cousin twice removed, came running out with a baseball bat. Both the bat and Gemma looked pretty darn lethal, but Reese didn't intend to let someone else fight her battles for her. She went old-school and rammed her knee into Chucky's nuts.

If he had nuts, that is.

Again, he didn't look endowed in any area except for that beak-like nose. However, even his tiny nuts must have been sensitive because he grabbed his crotch with both hands and howled in pain.

Gemma kept the bat lifted like an ax aimed right at

Chucky's head. "You want me to call the cops?" she asked Reese.

Reese didn't get a chance to tell her no, that she would handle this. That's because she heard the footsteps, and glanced behind her to see Logan sprinting toward her. He made it to her with gold-medal-winning speed.

"What the hell's going on here?" Logan demanded.

"This brainless wonder shoved Reese," Gemma explained. "I saw it with my own eye." Gemma hadn't mistakenly omitted the plural. She really did only have one eye, and she wore a patch on the other one.

Judging from Logan's reaction, he'd seen it, too. With both of his eyes. Probably because he'd been looking at her from his window.

Reese doubted that window-looking had anything to do with the kissing, either. No. He was making sure she wasn't stirring up trouble, and here trouble was being stirred up right in front of them.

"I'm calling the cops," Gemma said, turning to go back inside.

"Thanks, but I can handle this," Reese assured her. Possibly a lie.

Probably a lie, she silently amended.

Reese could handle Chucky, all right. That metaphorical three-year-old with a laptop could handle him, but the old memories were washing over her like acid. Plus, there was the new layer added to this. The mess that Chucky would start slinging that would make her not want to handle it. Because this was exactly the sort of thing Logan had been sure she would bring into his life.

"You want to tell me what's going on here?" Logan asked.

Not particularly, but Reese doubted he was just going

to walk away. Neither would Chucky, once he could walk, that is. He was still wheezing and holding his bruised nuts as if they were Fabergé eggs.

"This is Chucky Dayton," Reese explained. "My parents conned him, and now Chucky likes to find me and try to intimidate me. In turn, I end up kicking him in the balls."

Logan didn't roll his eyes exactly, but it was close. And he did groan. It had an "I knew it!" ring to it.

"I do intimidate her," Chucky said. Not easily but he got the words out, and his voice was even more high-pitched than usual. "She always runs from me."

"I always move," Reese corrected. "But then I move for all sorts of reasons." The bottom line was that she moved, period, and it rarely had anything to do with Chucky.

She would in this case, though.

"I'm not gonna let Reese get away with this," Chucky snapped. "She kneed me in the privates."

"Because you pushed her against the wall," Logan snapped right back.

So, he'd definitely seen that, and it had probably looked worse than it was, but repeating the analogy again, Chucky had the strength of a three-year-old.

Logan took a step closer to Chucky. He didn't get in his face. Didn't have to. In fact, he didn't even have to take that step to look intimidating. Simply put, Logan did not look like a friendly sort.

"If you don't leave town," Logan told Chucky, the muscles in his face squirming against each other, "I'll have you arrested."

"And who do you think you are?" Chucky fired back.

"Logan McCord."

It wasn't just the name. It was the way he said it. His tone, narrowed eyes and glare were about a thousand steps past the unfriendly stage.

But apparently the name meant something to Chucky, too. Of course, he would have had to be blind and deaf not to know that the McCords were the big guns in this little-gun town. However, it wasn't just fear that crept into Chucky's chicken eyes. It was greed. It was possible he saw Logan as a source for recouping his money.

Damn.

Chucky wasn't dangerous, but he was persistent and annoying, and he would peck away at her by using Logan. And it wouldn't take much. Just dropping the truth about her parents, and that truth would spread like wildfire. It would hurt Logan's good name just because he was standing here protecting her.

Maybe it was Logan's glare, but Chucky finally turned and hobbled away. Reese wished it was the last she'd see of him, but she knew it wouldn't be.

"I'll leave town this afternoon," she said to Logan. "After I finish the lunch shift."

Logan turned that glare on her, and while it did soften just a smidge, it still let her know that he was not happy about this situation. "You're shaking," he pointed out.

"Nerves." Not a lie. Every nerve in her body was just beneath her skin and was zinging.

"He scared you," Logan added.

It was something a normal person said in situations like this. Perhaps meant to give her some kind of comfort, but it sounded as if there was something more to it.

God, did Logan know?

"I need to get to work," Reese insisted. "My shift starts in a half hour."

That was plenty enough time before the café opened at eleven for lunch. Besides, Reese had finished most of the prep after the breakfast shift when she'd clocked out at nine-thirty. The break in between the shifts had given her just enough time to go home and fix herself a bite to eat. Something Reese wished she hadn't done because she could have avoided a Main Street showdown/nut-kicking with Chucky.

Reese started in the direction of the café, fully expecting Logan to follow her. And he did.

"Chucky will be back?" he asked.

She nodded. "But not before he spreads every rumor that he can think to spread. Thankfully, Chucky's not very smart so he might not think to connect the two of us to make the dirt seem dirtier."

Logan stayed quiet a moment. "There's no way he could know about what happened in San Antonio?"

"No. If he had known, he would have blurted it out when you told him who you were. Chucky's not big on keeping secrets. But he probably has heard you and your family have money. That's why I'll leave. When I go, he'll go, too. I'm sorry, though, that you might have to do some damage control."

She wasn't sure what to make of the sound that Logan made or the fact that he followed her all the way to the café. Maybe because he thought Chucky might return for another pushing match.

Or maybe because he wanted to confront her about something else he'd learned about her ugly past.

Reese unlocked the café door and went in. When Logan continued to follow her inside, she steeled herself up for the lecture he was no doubt about to give her. Since that would put her in an even worse mood, she went into the kitchen and washed up so she could put the scones in the oven.

Or rather, biscuits.

Bert had assured her that no one would order a scone, but that everyone in town would want to sample a biscuit even if it had berries, cream or other stuff in it.

He'd been right.

"So, are those the lemon thingies everyone's talking about?" Logan asked.

Reese blinked. She hadn't expected that to be part of the lecture or confrontation. "No. These are butterscotch. I do the lemon ones every other day. If you want, I'll send Della the recipe so she can make some for you."

He mumbled a thanks, watched as she started some dough for the next batch of scones.

"Baking calms my nerves," she explained. "If you were to ever come in and see the counters filled with cakes, pies, scones and cookies, you'll know I've had a bad day."

She meant it as a joke, but her tone must have let Logan know it was too close to the truth. He kept watching, and when Reese could take no more, she whirled around to face him.

"Go ahead," she demanded. "Tell me what a piece of scum I am and that I should stay out of your life and your town." Reese hoped that was all he would tell her, though.

"It seems to me that the scum in this scenario is your parents. Did you help them con Chucky?"

"Of course not." She hadn't helped them since she was a child and didn't know any better. But at least

Logan had asked. Most people just assumed she was guilty because of her gene pool.

"Then there's no need for a lecture. Not in this scenario," he added.

"No, but my lack of guilt won't stop Chucky from blabbing. My advice is just to ignore the gossip he stirs up. It'll go away pretty fast after I leave today."

She hoped. But then again, folks were still gossiping about Logan, Helene and the clown.

"You're really leaving?" he asked.

"Yes." Reese didn't have to think about that. It was the only way to get Chucky to budge. The only way she could outrun the memories.

Logan nodded. "I imagine you'll have to work things out with Bert. You might not be able to do that today. He's at a doctor's visit with Maggie in San Antonio. They probably won't be back until late."

True. "I can leave in the morning, then."

Another nod. He checked his watch. Checked the windows behind them. Basically, he was doing something she'd never seen Logan do.

Fidgeting.

"You're doing the dinner shift, too?" he asked.

"No. Sissy Lee's brother's doing it."

A third nod. "All right. I've got to leave for a meeting, but come by my place tonight around eight, and I'll give you the watch."

It was her turn to nod and mumble a thanks. A mumble because she was shocked that Logan was going to carry through on his promise to return it.

Logan didn't say anything else. He just turned and walked out. But he didn't have to say anything for Reese to know what this meant.

He'd essentially just told her not to let the door hit her butt on her way out. But that was better than the alternative. Logan could have said something worse to her. Much worse.

Logan could have told her that he knew all about Spenser O'Malley. And what Spenser had done to her.

And what Reese had done to him.

CHAPTER EIGHT

THE GOSSIP WAS waiting for Logan when he got back to town after his meeting. And so was the person who'd started the gossip.

Chucky.

The weasel was in Logan's office, and he was leaning back in the chair, hands tucked behind his head as if he were lounging.

Apparently, Greg had found Chucky, invited him in for a chat and made Chucky feel right at home—exactly as Logan had instructed his assistant to do. But judging from Greg's raised eyebrows and under-the-breath mumbles, he didn't think Chucky was worthy of the kid-glove treatment.

"It's about time you got here," Chucky snapped the moment Logan walked in. "When you send for a man to come and see you, you oughta be here to see him. Especially when you send a girlie man to fetch me. Why you got that prissy pants working for you, anyway?"

Logan didn't respond. Didn't care a rat's ass about how long Chucky had had to wait, but he did care about this tool insulting Greg. Keeping that to himself for the moment, Logan went to the side of the room, to the panels that concealed a bar, and poured himself a drink. He sipped it slowly while Chucky cleared his throat.

"I'll take one of those," Chucky demanded.

Logan ignored that, too. "Tell me about this con Reese's parents supposedly pulled on you."

"It's not supposedly." But Chucky pronounced it *suppossedly*. "They did it. They got me to invest in some land deal that didn't exist. They took me for twenty grand."

"Funny, the police report you filled out said it was five grand. If you want to look at that report to refresh your memory, I can have Greg bring it in."

Chucky didn't seem especially bothered that he'd just been caught in a lie. "It started out as five grand, but I'm adding interest. And payment for my pain and suffering."

"If you're interested in payment, why not go to the source—to Reese's mother?"

Now he was bothered. "Can't find her or I would. I caught up with her mother a few years back, but she gave me the slip. Her mother is scum, and that scum's rubbed off on Reese. She might claim she's all innocent, but she's not."

The jury was still out on that.

"You've been spreading lies about me," Logan tossed out there after he'd finished his drink.

"Not lies. The truth. I saw the way you came running to defend Reese. My guess is you're doodling her."

Logan figured that was a euphemism for fucking her. He wasn't, but since he had at one time, he didn't deny it. "The lie you told said Reese is running a con on me, and that I'm paying her off so she'll stay quiet."

"So?" said with the arrogance of an idiot who didn't know who he was dealing with.

"So, it's a lie," Logan answered. "The con is on you."

Chucky gave him a blank stare. "Huh?"

"I wanted you arrested and put behind bars in a town that my ancestors built. The police chief is a good friend. In fact, just about everybody in Spring Hill is either a good friend or works for me. I've been waiting for a reason to have you locked up, and you gave it to me today when you pushed Reese."

"What?" Chucky howled, and jumped to his feet. "She kneed me in my privates."

"Only after you assaulted her. I saw it. So did eleven other people. They're all willing to testify against you."

Chucky sputtered out a few syllables. "But she owes me money. Money that either Reese—or you—is going to pay."

Logan tried to rein in his temper. Sometimes, he could put his temper to good use, but there wasn't any reason to bring out the big guns when dealing with a little moron. "No, her mother owes you the money, and neither Reese nor I will pay you a penny."

While Chucky continued to sputter and howl, Logan went closer to him. Too close. He could smell the onions and beer on the guy's breath.

"Here's how this works. I give you a fifteen-minute head start," Logan said, using his low and dangerous voice, "and as long as you leave town and never see or speak to Reese again, I won't have the police chief arrest you."

"You can't do that. Go ahead. Have him arrest me. I'll make bail and be out in a New York minute."

Logan shook his head. "My town. My rules. You'll be lucky if you're out by Christmas."

It was a bluff. It was his town, all right, but Logan had never called in favors like that. So, he added something that wasn't a bluff.

"If you don't leave and if you ever call my assistant prissy pants again, I will destroy you." Since that wasn't a bluff, Logan had no trouble giving Chucky the glare that went along with it.

The man backed away from Logan, and even though Logan couldn't see them, he could practically hear the guy's bruised balls shriveling. He went out in the hall. "I guess you're not worried about Reese getting violent again?" Chucky asked.

Logan tried not to look surprised by that question, but he must have failed because he saw the gleam of victory in Chucky's eyes.

"Reese didn't tell you, huh?" Chucky chuckled. "You should sleep with one eye open when you're around her. And if you don't believe me, just ask her about Spenser O'Malley."

REESE WAS ALL packed up. Not that it was a big deal since all of her belongings fit into the backpack. She'd added a few things during her stay in Spring Hill. She did in most places. In this case she'd bought an old bronze key from the Lookie Here Thrift Shop. It was a silly purchase, but since the initial *R* had been on it, Reese had thought it was some kind of sign.

Perhaps just a sign for her to part with the eight dollars and twenty-five cents it had cost her, but it was something small enough she could carry with her as a reminder of her time in Spring Hill. Of course she'd left enough space for the watch.

She glanced around the room where she'd been staying. Not home exactly, but it had felt better than most places. In fact, it had started to feel, well, good, until Chucky had shown up. She'd told Logan about her con artist parents, but it was another thing for him to get a dose of what that meant.

In this case—gossip. And lots of it.

According to Sissy Lee, nobody believed the gossip about Reese being there to con Logan, but the buzz was going strong, and with each new buzzing, Logan's reputation and business could be hurt. And here he was finally recovering from the ordeal with Helene.

There was fresh gossip about that, as well.

Gossip about a crew that spent most of the afternoon cleaning out Logan's loft and bringing in new furniture. Reese figured after what she'd seen there, that change was good.

She went out the back exit of the Bluebonnet Inn, making her way to the McCord building. As she always did, she checked around her, but tonight she double-checked just in case Chucky was somewhere nearby waiting to go another round.

There was gossip about Chucky, too.

Sissy Lee had heard that Logan had brought Chucky to his office, but Reese figured that had to be just a rumor. There was no reason for Logan to talk to Chucky since in a few hours Reese would be on her way out of Spring Hill, and Chucky would be gone, as well. There was a six o'clock bus leaving in the morning, and she'd already bought her ticket.

Reese pushed aside the twinge she felt in her stomach and went to the back door of the McCord building. Unlike her other visit, this time it was unlocked, and Greg was still working at his desk.

"Logan's expecting you," Greg greeted. He stood, went closer to her and leaned in as if to tell her a secret.

"Explain to Logan that the brown sofa doesn't work. It's the only one the store had in stock, but it's butt ugly."

Reese doubted she'd be staying long enough for a conversation about sofas, butt ugly ones or otherwise, but she assured Greg she would do just that if it came up. She made her way up the stairs, and like during her other visit, his loft doors were wide open. Unlike her other visit, though, she smelled chicken, onion and rosemary.

The first thing she saw was the sofa. Yes, it was ugly. The sort of piece that would probably be okay in a family room but not on gleaming hardwood floors against the backdrop of all those windows. It looked out of place.

As did Logan.

He was in the kitchen area of the loft, amid all those high-end appliances, and he was dishing up something from a skillet.

"Della fixed it," he said. "It'll actually be edible."

That's when Reese saw that he had two plates sitting on the new table. She watched, uncertain of what she should do, but then he motioned for her to sit. Apparently, he was sharing his dinner with her. And his wine. Logan opened a bottle that he took from the counter and poured two glasses.

She'd been right about those smells. It was chicken with rosemary and onions, and Della had done a baby potato dish and some steamed veggies.

"The place looks better," she said, and because Reese thought they could use some levity, she added, "I do miss the broken porcelain boob, though. It was a great conversation piece."

"I can have the work crew fish it out of the Dumpster for you."

Good, he was going for levity, too. She hoped. She really didn't want that boob.

"I'm supposed to talk you out of keeping the sofa," Reese said, still aiming for light.

"Greg." He looked over at the sofa. "It's simple, and simple works for me right now."

Reese wasn't sure if they were talking about furniture or life. Or even her. Yes, his life would be simpler when she was gone. Hers, too, she supposed. But she wanted the watch first.

He sat across from her at the bistro-sized table, eating and drinking as if this were a dinner date or something. Reese was instantly suspicious. But she was also hungry. So, she ate. It wasn't just edible, it was delicious.

"Tell me about Spenser O'Malley," Logan said.

Just like that, the food wasn't so delicious anymore. Her stomach tightened into a cold, hard knot.

"Who told you?" But she immediately waved off her question. "Chucky did." Ironic, though, since the man knew almost nothing about it.

Logan didn't press her for anything more, and Reese considered just clamming up, but he'd probably already gotten every last detail from another background check.

"What do you want to know about him?" she asked.

"What do you want to tell me?" he countered.

This was easy. "Nothing. I don't want to talk about him at all, but it's my guess that Chucky told you I was violent and then he dropped Spenser's name."

"Pretty much," Logan admitted. "All the details, though, are sealed in your juvie record."

And apparently Logan's dirt-diggers hadn't been able to get into the sealed record. Which meant she could tell Logan anything. It surprised her that she wanted him to know the truth. Well, what part of the truth she could say aloud, anyway.

"I was sixteen when I met Spenser. He was nineteen. Things were fine between us in the beginning, and then they weren't."

"He was from a good family," Logan tossed out there. He didn't add "like mine" but Reese heard the unspoken words loud and clear.

"He was, but Spenser had anger-management issues. And clout. A bad combination."

A muscle flickered in Logan's jaw. "He hit you?"

Again, there were things unspoken here. Logan had noticed how shaken up she'd been when Chucky had pushed her so maybe he'd put two and two together.

In this case, though, it didn't exactly equal four.

"He did," she admitted. "And that's all I want to say about him."

Reese expected Logan to press for more. He didn't. Maybe because it didn't matter. After all, she would soon be out of his life.

She made the mistake of looking at him, and Reese saw something she didn't want to see.

Sympathy.

Crud on a cracker. Not this. Not from Logan. She needed to get this conversation far away from Spenser, Chucky or anything else in her past.

"Before I forget," she said, and she took out the piece of paper from her jeans pocket. "That's the recipe for the lemon thingies." Reese slid it across the table just as he reached for it, and his fingers brushed across hers.

Good. This was a distraction she actually welcomed.

It felt intimate. Strange. Because this was a man she'd had sex with so a simple touch should have been just that: a simple touch. Of course, maybe nothing was simple when it came to Logan.

"I talked to Della about getting someone else to do Mia's party," Reese explained. Best to keep the conversation moving. "She was a little disappointed but said it wasn't a problem."

Reese hadn't wanted to tell Della that she'd been disappointed, too. She wasn't a kids' party expert, but she had been looking forward to doing the cake and food for the little girl.

"Did you really bring Chucky to your office?" she came out and asked.

He nodded. "I don't think he'll be bothering you again, but I could be wrong. You should be careful just in case."

"Uh, what did you say to him?"

"We just talked." He topped off their wine, and when he set down the bottle, he took out the watch from his pocket. As she'd done with the recipe, he slid it toward her.

No finger graze this time, but the emotions hit her pretty hard when she closed her fingers around it. For such a small piece of gold, it always packed an emotional wallop.

"Thank you," she managed to say, though now there was a lump in her throat.

"The watch is important to you." Not a question, but it was still an understatement.

"Very. It doesn't work. Hasn't since, well, in a long time. But it's still the only thing I actually treasure."

She'd always said she would get it fixed but had never gotten around to it. It didn't have to tell time for her to feel the connection to the man who'd given it to her.

"You loved your grandfather?" he asked.

It took her a moment to trust her voice. More wine helped. "Yes. He was the only sane thing in my life when I was growing up. He died when I was twelve. After that, no more sanity until I was able to escape at sixteen."

"You ran away from home?"

She hoped this didn't take them back to the subject of Spenser. "More like my parents ran away from me. I called the cops on them when they took some things from one of our elderly neighbors. They were arrested, and when they made bail, they didn't come back to the apartment. I figured if I stayed, I'd end up in foster care so I took off."

This probably sounded like a nightmare to someone who'd been raised on that massive McCord Ranch. Then again, Logan had had his own version of a nightmare. "You were…what…nineteen when your parents died?" she said. "So, you weren't much older than I was when you were on your own."

Reese instantly regretted bringing that up. Logan dodged her gaze, and he took a moment before he shook his head. "I wasn't on my own. I had Della and Stella. My brothers and sister. The whole town rallied around us. Plus, I had finished high school and was in my first year of college."

Still, a town, housekeepers and siblings couldn't replace loving parents, and from everything she'd heard, his parents had been exactly that—loving. However, there seemed to be something missing, something he wasn't saying that made her believe their deaths were still a wound that hadn't fully healed.

They finished their meal and gathered up the dishes to take to the sink. "Did my friend Jason say anything to you today?" he asked.

The question was so out of the blue that it threw her for a moment. Good grief. Who had tattled? "He came into the café at the end of the lunch shift and asked me out. I didn't think anyone heard him."

"Word gets around."

That was it. No opinion on how he felt about that. Which meant Logan probably didn't have an opinion. Still, this whole eating-chicken deal seemed as if he did indeed have something to say to her. If he'd just wanted her out of his life, he could have had Greg bring over the watch, and it would have saved him from washing an extra plate and wineglass.

"In case you're wondering, I told Jason no, that I was leaving town," Reese explained.

"And if you weren't leaving?"

Logan didn't seem like the type to pose what-if questions. "What's this all about?" she came out and asked.

He took his time. "Jason doesn't know what happened between us."

Oh, she got it then. "You're worried I'll say something to him. I won't. What happens in San Antonio..." Reese stopped. "Or maybe you're just concerned that I'm not the right kind of woman for him."

"You're not."

Reese pulled back her shoulders, was ready to say a quick goodbye, but then Logan added, "Jason moves pretty fast from one woman to another without thinking things through. He tends to hurt women without even realizing it."

She pulled back her shoulders even more but this time for a different reason. "Are you actually looking out for me?"

He stared at her and leaned against the sink. "I can't get involved with you."

A burst of air left her mouth. It sounded like a laugh, but it definitely wasn't humor driven. "Believe me, I understand."

"No, you don't. You think it's because of what people will say. And that was part of it in the beginning. It's because I'm not ready to get involved with anyone."

"Believe me, I understand," she repeated, this time without the humorless burst of air. "It's only been a couple of months, and you were with Helene for a long time. Plus, there's the whole thing about us not being compatible."

The moment the last word left her mouth, she got a flash of them in bed together. Naked. With Logan's toned and perfect body stretched out over hers. The brief image was more than enough for her to remember everything. To feel everything. And the heat slid through her, settling in her female nether regions.

"Opposites," she amended. Because they had been compatible in bed.

He nodded. Gave her a long, lingering look that singed her toenail polish along with frying some brain cells. The man should come with a warning label attached to his zipper.

She headed to the door, and Logan followed her. Reese turned back around to tell him good, but Logan spoke before she could say anything.

"I want you to stay," he said.

Because she was still dealing with the singeing and frying, it took her a moment to hear him.

"In town?" she clarified. Because her mind was already starting to weave a nice little fantasy where they got naked and landed in bed.

"In town," he verified. Though she thought he might be dealing with his own singeing feelings. Feelings he definitely didn't want to have even though it was just old-fashioned lust.

"You're okay with that?" she asked.

He shrugged. "Sure."

Boy, talk about a conflict in body language so she repeated it. "You're okay with that?"

"Della said I was being an ass," he explained. "She guessed the reason you were leaving had something to do with me. I don't know how. I swear the woman has ESP. So, I told her that I would let you know it was okay for you to stay."

Reese gave that some thought. "If I stay, we'll end up in bed again."

"Yes." No hesitation. Not a drop. And neither was the kiss he gave her.

He didn't linger with the kiss as he had done the look. Just a quick brush on her mouth to let her know that if she stayed, she could have a whole lot more of Logan.

But not without risks.

She figured those risks were too big to take. Not just for Logan but for herself.

"Goodbye," she told him.

Reese walked away and didn't look back. The best thing she could do for Logan and for herself was be on that 6:00 a.m. bus out of town.

CHAPTER NINE

EVEN THOUGH LOGAN knew it was a dream, he couldn't force himself to wake up. Images of the accident that felt so real he could practically feel the cold rain on his skin, could smell the stench of the gasoline spewing from the cars.

Logan didn't remember getting out of his truck. Not then, not now in the dream. He was just there, his feet on the asphalt, running in the rain to get to them in time.

The steam from the radiator had fogged up the windshield and windows, but even through the cloudy glass, he saw Claire. His folks had given her a ride home from a ball game, and she was in the backseat. She appeared to be dazed. Even though she'd been seventeen at the time, she looked much younger in her band uniform.

And helpless.

It seemed to take an eternity to get to the car, and Logan threw open Claire's door first. She tumbled out into his arms, no longer conscious. That's when Logan looked in the front seat.

That's when he knew he'd fucked up.

He hadn't called for help yet. And that skid had cost him seconds. Seconds he didn't have.

His parents weren't moving, though his mother was making some kind of gurgling sound in her throat. And the blood. God, there was so much blood.

Logan took out his phone. His hands were shaking—costing him even more seconds. And in each of those seconds, his mother was still making those sounds.

No sounds from his father, though.

Logan pressed in 911, and like that night he didn't know who answered or what he said. The only thing he remembered was the emergency operator told him that help was on the way.

Claire moaned, a reminder that she was still alive, and for her to stay that way he needed to get her off the road. Away from that spewing engine, too. There was enough spilled gasoline to start a fire.

"What happened?" Claire mumbled.

He didn't answer. Couldn't. Logan just put her on the gravel shoulder and threw open the front passenger door. His mother's eyes fluttered, threatening to close, but she managed to turn her head and look at him.

Had she said something?

She didn't in the dream. Perhaps she didn't that night, either, but there were times when Logan let himself believe that she had spoken. That she had said the words that he wished she'd said.

It's all right. I forgive you for not saving us.

THERE WERE PLENTY of days that Logan loved his job. This wasn't one of them. He always felt a little like a circus monkey whenever he had to pose for a photo shoot for a magazine. No way could he do this for a living, but a magazine article was always good promo for the business. Considering the crap rumors that were still floating around about Helene and him, Logan figured the family and business could use all the good publicity they could get.

Plus, as bad as this was, it was also a distraction. Something he'd found himself wanting today. And no, it didn't have anything to do with Reese. Or that shit-brown sofa in his loft. Or the paperwork that'd been screwed up on a recent sale. Or the nightmare still rifling through his head.

Okay, maybe it did have a little to do with Reese.

But that was just the tip of this iceberg of a bad mood.

Perhaps Lucky was right. He did need to start dating again, especially since even a seventy-hour workweek wasn't enough to keep his mind off things it shouldn't be on.

Like Spenser O'Malley.

Even though Logan wanted to know what had gone on between Reese and the man, he hadn't asked the private investigator to dig any deeper. Heck, Logan hadn't even done an internet check on the guy's name. It hadn't been easy to hold himself back. Logan preferred to know anything and everything about people who came into his life, but it'd been obvious that the topic was off-limits for Reese.

And for once, he had respected that.

Still, that didn't mean he could stop himself from speculating. The guy had obviously hit her, maybe even done something worse to her. But then Reese must have done something to him, too, to get that juvie record. It was probably a good thing she wasn't around to tell him because Logan wasn't sure he wanted to hear about it.

"Uh, you probably need to soften your expression a little," the photographer told him. "We've already got enough resting-bitch-face shots."

Logan didn't ease up on his scowl. In fact, he made

it even worse so he could let the photographer know he wasn't pleased with that remark. Men didn't have bitch faces. Asshole faces, maybe.

"Why don't you just get your brother to do these photo shoots?" the photographer asked, clicking off some more pictures. "I photographed him at a rodeo last week, and he seemed to like it."

It wasn't the photo session but rather the bull riding that had probably made it enjoyable for Lucky. But the guy had a point. There were some benefits to having an identical twin, and this could be one of them. But he was still walking a fine line when it came to his brothers finally working in the family business. Logan had run the company for a long time, and it was hard for him to give up control. Hard, too, for his brothers to accept him as their boss.

"Resting bitch face again," the photographer grumbled.

Logan gave him a look that could have frozen hell, and the guy must have gotten the message that this was not a good day for a photo shoot. "Maybe we can try this again next week," he said, gathering up his equipment.

Logan didn't stop him, though it would have been easier just to finish this now. The guy left, and Greg came right in and put a small brown paper bag on Logan's desk.

"I popped over to the café and got one of those lemon thingies," Greg said. "Thought you'd like one, too. It's right out of the oven."

Logan glanced in the bag. It didn't look like something that'd caused such a fuss. Then he took a bite, and his taste buds applauded.

Yeah, it was worth a fuss, all right.

"I guess Reese left the recipe with Bert?" Logan asked.

"Nope. Reese baked these herself." And with that bombshell, Greg was halfway out the door.

"Reese baked it?"

Greg stopped, stared at him as if that were a trick question. "I thought you'd heard by now. She didn't leave town, after all. She's staying a while longer so she can do Mia's birthday party."

Logan cursed the flip-flop feeling he got in his stomach and hoped it was from the lemon thingy and not because Reese was still around.

Greg kept staring at him. "Say, you're not going to try to run her out of town again, are you?"

He was about to blast Greg for that, but then Logan had to mentally shrug. He had indeed nearly run her out of town. It hadn't worked, though. Even after she'd spelled it out that if she stayed they'd end up in bed together.

Which they would.

Logan only wondered if it was too soon for them to do just that. Yeah, it was stupid. He needed to stay away from her, but since that clearly wasn't going to happen, he might as well find out what it would be like to be with her when he was sober.

He checked the time. Reese's breakfast shift should be over in ten minutes so he grabbed his cowboy hat and headed for the door. He didn't make it far. Logan got another whiff of lemon, and Jason came in, stuffing his face with one of Reese's tasty pastries.

"Hey, did you hear?" Jason asked. "Reese didn't leave town, after all."

"I heard."

And apparently Jason had not only heard the news, he'd paid her a visit since he was chowing down on the lemon thingy. That visit had no doubt been to ask her out again. Even though this was going to sound like he was calling dibs or marking his territory, Logan figured it was time for his friend to hear the truth. There were man-rules about this sort of thing, and Logan had gotten to Reese first. That meant she was hands-off for Jason.

First, though, Logan shut the door. There was no reason for Greg to hear his dibs-calling. "The night after my botched proposal to Helene, I went to a hotel in San Antonio, met Reese and slept with her," Logan told his old friend.

Jason stopped chewing, his jaw frozen in a twisted angle. Then he laughed. Really, really laughed. "Right. Like you'd go for someone like Reese."

Logan huffed. "It happened."

Jason finally quit laughing and swallowed the rest of the pastry. "Oh, I get it. You were drunk."

"Drunk-ish." Which, of course, sounded stupid. Yeah, he was drunk, but judging from Jason's tone, he was about to dismiss it as something that wouldn't violate a man-rule of a guy going after a woman who'd been his drunk best friend's lover.

Jason kept staring, perhaps processing that, and he shook his head. "I just don't see you two having a one-nighter. *Any* nighter for that matter. So, are you the reason she came to town?"

"Only in a roundabout way. She gave me something and wanted it back."

More staring, more processing. "You didn't knock her up or anything, did you?"

"No. I used a condom." Several of them, in fact, but there was no reason to share that with Jason.

Jason made a sound of amusement. "Well, I gotta say, I didn't expect this. But obviously you haven't picked up where you two left off." He paused. "Have you?"

"No," Logan repeated after a pause of his own.

"Where do you see things going with Reese?" Jason came out and asked.

It was a good question. Logan didn't have a remotely good answer. It would sound shallow for him to say he was only interested in having sex with her, especially when he was still concerned that with her family history she could tarnish the reputation of the company.

"I'm not sure," Logan admitted. "But Reese doesn't tend to stay in one place for long. Six months at most so I suspect in a couple of months, or even sooner, she'll be leaving for greener pastures."

Logan couldn't blame her. It wasn't as if he could offer her anything but sex. Hardly an offer that would tempt a woman like Reese to stay put. As attractive as she was, she wouldn't have any trouble finding another guy to sleep with. One who wasn't accusing her of running a con.

"Until she leaves for those greener pastures, is she hands-off for me?" Jason asked.

"Yes," Logan said without hesitation. It was hard enough being around Reese, but it would be very unpleasant to see her with his best friend.

"All right." Jason bobbed his head. "I guess this means you're finally getting over Helene. You *are* getting over her, right?"

Logan nodded. It wasn't a lie, either. He was getting over her. He wasn't there yet, though, but this thing with

Reese didn't have anything to do with what he'd felt for Helene. It had to do with trust. He just didn't want to put his heart out there for another stomping.

There was a knock at the door, and a second later, Greg opened it and stuck his head in. "Logan, you have a visitor."

"I need to be going, anyway," Jason said, checking the time. "I'll see you at Lucky and Cassie's engagement party next month."

This was the first Logan was hearing of a party, a reminder he needed to get his head out of the clouds and keep better tabs on what was happening in his own family.

"Who's the visitor?" Logan asked Greg after Jason was gone.

"A woman. She says she's a friend of Reese's."

Logan hadn't meant to groan, but he hoped this wasn't another "friend" like Chucky. "Show her in," Logan said.

He wasn't sure what to expect, but at least the woman who came through the door didn't look like a con artist or a rooster. She was in her twenties, tall and looked like a model. Logan figured if Jason had gotten a glimpse of her, then he'd be hanging around for a while longer.

"I'm Jimena Martinelli," the woman said, "the closest thing Reese has to a sister, and I'm here to warn you that if you're dicking around with her, I will cut off that dick and roast it in a fire pit."

Okay, maybe not as normal as he'd originally thought. Logan hoped this woman's idea of dicking around didn't mean just sex.

"Is there something specific I can do for you?" he asked. "Something that doesn't involve my dick?"

"Yeah, you can stop treating Reese like she's a gold-digging slut. She's not." Jimena folded her arms over her ample chest. "The only reason she slept with you was to tick off a box on her bucket list."

Logan nodded. "She told me."

Jimena seemed a little surprised that he knew about the list. "Did she also tell you that she really liked you?"

Now Logan was the one who no doubt looked surprised. "No. But then she hardly knows me."

"Right." Said with all the sarcasm one word could have.

Apparently, Jimena thought a night of sex equaled getting to know someone. And in some ways it did. But there was still plenty Logan didn't know about Reese.

"I just want you to understand that Reese isn't as tough as she looks," Jimena went on. "You were the first man she slept with in nearly two years."

Again, Logan was sure he looked surprised. But then he remembered that might not even be true. Maybe this was Jimena's weird attempt at matchmaking.

"I have several things I need to do," Logan tossed out there. Including a chat with Reese to find out why she'd decided to stay in town, after all. "Was there anything else?"

Figuring there wasn't, Logan took out his phone so he could make some calls on his walk to the café. But Jimena didn't budge. She also didn't look as much in a dick-roasting mood as she had when she'd first come into the office.

"Was there anything else?" he repeated, sounding as impatient as he suddenly was.

"Uh, I heard about your ex. About you walking in

on her with another man. A man who was dressed like a clown."

Logan groaned again. "I won't discuss that with you."

"There's something you should know." Jimena took out her own phone. "I've been seeing a guy. Elrond Silverman. He's not the right letter of the alphabet, but sometimes I let that slide."

Logan didn't have a clue what that meant, and he could possibly be dealing with someone who was mentally unstable.

"Elrond worked for you," she added.

"So? A lot of people work or have worked for me."

She nodded and came closer, holding out her phone screen for him to see. "Last night, we got a flat tire when we were in Elrond's car, and this was in the trunk."

Logan figured there was absolutely nothing on the screen that he wanted to see. But he was wrong. The first thing he noticed was the porcelain tit. One that he recognized because it was a perfect match to the one Helene had given him.

Of her own right breast.

Hell. Had this Elrond stolen it?

Logan tried to remember the story Helene had told him about it, but all he could recall was that she'd said it had gone missing.

"Does it look familiar?" Jimena asked.

It took him a moment to realize she wasn't pointing to the boob but rather to what was next to the boob.

A clown suit complete with a big red nose.

CHAPTER TEN

REESE FELT THE flutter in her stomach when she saw the man in the doorway of the café. But the flutter fluttered away when after her initial glance she realized it wasn't Logan but rather Lucky.

"Glad I caught you before you left," Lucky greeted.

Since she already had her purse in her hand and had been going to the front door to lock it, he'd barely caught her in time. Even if she hadn't been there, it wasn't as if she would be hard to find since Reese had managed to keep her apartment at the Bluebonnet Inn.

"First, I'm pleased you're staying," Lucky continued. "Logan needs someone to keep him off-balanced a little."

She wasn't so sure of that at all. "There's nothing going on between Logan and me." Something she'd been saying to Bert, Sissy Lee and Sissy Lee's brother when they brought up that Logan was the reason she was staying on a while longer.

Lucky made a sound that he didn't quite buy that. "All right. I'm glad you're staying, anyway. I heard about Chucky. You know if he bothers you again, all you have to do is tell Logan or me."

For some reason that put another flutter in her stomach. Not a sexual one this time but a warm unfamiliar feeling. "Thanks. I'm not used to people having my back."

"Well, your friend Jimena seems to be looking out for you."

No more flutter. Just confusion. "How do you know Jimena?"

"Ah, hell." He groaned. "I just figured Logan had told you that she paid him a visit earlier today."

"I haven't spoken to Logan since last night."

Lucky tried to dismiss her words with a shrug. "I'm sure he'll tell you about it when you see him." Reese wanted to hear about it now, but Lucky just continued talking, and it wasn't about her friend. "Cassie and I are excited about you doing our engagement party."

Reese nodded. "Cassie called this morning, and we talked about that. She said she was looking at the end of next month."

"Uh, could you do it sooner? Like maybe the end of *this* month?"

"Sure. That works out better for me, anyway." In case she decided she needed to get out of town.

The end of the month was only two and a half weeks away, and at first Reese thought the short notice was what was causing that funny look on Lucky's face.

"And maybe don't fix anything with bacon or coffee," he added.

It was a strange request, but maybe Cassie simply didn't like those things. "No problem. Since Cassie wanted a brunch, I could do—"

"We'll need to make it an afternoon or evening party instead. Will that be a problem for you?"

She shook her head, and maybe it was the shaking that caused Reese to connect the dots. "Is Cassie pregnant?" Judging from the deer-caught-in-the-headlights look, Reese wished she hadn't asked.

Or guessed correctly.

"You can't tell anyone," Lucky insisted. "Not yet. Cassie and I need to figure out a way to tell the girls first. And we don't want to do that before Mia's birthday party. We don't want to take anything away from her special day."

"I understand, though in this town nothing stays secret for long," she reminded him.

"Yeah," he said without hesitation. "But don't even tell him." Lucky tipped his head toward the glass front door where Logan was standing.

Reese felt another stomach flutter. Logan had finally come. It was about time. She figured he must have heard by now that she was staying in town, and after the warning she'd given him about them landing in bed, Reese figured he'd either run for the hills...

Or run for her.

She was hoping for the latter.

Reese made a zipping motion across her lips for Lucky. A motion that she prayed Logan hadn't seen because he seemed suspicious when he came in.

"Engagement party stuff," Lucky explained to his brother. "Did you get some of those meetings rescheduled?"

"No. I've got to leave tonight for Dallas."

Reese hated to feel disappointed by that. She should just hit herself in the head with a frying pan. It would be less painful than all this second-guessing, fluttering and fantasizing she was doing about a man she could never have.

"What about you?" Logan asked Lucky.

"I've got to head over to the school right now for Mia's program. Apparently, the pre-K did picture poems complete with painted macaroni borders." He grinned. "Bet you never thought you'd hear me say something like that, huh?"

From all accounts, Lucky had been a serious player so it probably was a surprise that he was now attending school programs and talking about macaroni art projects. Still, it seemed to suit him, and he appeared to be happy. If not a little shaken by the news of Cassie's pregnancy. She wondered how Logan and the rest of his family would take it.

Wondered, too, why Logan was here.

He certainly didn't pull her into his arms and drag her to the floor after Lucky left. Not that Reese especially wanted him to do that…or maybe she did…but it didn't look as if he had kissing, sex, floors or flutters on his mind. And she soon remembered why.

"Did Jimena really visit you?" she asked. She also locked the front door so that no one else would come wandering in.

"She did. She threatened to cut off my dick and roast it."

Reese groaned. "She doesn't mean it. And she had no right. I'll call her and set her straight."

"No need. That wasn't the only reason for her visit." He took out his phone and showed her a picture. "Jimena texted this to me so I'd have a copy."

It took Reese's brain a moment to make sense of what she was seeing A porcelain boob and a clown suit.

"Please tell me Jimena got that boob from the Dumpster," Reese said.

Logan shook his head. "She found this in the trunk of her boyfriend's car."

"Elrond," Reese provided. Then she knew the reason for Logan's look. And the reason he'd come. He wanted to find out if she knew anything more about this. "You believe Elrond was the one with Helene that night?"

"It's not just possible, it's highly likely. After all, Helene was the one who hired him. I didn't have any dealing with him or the rest of the crew who redecorated the building." Muscles flickered in his jaw.

Obviously this was bothering him, and Reese couldn't let it bother her that he was bothered. After all, he had a right to know if this clown had indeed been the one who'd had sex with the woman Logan had intended to marry.

"What will you do if you find out he's the one?" she asked.

He shook his head, put his phone away, and that was apparently the only answer Logan was going to give her. "So, what made you decide to stay in town?"

Reese was thankful for the change in subject but probably not as thankful as Logan was. "I'm surprised you don't know that from the gossip."

"I heard a couple of theories. One was that you wanted to give me food poisoning for trying to run you out of town. Another was that you were too broke to leave. The dark-horse gossip was that you were pregnant with either my baby or the clown's."

Even though she hated to be the center of that much speculation, of any speculation, really, Reese had to laugh. "The clown's? When and where exactly was I supposed to have slept with the clown?"

He lifted his shoulder. "The gossips didn't exactly connect that thread."

And never would because a thread didn't exist. "Well, I'm definitely not pregnant, and I'm not flat broke. And as for the food poisoning, I only do that when I'm really pissed off at someone."

Of course that last statement was a joke, but Logan didn't crack a smile. In fact, it seemed to frustrate him.

"I can't stay long," he said without taking that frustrated stare off her.

"Yes, you're leaving for Dallas. When will you be back?" She tried to make that sound like a casual question. She failed big-time.

"A couple of days. Maybe more. You're not flat broke?" he tacked on to the end of his answer.

She shook her head. "Please don't make me show you my wallet and bank statement." Again, another attempt at a joke, but he still didn't smile.

"Why did you stay, then?" he asked.

Mercy, no matter what she said to that, it would require some soul-baring. Something she wasn't ready to do just yet. Reese couldn't tell him that she'd stayed because of him. That would send Logan running.

"Maggie's uterus," she lied. That poor woman's anatomy was getting a lot of buzz.

He nodded, mumbled something she didn't catch, but Reese certainly *caught* the next thing Logan did.

Logan pulled her to him and kissed her.

It happened so fast she didn't see it coming, but Reese didn't need to see anything to feel it. With just a touch of his mouth to hers, the man could perform some magic, and the flutter turned instantly into a sweet spot of pleasure. She felt as if she were melting sugar in a really hot pot.

He didn't exactly experience the melting, though. Logan seemed to be angry. Maybe with her, maybe with himself. And that anger went into the kiss. He probably soon figured out, though, that when kissing, the anger just made it all seem more intense. More urgent.

Reese figured once they had to break for air that it would be the end of it. That Logan would say he was sorry and that it wouldn't happen again.

He didn't.

He went right back to her mouth for a second round, this one deeper and even longer than the first. The problem with deep, long and intense was that everything revved up. Not just the kissing but the body-to-body contact. Logan snapped her to him, her breasts landing right against his chest.

All in all, a really good place for them to be.

Reese's nipples especially liked the idea because they tightened and hardened. The rest of her body, however, started to soften. Everything below the waist preparing for something it wasn't going to get.

When oxygen became an issue again, Reese was certain it was time for Logan's apology and departure. But no. His arm tightened around her, and with a clever little adjustment, he had their midsections aligned in just the right way for her to feel his erection.

Oh, man.

That wasn't a good thing to feel. Her body was already whining for Logan, and that didn't help. It especially didn't help that Reese already knew that Logan's cleverness didn't just happen with his kisses. He could do marvelous, wonderful things with his erections.

She broke away to give him a second to rethink this. Their gazes met, held, and Reese thought maybe she could regain her footing now that he wasn't kissing her. But without breaking the eye-lock he had with her, he slipped his hand beneath her top and touched her.

Reese made a sound. Way louder than it should have been. All pleasure. It was too schoolgirl for her to react this way to a simple hand on her bare skin, but her sound and reaction were a drop in the bucket compared to what he did next. Logan turned her, lifting her in the same motion, and sat her on the counter.

He probably didn't notice the plate of scones sitting there.

It was incredible what he could do with just a few deft shifts of their bodies. Since this part of the counter was table-high, it gave her the perfect height for him to step between her legs. All the while kissing her, touching her and generally making her crazy.

Of course, she'd felt all of this that night in the hotel, but Reese realized now the tequila had dulled things more than quite a bit. She was getting a full dose of Logan without the boozy haze.

"How far are we taking this?" she managed to ask.

"Not far."

He was lying, delusional or else he had no concept whatsoever of what *not far* actually meant. Because somehow he made their new counter position work so that his erection was now in the V of her thighs. Some well-placed pressure, some more kisses, his hand sliding over her breast, and Reese no longer cared if he took her right then and there.

She didn't even care that she was sitting on a plate

of scones that would give her a greasy stain on the butt of her jeans.

What she did care about was more of everything Logan was giving her. She found herself wiggling to get closer and closer until the only way for more closeness to happen was for her to unzip their jeans and go at it right here amid the scone crumbs.

And that might have happened if she hadn't caught the movement from the corner of her eye.

Logan must have seen it, too, because he let go and moved in front of her. However, he was clearly too late.

Bert, Maggie, Sissy Lee and three people whose names Reese didn't know had their faces pressed against the window. Unless they'd all been struck with a sudden bout of blindness, they'd just seen Logan and her kiss each other's lights out.

ACCORDING TO THE hottest gossip that Logan had heard, Reese was definitely pregnant with his child. Of course, that gossip had been fueled by what folks had seen through the window of the Fork and Spoon. So far, the gossip hadn't made it to any of his business associates, but if it did, well, Logan didn't want to go there. He wasn't exactly a celebrity, but that kind of talk could hurt.

Something he'd known right from the start.

That meant he should just make a clean break with Reese and start dating someone. Someone who could help the gossip die down so he could go back to his normal life.

If his dick could laugh, it would have laughed at that.

For reasons he would never understand, his dick wanted Reese. His mouth, too, and while he hated to let stupid parts of him like that rule his life, it was as if the other parts no longer had a say in it. That's why Logan had decided to go ahead and have an affair with her. That would make his dick and mouth happy, and if he fucked her enough, it might burn this heat to a crisp.

There, that was the plan.

But the plan went a little south when Logan went into the ranch house and saw Reese there in the family room. She was on a stepladder, putting up twinkling lights for Mia's birthday party, and she turned, her gaze connecting with his.

And he forgot how to breathe.

Hell. Now his lungs had gotten in on this stupid attraction.

He could hear chatter in the kitchen. Della, Stella, Cassie. And there were kids running around in the backyard, but Logan's eyes froze on Reese.

"You made it," Reese said as if his arrival were nothing short of a miracle.

In a way it was. Logan had had three days of intense meetings, interviews and the makeup photo shoot, and what he should be doing was heading to the office to clear out what would no doubt be a mountain of work on his desk. But Mia had sent him a personal invitation to her fifth birthday party, and while he often declined personal invites, Logan hadn't declined this one.

He would put in an appearance, and since the party wasn't due to actually start for another half hour, he figured he could also see Reese and the rest of his family. A way of killing three birds with one appearance.

Reese was smiling when she went to him, and she leaned in as if to kiss him. But no kiss. Just a whisper. "Everyone thinks I'm pregnant."

He wasn't surprised the gossip made it to her. The café was usually a hotbed for that sort of thing, but he heard just as much worry and concern in her voice as there was in Logan's head.

"I'm thinking about smoking a cigarette or drinking a shot of tequila in front of them," she added. "Maybe talk about skydiving or some other sport that a pregnant woman wouldn't do."

"It won't help." Then the gossip would be about what a reckless pregnant woman Reese was. "The talk will die down as long as you don't go see the doctor for any reason or if you don't gain weight."

Her eyes widened enough for him to know that those simple instructions were a problem. "I'm guessing that look doesn't have anything to do with any weight gain you might be considering?"

She shook her head. "I went with Cassie to the doctor in San Antonio. Lucky was tied up in a meeting, and Cassie said she wanted to discuss the engagement party on the drive. Cassie didn't tell anyone about what doctor she was seeing or why, not even me, but then she had a script filled at the pharmacy."

Logan picked through that explanation and realized his soon to be sister-in-law was pregnant. For once, he was hearing something ahead of the gossip.

"Prenatal vitamins?" Logan asked.

Reese winced. Groaned. "I'm sorry. I shouldn't have said anything."

It stung that the news hadn't come from his brother or Cassie, but things had been plenty hectic lately. Soon though, he hoped Lucky would come to him with the announcement.

"I don't think Cassie planned to tell me," Reese went

on. "It was hard not to know, though, when I saw the script. It was written out to Cassie, but apparently everyone thinks she was getting the vitamins for me. But Cassie and Lucky didn't want anyone to know until after Mia's party. They don't want to steal any of the limelight."

Logan was betting if anyone in town suspected that Cassie was pregnant, then the news wouldn't have made it yet to the girls. And even if it did, Mia was such a sweet kid that she wouldn't mind sharing the limelight.

"Lucky knows, though, right?" he pressed.

Another nod. "So do Della and Stella. They guessed because Cassie's been having some morning sickness—apparently whenever she smells coffee or bacon. Lucky and Cassie want to tell Riley and Claire after the party."

And speaking of the party, the room looked great. Very girlie fairy-tale-ish with the lights and the sparkly decorations. Reese had moved a table into the room, and it was filled with all sorts of kid goodies, including a large pink birthday cake.

"How did the meetings go?" she asked.

"They're done." And that was the best thing he could say about them. Logan had been distracted through most of the past three days.

"I talked to Jimena," Reese said. "She won't be threatening you again. And there's been no sign of Chucky." Another pause. "I also talked to Elrond."

"That was on my to-do list."

"I figured it was." And judging from the way she glanced away from him, that didn't please her. Well, talking to the clown who'd screwed his ex probably wouldn't please him, either, but Logan had felt it was necessary.

"Elrond said Helene gave him the porcelain breast, but he insists that he didn't have sex with her."

"He's lying," Logan snapped. "At least about the porcelain breast. Helene had two of them made for me. Bookends," he clarified, "and she told me that one of them went missing before she could give me the pair. Elrond probably stole it."

Maybe it was his suddenly pissed-off tone, but Reese no longer looked so happy to see him. "It's important for you to find out the truth," she said. Not a question. But Logan wondered if it should be.

Was it important?

Hell, yes. But he had no idea what to do with the information once he had it. Clearly, the clown hadn't taken advantage of Helene. Logan had walked in on her at the tail end of an orgasm so this wasn't a situation where he was trying to defend Helene's honor. Or would make sure he got the guy arrested.

So, what was it?

Logan figured it was something he didn't want to examine too closely, and he put it in the guy-thing category. His brother Riley had all kinds of man-rules for situations like these so Logan's new man-rule was that he intended to confront the Bozo who'd contributed to bashing his life to smithereens.

Reese touched his arm to get his attention. "Do you still love her?"

Now, that was a question he seemed to be having to answer a lot lately. "No." And since it wasn't something he wanted to talk about, Logan went with something he did want to say. "I think we should have sex."

She blinked. Obviously, that didn't come out as smoothly as he'd planned.

"Now?" she joked.

Those stupid parts of him wanted to jump at the chance, but Logan figured he had to at least try to act like an adult and not a teenager. "Tomorrow night around eight?"

Reese certainly didn't jump at the invitation.

"I could serve Cheetos and Milk Duds," he joked, too. Except it wasn't just a joke. Logan wanted her to say yes, and he'd obviously botched this.

"Jimena told you about my snack favorites."

He nodded. "She also said you carried a really sharp knife in your backpack."

That got the reaction he wanted. Reese smiled. "Two of them. I'll see you tomorrow night."

However, she didn't get a chance to add more because Della, Stella and Cassie had joined them. Logan got hugs from all three women, and it was from over Cassie's shoulder that he saw Claire, who was standing back from the rest.

"Could you help me with something?" Claire asked.

Logan went to her, but he hoped he didn't have to do anything that required decorating skills. But it wasn't decorating stuff. The moment he made it to Claire, she took hold of his arm. "You think we could maybe go to the sunroom for a chat?"

Uh-oh. She'd heard the rumors about Reese being pregnant. Or maybe she'd guessed about Cassie and wanted him to confirm it.

With Claire's fairly tight grip on his arm, they went into the sunroom on the far side of the house. Away from the playing kids. Away from anything remotely resembling a party. When she stumbled, Logan caught onto her.

"Sheez, are you all right?" He had her sit on the sofa, and he went to the wet bar to get her a bottle of water.

Claire mumbled a thanks, sipped some of the water and looked at him. "What I'm about to tell you stays between us. Sorry to dump this on you," Claire added, "but I thought I was about to pass out. If I'd told Della or Stella that, they would have guessed right off."

"Guess what?" he asked, clueless.

Claire clued him in. "I haven't done the pee stick yet, but I'm pretty sure I'm pregnant."

Oh.

Apparently, he was the only male in the McCord family who hadn't knocked up somebody.

And for some reason, that made Logan feel like shit.

CHAPTER ELEVEN

"You're sure about this?" Jimena asked Reese.

Reese looked at herself in the mirror. "Sure about which part?"

Because there were a lot of cogs going right now. Her dress, her shoes, her makeup. The perfume she'd borrowed from Jimena. And, of course, the biggest cog was the reason she was doing all these things.

For Logan.

The new-to-her dress was one that Reese had bought at Lookie Here. It was sunshine yellow, perhaps not exactly her color with her hair, but it'd been one of the few dresses in her size. Reese had been afraid to ask for a larger size for fear it would keep the pregnancy rumors going.

"The sex-date part," Jimena answered after she washed down a mouthful of the scone she was eating.

There was no easy answer for this. No, Reese wasn't sure about it, but yes, she was going to do it, anyway.

It would probably be a huge mistake, something she'd spent her adulthood trying to avoid, and this one had more pitfalls than most. Logan was looking for an affair. That was it. And he'd never tried to make her believe otherwise. Considering their relationship had started with a one-night stand, though, what did Reese expect?

"Whose idea was this, anyway?" Jimena pressed.

"Mine," she lied. It would save time on this conversation. Jimena was worried about her, that was obvious, but her friend would only worry more if she knew Logan had been the one to set this up.

Jimena didn't call her on that lie, but she did stare at Reese from over the top of her diet soda. "Are you even sure he's over his ex?"

"He is." Another lie. If he were over Helene, then why was Logan so insistent on speaking to Elrond? Of course, she wouldn't mention that to Jimena.

"If Logan's over his ex, then why does he want to talk to Elrond?" Jimena added.

Apparently, the woman's telepathic skills were working well tonight because she took that question right out of Reese's head.

"Wouldn't you want to talk to the person if they'd broken up a long-term relationship on the very night you'd planned on proposing?" Reese argued.

Jimena just looked confused. Probably because she couldn't wrap her mind around the long-term relationship part. Jimena didn't stick with men. For her, a week was plenty enough.

Reese checked her hair one last time and hated that she was fussing with it. Hated that she was fussing, period. She hadn't actually had a date in high school, but she remembered the nervous excitement from the girls when they'd talked about dates and such. It'd seemed vain and frivolous to Reese, especially since she was working full-time by then, and yet here she was doing it herself.

Enough.

"You can stay the night if you like," Reese offered.

Jimena shook her head. "I've got a dinner date."

Since the woman had just consumed several pounds

of junk food, Reese wasn't sure where she'd put dinner, but she wished Jimena a good night, grabbed her purse and the pie that she'd baked and headed out. It was already dark, but as Reese always did, she stuck to the back street. Old habits. In her youthful con days, it was a way of keeping out of sight, of making herself as invisible as possible.

Tonight, it was so no one would see her going to Logan's.

Of course, the gossips assumed Logan and she were already carrying on a hot affair, but Reese was still mindful of Logan's reputation. Spring Hill wasn't exactly a prudish place, but she was certain the members of the old guard—i.e., those who wanted Logan back with Helene—wouldn't care much for her spending time beneath the sheets with their golden boy.

She spotted Logan's truck as soon as the parking lot came into view, and Reese released the breath she'd been holding. Part of her had worried that he would come to his senses and cancel. Or forget.

Reese went to the back door and was about to test the knob when she glanced in Logan's truck and saw someone. Since the windshield was heavily tinted, she couldn't be sure, but her first thought was that someone had broken into it. She was about to call out for Logan when she realized the person inside *was* Logan.

And something was wrong.

He wasn't just sitting. He had slumped forward, his forehead leaning against the steering wheel.

Reese's heart jumped to her throat because he didn't look as if he were merely in deep thought. He wasn't. The moment she tapped on the window and he lifted his head, she saw the pain etched all over his face. She threw open the door, and he practically tumbled into her arms.

"Migraine," he managed to say.

She would have been relieved that it wasn't something more serious, but she knew about migraines and how bad they could be. Her grandfather had suffered from them.

"Let me get you inside," she said, trying to keep her voice at a whisper. Logan winced and grunted in pain with each little movement of his head.

She got him to the back door. It was locked. Damn. That meant she had to lean him against the building and go back for his keys. They were still in the ignition. Then she had to figure out which one, all while Logan stood there suffering.

It seemed to take an eternity, and her hands were shaking now, but Reese finally got him into the building. No sign of Greg. Too bad. Because the assistant could have helped with getting Logan upstairs.

"I can walk on my own," Logan said. Each word seemed an effort. "It's okay. You can go now."

Not a chance. Reese didn't argue with him about it, either. She merely hooked her arm around his waist and got him moving. Step by step. There were suddenly a gazillion of them, and both Logan and she had broken out in a sweat by the time she reached his loft.

The brown sofa was gone so she led him to the bed. He eased down onto the mattress and pulled a pillow over his head.

"Meds," he mumbled.

Reese hurried to the bathroom, threw open the medicine cabinet and spotted the prescription bottle of pain pills. Plus, some lavender oil. She grabbed both and a glass of water.

"Don't tell anyone about this," Logan said when she gave him the pills.

"I won't. I'll tell them we had sex instead."

He managed a smile. A very short-lived one that told her how much pain he was in. She put some of the lavender oil on her fingertips and began to massage his forehead, temples and the back of his neck.

"You've done this before," he whispered.

"Yes, for my grandfather. Peppermint oil helps sometimes, too." Though she also knew that sometimes nothing at all helped. Still, the pain didn't seem to be getting worse.

"The grandfather who gave you the watch?"

She nodded. "I lived with him on and off."

"Keep talking," Logan said.

Reese did. She kept massaging his head, too. "He was the night manager of a pizza place so we ate lots and lots of pizza—especially the ones they couldn't sell or the ones customers didn't pick up. I think it set me on my course of the love of junk food."

"Were your parents there, too?"

"On and off," she repeated. "When I was about ten, I think they got fed up and left me with him for good." Or so she'd thought at the time. "Then he got sick and died two years later."

Even though she knew it had to be painful for him, Logan opened his eyes, met her gaze. "I'm sorry."

Yes, so was she. Losing him had crushed her heart. Still did.

"For a long time I blamed myself for his death," Reese said before she even knew she was going to say it. And she was instantly sorry. Logan looked at her as if waiting for more.

Reese wasn't even sure she'd ever said this aloud, but

she had certainly thought it plenty of times. "When I was living with him, my grandfather started working extra hours to pay for my school things and clothes. I think that's why he didn't go to the doctor right away when he started having symptoms."

Maybe with all the pain, Logan wouldn't even remember her telling him this. It was bad enough that he thought she was beneath him, but now he would know that she had the dreaded emotional baggage. Just what no man wanted to hear.

"Keep talking," he repeated.

She had to pause and take a deep breath. Had to pause again to think about how to say what she wanted to say. Best just to get it out there, and hope that Logan didn't remember.

"He died of lung cancer. I watched him waste away, and that's one of the reasons my misdiagnosis scared me. I didn't want to die that way. Now, see? Aren't you sorry you asked? You should have asked me for recipes or something that didn't involve picking at these old scabs."

"We all have scabs." Logan stayed quiet for several long moments. "I should have been able to save my parents, but I didn't."

Judging from the way he suddenly got so stiff, she was guessing that wasn't something he'd expected to share. However, it was something she'd already heard about.

Gossip, again.

But in this case the gossip seemed to be reliable since it had come from Bert. Logan's parents had died in a head-on collision when he'd been nineteen, and Logan had been the first to arrive shortly after the crash.

"They died at the scene," Reese reminded him,

though she was certain he needed no such reminder. "I don't think anyone could have saved them."

He didn't agree. Logan only closed his eyes, and he didn't open them until she stopped massaging his temples. "Thanks, but you really don't have to stay."

She could see him already shutting down, already regretting that he'd let her have a little glimpse of what was in his head. "It's okay. I don't have anything else to do." Reese wiped her hands, took off his boots and pulled the covers over him.

"You're being nice to me because I'm in pain. I don't like that."

"Would you rather I yell at you?" she joked.

"Only if you whisper when you do it." His voice was groggy now, which meant the pain meds were knocking him out. Maybe they would knock out the pain, too. "Will you ever tell me about Spenser O'Malley?"

Obviously, though, the pain meds weren't erasing the things on his mind. "One day." Maybe. Probably not, though.

That wasn't just baggage but rather a mountain of it.

"Is he the reason you're scared of getting involved with me?" he asked.

Definitely not an easy question, and Reese only answered him because she was certain Logan wouldn't remember any of this. "No. I'm scared for other reasons."

She was scared he'd break her heart. And he would. Reese didn't have any doubts about that.

THE SMELL OF coffee woke Logan. Not easily, though. Despite the enticing scent, he practically had to pry open his eyelids. That was thanks to the effects of the pain meds. They'd knocked him out cold, had gotten him through the migraine, but he would pay for the relief for the rest of the day.

It felt as if a bug bomb had gone off in his head.

He finally got his eyes open and came fully awake when he saw how close the coffee cup was to his face. How close Reese was, too. She was standing right over him. A surprise. He'd thought for certain she would leave after he fell asleep. Just because they'd had a one-night stand didn't mean she was obligated to play nursemaid.

Hell. He hoped he hadn't said anything stupid to her, but he did remember a garbled conversation about his parents. Some things she'd told him about her grandfather, too.

Had she mentioned that guy Spenser?

If she had, Logan hoped he remembered what she'd said. From what he could sense, the man from her past was an emotional land mine that he should probably avoid.

"I was going to let you sleep," Reese said. "But Greg slipped a note under your door to remind you about an important meeting you have this morning. The meeting's in thirty minutes, and I didn't think you'd want to miss it."

"I don't," he assured her.

Logan groaned. It was a meeting he had to take, too, because he'd already rescheduled it twice. A third cancellation could create some ill feelings between him and a seller he needed.

Since Greg usually texted that sort of reminder, it probably meant his assistant realized Logan wasn't alone. Or maybe someone had seen Reese helping him into the building the night before and spread the word.

Logan had never told Greg that he had migraines, but the man had no doubt figured it out.

Logan forced himself to a sitting position, took the coffee and gulped as much as he could without burning his mouth. He prayed the caffeine would kick in soon and maybe rid him of the rest of the pain. It wasn't bad now. Just little pinging reminders that he didn't need. Especially because Greg had been right—this meeting was important.

"I didn't open the blinds," Reese said. "It's pretty sunny out there already."

"Thanks." The blinds would stay closed. Ditto for the lights being off. He'd have to ease into the whole light thing unless he wanted the headache to return.

"If you want to grab a shower, I can fix you some breakfast," Reese offered.

She was still being nice to him, and he would have told her to knock it off, but breakfast did sound good. He wasn't even sure the last time he'd eaten, but his stomach was growling.

"Don't you have the breakfast shift at the café?" he asked.

"Not this morning. I can stay a little while longer. If you want, that is."

He did want that. More than he should. And it wasn't all food related, either. Despite what had been a lousy night for both of them, Reese somehow managed to look amazing. Jason had said she was attractive in an unmade-bed sort of way, and while Logan didn't agree with that, looking at her did remind him of bed.

And sex.

Especially sex.

It was her mouth, he decided. Full and kissable. The

rest of her body, though, was kissable, too. So that's what he did. Nothing long and deep. Just a taste of her mouth that he'd hoped would tamp down this little fire that was starting to simmer in his body. It didn't. The one kiss only made him want more.

More of something he really didn't have time for.

"Sorry about all of this," Logan said, moving away from her and getting up. "Both the half-assed kiss and the half-assed night. Last night qualifies as the worst dinner date ever."

Reese smiled. "Sadly, I've had worse."

She was probably being nice again, and because the niceness was making him want to pull her back to him, Logan headed to the bathroom for that shower. He didn't take long, mainly because his head was still sensitive, and it actually hurt to have the water hit his scalp. Also because he wanted a chance to say goodbye to Reese before he ate and headed downstairs for the meeting.

His dressing room was off the bathroom, which was a plus. Best not to run around half-naked with Reese still in his house. Well, best not to do that when he had someplace else to be.

Logan finished dressing and hurried back out to find breakfast sitting on the table. Scrambled eggs, and a glass of OJ next to the plate.

But no Reese.

"Reese had to leave," someone said. "She said something about having to go to work."

Maybe it was the fog in his head, but it actually took Logan a moment to recognize the voice. Another moment to pick through the dimly lit room and see the woman standing by the door.

Helene.

CHAPTER TWELVE

SHIT. AND BECAUSE Reese didn't know what else to say, she repeated that a couple more times as she hurried out of the McCord building.

Helene was back.

And Reese didn't know who'd been more surprised about that—Helene or her—when Reese had opened the loft doors. Reese had expected Greg to be standing there when she heard someone knock, and her stomach had landed near her ankles after she saw Logan's visitor.

His *perfect* visitor.

Reese had heard that Helene was beautiful, and it hadn't been an exaggeration. The woman looked like a pageant contestant, moved like a ballerina and smiled like the *Mona Lisa*.

Reese hated her.

But even more than that, Reese hated that she hated her.

She had always known Helene could come back. After all, the woman owned several businesses in town, but Reese hadn't thought her homecoming would have happened with Reese looking and feeling like a piece of gutter trash.

It hadn't helped, either, that Helene had turned that *Mona Lisa* smile on Reese. If Helene had been angry about finding another woman in her ex's loft, she had shown no traces of it. Helene had merely introduced herself and politely asked to see Logan.

Reese had exchanged introductions, shaken Helene's hand and then had somehow managed to rattle off an excuse of needing to get to work. Part of her, the part with a spine, wanted to hold her ground and stay until she could at least say goodbye to Logan. Maybe even kiss him in front of Helene. But Reese had been afraid that any kisses he might have given would have landed on Helene's mouth, not hers.

"Reese?" someone called out.

Lucky.

Definitely someone she didn't want to see right now. Of course, she could say that about anyone. The tears were threatening, and if Reese did disgrace herself by crying, she didn't want a witness. But this was one witness she couldn't avoid because Lucky was running to catch up with her.

"You okay?" he asked.

He stepped in front of her, blocking her path. The question alone meant he no doubt knew about Helene's return, but the look in his eyes let her know that he was also aware that Helene was with Logan right now.

"I'm fine." The lie just sort of stuck in her throat. "You knew she was back?"

"I just found out. Greg told me when I came in for the meeting, and he said you'd left in a hurry."

Reese shrugged. *Don't cry. Don't cry.* Better yet, she told her heart to knock it off. That crushing feeling in her chest was making it hard to breathe.

"I knew she was coming home, though," Lucky continued a moment later. "Her mother, Mary, called me last night to give me a heads-up. She said she tried to call Logan, but he didn't answer."

"Logan wasn't feeling well," she settled for saying.

"Migraine?"

Since Logan had told her not to tell anyone, Reese only shrugged. "For the record, nothing happened between Logan and me last night."

Lucky shrugged, too. Probably because he didn't believe her, and then he huffed. "Look, there's no easy way to say this, but I think you should know. Helene is planning to stay. *Really* stay," he added. "Her mother said Helene is organizing several big charity events and that she's going to donate money to build an addition onto the civic center."

"She's trying to mend her reputation," Reese concluded.

"You bet she is. But Helene's good at this sort of thing, and if anyone can make this shit stink less, it's Helene."

Reese didn't doubt that for a minute. Nor did she doubt something else. "Helene is planning to reconcile with Logan, too."

"She'll try." Lucky pinched his eyes together a moment. "And she might succeed. That'll suck for Logan."

It took some more blinking to stave off those tears. Reese gave up on coaxing her heart out of the crushing feeling and just went with it. After all, she'd known it was coming.

"Helene's perfect," she said. "I mean, I kept hearing people say that, but I didn't know they actually meant it."

"She's not perfect," Lucky argued.

"She certainly looks it. Please tell me she had a boob

job because, in all the gossip, no one mentioned those huge breasts of hers." The porcelain bookends hadn't been to scale at all.

"Funny, it's what most people mention about her first. Guys, anyway," he added in a mumble. "Still, big boobs don't equal perfect."

"She's beautiful, and that outfit she was wearing probably cost more than I've made in a lifetime. Plus, she used a word I didn't even understand. I'll have to look it up to see if she insulted me or not."

"It wouldn't have been an obvious insult. Helene doesn't work that way. She's more the 'silently put a curse on you while conniving to make your life miserable' type."

Reese stared at him. "Did you start to feel that way about her before or after you saw her with the clown?"

"Before." He held up his hands in defense. "But hey, I kept my mouth shut because I thought she was what Logan wanted. God knows Logan never approved of any woman I dated before Cassie."

She didn't know if Lucky was just trying to make her feel better. Reese couldn't imagine anyone disapproving of Helene. Well, not until after the clown incident, anyway.

"Did her mother happen to mention why Helene cheated on Logan?" Reese asked.

He shook his head. "I've got my own theory, though. High-end upbringing and she wanted to sample something down and dirty. Something a little perverse."

"Perverse? I'm not sure you can call it that—"

"You don't know what the clown was doing with his big red nose," Lucky interrupted.

Oh. So, maybe perverse, after all. Perhaps this was

something akin to an heiress sleeping with the pool cleaner.

Or Logan sleeping with her.

Reese hadn't actually wanted to ask him if he'd been playing out a dirty fantasy that night with her at the hotel, but it was possible he had. Maybe Logan had wanted a pool cleaner experience, too.

Mercy. Had that been it?

"Fight for him," Lucky insisted.

Reese wasn't sure she heard him correctly at first, but then Lucky repeated it.

"Fight?" she questioned.

"Not with your fists." He shrugged again. "Though, if I thought it would work, I'd say go for it. I just don't want to see Logan hurt again."

"Neither do I. But he's a grown man, and if he wants to get back with his ex, then it's his decision. I gotta go," she said.

And Reese hurried away so she could get inside her room before the first tear rolled down her cheek. There was only one word she had for herself.

Idiot.

"HELLO, LOGAN," HELENE SAID. She was smiling as if this were a normal visit. It wasn't. Far from it.

Logan felt as if a heavyweight boxer had just slugged him in the gut. Twice. Not just at the sight of Helene but because Reese wasn't there.

"What did you say to Reese to make her leave?" he asked. And he didn't bother to sound even a little friendly.

"Reese?" she repeated.

"Quit the innocent act. You know her name. You know who she is."

No way would Helene not have heard the gossip, especially considering her mother still lived in Spring Hill. Logan didn't want to know the picture her mother had painted of the fry cook at the Fork and Spoon.

Helene's smile faded, and she flexed her eyebrows. "Yes. Reese is an interesting woman. People seem to love those lemon things she bakes. Have you been seeing her long?"

"You know the answer to that, too." Logan would let Helene sort out fact from fiction all on her own.

"You're angry," Helene said, sitting down at the table where his breakfast was waiting. "And you have every right to be."

"You're damn right I do." He hadn't meant to raise his voice and instantly regretted it because it let Helene know that what she'd done had put his heart through the shredder.

"I want you to know that what happened that night wasn't planned," she explained.

"Various parts of a clown just happened to fall into your vagina?" Logan snapped.

Her mouth tightened a little but not for long. She quickly regained her cool composure. "It was a mistake. One I'll regret for the rest of my life, and I'll spend the rest of my life trying to make it up to you."

Even that wouldn't be enough time, but Logan had something more important on his mind right now. "What did you say to Reese?" he repeated.

"I only introduced myself."

Maybe that was true. Helene could intimidate with just a smile. It was one of the things that had actually attracted him to her in the first place. He'd wanted a woman who could hold her ground, go toe-to-toe with him. And Helene had done just that. Or rather had pretended to do it. Like the gossip, Logan didn't know what was fact and what was fiction when it came to his years with Helene.

"I didn't come here to spoil things with Reese," she said, pausing right before Reese's name. There was some disdain in her voice. Maybe some jealousy. Or fake jealousy at least.

"Then why did you come?" he asked.

"Forgiveness."

Logan would have laughed if he could have gotten his jaw unclenched. "Try something simpler. Something you actually stand a chance of getting from me."

In that moment he wanted to ask her why she'd fucked a clown. Why she had betrayed him, but Logan figured there wasn't nearly enough time to get into that. He needed to go to the meeting and then find Reese and discover the truth behind what Helene had said to her while he'd been in the shower.

"All right," Helene finally said. "I don't want you to stand in the way of my return. For the past month I've been in therapy to help me understand why I cheated, and I'm in a much better place in my life now. I want to come home."

"It appears you're already here."

"Yes, and I plan on staying." She took a deep breath, patted her chest as if to steady her heart. Or maybe it was just to remind him of her huge breasts. "I know I have fences to mend, not just with you, but with the entire town. I've already gotten started on that."

Logan didn't ask her how. "I have a meeting. I have to go."

"Greg told me. I won't keep you, but I wanted you to know that I'll be hosting a fund-raiser reception this Friday at the civic center. I'm donating money for the building extension, and this will be a good first step to repairing my image."

The only image Logan had was of a naked Helene on her desk, getting intimate with the red clown nose.

"I hired a publicist, and she's the one who suggested the civic center donation and reception," Helene went on. "She specializes in human branding, which isn't as BDSM as it sounds." She laughed.

Logan didn't.

"Anyway, I'm inviting the entire town to the reception, and I want you to come, as well," she added.

Now he did manage a laugh. He also opened the door and headed out. Helene followed him down the stairs.

"Just think this through," Helene said. "If you don't go, people will say you're too torn up to face me. They'll say your heart is broken."

Hell. The woman knew just how to go after him. Had she always been this way, or had she honed her bitch skills in the past three months?

"Well?" she asked when they reached the bottom of the stairs. "Should I put you down as a yes for the reception?" And Helene made the mistake of smiling at him. An "I've got you by the balls" kind of smile.

But two could play this game. "Yes, plus one. I'll be bringing Reese as my date."

Logan did enjoy the glimpse of Helene's bitch face to go along with her bitch skills. But it was only a glimpse. He didn't wait around to see what else Helene would do or say. He went up the hall to the meeting wondering just one thing.

How the hell was he going to talk Reese into going with him to his ex-girlfriend's party?

CHAPTER THIRTEEN

"No way in hell," Reese told Sissy Lee.

Reese didn't have to think about it, either. If Sissy Lee was right, Helene was throwing some kind of big party on Friday night, and Logan would be expecting Reese to go with him. But Sissy Lee had to be wrong about this.

"You're sure you wouldn't want to show up at Helene's fancy to-do and give her what for?" Sissy Lee asked.

Reese wasn't exactly sure what Sissy Lee meant by that, but if it involved her going to a party as Logan's date, then it wasn't happening. Of course, Logan wouldn't allow it to happen, either.

Probably for several reasons.

When Reese had left Helene in Logan's flat earlier, the woman's smile had made it crystal clear that she was there to reclaim her man. A man Reese was unworthy of. Helene had punctuated her claim with the scalp-to-soles glance she'd given Reese. The woman didn't have to say a word to let Reese know that she wasn't acceptable in Logan's and her social circles.

And Reese didn't want to be acceptable.

All right, maybe she did, but not like this. Not showing up with Logan just so she could rub it in Helene's face.

"What are you going to wear?" Sissy Lee asked.

"I'm not going." Reese finished the burger she was making, plated it and slid it to Sissy Lee, hoping that would put an end to this conversation.

Apparently not.

"I'm wearing the purple dress I wore to my prom," Sissy Lee declared, helping herself to one of the fries on the plate. Since Sissy Lee was in her midthirties, it had been a while since that prom had taken place.

"You might want to take that order to the customer," Reese reminded her when Sissy Lee ate another fry. Much more of this, and Reese would have to make a second batch, and since the lunch shift was nearly over, she didn't want to do that.

Sissy Lee finally headed out into the dining room, but she had no sooner walked out when the swinging doors to the kitchen opened again. At first Reese thought Sissy Lee had forgotten something, but it wasn't the waitress.

It was Logan.

"No, I'm not going to Helene's party," Reese said right off.

He huffed. "I see the gossip made it here ahead of me."

"Hours ahead of you."

Which was her way of reminding him that it'd been nearly half a day since Helene had shown up, and he hadn't called Reese to give her any hint of what had gone on in the loft after she left. Judging from the buzz that Logan wanted to take Reese to the reception, it hadn't gone well.

Reese tried not to smile about that.

Logan opened his mouth to say something, glanced out at the diners who were watching them and then he pulled her to the side so they'd be out of sight.

"Look, I'm busy," Reese said. "Lucky and Cassie's engagement party is only a week and a half away." Of course, what she wouldn't tell Logan was that she already had everything planned out because then he would argue she was free to go with him to the reception.

But even though she didn't say that, he argued, anyway. "I can hire someone to help you with the engagement party, but if I don't show up at the reception, it'll look as if I'm licking my wounds."

"Are you?" Reese came out and asked.

He made a face. "I hadn't realized how disgusting that sounds. But no, I'm not. And I want you to go with me."

"So you can…what? Show Helene that you've moved on? I'm sure you can find a more acceptable date for that. Besides, I don't have anything to wear."

"I'll take you shopping." Judging from his dour expression, doing that would be about as much fun for him as sliding down razor blades while naked.

"I don't need you to take me shopping. If I were going, I could find something on my own." That was possibly the truth. Possibly.

Logan glanced around, then up at the ceiling as if asking for divine guidance as to what he could say that would make her change her mind. But there was nothing he could say.

Except what he said.

"Please."

That was it. A single word from him attached to a desperate expression.

Reese considered having another go at convincing him to take someone else. Anyone else. Or even his going alone. But then she gave that some thought. Did she really want Logan alone at the party with Helene? Helene might see that as an open invitation to pursue him.

Something she was likely to do, anyway.

Still, why make it easier for her by serving up Logan on a silver platter?

"You're going, aren't you?" Logan asked. He pulled out the big guns. A smile. And a dimple flashed in his cheek.

Good grief. How could she say no to a dimple like that? And the *please*?

Reese huffed first before she answered. "All right, I'll go."

Another smile. Logan dropped a quick kiss on her mouth. "You won't regret this."

He was wrong about that. Because Reese already did regret it.

AND REESE CONTINUED to regret her decision to go.

However, what she regretted even more was that she'd brought Jimena with her on the shopping trip to the San Antonio mall. Her friend and she clearly had different ideas about what constituted a suitable dress.

Jimena studied the latest one Reese had tried on. Electric blue and with enough sparkles to possibly trigger seizures in some people. It was also far shorter and tighter than Reese preferred. Call her old-fashioned, but she didn't like the idea of someone discovering the color of her panties if she happened to lean even an inch in any direction.

"It's not slutty enough," Jimena insisted. "You want to wow Logan's ex when you walk into that party."

She would wow Helene, all right, but not in a good way. The woman already thought Reese was trash, and this dress would go a long way toward proving it.

"In a slut contest, this dress would win," Reese argued. "I'm definitely not getting it."

Jimena looked shocked, though Reese didn't know why. So far, Reese had vetoed every dress that Jimena had chosen for her to try on. In several cases, she had vetoed without even trying on the outfit.

Maybe it wasn't too late to tell Logan to find another date. Or for her to leave town. Of course, that was probably what Helene wanted her to do, and the reminder gave Reese enough of a resolve to go back into the dressing room and try the next one. It was another of Jimena's selections.

Acid green and, yes, sparkles. The back was what Jimena called a crack back. Reese hadn't asked for clarification, but she doubted her friend had meant the dress was suitable for selling drugs or a spinal adjustment.

"So, did I tell you I dumped Elrond?" Jimena asked.

"Really?" She gave Jimena a dose of that same *shock* Jimena had given her with the dress. It wasn't a shock at all. Jimena went through men as quickly as Reese was going through these dresses. "Was it because of the clown outfit?"

"No. I actually sort of got into that. Did you know there's an entire clown fetish thing?"

"Didn't have a clue." She paused. "Did he ever confess if he was the one with Helene?"

"Never. In fact, he denied it all the way up to the time I dumped him. And you know what? I believe him. Who does Logan think it was?"

"He doesn't know." And this conversation wasn't

making her feel any better about any of this. Here she was trying on dresses to go with Logan to his ex's reception, and he was still obviously concerned about the identity of Helene's lover.

Nope, there was no chance of Reese getting a broken heart over this.

Reese put the crack back dress aside and went to the next one. One of her own selections. It was black, plain. And boring. She could be a wallflower in this dress, which was the exact reason she tried it on. She came out of the dressing room ready to hear Jimena make the fake gagging sounds she'd made at all of Reese's selections.

And that's exactly what happened.

"The idea is for you to look good," Jimena pointed out, her voice flat. "So good that the ex will turn green and Logan will want to have sex with you on the hors d'oeuvres table."

Those were high expectations for a mere dress, but Jimena did have a point. As long as she was going to be there at the party, she might as well wear something she knew Logan would like.

With her mission clarified, Reese went back into the dressing room, looked through the choices she had left and came up with a tomato-red dress. No sparkles, but it was silk and had a shimmer to it. That silk whispered over her skin when she put it on, and Reese knew that even without Jimena's approval, this was going to be the one. Not because she loved, loved, loved it, but because she was tired of shopping, and it was on sale.

As she'd done too many times to count, Reese came out of the dressing room, prepared to twirl around to show Jimena how *enthusiastic* she was with this choice, but her enthusiasm sort of stalled in her throat.

Helene was standing there.

"Well, hello," Helene said, giving Reese another dose of that creepy smile. "What a coincidence, running into you here."

Reese doubted it was anything but a coincidence. Helene was checking her out. Literally. The woman's attention was lingering on Reese's bust area. Reese's B-cups obviously weren't measuring up to Helene's DDs.

Jimena looked at Reese, and she didn't think it was her imagination that Jimena was silently asking if Reese wanted her to punch the woman's lights out. She did, but that wasn't going to happen. If anyone punched out Helene's lights, it would be Reese.

"Is that what you're wearing to the reception?" Helene asked. A glacier wouldn't melt in that cool mouth of hers.

"No," Jimena said at the same time Reese said, "Maybe."

Helene's expression tightened, just enough to show her disapproval. "It doesn't do anything for your skin, does it? It washes you out. May I suggest something in yellow or green?"

Colors that were certain *not* to look good on her. Maybe Reese should put on the electric-blue one and try to trigger a seizure in Helene.

"Then again," Helene went on, tapping her chin as if she were truly giving some input that Reese might take. "This one does make your stomach look flat since it skims over the body rather than hugging it."

Reese figured that was a dig about the pregnancy rumors.

"I think it's perfect," someone said.

Logan.

He wasn't exactly hurrying when he came into the viewing area of the dressing room, but judging from his slightly rapid breathing, there'd been some hurrying involved before his arrival.

"Logan," Helene greeted as if everything were hunky-dory between them. She moved in for a handshake, maybe even a hug, but Logan made a beeline toward Reese.

"Sorry, I'm late," he told Reese.

Reese didn't dodge the hug he gave her. Or even the quick kiss he dropped on her mouth.

Oh, Reese got it then. Logan must have heard that Helene had followed Jimena and her here to the mall, and he'd come to run interference. Or maybe he'd come to give Helene a little payback. Either way, Reese was glad to see him. Glad about the kiss, too, and not because it was possible payback but because a kiss from Logan always made things feel right.

Even when it was a fake kiss.

"There's a purple one in the dressing room that I think Reese should pick," Jimena piped up. She gave Helene some stink eye, and coming from a woman who was even more beautiful than Helene, it was far stinkier than anything Reese could have squinted out.

"Purple, huh?" Logan said. "Maybe I should see it." He took hold of Reese's arm, leading her back to the dressing area.

Thankfully, there were no other customers trying on clothes because this wasn't exactly a man-friendly zone.

"Sorry about that," Logan added once they were in the dressing room. "Greg heard that Helene was coming here to the mall to shop, and I figured it was so she could follow you. I didn't know which store you were in so I had to go to six of them before I found you."

It touched her far more than she wanted that Logan was looking out for her. "Thanks, but it wasn't necessary. Helene is just sizing up her competition, and I'm pretty sure she's decided that I'm not much competition at all."

"You're wrong."

It was one of those perfect things to say. Then Reese realized why he might be saying it. "Don't worry. I said I'd go to the reception with you, and I will. I just won't be going in this."

She plucked out the purple dress Jimena had mentioned. The opposite of a crack back. This was more of a cooch front since the neckline plunged all the way to the navel and then some.

Logan eyed it, not at the absurdity of the design but with an interest that any red-blooded straight man would have. "It would, uh, get everyone talking. And drooling."

"You're not the drooling type. But thanks for coming to my rescue." She was about to usher him out, but Logan didn't budge.

The cooch front must have put some thoughts in his head, or maybe he was still in the "I'll show Helene" frame of mind. Either way, he kissed her again.

"Helene can't see us," Reese reminded him.

Reese had figured that would get that gleaming look out of Logan's eyes. It didn't.

"Good," he said. And he kissed her again.

This one definitely wasn't just some little peck on the mouth to get back at his ex. This was a full-fledged, openmouthed kiss that sizzled in all the right places.

Of course, Logan had a way of sizzling just by looking at her.

"So, is this the dress?" he asked. But he wasn't really looking at it. He dropped a kiss on her neck. Then lower.

More sizzling, but Reese knew she had to get some things straight before he sizzled her right out of the dress. She took hold of his chin, lifted it. "What's this really about?"

Logan stared at her. "If you don't know, then I'm doing this all wrong."

"No, it's right." Reese winced at the confession. Best not to bare her soul when the soul-baring needed to come from him. "I just don't want this to be about Helene."

The stare turned a little glare-ish. "Yesterday I invited you to my place to have dinner and sex. The only reason it didn't happen was because of the migraine."

Yes, and then the morning meeting. Then Helene's arrival. Reese was about to remind him of all that, but then Logan pushed away the grip she had on his chin and kissed her again. That caused her breath to vanish, and she couldn't very well give him reminders when she couldn't speak.

But Logan gave her a reminder, all right.

A reminder of just how hot this attraction was between them. Of course, it was just that—an attraction— and Reese should have held back as a self-preservation thing. But then Logan kept kissing her, and thinking about anything except the pleasure seemed to be well beyond her present mental capacity.

Logan kissed her neck again. Then he went lower and used that clever mouth on the tops of her breasts. The dress was cut just so that he didn't have to work too hard to hit his target. However, he did have to work when he dipped lower to catch on to the hem. He slid up the slinky dress, all the while his hand sliding along the outside of her leg.

Then the inside of her leg.

Mercy, that felt good even though his fingers landed against her panties and not bare skin. It rid her of what little breath Reese had managed to gather, but it also did something else.

He's not stopping.

That flashed in her brain along with remembering one teensy little detail. They were in a women's dressing room at a department store while Jimena and Helene were just yards away.

"I don't do things like this," she managed to say.

He didn't laugh, but he could have considering their one-night stand. A one-night stand that had been amazing but was still complicating her life. Like now. Reese wanted him to keep kissing and touching her, but she didn't want him doing it for all the wrong reasons. Considering the timing and the place, it seemed wrong.

But then Logan lowered himself, drawing up her knee to his shoulder, and he gave her such a well-placed kiss that wrong suddenly seemed very, very right.

He slid down her panties and made the kiss even more special.

Reese groaned. Too loud. So she clamped her teeth over her bottom lip in case she did it again.

"Is everything okay?" Jimena called out.

"Fine," Reese answered, her response too fast and clipped. Jimena would certainly know what was going on.

Or not.

"Can I see what you're putting on now?" Jimena asked.

"Not just yet. I'm not ready."

But Reese was certainly nearing the readying point with each kiss. She gasped, then groaned when Logan flicked his tongue.

"That must be some dress," Jimena remarked.

Reese figured if Helene had said anything that would have pulled her right out of the moment. Heck, Jimena might have pulled her out of it, too, but Logan seemed to sense that speed counted here.

"Is Logan helping you?" Jimena again.

"Yes." He was helping. Helping a lot.

Reese pressed her back against the wall to anchor herself. A hanger poked her in the side, and her one foot on the floor was suddenly feeling as it were on the verge of a charley horse. She hung on by latching onto Logan's hair. And it didn't take long for the pressure to build, build, build.

Until the climax rippled through her. Except it wasn't really a ripple. It was more like a tsunami.

"Reese, are you okay?" she heard Jimena ask. Heard the concern, too, in her friend's voice.

But Reese was past the point of answering and worrying about the concern. She just held on and let Logan finish what he'd started.

CHAPTER FOURTEEN

LOGAN GLANCED OUT the window of his office to make sure a real storm wasn't coming. It wasn't. The sky was clear, not even a hint of a cloud. So, the only storm warning was the one inside him, and there was nothing he could do to stop it.

Helene had something up her sleeve.

But what?

Logan hadn't been able to figure it out yet, but he was certain she was going to use this reception tonight as some kind of ploy to do something he wasn't going to like. That concern alone nearly made him want to cancel, but that could be playing right into Helene's hands. If Reese and he didn't show, then Helene could play spin doctor and somehow make herself the victim.

However, he got the feeling that his ex was planning something much worse. And he'd had that particular feeling since she'd followed Reese to the mall two days earlier. Thankfully, Logan had gotten to Reese before Helene could try to sabotage things. Again, he wasn't sure how she'd planned to do that, but he had considered lots of possibilities.

Some stupid.

Like maybe Helene talking Reese into choosing a dress that would fall apart when she stepped into the reception. Or a dress that would turn see-through in the lights Helene was planning to use.

Of course, maybe Helene just wanted to get inside Reese's head. It was that possibility, and the stupid ones, that had sent him running to the mall.

Logan had no idea what had sent his mouth running into Reese, though.

It had started as a way of, well, thanking her. Not just for going to the reception with him but for putting up with all the other shit he'd pulled. Any other woman would have plotted his castration if he'd accused her of conning him and then trying to run her out of town.

In hindsight, though, an orgasm probably wasn't the best way to thank her.

Especially an orgasm in a mall dressing room.

Reese probably wouldn't believe he hadn't planned that down to the final ripple of her climax. He hadn't. She had mentioned something about her not doing things like that. Well, he didn't, either, but Logan hadn't figured out yet why he'd thought it was a good idea.

Why he still thought it was.

Hell, fucking her was an even better idea. But he wanted to make sure that Reese understood that sex between them didn't have anything to do with Helene. First, though, he had to make sure that was the whole truth and nothing but the truth.

Logan signed a contract that he should have been reading just as there was a tap at the door. Part of him expected it to be Reese, coming to cancel out of the reception, but it was only Greg. His assistant was wearing an orange suit with a pink bow tie. Probably the outfit he was planning on wearing to the reception since the event was only an hour from starting.

Greg had some papers under his arms, some in each hand, and he was also balancing a large mug of coffee that Logan figured he would need. He hadn't gotten a lot of sleep the last couple of nights, mainly because Reese had seemed to be keeping her distance. She hadn't called, and Logan hadn't called her for fear of that cancellation thing.

And her dumping him.

Though they'd actually have to have a relationship first before he could become a dumpee.

Greg handed Logan the coffee first. "The McMillian contract," Greg said, placing some of the papers in front of Logan. Then he added another batch. "This is the work contract for the vet you're hiring."

"What vet?"

Greg gave him a blank stare. "The one to deal with the rodeo bulls and cutting horses. Remember, you and your brothers thought it was best if you had a vet assigned just to the ranch."

Logan had some vague memory of that. Hell. He was going to run this business into the ground if he didn't get his mind off Reese and back where it belonged.

"I had your car filled up with gas," Greg went on. "I assumed you'd be using it to pick up Reese. I mean, instead of your truck."

"I'll use the truck." It would seem less of a big deal that way, and he figured Reese wanted to stay as far under the radar as possible. "But there should be enough gas in it." And even if there wasn't, they could walk. The civic center was just a few blocks from the Blue-bonnet Inn.

Greg nodded. He had two more sets of papers, and he put one of them on top of the vet contract. This one was in a manila envelope. It was sealed with a large swatch of tape. "It's a report from the private investigator," Greg explained. "He finally managed to get Reese's juvie record."

Logan looked at the envelope as if it were coated with anthrax. He certainly hadn't forgotten about the request he'd made to the PI, but the timing sucked. A couple of weeks ago, he would have been plenty glad to read what was inside.

Not so much now, though.

It felt like exactly what it was—a huge violation of her privacy. Since it was obvious Reese wasn't trying to con or scam him, there was no reason for him to know what she'd done that had caused her to be arrested.

No logical reason, anyway.

Hell.

Logan might have been tempted to open it if Greg hadn't stayed hovered over his desk. "Anything else?" Logan asked.

Greg nodded. "It's about Helene."

"What now?" Logan pressed when Greg didn't continue and didn't budge.

His assistant took a long breath. Then a second one. When he got to the third one, Logan figured this was either bad news or the guy was about to do some yoga or meditation.

"Well, I thought you should know that Helene has been doing some good things," Greg finally said. "Today she paid off a bunch of medical bills for people over at the clinic. And she bought a lot of supplies and even some computers for the elementary school."

Good things indeed, but Logan had to shake his head. "Why are you telling me this?"

For the first time since Logan had known the man, Greg fidgeted. This was different from him twitching and twittering about. He twisted the corner on the final envelope he was holding.

"I think you should give Helene a second chance," Greg blurted out.

Logan had already used his *screw-this* quota for the day. Heck, maybe for the rest of his life, so he just sat there and stared at Greg, daring him to continue with this stupid idea.

"She's trying so hard," Greg went on, "and it's obvious the reason she's doing all of this is to win you back. Do you have any idea how much it'll humiliate Helene to have you bring Reese tonight?" He didn't wait for Logan to answer. "Don't get me wrong. I like Reese, but you and Helene were together a long time, and it seems wrong for you to throw that all away because of one mistake."

It wasn't as if Logan hadn't already considered this. Had dismissed it, too. "It was a *big* mistake," Logan reminded him.

"I know you're thinking this isn't any of my beeswax," Greg continued.

Yes, he was.

"Then why are you bringing it up?" Logan snapped. He stood, went to the bar—not for a drink but so he could check his suit in the mirror.

"Because, well…" After the third time Greg repeated that pair of words, Logan turned back around to face him.

"What's going on?" Logan demanded.

"That." Greg put the last piece of paper he'd been holding on Logan's desk.

Greg didn't offer any explanation to go along with it. In fact, he didn't say anything. The man just headed for the door so Logan went to his desk to have a look.

It was Greg's resignation.

Greg stopped in the doorway. "I figured you'd want that. I've already cleared out my desk, and I've left you a list of suitable replacements to fill my position."

Logan didn't consider himself clueless very often, but this was one of those times. "And why would I want you to resign?"

"Because I was the clown that night with Helene," Greg confessed.

Logan wasn't easily surprised, but that did it. It took him several seconds to get his tongue working, and by then, it was too late.

Like Elvis, Greg had left the building.

LOGAN WAS LATE.

Reese didn't think she'd get so lucky, though, that he would skip out of picking her up for Helene's reception. No. He'd show, but if he didn't make it soon, they were going to be one of the last ones to arrive, which would mean everyone would be there to see them go in. Reese was hoping for the wallflower mode tonight.

The dress might help. Much to Jimena's disgust, Reese hadn't chosen any of the slut-ish dresses but had instead opted for one with more wallflower appeal. A little black number with subtle sparkles. Of course, it wasn't without some controversy.

After giving her that amazing orgasm, Logan had offered to pay for the dress. He probably hadn't meant it as anything more than a nice gesture since she was going to this reception for him, but there was no way Reese would take Logan's money.

No way apparently that she could force herself to calm down, either.

She wasn't a pacer, but that's exactly what she was doing now even though pacing in her small apartment amounted to about eight steps max in any direction. Reese checked her phone. No missed calls or texts, and she was about to call Logan when he finally appeared at her door.

One look at him, though, and Reese knew something was wrong.

"Are you here to tell me you're getting back with Helene?" she asked.

Logan opened his mouth, shook his head and stared at her as if that'd been the last thing on his mind. Reese was so relieved that she kissed him. It wasn't nearly as hot as the ones in the dressing room, and it seemed as if kissing her was the next to the last thing that'd been on his mind.

"Greg was the one with Helene that night," he said.

Reese certainly hadn't seen that coming. Apparently, neither had Logan, judging from the stunned look on his face. She led him into the apartment and shut the door. The walls in the inn weren't exactly thick, and she didn't think he wanted anyone else to hear this conversation.

"How do you know that?" Reese asked, and she was about to launch into a warning for him not to jump to conclusions and believe gossip. Greg seemed like the last person in Spring Hill who'd carry on with Helene.

"Greg told me."

All right, so no warning necessary, though Reese

still couldn't quite wrap her head around it. "I thought he was gay."

"So did most people in town. Evidently he's not." Logan scrubbed his hand over his face, sat on the edge of the bed. "He told me about a half hour ago, gave me his resignation and then walked out. I didn't even get to ask him if it was a one-time thing or if Helene and he had been carrying on for years."

Reese wanted to ask him if it mattered, but obviously it did. Maybe Logan could forgive a single lapse. Maybe that's what was putting those worry lines on his forehead.

"Did I ever tell you that I fucking hate clowns?" he added. "I have since I was a kid."

In the grand scheme of things, that seemed minor, but maybe it was a phobia. If so, that would add a little more salt to an already salted wound. His trusted assistant and his longtime girlfriend together, and now that Greg had just resigned, Logan might never get the answers that he clearly needed.

"Here," he said, handing her an envelope.

She sat down next to him. "Is it Greg's resignation?" Though she couldn't imagine why Logan would want her to see it.

"No. It's the report from a PI I hired. He was able to get into your juvie records."

Her heart flip-flopped. Then fell straight to the floor. Not a good place for a heart to be. Reese's first response was to lash out, to tell Logan he had no right, but then she noticed that the envelope was still sealed.

"I asked the PI to get that before," he added. "Well, *before*. And no, the PI didn't tell me what was inside.

If you want to tell me at some point, then fine. If not, it'll stay your secret."

That was generous, considering that Logan was a cautious man. Also considering that he had to know there was something inside that could possibly hurt his reputation simply because he was associating with her.

"Does this have something to do with what happened in the dressing room?" Reese came out and asked.

"Yes."

So, he was letting his emotions play into this. Reese wasn't sure if she should be flattered or tell him that, in this case, it wasn't a good idea. Nor was it a good idea for her to continue to put her head in the sand on this. She needed to come clean with Logan.

And then find a way to get out of his life.

Reese stood to start talking, but Logan stood, too. "Come on. Let's put in an appearance at this reception."

"You're sure you're up to this?"

"No." He was heading to the door but stopped as if seeing her for the first time. "You look amazing by the way. You didn't choose the red dress."

She shook her head, put the envelope on the kitchenette counter. "This is the 'blend in with the crowd' black one." Not dowdy exactly, but definitely not flashy, either.

He managed a smile and kissed her again. This one was very much like the others that'd started the firestorm in the dressing room. "Thank you for doing this," he added.

Considering the extreme swing of emotions she'd just had, Reese was surprised she was able to get her feet moving. Logan helped with that. He took her hand

and led her down the stairs to the front of the building where he'd parked.

"My advice…" he said as he drove toward the civic center. "Avoid Helene as much as possible."

That had been her plan, but Reese thought of something. "Does she know that Greg told you?"

Logan shook his head. "Like I said, Greg didn't hang around to answer any questions. But I figure he's probably let her know. And she probably told him to lie low to give her a chance to put a spin on the gossip. No one overheard Greg's confession, but it will get around."

Yes, it would. And while it seemed selfish to think it, at least this meaty gossip could maybe finally put to rest the rumors that she was pregnant with Logan's baby. Of course, it would also give Logan something else to get over because he now knew the betrayal had come from someone he trusted.

The parking lot at the civic center was packed, and Logan wound up parking on the street. No one was milling around the building, which meant everyone was already likely inside.

"One drink, a few handshakes," he said, "and we can leave."

Reese wasn't sure if Logan was talking to her or if he'd said that just to steady his nerves. Her own nerves certainly needed some steadying.

As they approached the building, the double doors opened, and Reese saw Jimena step out. A surprise. She hadn't known her friend was coming. Or that Jimena had bought the cooch front dress.

"I came for moral support," Jimena said. "You're going to need it."

That didn't help Reese's already churning stomach.

Hand in hand Logan and she approached the doors. And considering that Reese could see dozens of people inside, she noticed right away that something was missing.

Chatter.

No one was talking, and everyone had their attention focused on the stage area. At least they did until Logan and she walked in. Almost immediately, the whispers went through the crowd like a wave, and the wave didn't take long to make it to the front.

And that's when Reese noticed the person on the stage. Not their hostess, Helene. But rather a clown with a microphone.

If this had been an ordinary situation, Reese would have thought he was part of the entertainment, especially since the clown was onstage with a three-piece band. She wouldn't have given a second's thought to whoever it was behind that makeup, big floppy shoes and the squishy red nose.

However, this situation wasn't ordinary, and she was afraid the clown was Greg.

It was.

Reese got confirmation when the clown spoke, and thanks to the microphone, everyone in the room had no trouble hearing every word.

"I'm here to help mend some fences." Greg raised his glass to Logan.

Until then, everyone had been volleying glances between Logan and the clown, but the volleying stopped, and everyone's gaze now settled on Logan.

"Logan," Greg continued. "When you hear what I have to say, I'm sure you'll be proposing to Helene—tonight. And this time, she'll get the chance to say yes."

CHAPTER FIFTEEN

SHIT ON A STICK.

So much for the quick in and out that Logan wanted.

There was zip that Greg or anyone else could say to make him propose to Helene, and the only *yes* Logan wanted to hear was Reese answering his plea to get the heck out of here. Logan considered just turning around and walking out with Reese, but Greg apparently had something else to say.

"Don't leave, Logan," Greg called out, his voice very loud with the microphone. "This is a public apology to both Helene and you." Greg looked at the people in the crowd who were hanging on every word. "You see, I'm the one who had an inappropriate relationship with Helene."

That started some whispers through the crowd, and Logan heard a couple of X-rated comments about what had possibly gone on during clown sex. The red, bulbous nose came up.

Logan glanced around and spotted Helene. Like him, she was trying to inch her way to the side of the room and out of sight. That wasn't going to happen, though, unless she headed out of the county. With the volleyed glances going on among Greg, Logan and her, the party-goers looked as if they were watching a three-way tennis match.

"It wasn't Helene's fault," Greg went on. "I seduced her, and I caught her at a down moment. She'd just lost a sale on a sideboard. She really wanted that sideboard," he added as if it would help. Ditto for the part about seducing her.

Maybe that's why he'd worn the clown suit, so that maybe people would forget he wasn't exactly the sort of man who could seduce a former beauty queen.

"Greg, please," Helene said, shaking her head. There were tears in her eyes, and even though Logan didn't want to, he felt a little sorry for her.

For a second or two, anyway.

Then he remembered where that red nose had been when Logan walked in on them.

"Anyway, Helene has paid and paid hard for what I did," Greg went on. "Logan, too. And I'm truly sorry for all the trouble I caused both of you. You're obviously meant to be together. Logan used to tell me that all the time, that Helene was the perfect woman for him."

Because Logan still had his arm around Reese, he felt her muscles tighten, and he wished he could tell her that the last part wasn't true. But he couldn't. Because he had indeed said that not just to Greg but to everyone in his family.

"I'm leaving town," Greg went on. "No, it's necessary," he added, though no one had objected. "Once I'm gone, Logan and Helene can find their way back to each other without me around to stir up bad memories."

Greg sniffed as if crying. It was hard to tell because he had fake tear streaks on his cheeks, but his shoulders were slumped when he walked away, his floppy shoes squeaking as he exited the stage. He disappeared out the back door.

No one else moved or said anything. It was as if everyone held their breaths and then released them at the same time. The band started moving, too, and they jumped right into playing a soothing classical tune that didn't go with the tension in the room. Several people rushed to Helene. Riley, Claire, Cassie and Lucky rushed to Logan.

"You knew?" Lucky asked him right off.

Logan nodded. He'd explain more later, but for now he looked at Reese to see how she was handling this.

"I think that went well, don't you?" Reese asked.

Of course, that made Logan smile, but he knew her attempt at a joke wasn't from humor as much as it was from nerves. Worse, some people were now glaring at Reese as if she were somehow responsible for Logan not rushing to console Helene. He'd rather eat the clown nose—and that was after he knew where it'd been—than console his ex.

"Want me to do something stupid to get everyone's attention?" Lucky asked.

It was a generous offer, but considering Lucky and Cassie were finalizing custody of Mia and Mackenzie, it was best if the antics stayed clown-related. Of course, Helene was doing her own antics, too, and more and more people were heading her way to offer hugs and no doubt kind words. Logan got his share of them as well, and not that he was keeping count, but he was getting more than she was.

"Please," Jimena said in an "I've got this" tone. "Wardrobe malfunction," Jimena yelled after she shoved the skinny strap of her dress off her shoulder.

The dress hadn't covered up much before, and now her left breast was exposed. She had a nipple ring and a Lick Me Here tattoo complete with a tattooed arrow that pointed right toward her nipple.

Jimena got more attention than Logan or Helene. In fact, even the band stopped to see her tattooed tit.

"Wardrobe malfunction," Jimena said again.

Jimena paused a couple more seconds before she fixed the dangling boob and dress strap. There were still plenty of dangling tongues, though, and Logan realized that even with Greg's clown appearance, that the gossip about Greg and Helene would be tempered some with the breast reveal.

"Thank you," Logan told her.

"Anytime." Jimena winked at him and Reese. "If that doesn't work, I'll drop something and bend over to pick it up."

"No!" Reese said so quickly that she choked on her own breath. "Jimena only goes commando," she added in a whisper to Logan.

Well, that would definitely be the talk of the town. But Logan didn't think it would be necessary. However, he could use that drink right about now, and he led Reese through the crowd toward the bar at the back. Apparently, Reese needed a drink as well, because she downed the glass of champagne she'd gotten at the bar. Jimena downed two, plus the one she'd already been holding.

Logan wanted to do the same thing. Actually, he wanted a shot of something much stronger, but he sipped the champagne and got to work. His brothers and their partners did, as well. Cassie and Lucky went in one direction. Riley and Claire in another.

Logan greeted all the people he should greet. Bert and some of the town's other business owners. He had to listen to an update on Maggie's uterus. Then more about Walter Meekins's latest gout flare-up. Other ailments included a wart with an infected hair in it and hemorrhoids.

Clearly, the people of Spring Hill knew how to make good party conversation.

Of course, none of the men actually looked Logan in the eye when they spoke to him, and that wasn't because of the clown-Helene thing. It was because all male eyes went to Jimena, perhaps hoping for another wardrobe malfunction.

Reese fared somewhat better with the eyeballing and conversation. She got three requests for the recipe for her lemon thingies, though Elgin Tate, who had been a horn-dog since he'd first sprouted chest hair twenty years earlier, had asked without adding the lemon part.

"I just gotta have that thingy of yours," Elgin had said.

Elgin smiled until he happened to glance at Logan, and then the man scurried off. Logan rarely had to use words to threaten to bust a guy in the nuts.

"Well, of course, I know you'll reconcile with Logan," he heard someone say. Tiffany Halverson, Helene's old college friend.

Somehow, even over the other chatter in the room, that made its way to Logan's ears. To Reese's, as well. And Logan soon realized why.

Helene and Tiffany were inching their way over to them. Logan figured that was by design. Heck, they'd probably rehearsed every word of the conversation, too.

"Logan's the love of your life," Tiffany declared, and she then acted surprised to see him when her gaze landed on him.

"You're sure about that love of your life thing?" Jimena asked. "Because I heard you fucked a clown."

Neither Helene nor Tiffany spared her a glance. Or Reese. Talking to Reese and/or her friend probably wasn't in the script. Yet. But Logan figured Helene and/or her friend had some zingers planned for Reese.

Tiffany did answer Jimena's question, though. "Absolutely, Logan is the love of Helene's life. I look at all of this as just a hiccup, and my prayer is that ten years from now, when Logan and Helene are playing with their children, that this will be just a distant memory. Helene and Logan have both been so hurt by what happened."

This was the first time Logan had ever heard the mention of children, and he had no doubts, none, that Helene had put her up to saying it. Maybe it was the first time he actually saw the woman he'd thought he loved enough to marry. For once he was glad he'd walked in on her with that clown.

"You're smiling," Helene said, but she didn't look especially happy about that. Maybe because he was smiling at Reese. And Reese was smiling back as if they were sharing some kind of secret.

And that didn't please Helene one bit. Logan heard the hitch in her throat and saw just a glimmer of the hurt, and maybe the jealousy, simmering behind those cool blue eyes. However, she concealed it as quickly as it came with a smile of her own.

"Tiffany, I don't believe you've met Logan's date," Helene said. She made the introductions. Polite ones, too, though he was certain that Tiffany already knew who Reese was. "Reese, I'm so glad you could come, and the dress is perfect. Logan helped her pick it out," she added to Tiffany.

No doubt something else Tiffany knew, but the woman smiled as politely as Helene did. "How did you two meet?" Tiffany asked Reese. It was possible Helene had somehow found that out, but Logan had no intentions of confirming it. But Jimena did.

"In a bar," Jimena provided. At least she didn't add anything about the bucket-list one-night stand. Not at first, anyway. "Reese picked him up because he was hot and because she thought she was dying. Logan was a bucket-list thing, but now Reese has to undo all of that."

"Oh," Helene said.

And then she smiled a little smile probably because she quickly put everything together and thought she'd come up with what had actually happened. That Logan had been nursing a broken heart and that's the only reason he'd landed in bed with Reese.

That didn't explain what'd gone on in the mall dressing room. Or all the kisses they'd shared since. It also didn't explain why he had every intention of having sex with Reese again.

Tonight.

Logan glanced around to see if they were the center of attention. They were. Even the band had softened the music, and Logan was betting every word, every expression, was being cataloged and examined so it could be gossiped about later. The trick was not to give them anything more to talk about.

Because if this conversation got out of hand, he might have to ask Jimena to pick something up off the floor, after all.

"So, what do you do?" Tiffany asked Reese.

Again, it would have been a question Helene fed to her friend. Tiffany didn't live in Spring Hill, but Helene had probably filled her in on everything she knew, including the plan Helene had no doubt concocted on how to get back in Logan's good graces. And his bed.

"I'm a cook at the Fork and Spoon Café," Reese answered.

"She's being modest," Helene piped up. "From what I've heard Reese was top in her class at culinary school."

Logan glanced at Reese to see if that was true, but apparently she was still being modest because she shrugged. But Logan didn't shrug. To the best of his knowledge, no one was gossiping about Reese's placement in culinary school. They were only discussing her possible tattoos and the equally possible pregnancy.

So, how had Helene known?

Hell. She'd probably had Reese investigated, and it was hard for Logan to blast her for that since he'd done the same thing. But Helene was almost certainly doing this so she could find some dirt on Reese. Dirt that would send her running.

Perhaps like the dirt in that sealed envelope he'd given her earlier.

Logan wished now that he'd at least gotten a glimpse of the information so he would know how to fight this shit that Helene was no doubt about to sling at her. When he'd been with Helene, he'd seen her make plenty of ball-busting deals, but it was another thing to be on the other side of that.

"I'll see you at Lucky and Cassie's engagement party," Helene said, and she would have just slipped away if Logan hadn't stopped her with a question.

"You're going to that?" He didn't add a "why," but his tone certainly implied it.

"My mother was invited, and I'm her plus-one."

Great. This was Della's doing. Except Della had probably invited her mother more out of a social obligation. She likely hadn't realized that the woman would be bringing Helene. Since it would seem petty to un-invite them, Logan and Reese would be forced into another uncomfortable situation.

"Are you ready to get out of here?" Logan asked Reese.

She was hugging Jimena goodbye before Logan even finished asking. He hated that he'd put her through this, and he had every intention of making it up to her. Jimena didn't seem to mind, either, being left behind, because she started line dancing with the Nederland sisters. Those women were bad news, but Logan figured Jimena wasn't on anyone's good-news list, either.

Logan threaded Reese and him through the crowds, speaking to those that he'd missed, and he made his way to the door. He didn't release the breath he'd been holding until he was outside.

"Are you okay?" Reese asked.

She looked good enough to kiss so that's what he did, and he could almost feel the tension slide right out of him. Whatever this was between Reese and him, even if it was just temporary sex, he was going to take it and not look back.

Logan was still kissing her when he led her to his truck, and it was because of the lip-lock that he didn't see the person leaning against his door until she moved. It was a woman smoking a cigarette, and when they approached, she flicked the cigarette to the ground and crushed it out with the toe of her stiletto.

"Good to see you, Reese," the woman said.

Reese had gone stiff a couple of times in the reception, but it was nothing compared to this. Every muscle in her body seemed to turn to rock.

"You know her?" Logan asked when Reese didn't say anything and didn't move.

"Of course she knows me," the woman purred. She went to Reese, pulled her into her arms. "I'm her mother."

REESE HAD HOPED that the worst part of the night was over, but she'd obviously been wrong. If she knew her mother, things were about to get much, much worse.

The first thing Reese did was untangle herself from her mother's embrace. It was as fake as the smile on her face, and after seeing so many fake smiles at the reception, Reese knew one when she saw it. Of course, anytime her mother smiled, it was likely just to play a con or because she was drunk. Since Reese didn't smell any booze on her breath, it had to be the latter.

"Why are you here?" Reese snapped. She also checked her purse to make sure her mother hadn't already managed to snatch her wallet. It was there, for now.

"Where are your manners?" Her mother turned to Logan, extended her hand for him to shake. "I'm Vickie Stephenson. Reese probably hasn't mentioned me—"

"She has." And he left it that. His tone, however, implied he knew all about her criminal ways.

"That's a surprise," her mother said. "Reese doesn't

usually tell her…friends about me." And yes, she actually glanced at Logan's crotch.

In addition to being a con woman, her mother slept around a lot. With anybody. One of her favorite things to do was to seduce Reese's boyfriends, and that had started when Reese was a teenager.

"Watch your wallet and your zipper," Reese warned Logan, and she hated that she even had to bring it up. Still, she didn't want him to be robbed. Or groped. Both were possibilities.

"Why are you here?" Reese repeated.

Of course, she could have added a bunch more questions to that including but not limited to, how did you find me and what do you want? Because if Vickie was here, she definitely wanted something.

"Can't I visit my own daughter without my motives being questioned?"

Vickie was using her "high-end" voice tonight. She had many voices and used them to fit the situation. She apparently thought she shouldn't sound like a thug or a hick around Logan. That included dressing high-end. Or her interpretation of it, anyway. She was wearing a black skirt with a leopard print top.

"No, I'll always question your motives," Reese quickly assured her. "Whenever I see you, I know you've brought trouble with you."

Vickie made a sound of frustration that couldn't possibly be genuine because she had to have known Reese wouldn't trust her. Not after their last encounter. She'd taken Reese's keys, broken into the restaurant where she worked and stolen thousands of dollars' worth of knives. Since there probably wasn't a black market for them, Vickie had likely just done it to prove to Reese that she could screw up her life.

Reese had a bad feeling in the pit of her stomach that Vickie was here to do that all over again.

"Can we go somewhere and talk?" Vickie asked. She motioned up the street. "Maybe we can go to that pretty Victorian place where Logan has his office? I'll bet you have some good whiskey in there, and I could use a drink. Could use some other things, too." Vickie glanced at his crotch again.

Good grief. The woman was sixteen years older than Logan, and every one of her forty-nine years showed on her face. She would have had better luck picking up Greg the clown than a guy like Logan.

"How did you find out I was here?" Reese asked.

"Does it matter?"

Well, it mattered even more now that Vickie had dodged the question. "Did Chucky tell you?" Not that Chucky would have just volunteered information like that, but it was possible Chucky had found her and then mentioned it.

"Chucky," Vickie repeated. "Yes. He told me."

For a woman who made her living doing cons, that wasn't a convincing lie. But the problem with Vickie was if she made it seem like a lie, then it wouldn't put the blame back on Chucky, and it didn't let Reese know who'd really ratted her out.

Reese glanced at Logan, and even though he didn't say anything, she thought they might be thinking the same thing.

Helene could have done this.

After all, Helene had known about Reese being number one in her culinary class, and that wasn't even something Jimena would have mentioned—since Jimena had graduated last. It made sense that Helene would have Reese investigated, and if so she could have been the one to find Vickie.

And bring her here to Spring Hill.

Where Helene could see how much trouble she could stir up.

"Can we have that talk now?" Vickie asked. Judging from her tone, the pot stirring was about to start. "Maybe in private? Maybe over drinks? Or would you rather we just chat in front of your friend?"

"I know about Reese's past," Logan volunteered.

"Do you, now?" Vickie said in a tone that implied Logan didn't know everything.

And he didn't.

But her mother did.

Vickie didn't have to mention Spenser's name, but it was there, part of the pot stirring, and it wasn't something Reese was ready to share with Logan. She might never be ready for that.

Reese turned to him, but Logan must have known what she was going to say because he shook his head. "I'm not sure it's a good idea for you to be alone with your mother."

It wasn't, but she didn't have a lot of options here. Reese kissed him but kept it chaste and brief. "I'll take my mother to my place and will call you when we're done."

"I can drive you there," he said, taking out his keys.

But Reese shook her head. "We can walk." She didn't want her mother around Logan for another minute. "Don't worry. This won't take long."

Considering that she'd started out with a string of

lies when she met Logan, Reese hated to lie again, but she was pretty sure this would take more time than "not long."

Reese started the questions as soon as Logan walked away from them, heading for his truck. "Did Helene Langford contact you?"

Vickie made a show of thinking about that. She made a hmm-ing sound and tapped her chin. "Doesn't sound familiar. Refresh my memory."

Reese didn't bother. Even if her mother admitted it was Helene, it could still be a lie, but Reese did need to check with Jimena to make sure she hadn't let anything slip.

"You got a nice thing going here," Vickie said when they reached the Bluebonnet Inn. "Nice dress, and that cowboy you were kissing is dreamy."

Coming from Vickie, it sounded perverse, and it would no doubt lead to demanding that Reese let her in on some of that dreaminess.

"Well, this is a disappointment," Vickie said when Reese unlocked her room and they went in. "I'd have thought you'd be staying in the cowboy's fancy house."

"Even the cowboy doesn't stay in his fancy house. And this place suits me just fine since I won't be in town much longer."

"Oh?" Vickie went to the kitchenette and would have helped herself to a glass of wine from the fridge if Reese hadn't stepped in front of her.

Reese didn't dare move the envelope that Logan had given her. Didn't even glance at it or else her mother might have realized it was something important.

"This isn't a social call," Reese reminded her, "so just tell me why you're here and then leave."

Vickie certainly didn't move any faster. Maybe she would, though, if Reese kept blocking her from getting her booze fix. She would also block the bathroom. And watch to make sure Vickie didn't steal anything. Of course, that was the advantage of not having much because it meant there was nothing much to steal.

Nothing but the watch.

It was the one thing Reese had managed to keep secret from her, and that was in part thanks to her grandfather's warning. "Don't let your mother get her greedy hands on this," he'd told Reese.

Even though she'd been only twelve, she had known it was sound advice. Because although the watch itself probably wasn't worth much, Vickie would want it simply to pawn it for whatever few bucks she could get for it.

Heirlooms had a short shelf life in the Stephenson family.

"You're leaving, you say?" Vickie asked, her gaze combing the room. Thankfully, it was so small the combing didn't take long. "It appears you've got a good thing with the cowboy. Don't know why you'd just give that up."

"I flip burgers at a café, and I live here." Enough said about that. Not a dream job or dream apartment. "The cowboy is temporary just like everything else in my life. You know I don't stay in one place for long. In fact, I'm already antsy."

Reese was afraid that sounded like the huge lie that it was. The not getting antsy was a problem. Because she really wasn't in a hurry to leave. Or at least she hadn't been until Vickie had shown up.

Vickie finally sat down on the love seat. "So, what kind of game are you running on the McCords?"

"No game."

Vickie didn't believe her, of course. "Well, I want a cut of it."

There. It'd taken way too long for Vickie to finally spell out why she was here. "There is no cut because I'm not getting a dime from Logan."

Her mother made a sound of disgust. "That'll have to change. I'll expect payment, and I expect it by tomorrow morning. I have places to be, people to see."

Everything inside Reese went still. "Or?" Because with her mother, there was always an "or."

"Or I'll tell Logan about Spenser."

Reese tried not to react. Was sure she failed. Since she didn't trust her voice, she just stayed quiet and listened as she could feel the proverbial rug being yanked from beneath her feet.

"I know you haven't told him," Vickie went on. "This town is a hotbed of gossip, and I would have heard it by now. By the way, you don't look pregnant."

"I'm not. Hotbeds aren't always accurate."

"That's a shame. You could have gotten a bundle for a McCord heir."

Reese didn't even bother telling her that she would never have a baby just to get money from the father. When and if she had children, it would be for all the right reasons. There wasn't much right about her situation with Logan.

Nothing other than the attraction.

But even Logan wouldn't want to be ruined because of this heat between them. In another month or so, maybe less, he'd find another source of heat.

"So, let me get this straight," Reese said. "If I don't get you some money, you'll tell Logan about my past?"

She nodded. Smiled. Oh, no. That was her snake-oil smile. "And I'll call Logan's business associates. Think how all those ranchers with their down-home values will react to Logan carrying on with the likes of you. I can destroy him."

Reese wished she could argue with that. She couldn't.

Vickie stood. "I'll give you twelve hours," she added. "If I don't have ten thousand dollars by then, I start making those calls and talking to people."

Reese blocked her path when Vickie reached for the door. She knew she had zero bargaining power with this woman. And the calls might not even do the damage that Vickie was claiming they could.

Still, Reese didn't want to take the chance.

"Please don't do this," Reese said, and yes, she was begging.

But got exactly the reaction she expected. Vickie's smile only widened. "All right, I'll give you twelve and a half hours. I'll meet you at the café then. Oh, and bake me something special to go along with the money."

God, Reese couldn't stop this. Well, not without hitting Vickie with a skillet and tying her up in the closet. Extreme, yes, but she was furious enough to want to do it. Of course, she'd been wanting to hit her with something for a while now.

Reese stepped aside and let her leave, knowing there was nothing she could do to stop this train that was speeding right toward Logan.

Nothing she could do here in Spring Hill, anyway.

She grabbed her backpack and headed for the door. Once she was far away from here, Reese could call the same business associates of Logan's and assure them that she was no longer part of his life.

The first tear slid down her cheek before Reese even made it to the back stairs.

CHAPTER SIXTEEN

LOGAN SAT IN his truck and watched the Bluebonnet Inn. The light was still on in Reese's apartment, but he couldn't see anyone moving around in there from the window. Of course, it didn't take much moving around for Vickie to spell out whatever blackmail scheme she had in mind.

Something that involved him, no doubt.

He'd read her arrest record, and her favorite con was to get friendly with a senior citizen and then rob him blind. The coziness often involved sex, and in many cases, the victim had to be coerced into bringing charges against her because they were either too embarrassed or had fallen for her. Which meant there were likely countless victims out there.

Including Reese.

Reese wouldn't see herself as a victim, though, but she wasn't nearly as tough or guarded as she wanted people to think.

He frowned.

Since when had he become an expert on the inner workings of Reese's mind? Yes, he knew how to bring her to an orgasm, but that hardly made him a Reese expert. Still, he sat and watched, his stomach in knots over the idea that Vickie would use him to get to her own daughter.

His phone buzzed, and Logan nearly sprained his hand yanking it from his pocket. Not Reese, though. Lucky. He considered letting it go to voice mail, but that would only unnecessarily worry his family.

"I'm fine," Logan answered right off to save them some time.

"Good to hear it. Since you're with Reese, I figured she'd kiss any boo-boos you got from Helene's chatter."

"I don't get boo-boos. If you're not calling about my well-being, then why are you calling? And if it's about Helene, save your breath."

"It's about clown shit."

Logan was sure he made a face. "Have clowns been crapping in the pastures, too?"

"No, but one clown crapped his pants. Greg. Apparently, the Nederland brothers followed him out of the reception and gave him a butt-whipping on your behalf."

Hell's Texas bells. The Nederlands were hardly champions of justice. They were three linebacker-sized brothers, probably suffering from some kind of glandular issues because of their size, and they liked to do two things—drink and fight. They had three sisters, same glandular problem, who were even worse than the brothers. Greg was lucky the Nederland males had been the ones to go after him.

"Is Greg okay?" Logan asked.

"Other than crapping his pants, some bruises and a missing tooth, he should be fine. But the Nederland brothers have him pinned down on the ground in the back of the civic center and have said they won't let him up until you give them the say-so."

"Call the cops," Logan instructed. "I don't want to go back to the civic center. I'm tied up."

"Oh, yeah? Didn't know Reese was into that sort of thing." And he probably wasn't joking. "Someone did call the cops, and that's why I'm calling you. Deputy Davy is on the way."

Logan didn't just groan. He cursed. Deputy Davy Devine looked like a zombie and had the IQ of a shrimp. He could start a brawl just by showing up on the scene. Greg could get seriously hurt since he wasn't much of a fighter. Heck, lots of people could get hurt.

But Reese was in the same boat. It was just that her injuries wouldn't be bruises and crapped pants. He hoped.

"Pretend to be me," Logan told his brother. "And tell the Nederlands to back off, that my honor doesn't need defending. Just use small words so they'll understand what you're saying."

"You're sure? You hate it when we've played the switch."

Yes, he did. Mainly because Lucky had used him to break up with girls, and a couple of times it had involved getting smacked upside the head with things that the girls threw at him.

"I'm sure," Logan answered. "The Nederlands are probably drunk enough they won't notice you're not me, and we're dressed almost the same."

Helene would notice, though, but maybe she wouldn't say anything. It did make Logan wonder, though, why she wasn't out there trying to save her clown lover.

Logan ended the call, but the second he did, his phone buzzed again. Speak of the devil—it was Helene—and this time he did let the call go to voice mail. It was probably just her asking him to intervene on Greg's behalf, but Logan had his own intervention right now.

Vickie came out of the Bluebonnet Inn.

She must have recognized his truck because she came his way, and Logan stepped out so she'd be sure to spot him.

"I figured I'd see you again," Vickie purred, and yeah, it was a purr. She was coming on to him, and for some reason she thought it would work. She moved in much too close. Close enough that she brushed the front of her body over his.

Logan took her by the shoulders, lifted her and maneuvered her away from him. And he took back his wallet that she'd lifted.

She smiled, shrugged. "Must be losing my touch with both the wallet and the, well, touching."

"I doubt your touch would have ever worked with me."

"No? Well, plenty of people say that Reese and I look like sisters."

Blind people, maybe, but Logan wasn't here to exchange pleasantries with this turd. It'd been a long night, and he still needed to talk to Reese.

"Here's how this is going to work," Logan started.

But he didn't get to finish because Vickie interrupted him. "You're going to threaten to put me in jail the way you threatened Chucky. Well, that won't fly with me. I keep a lawyer on retainer and will be out in minutes."

Not in the Spring Hill jail, but she was right—an arrest for trying to steal his wallet wouldn't get her much time behind bars. He could goad her into slapping him, but it would have the same results. The only thing he could do is take away what power she thought she had.

"There's nothing you can tell me that will come between Reese and me." That possibly wasn't true.

"Even Spenser?" And she smiled when she asked that.

"Even Spenser O'Malley."

She flinched, maybe surprised that he knew the man's full name, or maybe a gnat just flew in her eye.

"I hired a PI to investigate Reese. And you," Logan added. "I know everything about both of you."

Definitely not a gnat that time. It was a real flinch. "Are you still seeing her because you knocked her up?"

Logan rolled his eyes. He couldn't wait for a couple more months to pass, and then people would see that Reese wasn't showing, and it would put that rumor to rest. Well, they'd see if Reese stayed around, anyway. The jury was still out on whether or not that would happen.

"It's none of your business why I'm seeing her," Logan went on. Good thing, too, since if he couldn't explain it to himself, he damn sure couldn't explain it to this piece of navel lint.

"It'll be my business when I tell your friends about you seeing a criminal."

Now Logan smiled and shrugged. "My friends already know, and just in case you're going to threaten my business associates next, they know, too. I took Reese to a reception tonight where everyone in town saw us. If there was someone who didn't know, they will by morning."

Of course, Jimena's tit slip and the clown crap might take top billing. No way could Reese and he match up to that.

Vickie huffed, glanced around as if trying to figure out what to say to salvage this. "All right. Give me ten grand, and I'll leave town. You'll never hear from me again."

That didn't salvage it. And while she might indeed leave, Vickie was crap. She would just keep showing up. And Logan frowned at all the crap references he was making tonight.

"Listen carefully," he said, making his voice take on that dangerous edge that he liked to have in situations like these. "I didn't give Chucky a dime, and I'm not giving you one, either. Leave town before you see a side of me that most people don't like to see."

That was it. The only warning he intended to give her. It might work. Might not. Which meant Logan needed to be prepared for the fallout. Preparing started with seeing Reese. And he knew where she wouldn't be.

In her room.

Nope, she was probably already trying to outrun the stink her mother was using to smell up her life. And his.

"That's it?" Vickie howled when he got back in his truck. She called him a name, one that questioned his paternity, sexual habits and the size of his dick. Logan didn't care how many names she called him if she just left.

He drove away with her still swearing at him.

Logan went in the direction of Walter Meekins's place first. Since Walter had the only taxi in town, Reese might head there, but no, the taxi was parked right out front and had two cats sleeping on it. So, Logan drove toward the bus station, the only other way for Reese to make a getaway.

Unless she'd called Jimena to pick her up.

That caused his stomach to churn.

Jimena hadn't exactly been in any shape to drive, but that didn't mean Reese hadn't arranged to meet her friend at her car. If so, they could be anywhere by now.

Even though the bus station was only six blocks away from the Bluebonnet Inn, the sidewalks ended after about three of those blocks. And there were ditches. Since there were no streetlights in that section of the road, Reese could twist her ankle. Or get picked up by a serial killer.

And apparently he was imagining worst-case scenarios now.

Logan was about to call Reese, but he spotted something just ahead. At first it looked like fireflies, but then he realized it was his headlights catching the sparkles on Reese's black dress. She had her backpack looped over her shoulder, and yep, she was going straight for the bus station. Except she was limping.

He pulled off the road in front of her, blocking her path.

"I'm leaving," she said, glancing at him.

"I see that." He had to step in front of her when she tried to go around his truck. There was no traffic and probably wouldn't be this time of night, but Logan didn't want to risk her being hit. "Did you hurt your foot?"

"No, these heels are hard to walk in."

They sure looked it, and coupled with the snug dress, she definitely wasn't dressed for a trek to the bus stop.

"My mother's going to ruin you," she added, and that's when the headlights caught something else. The tears in her eyes.

Hell. She was crying.

"Your mother will try," he argued. "But you do know I don't need protecting, right?"

Judging from the tears mixed with a huff, Reese didn't know that. "I can't let her do this to you."

"Leaving won't help. If she comes after me, she'll do

that whether you're in town or not. Vickie smells money, and she thinks she can get it from me."

A sob left her mouth, and she sagged against him. "God, Logan. I'm so sorry."

He knew that, and he was also pissed that Reese felt the need to apologize for something she hadn't done. Also pissed that she'd tried to limp her way away from town. And from him. He scooped her up in his arms, kissing her to catch the sound of surprise she made, and he carried her back to his truck.

"At least if I go, you can tell your business associates that you're no longer seeing me," she reminded him when he set her on the seat and then followed in behind her.

Since it appeared that argument might continue, Logan kissed her again. Then he kissed her just because he felt like doing it. The third kiss, though, was all pure lust. That's because kisses one and two gave him a hard-on.

"You're staying," he told her, but it was possible Reese didn't hear that because he was still kissing her when he said it. Possible, too, that she didn't hear it because she really got into the kiss, as well. Not just with her mouth.

But also with her hands.

She took hold of him and yanked him to her.

Logan hadn't expected the kiss to get this frantic and this deep so fast, but heck, he just went with it. In his way of thinking, Reese and he had been to hell and back today, and they deserved this.

But the question was, did they deserve it right here, right now?

Apparently so. Because Reese kissed him as if this

were the last kiss she was ever going to get. Not just from him but from anyone. It wasn't true because Logan intended to do a lot more kissing.

And that's what he did.

Her dress was stretchy and clingy, but thankfully stretchy and clingy worked for what he had in mind. He pushed it up, found only a tiny pair of panties underneath, but even the millimeter of silk fabric was too much. He shoved the panties down, too, and kissed her stomach. The inside of her thigh. He would have sampled the part of her he really wanted to sample if she hadn't caught onto his hair and yanked him back up.

"We do this the old-fashioned way," she insisted.

That was fine by him except her idea of old-fashioned and his weren't quite the same. She went after his zipper, and while her frantic hands were giving him some pleasure, there was pain, too. But not enough pain and pleasure to knock the common sense right out of his head.

They were on the side of the road. In his truck. And while he did have tinted windows, anyone driving by could get a glimpse inside if they looked hard enough.

Oh, hell.

She got him unzipped and had him in her mouth before he could stop her.

Logan cursed, all from pleasure this time, and while he did enjoy her particular version of old-fashioned, he couldn't see. His eyes had glazed over. Or so he thought. But they were just fogging up the windshield.

Reese kept him in her mouth long enough to make him want a whole lot more of her. She made a sound of protest when he caught onto her and moved her onto his lap so that her dress was up to her waist and she was straddling him. He made his own sound of protest because this was not the way he wanted to have sex with her. He'd wanted a slower pace. Foreplay.

A bed.

It wasn't the first time he'd had sex in a truck, but the last time had been when he was seventeen. He hadn't realized then just how dangerous it could be. With the steering wheel in the way, Reese and he were teetering between the bucket seats and the gearshift. It didn't help that they were both still jockeying for position. That they were both still trying to kiss each other blind. Or that she had her hands in his boxers.

Or that he had to get a condom out of his wallet.

Getting the condom on was even more of a challenge. He nearly gave her an orgasm just because the back of his hand was moving against her in the wrong place. Of course, it was the right place if he'd been going for a quick end to this. He wasn't. Logan wanted to be inside her this time when they finished this insanity they'd started.

It felt like a juggling act, and when Logan bashed his elbow into the steering wheel, he nearly put this on pause so he could take her back to his place. However, the *nearly* notion went south when Reese lifted herself and then slid right down onto his erection.

Yes, the truck was still uncomfortable, but Logan no longer cared.

He no longer cared that his phone was buzzing, either. Reese started to move, and he caught onto her hips to guide that movement. Not that he had to do much. She'd already found the right pace and angle, and she was working to get him the only thing he wanted right now.

A mind-blowing climax.

She got there ahead of him, which was a surprise

considering he'd botched everything about this. Well, everything but the pleasure. Hard to botch that when he was with Reese.

Despite her own orgasm slamming through her, she managed to keep moving her hips. Kept sliding against him to give him exactly what he needed to finish.

Logan let the mind-blowing take over.

Reese collapsed against him, and Logan would have been content to sit there for a couple of minutes to let them both come back to earth. No such luck, though. The approaching headlights caught their attention, and then it did more than just that when the car pulled to a stop ahead of Logan's truck. A car he recognized.

Della and Stella's.

Logan would have rather faced Satan because he wouldn't have been required to explain anything to him.

Seeing the car, and the two occupants inside, had both Reese and him scrambling. Reese crawled off his lap and dragged down her dress. Logan stood no chance of zipping up just yet, but he grabbed his cowboy hat and put it over his crotch. Not a second too soon because the car door opened, and Della stepped out.

"Is everything okay?" she called out. Since she was wearing a party dress, she'd probably come straight from the reception.

Logan lowered his window a couple of inches. "We're fine. I just pulled over to answer a text."

He'd hoped that would satisfy Della enough to wave and get back in her car. It didn't. She came walking toward him, and thankfully at the last second Reese noticed her ripped panties on the gear stick. She grabbed them, shoved them beneath the seat.

"Coming from the reception, are you?" Della asked.

She leaned against the door as if this were going to be a long conversation.

It wouldn't be. Not with a cowboy hat on his dick.

Logan nodded. "And now I need to get Reese back to her place."

Della smiled, looked at them. Smiled some more. "It's good to see you two together."

Her smile faded, though, and Logan made sure that wasn't because she'd seen something out of place. Like an open condom wrapper. Logan wasn't sure exactly where that had landed. But then he realized Della wasn't looking in the truck itself. She was dodging his gaze.

"I'm sorry about accidentally inviting Helene to Lucky and Cassie's party," Della said. "Cassie said to do a plus-one—"

"It's okay, really." It wasn't, but at this point Logan would have agreed to a lobotomy to get her out of there. He even moved as if to put the truck into gear.

"Are you okay with it?" Della asked, talking to Reese now.

"Yes, of course." Clearly, she wasn't, but Reese might have agreed to a joint lobotomy at this rate. "But I need to be getting back now."

Della still didn't move. Nor did she make any indications whatsoever that she had immediate plans to do so.

"Is there anything I can do for you before we go?" Logan asked, and he did put the truck in gear while keeping his foot on the brake.

Another smile. "No, but you should probably both put on your seat belts." With that Della finally headed back toward her car but then stopped. "Oh, and you should probably move that condom wrapper. It's stuck on your shirt." She laughed all the way to her car and was still laughing when she got inside.

At least Della wouldn't gossip about this to anyone but Stella. Stella, however, would probably let something slip so by tomorrow it would be all over town that he'd screwed Reese in his truck. But at least there'd be the mention of safe sex, which might finally dispel the pregnancy rumors.

Reese groaned, and for a moment he thought she was going to cry again. But nope, she laughed, too, and it was a wonderful sound to hear. Not quite as good as her orgasm moan, of course, but it made Logan smile.

Until his phone buzzed again.

That's when he saw he had two missed calls from Lucky. He took this one and put it on speaker so he could start driving back to his loft.

"Anything wrong?" Lucky asked him right off.

"I was about to ask you the same thing."

"Nope. I just wanted to give you an update and got a little worried when you didn't answer. Then I got a text from Della, who said she saw your truck on the side of the road—"

"I'm with Reese," Logan confessed. The confession would save time because Lucky would know exactly what that meant.

"Good. Then I won't keep you. I just wanted to let you know that the switch worked, and the Nederlands let Greg go. We took him to the ER after he changed his pants. You're not gonna believe this, but Greg had that clown nose fixed like a dildo to the end of his dick."

Logan believed it. Tonight, he would believe anything including clown dick dildos. "The doc patched

Greg up," Lucky added, "and we're all heading out now. See you when I see you."

Before Logan could even put his phone away, it buzzed again, and he quickly answered it, figuring there was something his brother had forgotten to tell him. But it wasn't Lucky.

"Logan," the woman said, her voice so breathy that it took him a moment to realize it was Helene.

He hadn't meant to groan, but Logan didn't want to go another round with her tonight.

"You have to help me," Helene said. "Please. I need to talk to you right away. Logan, I'm in trouble."

CHAPTER SEVENTEEN

TROUBLE.

Even though Logan hadn't put the call on speaker, the cab of the truck wasn't that big, and Reese had no problem hearing what Helene had just said to him. Since Reese had started this so-called affair with Logan, she had been waiting for the other shoe to drop.

But she hadn't gotten one shoe but rather three.

First Chucky, then her mother. Now this. Of course, the first two shoes had been expected. Not this one, though.

Because *trouble* was a synonym for *pregnant*.

"I'll call you back," Logan told Helene, and he hung up. He didn't say anything for several long moments, but even in the dim light Reese could see his jaw muscles stirring against each other.

Then he cursed.

"Helene isn't pregnant with my baby," Logan said right off. "And she might not be pregnant, in any trouble or anything else. She could be lying to get me to see her."

Yes, she could be, but considering Reese's luck, the woman was in fact pregnant and expecting quadruplets. Even one baby, though, would be more than enough to put an end to whatever this was between Logan and her.

"Just drop me off at the Bluebonnet Inn," Reese insisted. "Then you can, uh, freshen up before you see Helene."

And she was certain he would be seeing the woman tonight. No way would Helene have made that call if she hadn't planned on a face-to-face meeting.

"I haven't been with Helene in over four months," he continued. "If she was really pregnant, she would have told me before now."

It sure seemed as if she would, especially since the woman was trying to win him back. A baby would do that in a heartbeat. Reese wasn't even sure if Logan wanted children, but he wasn't the sort of man to run from fatherhood. And Helene would certainly know that.

"Just drop me off out front," Reese said when they reached the Bluebonnet Inn. She gave him a quick kiss and got out, fast, before he could try to say anything. But there wasn't much he could say, not until he found out what was going on with Helene.

Reese used her key to get in since it was past regular check-in hours. She tried not to look back at Logan as he drove away. And she failed at that. Failed at keeping the sucky feelings at bay, too. It was amazing how good she could feel one minute and how lousy the next.

She made her way toward the stairs, hoping for a quick shower, a drink and then sleep. Maybe not even in that order. However, when she heard the voices out back, Reese knew none of those things would probably happen anytime soon. That's because she heard Jimena and her mother.

"What did you say to me?" her mother snarled.

Jimena repeated it, and from what part of it Reese caught, it was one of her better insults. Something to do with blighted root vegetables and multiple body cavities. Knowing Jimena, though, this—whatever *this* was—

wouldn't stop with just bizarre insults. It could lead to a physical fight, and she didn't want to have to bail Jimena out of jail tonight.

Reese went out in the back parking lot, and yes, Vickie and Jimena were there, all right.

"What's going on out here?" Reese asked even though it was pretty clear.

"Your skank friend is trying to run me out of town," Vickie snapped.

"Not trying. I *am* running her out of town," Jimena assured her. "This persistent yeast infection from hell that calls herself your mother has spent enough time ruining your life."

It was true. Except for the *am* part. Vickie outweighed Jimena by a good forty pounds, and Vickie was a dirty fighter. She would bite, kick and pull hair. But Jimena wouldn't go down without kicking, biting and some hair pulling of her own, which meant someone would hear it and call that dorky deputy who kept coming in the diner to chat Reese up.

"Unlike Chucky I don't give in to threats," Vickie said.

"You've seen Chucky?" Reese asked.

Vickie kept her eyeballs pinned to Jimena. "Maybe. But it doesn't matter. I won't tuck tail and run like he did." And because she probably knew it would get Jimena's goat, Vickie smiled. Her smile changed a little, though, when her attention finally landed on Reese.

Reese had no doubts, *none*, that she looked as if she'd just had sex. Plus, she had Logan's scent all over her, possibly a hickey on her neck, another hickey on the top of her right boob, and while her mother didn't have X-ray vision, Reese figured she was standing a little differently since she wasn't wearing any panties.

"You've been with Logan." Her mother touched her tongue to her top lip. "I don't know why we all have to argue about this. We can all share. The man's got enough money and dick to go around and around and around."

"Logan's money's not going anywhere, especially in your pockets," Reese informed her. She didn't even address where his dick wouldn't be going.

Jimena agreed with a crisp nod. "Reese has got a good thing with Logan, and you're not messing it up."

No, she really didn't have a good thing. In fact, Reese might have no *things* at all with Logan if it turned out Helene was indeed pregnant.

"Then we'll agree to disagree," Vickie said, using her best smart-ass tone. "But I'm not leaving."

"Oh, yeah?" Jimena stepped closer and got right in Vickie's face.

Vickie chuckled. "Jimena, are you really going to punch me?"

"No. I'm going to let them do it." Jimena hitched her thumb to the side of the building. "You can come out now, girls."

The Nederland sisters stepped out.

Even though it wasn't very courageous of her, Reese took a step back. Her mother took six.

Reese knew the sisters, of course, because like everyone else in town, they came into the café. The smallest one was six-four. The biggest one could have played starting defensive lineman for the Dallas Cowboys, and with the size of her hips, she could have cleared out the entire football field with just a single shift of position. To say they were intimidating was like saying there was a small patch of ice in Antarctica.

"You talked these thugs into hitting me?" Vickie howled.

The biggest sister shrugged. "She didn't have to talk us into anything. We just like to fight."

Vickie glanced at Reese as if she might intervene, but Reese only gave her a flat look. She certainly wasn't getting between the Nederlands and their intended target, especially for a woman who was trying to extort money and dick privileges from Logan. Vickie must have figured that out right off because she turned and started to run.

The smaller sister moved as if to go after her, but the big one caught onto her arm. "No. Let her have a head start. It's more fun that way." The sisters then began to mosey on after her.

Reese supposed she should remind them not to actually hit—not hard, anyway—but she didn't have the energy. Besides, Vickie was like a cat with thirty-four lives, and she was sneaky. She had probably already scoped out a hiding place before she even let anyone know she was in town.

Jimena, however, didn't hurry to join the potential butt-whipping. "Thank you for trying to help," Reese told her.

Jimena sighed, patted her arm. "You want to talk about it?"

Reese didn't even have to think about that. The answer was no. She just wanted to go to her room and wait for that fourth shoe to drop.

LOGAN DIDN'T EXACTLY hurry when he heard the knock on his loft door. He took his time as he'd done in the shower, as he'd also done getting dressed. Even though he did indeed want to know what Helene considered "trouble," he wasn't sure he was up to dealing with it. Still, it was better than waiting until morning and stewing about it all night.

But when he opened the door, it wasn't Helene.

It was Jimena. And she wasn't alone. She was holding a purring, nuzzling Crazy Cat in her arms.

"Reese wouldn't talk to me about what's wrong so I came to hear it straight from the horse's mouth. What did you do to her?" Jimena quit nuzzling the cat long enough to jab her index finger against his chest. The cat wasn't hissing at her or anything.

Logan hated to be distracted by something like that at a time like this, but it was somewhat of a miracle. "How did you catch Crazy Cat?" he asked.

She looked at him as if his hair had spontaneously combusted. "The cat came to me when I walked in. And that's not an answer to my question. What did you do to Reese?"

Since Jimena seemed to be looking for something specific and wasn't asking in a general sense, Logan went with, "What do you mean?"

"She's upset and won't talk about it. I want to know why."

While Logan admired Jimena for watching out for her friend, he had to shake his head. "I need to have a conversation with someone first because even I don't know what's going on."

"You mean a conversation with Helene. She's sitting in her car in your parking lot. I don't think she saw me when I came in, but I got a pretty good look at her, and I believe she's crying."

Hell. Not tears. He barely had enough energy to deal with the talking.

"Not that I care if Helene cries," Jimena went on, "but I suspect her tears are connected to the love bite on Reese's neck. I've heard a few people say they saw one on Reese, and news like that would have gotten back to Helene."

Mercy, he hoped he hadn't left a love bite. Like his sex-in-a-truck adventure, he hadn't done that since high school.

Logan scrubbed his hand over his face. "Look, I'm not sure exactly what's going on, but when I do know, I'll fill in Reese, and if she wants, she can tell you."

He didn't expect that to work, but Jimena finally nodded. "Deal. Just swear to me you won't pull some shit that gets her hurt."

Logan wished with all his heart that he could promise that, but he figured someone was going to get hurt in this. Maybe Reese. Maybe him. The only thing he was certain of was the shit pulling wouldn't be done by him.

He reached to pet the cat, but Crazy Cat reacted as if he were coming at her with raptor claws. Full-pitch hissing, and she swatted at him. She started purring, though, when Jimena pulled her closer.

"Well, I'd better leave since someone just opened the back door," Jimena said. "Helene probably."

Logan hadn't heard anything, but then his head was starting to pound. No migraine. Not now.

"By the way," Jimena said, "you know that phone on your reception desk? Well, the lights are all blinking. Looks as if you've got a lot of messages."

He probably had a thousand. In addition to a messy personal life, his business wasn't going so great, either.

"What do you want me to do with Cuddles?" she asked. Apparently, that was the name she'd given Crazy Cat.

And Logan got an idea. A really bad one probably, but then good ideas seemed to be in short supply. "Are you staying in town?" he asked.

"Yeah, sure. For a little while. Reese's place isn't big enough for one much less two so I'm renting the room in that old building across the street from the post office. Wendell Wertz owns it."

Logan knew the building. It had been for sale for five years. "I didn't know there were any apartments in the place."

"Well, it's not actually an apartment. It's what used to be the storage room for a coffee shop."

Yes, back in the nineties.

She shrugged. "Anyway, I'll get something better if I can get hired at the café."

So, she was looking for work. That made his bad idea take even deeper root. "Can you fill in as receptionist until I can get someone in permanently?"

Jimena looked at him with all the suspicion of someone in a police lineup. "Are you offering me a job?"

"A temporary one, starting Monday morning," he clarified. He'd almost said tomorrow, but since that was Sunday, it could wait a day. "It would involve taking care of the cat, too. Oh, and fixing coffee. And answering the phone."

She stayed quiet a moment, giving that some thought. "I'll let you know," Jimena said, and hurried off, meeting Helene, who was coming up the stairs.

Crazy Cat hissed and swatted at Helene, too.

Jimena possibly did also.

Logan wasn't into hissing and swatting, but he wanted to set some ground rules to hurry along this conversation with Helene. At least, that had been the plan, then he did indeed see the fresh tears in Helene's eyes. Instead of giving her a shoulder to cry on, though, he offered her a box of tissues when she stepped into the room. Which she accepted.

"Explain what kind of trouble you're in," Logan demanded.

But Helene didn't jump to answer. Her gaze skirted around the loft. "You've, uh, redecorated."

Hardly the right word for it. He'd replaced the cheap furniture with even worse cheap furniture that'd been delivered earlier, and it now looked like one of those places in need of an extreme makeover. Or a torch. "If that's what you've come to talk about—"

"It isn't." However, that was all she said for a couple of snail-crawling moments. "May I sit? This isn't something I can just blurt out."

He motioned for her to take a seat, but Logan had some of his own blurting to do. "It's been over four months since we've had sex. So, if you're pregnant, the baby's not mine."

Logan had gotten some funny looks over the years—many of those coming this very night—but he had to say that one was the funniest. Helene's mouth dropped open so wide that he could see her tonsils.

"You thought I was pregnant?" she asked in the same tone one might if the world was ending in thirty seconds.

He lifted his shoulder. "You said you were in trouble."

"I said I was in trouble, not stupid. I'm on the pill, and we always used a condom."

"Yeah, I wasn't sure Greg had, though." Or maybe the clown nose had acted as a condom. If so, Logan really didn't want to know the details.

"Wow," she mumbled, and she repeated it a lot of times. "Okay, I'm not pregnant. Have no plans to become pregnant. Have no plans to repeat my mistake by being with Greg again." Another pause. "Is Reese pregnant?"

"No." And he wondered how many more times he was going to have to answer that question. "And I should have said right from the start that I don't want to talk about Reese."

Helene stayed quiet for way too long. "We have to talk about her. Because she's the reason I'm here." Tears sprang to her eyes again. "When I found out you were involved with her, I had Reese investigated. I know, it was wrong, but I needed to know that I hadn't sent you into the arms of the wrong woman."

Since Logan had also had Reese investigated, he decided it was a good time to stay quiet and listen to the rest of what Helene had to say.

"You know about Reese's past, of course," Helene went on. "I'm sure she's told you."

He settled for a nod. She'd told him some of it. Logan figured there was more, and then there was that juvie record he'd managed to get unsealed. Hell, he hoped Helene hadn't managed to get into that because Logan didn't know why Reese had a criminal record.

Helene nodded, too, and he had to hand it to her. She didn't seem disappointed that Reese had come clean. Or at least semiclean. A bitter woman would have probably taken some pleasure in springing the news of her shady past on him. But either there was no pleasure or else Helene was doing a good job concealing it.

"Anyway, I found out about Chucky Dayton." She looked up at Logan. "You know about him, too?"

"Yes." And Logan got a bad feeling in the pit of his stomach. "You're the reason he came to town." He cursed. "Did you contact Reese's mother, too?"

"No." She shook her head. "I mean, I told Chucky where Reese was, but I haven't seen or spoken to her mother. Is she in Spring Hill?"

Logan decided to go with a question of his own. "What does all of this have to do with the trouble you're in?"

"Everything," Helene said on a rise of breath. "Chucky's blackmailing me. He says if I don't pay him twenty thousand dollars, then he'll tell Reese and you that I'm responsible for him finding her. I considered just paying it, but I figured he'd keep coming back for more."

"He would."

Logan suddenly had a flurry of emotions about all of this. Helene had likely started a domino effect what with first telling Chucky and then Chucky had probably told Vickie. Or maybe Helene had been the one to tell Vickie, too. Either way, the domino tiles were already falling, and they were falling on Reese.

"Chucky tried to get rough with Reese," Logan said. "He pushed her against a building, and if I hadn't been there, he could have hurt her."

"Oh, God." More tears.

Logan hadn't told her that to make her cry but only so that she'd understand what a truly stupid thing she'd done. And the only reason Helene had done it was to send Reese running.

It had almost worked.

Heck, it still might work.

"If you stay with her," Helene said, her voice shaky, "you also invite these people into your life. Is that what you want?"

That didn't help with the flurry of emotions, but part of his frustration was that he didn't know the answer. He wanted Reese. For now. He wanted to continue to have sex with her, preferably not in his truck. But Logan couldn't see beyond that.

"It took me eight years to decide to propose to you," he finally answered. "I've known Reese a little less than four months. I don't have to make any decisions about what I do or don't do right this very second."

At the rate he was going, he might never make a decision. Or Reese might make it for him and cut out again.

"Of course," Helene agreed. She stood, looked around again. "You really are moving on with your life." She didn't sound happy about that. Or maybe her reaction was for the decor. His sofa was the same color of vomit.

"You'll move on with yours, too."

"Yes, but not with Greg. I know you wouldn't have asked, but despite the spectacle he put on tonight, there's no chance I'll ever be with him." She paused again. "In therapy I learned what happened with him was just sexual experimentation. Nothing more. It happens sometimes when a woman has my kind of upbringing where people expect her to be, well, perfect."

It sounded as if she wanted him to jump in there with

an "I understand." But Logan didn't jump. Instead, he made the mistake of rubbing his forehead.

"Headache?" she immediately asked.

"I'll take something after you leave." Which was a not so subtle way of telling her this conversation was over.

But Helene didn't budge. She did nod, though. "So, when Chucky contacts me again, I'll just tell him that I confessed to Reese and you, and the two of you are okay with what happened."

"FYI, we're not okay with it. In fact, Reese has a right to be really pissed off at you. But now that we know what you've done, it's taken away Chucky's bargaining power. You don't have to pay hush money."

Another nod, and she finally started for the door. She stopped, though, did another of those annoying looks around before her attention came back to him. "There's no chance of you forgiving me?"

He really did need those pain meds. "Good night, Helene."

Logan maneuvered her out the door and closed it. In the same motion, he reached for his phone and headed to the medicine cabinet. The migraine was chasing him, but if he could drug up in time, he might be able to fight it off. First, though, he needed to talk to Reese. She was no doubt playing some worst-case scenarios about this chat he'd had with Helene.

She didn't answer on the first ring. Or even the second. By the time it got to the fourth ring, Logan was playing out some worst-case scenarios of his own until she finally answered.

"Are you okay?" Reese asked, taking the question right out of Logan's mouth.

"Yes. How about you?"

Judging from the fact that she mumbled some profanity, Logan knew the answer to that. "Look, this would be a good time for you to stay put and not get involved."

"What do you mean?" And Logan really did want to know the answer. Something pretty big had to be going on for Reese not to ask about why Helene had wanted to talk to him.

Reese mumbled more profanity. "Please don't come down here. I'm at the Spring Hill Police Department. I've been arrested."

REESE UNDERSTOOD WHY people called Deputy Davy Devine by the nonaffectionate nickname of Deputy Dweeb. She couldn't figure out how anyone could look so twitchy and yet move so slow at the same time.

People in comas were more active than this guy.

The Nederland sisters were in the cell next to Reese and had said pretty much the same thing. Before they all passed out, that is. Now they were snoring and clearly didn't care about a hasty release. In fact, they seemed so at home in the jail cell that it made Reese wonder how often they had been here.

Unlike Reese. She definitely wasn't comfortable behind bars, though it wasn't her first rodeo, either. But it was her first one in a cocktail dress and without panties.

"If I find some firecrackers, I'm going to shove them up that deputy's ass," Jimena mumbled. She was sitting on the floor outside the jail cell where Reese was locked up. "That might get him moving."

Reese doubted it. It had taken him over an hour to read Reese her rights and start the paperwork for the charges against her. Heaven knew how long it'd take for Reese to post bail, though Jimena was there with the cash to get her out.

Of course, Logan was on the way now, too.

Reese had hoped to have all of this resolved by the time he called her but no such luck. At this rate she might not have it resolved before she reached the age of mandatory retirement.

And she could blame her mother for this.

Yet something else on the list of crappy things her mother had done to her and continued to do to her.

Vickie had run from the Nederland sisters, all right. She'd run straight to the jail and had told Deputy Davy that Reese had ordered the girls to attack her. It hadn't helped that the sisters had come into the police station at that exact moment and started punching Vickie. It also hadn't helped that the sisters had verified—in their drunken state, of course—that they were doing this for Reese.

Apparently, the Nederlands failed to remember that Jimena was the one who'd set all of this in motion, but Reese wasn't about to rat out her friend.

Sadly, being in jail wasn't the worst of what she was feeling right now. It was Logan. He would no doubt come down here, get mixed up in all this craziness that was her life, and he'd do that even though he had almost certainly been put through the wringer with whatever Helene had told him.

Of course, the wringer might be better than some of the other things Reese had figured could happen. It was possible that Helene and Logan were back together.

"I went to see him tonight," Jimena said.

Reese lifted her head. "Logan?"

"I know you didn't want me to do that, but I had to warn him not to shit on you."

Great. It was just yet another cog turning in this wheel of a nightmarish night. Reese forced herself to remember that there had been some good parts. Well, one good part, anyway. Sex in the truck. Even though it wouldn't sound like a good part to most people, the sex had been with Logan so that made it a shining spot in an otherwise awful day.

"Logan offered me a job," Jimena added. "A temporary one," she clarified. "He wants me to be his receptionist and take care of the cat."

It was as if Jimena were speaking a foreign language, and that's why Reese just stared at her.

"He didn't say he was offering the job because of you," Jimena went on. "I got the feeling he really needed some help."

"You've never been a receptionist," Reese pointed out.

Jimena shrugged. "I've never bailed you out of jail, but I'm managing that just fine."

Uh, no, she wasn't, and Reese was about to point out why working for Logan would be a really bad idea.

But maybe it wasn't.

After all, Vickie had threatened to call Logan's business associates and try to hurt his reputation. When Reese had told Deputy Davy that, he'd said it was too vague of a threat to have Vickie arrested, that it was a she said/she said kind of thing.

"If you're at Logan's office, you can let me know if Vickie succeeds in turning people against him," Reese suggested.

Jimena stared at her. Though she was staring at

Reese through bars, it wasn't hard to see that her friend was suspicious of that. "Why, so you can leave if it happens?" She huffed and didn't wait for Reese to verify it. "One day you're going to learn that you can't fix shit your mother keeps shitting on. She'll just follow you and shit up the next place, too."

That was a lot of shit to deal with at once, and Reese wished she could disagree, but she couldn't. But if she stayed after such a shit-fallout, then her mere presence would be enough to continue to fuel the gossip.

Reese heard the voices out in the squad room. Two she recognized as Deputy Davy and Logan. She didn't recognize the other man, but several seconds later, the trio appeared. She'd seen the third man in the café—Police Chief Luke Mercer—and he was sporting a scowl that was almost as bad as Logan's.

Almost.

Logan was aiming his scowl at the deputy.

"You're an idiot," Logan said to the deputy, and while Reese had heard him use his badass voice, she'd never heard it this lethal.

"Yeah, he is," the chief agreed. Since it looked as if he'd dressed in a hurry—he had a pajama top hanging out from underneath his shirt—it was likely he'd gotten out of bed to come and handle this.

The chief unlocked the cell door, and Logan immediately went to Reese and pulled her into his arms. "Are you all right? Sorry, bad question," he added when she just gave him a flat stare.

"Something needs to be done about Vickie," Jimena insisted.

Reese was about to say there wasn't much that could

be done, but Logan nodded. "Chief Mercer is arresting your mother for attempted extortion."

Reese gave him a blank stare for a different reason. Because she didn't have a clue what he was talking about. "It'll be her word against mine," she reminded him.

"No, it won't be," Logan assured her. "We're getting some help with that."

"Help?" Jimena and Reese asked in unison. "Who's willing to help me?"

"You wouldn't believe me if I told you." Logan took hold of her and got Reese moving toward the exit.

CHAPTER EIGHTEEN

"DID A CAT eat your homework?" Jimena asked.

Reese was in such deep thought that she heard Jimena's question, but it took a moment for what her friend was saying to sink in. She'd been distracted most of the night before and now the morning since Logan had managed to get her sprung from jail.

"I'm just thinking about what happened," Reese mumbled. Though that was probably as clear as a gypsy's crystal ball.

Logan had been right about Reese not believing who was helping them.

Chucky.

The man who'd been a thorn in Reese's side for years had now apparently decided to grow a pair. Reese only hoped it wasn't a pair that included some kind of back-stabbing or scam. She wasn't exactly holding her breath, but it appeared that someone had convinced Chucky to come forward and spell out Vickie's intentions of ex-torting money from Reese and/or Logan.

And that someone was yet another surprise for Reese.

Helene.

Chucky and Helene seemed an unholy alliance, but from what Reese had learned from Logan, Chucky had tried to blackmail Helene, and Helene and Logan had turned the tables on him. In exchange for Helene not filing charges against him, Chucky would testify against Vickie.

Reese still wasn't exactly clear about how Chucky had found out about her mother's plans, but she suspected that they had had their own unholy alliance before Chucky and Helene decided to do the right thing and go the holy route.

Still, the good news was Reese hadn't had to spend the night in jail, the charges against her had been dropped and Helene wasn't pregnant. The bad news was that her mother was nowhere to be found, and that meant the police chief couldn't arrest her.

"Did the cat shit on your homework?" Jimena asked.

Obviously that was a reminder that Reese's head was still in the clouds. "I left my backpack and panties in Logan's truck." Reese hadn't actually planned to say that, but it was yet something else that had been clouding her mind.

"And you're worried about…what? That he'll keep them? Look inside the backpack? Wear the panties?"

Since Jimena had never actually looked in the backpack, the second question was the only one that was legitimate. Though Reese was worried that one of Logan's brothers or a business associate might see the torn panties. Still, that wasn't her main worry, and Jimena knew it.

It was Logan.

He could tell her a thousand times that he could weather out whatever storms this bad press and her mother might cause, but Reese wasn't so sure. That meant she should be distancing herself from him, or at least thinking about distancing herself, anyway.

But she wasn't.

Here she was waiting for Cassie and Claire to show up to look at the building where Jimena was staying. A building that Cassie was thinking of buying for her new counseling practice. Reese still wasn't sure why the two wanted her in on this look-around, but Cassie had then said they could use the opportunity to go over the final details for the upcoming engagement party.

Instant guilt.

Because Reese hadn't done nearly enough for the party. Worse, less than twelve hours ago, she'd nearly skipped town without so much as a heads-up phone call to Cassie. That did make Reese feel as if the cat had pooped not just on her homework but on her, as well.

Cassie had also invited Jimena because Jimena was already renting a room on the second floor of the building and had a key. Since the owner lived in San Antonio, it would save him a trip to Spring Hill in case Cassie vetoed the place after one look.

Something she just might do.

The midcentury building was definitely nothing special. Gray peeling walls, a warped parquet floor and a trio of short halls off the reception area that led to a number of rooms. There was a metal sign in the corner for watch repair. Too bad that wasn't still there. For years, Reese had promised herself that she would have her grandfather's watch fixed, but with all the moving around, she'd never managed it.

In addition to the repair sign, there were boxes of old books, several industrial hair dryers, a saddle, a masseuse table and plastic riding horses. At least Reese thought they were horses. With the paint peeling off their eyes and faces, they looked like animal zombies.

"Did they used to make porn films here?" Jimena asked.

Reese wasn't sure how Jimena got that from the assortment of things surrounding them, but she supposed it was possible. No, wait. It wasn't. If there'd been a porn industry here, even if it had been sixty years ago, it would have still been gossiped about.

Jimena went to the glass front of the building and looked out, but then she immediately ducked back. Not just away from the window, but she scrambled behind the zombie horses.

"Elrond," she whispered.

Reese had a look for herself and thought maybe from Jimena's reaction that there was more to her friend's breakup than she'd mentioned. Like that maybe Elrond was an ax murderer and was charging toward the building to chop her into pieces. But no ax.

However, Elrond wasn't alone. He was with Helene.

Judging from their body language, they were arguing. At least, Helene was arguing and Elrond was listening. Neither was happy, and Helene stormed off, not even sparing him a glance.

"I'll bet that's because he stole her porcelain titty," Jimena said, still whispering as if they were right beside Elrond and not across the street from him. She pulled Reese back into the shadows with her. "Maybe they'll kiss or something."

Reese had to shake her head. "Why would I want to see Logan's ex kiss a guy who stole her breast?"

"Because then you'd know she's as phony as those tits and that she's still screwing around."

Reese doubted that. Helene was on her best behavior because she wanted Logan back, and no tumble with a boob-stealing clown was worth that. Helene had almost certainly learned her lesson along with sowing all the wild oats she'd ever sow.

As Helene was storming away, Reese finally saw the car pull up in front of the building. Cassie got out from the driver's side, Claire, the passenger's side, and both women immediately stopped, each catching onto the car.

And their stomachs.

Both looked as if they'd been doing some barfing with the possibility of more to come. Morning sickness.

"Sorry we're late," Cassie said, coming in ahead of Claire. Then she stopped, snickered. "And I guess that's in more ways than one."

"Yes, I told Cassie," Claire fessed up. "I'd wanted to keep it a secret until after the engagement party, but it's hard to keep extreme nausea that only happens in the morning a secret."

"You're both pregnant?" Jimena asked, and even though she hardly knew the women she hurried to them for a celebratory hug. It turned into a group hug because Jimena caught onto Reese and pulled her into the mix.

"And are we celebrating your, uh, morning sickness, too?" Claire asked Reese.

Reese shook her head. "Just a rumor."

Claire shrugged as if disappointed by that. "Oh, well. Maybe one day."

It almost sounded like some kind of acknowledgment that one day Reese would be part of this family to exchange such news. But the chances of that happening were akin to gelato freezing in hell.

Or Logan wearing her panties.

"So, I heard about your jail adventure," Claire went

on. "I was arrested earlier this year for a fight at the pub."

Claire looked as sweet as that gelato Reese had just been thinking about, and somehow the arrest gossip hadn't made it to her ears. So, maybe Jimena had been right about the porn thing, too. Maybe gossip in the town was selective.

"And I was committed to the loony bin," Cassie volunteered.

Reese had heard mention of that but only in whispered tones the way a person would mention yeast infections. In other words, something unpleasant but not serious.

But Reese knew where they were going with this. They were trying to make her feel better about what'd happened. Of course, the difference was neither Cassie nor Claire had a real police record. They were still suitable mates for the McCord men.

Reese wasn't.

"Thanks for being here to let us in," Cassie told Jimena, and she started to look around. "I haven't been in this place in ages." Judging from the sound Cassie made, she was seeing something Reese hadn't.

"Over the years, it's been a bookstore, a beauty salon, a jeweler's and a day care," Claire remarked.

That explained the zombie horses.

"When it was still a day care," Claire went on, "I used to bring over the lunches from the café. I was a waitress there," she added to Reese.

Claire was still trying to make her feel part of the group, but Reese felt herself pulling further away.

"Look, what you're doing is nice," Reese said. "In fact, you're both very nice, but the only reason Logan slept with me at that hotel in San Antonio was because of what happened with Helene. And the only reason I slept with him was because I thought I was dying."

No surprise whatsoever on their faces. Zilch. And that's the reason Reese looked at Jimena.

Jimena shrugged. "So, I might have mentioned it to them, all right? But for the record, you've been with Logan since then, and it didn't have anything to do with mistaken brain tumors and clown sex."

No, it hadn't, but that didn't mean it was more than just sex.

"So, you really thought you were going to die?" Cassie asked. She no longer sounded just nice now. She sounded like a therapist.

"I did." Since Claire and she seemed to be waiting for more, Reese added, "I did a whole bucket-list thing. Ate what I wanted, gave away my money, quit my job."

"And Logan was on that list?" Claire said.

"A hot cowboy was." Sheez, Reese suddenly felt like a slut. A hot cowboy—*any* hot cowboy.

"Wow." Claire again. "So, it was like fate when you met Logan. I mean, what are the odds that you'd be looking for a hot cowboy—which he is—at the exact moment he was nursing a broken heart?"

Cassie nodded. "Logan's not the one-night-stand type."

Heck, he wasn't the broken-heart type, either, so Reese wasn't going to read much into this. For her own self-preservation, she needed to get her mind on something else.

"Let's look at the rest of the place," she insisted.

They got moving, but she also heard Jimena whisper

to Cassie and Claire. "Reese has a tough time trusting men. Old man-baggage stuff."

Great. Now they'd moved from bucket lists to man-baggage. With all this revealing going on, she might as well strip down and show them her tattoos.

Cassie made a sound of agreement. "It's hard not to have man-baggage once you're past twenty-one, but all it takes is one good man to help you put that baggage away for good. Did you have to deal with any lingering depression after learning you didn't have a tumor? I mean, did you have survivor's guilt?"

"Yes," Reese admitted.

Jimena admitted even more. "Reese didn't know the other woman who really did have the tumor, but she was worried she might be a mom or someone who'd be missed."

Reese was still worried about that.

"That's a natural reaction," Cassie went on. "But you seem to be handling it well now."

Reese ignored them and started opening doors. Some contained even more bizarre collections of building memorabilia. White Styrofoam wig heads. Disassembled cribs. The only reason Reese spent even a second glancing at them was so she wouldn't be looking at the other women. Eye contact might just encourage them to keep talking. All she needed to do was finish this tour and then get the heck out of here.

She opened one of the doors and had a serious wow moment.

"It's a kitchen." Reese went in, her gaze taking in the very high-end appliances.

"That's right," Cassie said. "About ten years ago, it was a bakery." She pointed to the sign that was propped up in the corner. Shirley's Sweets. "But it didn't last long. Only a couple of months."

Claire nodded. "That was the baker from Abilene, but she wasn't very good at business. One day she just up and left."

"You sure she wasn't murdered?" Reese asked. That got their attention. "I mean, because this isn't the kind of kitchen a baker would just leave behind. There must be twenty grand worth of appliances and equipment in here."

At the mention of that, all of their shoulders straightened. Because maybe there was a body in the oven. As if to prove that theory wrong—hopefully it was wrong—Reese opened the oven door.

And burst a lung screaming when spiders came scurrying out.

The four of them went scurrying out, too, some faster than others. Claire practically sprinted out of the room.

"Maybe that's why the baker left," Claire said, shuddering.

Cassie shuddered, too, and Reese was shuddering right along with them. Finally, this was something she had in common with the pair.

But Jimena didn't leave. She squished a few spiders, and as if this were the most mundane part of her morning, she strolled out of the kitchen. "I can clean that out for you if you decide to buy the building," she offered.

The spiders seemed to be the least of the problems, or maybe they were some kind of omen. Still, Cassie continued to look around as if she hadn't completely gone off the notion of putting her office in here.

"I have an idea," Cassie finally said. "I could buy the building, and the two of you could rent space from me."

It took a moment for Reese to realize Cassie was talking to her. "What?"

"You could open a bakery, and Claire could use a couple of these rooms for a photography studio. That'd still leave plenty of room for my office and for the apartments on the second floor," she added to Jimena. "Which I'd redo, of course. The whole place needs a face-lift."

"And a good exterminator," Claire added. She was still shuddering.

"Yeah, it sounds great," Jimena piped in. "You could call the bakery Reese's Lemon Thingies."

"No, it doesn't sound great." Reese hadn't meant to say that so loud—it was practically a shout—but she was still stunned that Cassie was making plans. Long-term plans. Plans that included her.

"I'm not the 'opening a bakery' kind of woman," Reese explained when they all just stared at her.

"So, you want to keep working for other people?" Jimena asked. But she didn't just ask it. She was on board with this, too, though Reese wasn't sure how.

"You know I move at least every six months," Reese reminded her.

The three women made varying sounds that they did know that. And that they disapproved. Worse, they looked at her with those looks of disapproval.

It was Claire who broke the silence. "You've been seeing Logan." Then she held up a finger. "Excuse me a sec." And she hurried to the bathroom. A few moments later, Reese heard a different kind of sound—retching.

"Anyway," Cassie said, picking up where Claire had left off. "If you want to have a fighting chance with Logan, then at least consider my offer. You wouldn't have to put up any cash until you actually opened Lemon Thingies."

"Or you could call it Queen of Tarts," Jimena suggested. She snapped her fingers. "Or how about Dough Play?"

"Or Wants and Kneads?" Cassie added. "Or Sweetie Pies?"

"For Goodness' Cakes would work," Claire put in as she came out of the bathroom. "Or Sugar Mama's."

Jimena did more finger snapping. "Or instead of Lemon Thingies, it could be Reese's Thingies."

For Pete's sake, that sounded as if she had testicles.

"Or Reese's Sweet Spot and Thingies," Cassie went on.

That sounded as if she were horny and testicular.

Reese groaned. Not only were they planning her future, they were planning it with really stupid names.

"I don't fit in here," Reese yelled. "And I don't fit into Logan's life. For Christ's sake, I have tattoos."

"Are they spelled correctly?" Cassie asked, and she appeared to be serious. "Because my grandmother had misspelled tattoos, and it drove Lucky nuts."

Reese tried not to groan again. Failed. "They aren't words but a rose and rosebud."

"Sounds tasteful," Claire remarked. "I remember my mother had tats that weren't tasteful at all. Snakes and a spider." Another shudder.

Of course, Reese had heard bits and pieces of Claire's and Cassie's not-so-perfect upbringings, but at least they'd had some semblance of a normal childhood.

"I was raised by con artists. We would have had to come up in status to be called trailer trash." Reese shook her head. "I'd never fit in here."

Cassie and Jimena opened their mouths, no doubt to argue that, but both their mouths stayed open. And Reese soon saw why when she followed their gazes and saw what had captured their attention.

It was Logan.

He was across the street in front of the post office where earlier she'd seen Helene and Elrond. Elrond wasn't there.

But Helene was.

Reese watched as the woman put her hand on Logan's chest, leaned in and whispered something to him. He didn't back away. In fact, Logan leaned in and whispered something right back to her.

Before both Logan and Helene exchanged a very intimate-looking smile.

LOGAN SCOWLED.

First at the stuff the guy had just put on his desk. Then at the guy himself. Logan couldn't remember his name, but the person he was scowling at was someone Lucky had hired to do maintenance on the company trucks and other vehicles.

The stuff the man had put on Logan's desk was Reese's backpack and panties. Red panties that had been visibly ripped.

"Found these when I was cleaning out your truck," the guy said, and he made the mistake of smiling.

Logan's scowled deepened. "Shut the door on your way out," he snarled.

That didn't lessen the guy's smile, and he added a knowing wink. A wink that Logan couldn't deny because he had indeed done some winkable stuff with Reese that had resulted in those torn panties, but there was no reason for someone he barely knew to point that out.

He pressed the intercom button to call Jimena, who should be in reception. Whether she was there was anyone's guess and whether she was working was another guess entirely. Since it was her first day, Logan didn't even know if she was at her desk.

And she wasn't.

That's because at that exact moment Jimena came in the door carrying a cup of coffee, something he was about to request she bring him. She also looked reasonably dressed for the job.

Of course, he was grading on a curve here since Greg had often been unreasonably dressed.

Jimena was wearing a tiger print dress that fit her like a sausage casing and purple glitter shoes. And she smelled like Cheetos. Since there were some yellow stains on her fingers, Logan doubted the finger stains were a coincidence.

Logan figured the sausage-casing clothes would impress Delbert Clark, his ten o'clock appointment. Delbert had an eye for good Angus cows and questionably dressed women. Since Logan had been doing business with the man for nearly a decade, he didn't exactly need to impress Delbert, but it was always good to start with a happy client.

"Your coffee," Jimena said, putting the cup on his desk. "Beans are ground fresh. Two sugars, a teaspoon of half-and-half just the way you like it. Greg left notes about things," she explained. "Building temperature, how you like your coffee, litter box cleaning, your somewhat persnickety personality. Had to look up *persnickety*, but I gotta say, I agree with him."

"I have to say I don't care for being called persnickety." Or having his coffee mentioned along with kitty litter maintenance.

"Greg said in his notes that you'd say that if I brought it up." She slid some papers his way. "That's the contract for those ugly bulls with the humps. The ones that the fella sent pictures of this morning."

"The Brahmas," he supplied. So, evidently Jimena could print out a contract and make coffee even if she didn't know squat about livestock and referred to him with insulting labels.

She scowled, too, when she saw the panties and backpack, and Logan quickly shoved them under his desk.

"You didn't give those back to Reese yet?" She sounded more like his sister than his employee.

"I haven't seen her since Friday night when I got her out of jail." And yes, it was Monday, three days later. But he'd had meetings most of the day on Saturday, had gotten a migraine and had spent a good chunk of Sunday in bed.

"You haven't spoken to her?" Another snap.

"Only for a couple of seconds. I called her, told her I wasn't feeling well and that I'd go by the café today for lunch."

She huffed. "Turd on a tire iron," Jimena grumbled. "I had a date yesterday and didn't check on her because I thought she'd be with you."

"Uh, why would you need to check on her?"

"Because of what she saw, you idiot."

Logan scowled again. There was no reason for her to call him an idiot. Was there? "What did she see?"

Jimena's hands went on her hips, and either the sausage casing was causing her eyes to bulge, or else she was truly pissed off. "You and Helene carrying on in front of the post office."

He had to shake his head, and Logan was certain he looked as confused as he felt.

Jimena made a "duh" sound. "Cassie, Claire, Reese and me were all there Saturday, looking at that building Cassie wanted to buy. Did you know it used to have a bakery in it?" But she waved off that question and continued. "Anyway, we saw you getting cozy with Helene."

"Cozy?" Logan wanted to throw up his hands. "What are you talking about?"

"Post office. Saturday. You. Helene. Whispers. Smiles. In-your-face contact." She spoke slowly as if he were mentally deficient.

Heck, maybe he was because Logan didn't remember…wait…yes, he did. "That wasn't cozy. Helene was just thanking me for getting her out of a sticky situation." The one with Chucky that could have ended up costing her a fortune. "And I thanked her for getting Chucky to testify against Reese's mother."

For all the good that'd done. The police chief had yet to find Vickie, which would only be a good thing if the woman stayed away from Spring Hill and especially from Reese. Logan figured a swarm of bees would have an easier time staying away from something sweet than Vickie did of staying away from Reese.

"You smiled at Helene," Jimena said like an accusation.

Yes, he had. He remembered that now. Logan also remembered why he'd done it. "Because people were watching, and I didn't want to seem petty."

"Well, Reese thought it was more than that. You

should have seen the look on her face. I thought she was going to throw up." She lifted her shoulder. "But that could have been because Claire just threw up, and that was making us all a little queasy. Plus, Reese was spooked because of all those spiders in the oven."

Logan hadn't known any of this was going on. And some of it, he just didn't understand. But one thing was clear; he needed to talk to Reese if she believed he was getting *cozy* with his ex.

He thought about calling her, only to realize she was working and wouldn't be able to answer. However, she should be finished with the breakfast shift in thirty minutes or so, and he could see her then in person.

"When Delbert Clark gets here, show him in right away," Logan instructed.

Jimena didn't acknowledge that. Didn't move. "Uh, about that," she finally said.

The *uh* couldn't be good, and the gloom-and-doom look on her face supported that notion. "What's wrong?"

She took several deep breaths, which no doubt tested the stretch of the dress fabric. "Delbert Clark called about fifteen minutes ago and canceled the meeting."

"Why didn't you put his call through to me?"

More deep breaths. "Because he said he didn't want to talk to you. He said he didn't want to do business with a man who was boinking a convicted felon."

Hell. Logan just had to sit there a couple of seconds and take that in. Vickie had obviously gotten to Delbert, but what surprised Logan was that the man had put gossip over business.

Of course, maybe it wasn't just gossip.

Maybe Vickie had shown Delbert some kind of proof to back up her claims. Then again, Vickie was a con artist so perhaps she was able to use those conning skills to convince the man.

"I told him no one uses that word—*boinking*—anymore," Jimena added. "And then I called him a jackass. Trust me, I could have come up with something much worse to call him, but I kept it PG-rated for your sake."

"Thanks," Logan grumbled, and he wasn't the least bit sincere. He didn't want his receptionist calling an old business associate any names since this was something Logan was sure he could smooth over.

He scrolled through his numbers and pressed Delbert's, and the man answered on the first ring. "I told your girl that I didn't want to talk to you," he said before Logan could even get out a greeting.

Several different emotions hit Logan. First the shock, then the hurt. Followed by the anger. "She told me that, but I didn't believe her. I just figured after all the business we've done together that you owed me a personal explanation."

"Well, I don't," Delbert snapped. "I don't care where you dip your wick as long as it doesn't come back on me."

Logan had to get his jaw unclenched to speak. "How would that come back on you? And please don't use any other reference about wick-dipping."

"Huh?" He sounded surprised that an outdated comment like that would offend Logan. "All right. Then what should I call her—your convicted felon of a lover?"

"You could just call her Reese since that's her name."

Delbert mumbled something that Logan was glad he didn't catch. "I don't plan on calling her anything because there'll be no more business between us unless you dump her. The woman… *Reese*…is a con artist, and I don't want to risk her getting hold of my bank account number and shit like that."

"Her mother's a con artist, not Reese," Logan corrected, "and her mother is no doubt the one who told you these lies."

"Lies aren't lies if there's proof to back them up," Delbert snapped.

Logan tried again to explain, but he was talking to the air because Delbert had already ended the call.

"Now can I come up with something worse than jackass to call him?" Jimena asked.

Even though Jimena only heard Logan's end of the conversation, she'd no doubt figured out the direction it had taken. Logan would have said, "Sure, why not?" but he saw Reese standing in the doorway.

Crazy Cat was at her feet, coiling around her ankles.

Logan wasn't sure how much she'd heard, but she had an even more troubled look on her face than Logan was sure he did. He immediately changed his expression because Reese would feel bad enough about this without his rubbing salt in the wound.

"I called her and told her about Delbert," Jimena volunteered, scooping up the cat. "Reese asked me to spy and find out if your business was getting hurt because of her."

Hardly an admission an employee should make, but in a way Logan was glad Reese was here. He could try to make her see this really wasn't her fault and explain that cozy smile that had apparently made her look as if she wanted to throw up.

Jimena sniffed her. "You smell like bacon."

Reese gave herself a whiff, too. "I didn't have time to shower after breakfast shift."

That was probably the reason the cat was stretching and arching to get closer to Reese. But Reese had her attention nailed to Logan.

"I'll leave you two alone," Jimena said, but she stopped after she was in the doorway with Reese. "Buns in the Oven," Jimena said.

"Uh, what?" Reese asked. Logan mumbled the same.

"That's the name I thought of for your bakery. Of course, most people would think you were naming it that because you're pregnant, which we know you're not, but it's a great name."

"You're opening a bakery?" Logan asked. Sheez. For a gossipy town, he hadn't heard a peep about this.

"No, I'm not." Reese huffed, gave Jimena a frustrated look that Logan was betting she had to use frequently when it came to conversations with the woman. "There's a kitchen in the building Cassie's thinking about buying—"

"Cassie bought it this morning," Logan interrupted. "She asked to use some of the ranch hands to help clear out the place." What Cassie hadn't mentioned, however, was anything about Reese and a bakery.

Jimena got moving again but stopped once more, this time in the hall. "I still think you should consider Cassie's offer." She snapped her fingers, obviously way too gleeful considering that Reese and he had something not so gleeful to discuss. "You could name it Stud Muffins."

Reese shut the door in her friend's face.

"Cassie's offer?" Logan asked.

Reese gave a weary sigh, shook her head. "Cassie

said I could rent the space from her. But I'm not going to do that because I'm not opening a bakery. Especially not one with a name like Stud Muffins."

She probably couldn't help herself—she smiled. Not all from humor, though. Logan could also see the frustration.

"I'm sorry about that business deal with Delbert," Reese said. "I should have already left town."

Because this might require more than just words, Logan got to his feet and went to her. Yes, she did smell like bacon, and while it wasn't exactly a turn-on, it sure wasn't a turnoff, either.

"I'm not ready for you to leave," he told her.

They weren't words of gold, and it sounded selfish. Because he was. Despite the mess that had just gone down, he really wasn't ready for her to leave town. Of course, that wasn't fair to her because that meant he wanted to talk her into staying around…until he was ready for her to leave.

Hell. It wasn't just un-golden words; it made him feel like the names Jimena was no doubt thinking of to call Delbert.

Still, that didn't stop him from kissing Reese. Or rather trying to kiss her. He got a quick brush of his mouth on hers before she eased back.

Oh, *that*.

"You didn't see what you thought you saw between Helene and me," he explained. "I'm definitely not getting back together with her."

"It'd be less trouble for you if you did."

"You're wrong. That would be the worst kind of trouble." Because if he were with Helene, he'd be with a woman he no longer wanted. A woman who didn't fire up every inch of his body. A woman he couldn't trust.

Ironic, though, that he could trust Reese. And the firing-up part was a given anytime he was within six miles of her.

Like now.

Logan kissed her again, and this time he made it more than just a brush of the lips. He drew her to him, hoping for something long, deep and satisfying, but she pulled back again.

Reese fumbled in her purse that she had hooked over her shoulder and came up with an envelope that she handed him. Logan instantly recognized it because it was the report from the private investigator that he'd given her. It was still sealed.

"Read it," Reese said, putting it in his hand. She told him the rest of what she had to say from over her shoulder as she was walking out. "And then you'll know why we can't be together."

CHAPTER NINETEEN

REESE WALKED. SHE DIDN'T know where she was going. She just put one foot ahead of the other and kept moving. Because if she stopped, she would fall apart for sure. That still might happen, but it was harder to break down sobbing if she kept moving.

God, what had she done?

She didn't regret giving Logan that report. It was something she should have insisted that he read when he'd first gotten it. That way, they would have never had sex for a second time. They wouldn't have made out in the dressing room at the store. They wouldn't have kissed.

That didn't help her mood.

Neither did thinking about what she had to do next. She had to leave town, of course, and she would do that right after the engagement party. It would be the first time she'd left a place not because of the wanderlust stirrings inside her but because she'd made a mess of Logan's life.

She cursed her mother. Cursed this bad hand of a life she'd gotten. But it wasn't just the life she'd been born into, though. It was some of the bad choices she had made on her own. That wasn't on her mother or Chucky. Reese could put that right on her own weary shoulders. She had been the one to get involved with Spenser O'Malley. She was the one with the police record.

"Reese?" someone called out. Summer Starkley. A college student who was also a part-time waitress at the Fork and Spoon. Thankfully, she was on the other side of Main Street so she probably couldn't get a good look at Reese's face. "I heard about the bakery idea. Love it. I'd be one of your first customers."

Reese just smiled, hoped it looked genuine and didn't show too much of the frustration over hearing about that damn bakery. Talk of it was probably better than the pregnancy rumors, but still, she might scream at the next person who brought it up or suggested some stupid name for a business she wasn't going to own.

"You're here," she heard someone else say. Cassie this time, and that's when Reese realized she was walking right past the building in question. "I was hoping I'd run into you today."

Cassie was in the doorway of the building, and she caught onto Reese's arm and tugged her inside. "Can't you just see a sign with Sweet Tooth on it?" And, God forbid, she was pointing to the kitchen.

Reese didn't scream, though, it took some effort to hold it back. "Cassie, I can't open a bakery here." Best just to set her straight once and for all. "In fact, I'll be leaving in seven days."

No way could Cassie miss the timing. It was the day after the engagement party. "Did something happen between Logan and you?"

Not yet. "I'm just ready to move on," she lied.

Cassie didn't exactly call her on that lie, but she made a sound that reminded Reese that the woman was a therapist. A sort of "oh?" sound that was probably a prompt for Reese to continue.

She didn't.

"Well, at least you're staying to do the engagement party, right?" Cassie asked.

"Of course."

Cassie blew out a breath of relief. "Good, because it's really going to be more of an engagement party–adoption celebration combined. The paperwork went through, and the girls are officially ours."

Cassie dragged Reese into her arms for a hug while she made excited squeals of joy. Reese was happy for her. She truly was, but Cassie seemed to be taking on a lot right now what with getting engaged, the baby and a new business.

Reese glanced around at that new business venture in progress. Even though Cassie had just bought the place, the reception area had already been cleared of the debris, and Reese spotted cleaning crews in the other rooms, including the kitchen.

"The place already looks much better," Reese said.

"Thanks." Cassie led her to the first room. "I thought this could be Claire's studio. Lots of light and space. Of course, she'll only be here a couple of hours a week what with her son and the new baby on the way. Plus, she'll still do wedding photos with her business partner, Livvy. But Claire wanted a local place to do portraits and such."

It was a good space, and a good idea, too.

"I'm having that wall torn down," Cassie said, showing her the next two rooms. "That'll give me an office and a private waiting area. A private entrance and exit, too, in case the clients don't want people to know they're in therapy. Not that something like that would stay private in this town, but still…"

It was another good idea.

The next two rooms were his-and-her public bathrooms, and they'd also been cleaned. And that left the kitchen. Reese didn't want to glance in there, but she found herself doing it, anyway. It was akin to an alcoholic eyeing bottles of booze. Too much temptation to tell the crew not to use those steel scouring pads on a wooden butcher's block. It would leave scratches. But she held her tongue. If she said anything, it would appear she had an interest in it.

"Can you keep a secret?" Cassie asked. She lowered her voice, though there was no way the cleaner could have heard her. Not with the way they were scraping away at those tables.

"As long as the secret doesn't involve me opening a bakery," Reese countered.

"Oh, it doesn't. I figured if you didn't want to open it, then I'd offer it to Jimena since she went to culinary school, too."

Reese hadn't meant to look horrified by that idea. Again because it would make her appear interested, but she felt she should warn Cassie. "I love Jimena. She's my best friend. But she's a horrible cook."

Apparently, that hadn't made the gossip mill yet, but it would if Jimena ever flipped a single burger at the café. However, there were no worries with this particular kitchen and its restaurant-quality equipment. Jimena would never figure out how to turn any of it on. Her forte was making coffee and opening a bag of Cheetos without getting a paper cut.

"Well, maybe I can entice someone else," Cassie

went on. "And now to the secret. Lucky and I are getting married right after the engagement party."

"Married?" Again, that wasn't in the gossip chain so it was an honest to goodness secret.

"I know. It's crazy, but we just wanted to say 'I do' and get on with our lives. Anyway, we're having the justice of the peace come to the house after all the guests have left. It'll be just family and close friends. And Lucky and I wanted you to be there as one of the witnesses."

Reese felt as if someone had punched her, and worse, it was hard to think of how to tell Cassie no what with all that scouring going on.

"One second," she told Cassie, and went to the door of the kitchen. "Uh, you don't want to use those steel wool pads on wood. It'll make it easy for bacteria to get into the scratches." Or in this case, into the gouges they were creating. "Just use a soft cloth."

Of course, Cassie was smiling when Reese turned back around. The woman was sneaky. But it wasn't going to work.

"I just don't want you to have to replace that particular prep table," Reese explained. "As big as it is, a replacement will run you close to a grand."

Cassie didn't smile at that. "Thanks. I had no idea. I guess I have a lot to learn about going into business."

Yes, like maybe it wasn't a good idea to have a photography studio, a therapy office and a bakery all in the same building. The smell of the baked goods would be everywhere.

But come to think of it—maybe that wasn't a bad thing.

Fatty, sugary things tended to cheer people up and

make them happy. Happy people smiled, and that would make it easier to take their pictures. It would also help with those in therapy.

"This was always a dream of mine," Cassie went on. "Not to buy a really crappy building that needs a lot of work, but to be part of this town."

Reese had to shake her head. "You grew up here."

"I didn't feel part of it, though. My father owns the Slippery Pole Strip Club. Hard to fit in with DNA like that."

"But you were a celebrity, a *somebody*," Reese reminded her. "I saw you on TV."

"There's that old saying—when the gods want to punish you, they give you what you wish for. I wished to be somebody, to be important and away from this messy life, and I got exactly that. Except the other life was just as messy, and I was miserable. I'm not miserable now. I'm exactly where I should be. Very, very happy."

Cassie moved closer, looped her arm around Reese. However, before Reese could say anything, not that she had a clue what to say, Cassie lifted her hand in a wait-a-sec gesture. "Bacon. You smell like bacon. I need a minute. I'll be right back." And she ran off to the bathroom to deal with what appeared to be another round of morning sickness.

"Sorry," Reese called out to her.

Apparently, morning sickness didn't mind intruding on something *very, very happy*.

Reese didn't doubt that Cassie was telling the truth, though. This probably was her dream, and she was probably happy with a couple of *very*'s thrown in. But telling Reese all of that was probably another sneaky therapist ploy to make Reese see that she, too, could have a life here.

But she couldn't.

Because once Logan read that police record, it wouldn't matter. He would be more than ready for her to leave.

LOGAN PUT THE envelope on the center of his desk and stared at it. Something he'd been doing since Reese had left it with him and then disappeared. Obviously, she hadn't wanted to wait around and see his reaction.

Because his reaction would be bad.

He had no doubts about that. After all, it was a police report, and even though what was inside had happened over a decade ago when Reese had been just seventeen, she must have thought it would still send him running for the hills.

Or in this case, send *her* running for the hills.

She probably wouldn't leave town immediately. Not with the engagement party coming up. But she was likely off somewhere, planning her escape so that she wouldn't have to deal with whatever fallout that police report would cause.

He decided to buzz Jimena first and have her bring him a fresh cup of coffee, but the moment he reached for the intercom, there was a knock at the door, and when it opened, Jimena was there, coffee in hand.

She put both the coffee and some papers on his desk. She also eyed the envelope and then cursed. "Is that what I think it is?"

"If you think it's Reese's juvie record, then yes, it is what you think it is. Reese gave it to me to read."

She blinked. "I thought you were firing me."

"Not at this moment." They stared at the envelope together. "Do you know what's in it?"

Jimena nodded. "Reese and I met right after it happened. We were in the hospital together."

"Hospital? What does that have to do with her being arrested?"

The woman looked around as if deciding what to say or do. "How much do you want to know?" Jimena finally asked.

"Everything," he insisted, though he wasn't sure that was true.

One second he hated the idea that something could come between Reese and him, and the next second he thought he might as well get it over and done. After all, no matter what happened between them, she would still leave.

"The police report won't have the backstory," Jimena said. She went to the door and closed it. "So, here's the skinny. When I met Reese, I'd just fallen off a two-story balcony because I was drunk. I had three broken bones, sixteen stitches, a dislocated shoulder, and I was still in better shape than Reese was."

Hell. Logan couldn't breathe. It felt as if someone had sucked all the air out of the room.

"Spenser O'Malley?" he managed to say.

"Oh, yeah. There are tools in the world, but he was a sick fuck of a tool. He beat her, and I don't think it was the first time. Then, after he beat her, he dumped her at the ER, went to the police station and had charges filed against her for theft and assault even though the cops never found the money she supposedly stole from him."

Logan could possibly see the theft charges since

Reese had admitted to doing some cons. "Assault? But he's the one who beat her up."

Jimena rubbed her middle fingers and thumbs together. "Spenser was rich. Well connected in that hick town, so the cops believed him, and they arrested Reese while she was still in the hospital bed."

Unfortunately, Logan had a much too vivid imagination and could see her there. Could feel it, too. And worse, it explained why Reese had been so hesitant to get involved with someone else who was well connected. Like him. Except he would never do that to a woman.

Something about this didn't make sense, though.

"Reese could have told me what happened," he said, talking more to himself than to Jimena, trying to work it out in his head. "She was a victim here..."

He looked up, his gaze connecting with Jimena's. "Reese went after Spenser when she got out of the hospital?" he asked.

"We both did. He stole Reese's grandfather's watch, and Reese wanted to get it back."

Logan had no doubts about that. After all, Reese had broken into his own loft to retrieve it. But he never would have assaulted her as Spenser had done.

"We were going to threaten to beat him up if he didn't give her the watch. By then, Reese was my friend, and I wasn't going to let that dickweed get away with what he'd done."

Logan agreed. If he'd been around, he would have done the same thing. In fact, he still wanted to do the same thing. And worse. Logan wanted to hurt the guy the way he'd hurt Reese.

Jimena tipped her head to the envelope again. "The rest of the details are in there."

"Accurate details?" he asked.

"We didn't lie to the cops. Guess whose idea that was?"

He didn't have to guess. It was Reese's. "Is Spenser completely out of the picture now?" And if he wasn't, Logan wanted to know where the guy was.

"He's out. Way out. Only because he's dead."

Good. Logan wasn't in the habit of wishing ill will on people, but he did in this case. In this case, dead wasn't even enough.

"Just know this," Jimena went on. "It took Reese a long time to be with another man. A *long* time. And you know what she called her night with you in San Antonio? Nice and good," she answered before he could decide if he wanted to know. "*Nice and good* might not sound like much to you, but it's the best thing she's ever said about any guy."

That didn't make everything he was feeling any easier.

"If you hurt her, as a minimum I'll brew cat shit in your coffee," Jimena added. And she walked out, leaving Logan to curse again.

He quit arguing with himself and tore open the envelope. It wasn't the actual police report but rather a summary from the private investigator. There it was—the details Jimena had just given—and more.

It was the *more* that got Logan's attention.

Hell.

Spenser O'Malley was dead, all right. He'd died the night that Reese and Jimena had gone to threaten him to give Reese back the watch. And Spenser had given it back in his true asshole kind of way. He'd tossed it on the ground, breaking the crystal watch face. Before Reese or Jimena could even lay a hand on him—or in Jimena's case, a bat—Spenser had run away.

Right into the street.

Where he'd been killed by the Houston-bound, 8:00 p.m. bus.

REESE HAD TO get out of the building. She needed to get moving again. If she didn't, she was going to think about what Logan was reading in that report. And right about now, he had probably already read it, and he was cursing himself for ever getting involved with her.

Her breath caught in her throat. Her heartbeat started to race. And the memories came. Memories that she didn't want to discuss with Cassie.

"Cassie, I have to go," Reese called out to the woman while she was still throwing up in the ladies' room. "Something important's come up."

Reese hurried out before Cassie could stop her.

Since she felt all clammy and sick, she headed in the direction of her apartment. Of course, it was a people minefield along the way, and it seemed as if everyone in town was suddenly out for a stroll. Reese had to smile again. Had to pretend nothing was wrong all the while she was falling apart inside.

How could she have let this happen?

And she wasn't just thinking about Spenser now but Logan. How could she have let herself fall this way? She wasn't a faller. Spenser had taught her that lesson, but here she was with her heart aching and the sick feeling that she had lost something that she could never get back.

By the time she made it to the Bluebonnet Inn, her face was hurting from the smiles and the too-tight muscles. Reese hurried up the stairs, hoping she wouldn't encounter anyone else along the way. And she didn't. Not until she reached her apartment.

Logan was sitting there on the floor with his back resting against her front door. It was such a relaxed pose, for a split second she thought it was Lucky. But it was Logan, all right.

"I called around," he said. "Various people saw you walking so I decided to head here and wait for you."

He stood slowly, met her eye to eye. He knew. She could tell. He'd read the secret that had put her stomach in knots.

Since Reese didn't want to air her dirty laundry in the hall, she unlocked the door, and Logan followed her inside. He didn't say anything until he shut the door behind him.

"Jimena said if I hurt you that she'd put cat shit in my coffee," he said. "Anything you can do to make sure that doesn't happen?"

That certainly wasn't the conversation starter she'd expected, but Reese nodded, anyway. "It's just an empty threat."

Logan lifted his shoulder as if he might not believe that. "We have a lot of cat shit she could use, and she's convinced I'm going to hurt you."

He came closer, and each step seemed to cause her heart to skip beats. However, there was no anger in his eyes, in his tone, not in any part of his body. It stayed that way when Logan slipped his arm around her and kissed her.

Oh, my.

It was a nice kiss, one that untightened those stomach knots and eased away some of the tension in her shoulders. It would have been so easy just to melt into that kiss, maybe melt into some sex, too, but Reese knew that kisses and sex were a temporary fix. And it would only postpone the conversation they had to have.

"Didn't you read the report?" she asked.

He nodded, tried to kiss her again, but she stopped him.

Oh, she got it. "These are pity kisses, aren't they?"

His forehead bunched up. "I don't pity-kiss, have pity sex or really anything else that has to do with pity."

That was probably true, but it didn't explain why he was trying to kiss her again when he should be telling her they were all wrong for each other. So, Reese was the one to say it.

"I could mess up everything for you and your family."

Logan gave a fake yawn. "Old news. We're rich. It's hard to mess up really big trust funds."

"You're making light of this?" she snapped.

"No." And he suddenly got very serious. "I'm just trying to make you understand I'm sorry for what happened to you."

"Aha! I knew it. Pity."

"No. Sympathy and understanding."

"Pity," she grumbled. Reese groaned. "Why don't you ask me why I was stupid enough to get involved with a man like Spenser?"

"You were seventeen. All of us are pretty much stupid at that age."

"I'm betting you weren't."

"Then you'd be betting wrong. At seventeen, I was

doing dumb things like switching places with Lucky so he'd take English tests for me. In exchange, I'd go on dates with very sexually aggressive girls who thought they were getting Lucky. Literally."

He was still trying to make her feel better, but it wasn't working. Nothing could. "The only reason I wasn't charged with manslaughter was because there were witnesses who said neither Jimena nor I forced Spenser into the street. But the bottom line is that I'm responsible for a man's death."

"How do you figure that?" he challenged.

"Spenser ran out of the alley because he was scared of me."

Logan shook his head. "I'm thinking that had more to do with Jimena's bat and a scary threat she probably made to go right along with it."

"No. It was me. Spenser could see in my face that I wasn't going to take any more of his punches. He knew I would fight back, and since he was basically a coward, he ran."

"And he ran into a bus, which I think is some kind of cosmic justice."

It sounded, well, forgivable the way Logan put it, and it wasn't. He pulled her to him again. Kissed her light and soft.

"What happened to you sucked," he said. "You didn't deserve it, but you were ready and willing to get out of a bad situation. And you did. You went to culinary school, got jobs. You made a life for yourself, and you did all of that without the benefit of a trust fund or a family who would walk through fire for you."

Reese dismissed all of that because of what'd happened to Spencer. But to say that to Logan meant she'd just have to keep reopening this wound she didn't want opened. It was a wound that hurt less when it wasn't discussed. And when no one else knew about it. Reese could keep it covered with thick imaginary bandages.

Since she thought they both could use some levity, Reese gave it a try. "You really had sex with Lucky's girlfriends?"

"It's how I lost my virginity. That wasn't a proud moment for me. I was ashamed. Very ashamed."

He was smiling so the levity worked. Or maybe he was just reliving that *ashamed* sexual experience.

"Are you being nice to me so I'll tell Jimena to cancel the cat-shit coffee plans?" she asked.

"In part. In part, too, because I want you in my bed later."

Oh, that got her toes curling. Probably her eyelashes, too, since Logan added a kiss to it. "How much later?"

"Tonight, maybe? I've got meetings stacked up for the next few hours. In fact, I'm running late for one now."

She stepped away from him. "Go. Don't be late." Reese didn't want to do any more damage to his business.

"He can wait. I just want to make sure you're okay."

"I'm fine." It wasn't a lie exactly. She was as fine as she could ever be considering she would always be broken. And that's why she had to tell Logan this now. "I still plan on leaving soon."

He took one short breath. "I figured as much. But I still want to make sure you're okay."

"I am, really."

Logan stared at her as if trying to figure out if that was true. "All right. I'll see you later, then." He moved to leave, but his phone buzzed. "Probably Jimena." But he shook his head when he looked at the screen. "It's the police chief."

Reese automatically moved closer to the phone because this could be about her mother.

"Please tell me you arrested Vickie," Logan greeted.

"No. Haven't found her yet, but we have a problem. By any chance have you spoken to Chucky in the past couple of hours?"

"No," Logan answered, and Reese shook her head, too.

"That's what I figured. Well, Chucky just called here, and he said he's no longer cooperating, that he's withdrawing his complaint. Sorry, Logan, but that means I can't arrest Reese's mother, after all."

CHAPTER TWENTY

LOGAN FOUND A spot out of the path of the other guests. He went to the corner of the sunroom so he could sip his drink and hoped it looked as if he were having fun. After all, this was his twin brother's engagement party, and fun and celebration should be at the top of his to-do list. For the next couple of hours, anyway. But it was hard to think of fun and celebration when Reese was so miserable.

She was trying to hide that misery, of course, and for most of the guests, she was succeeding. Reese was all smiles and friendly conversation as she chatted about the food all laid out on the table. Some of the stuff Logan recognized—various finger foods—but Reese had also included some fancier things, too, like pâté-wrapped brie cheese. All served with champagne, of course, and nonalcoholic sparkling cider for Mia and Mackenzie.

For Claire and Cassie, too.

Everything was picture-perfect. Which in his mind was different from ordinary perfect. It just meant everything looked the way it should. People smiling, having fun. Even Helene was working the room and pretending to be happy that she was there. Logan was pretending as well, but he was certain he failed big-time when he saw Lucky making his way toward him.

Lucky handed him a fresh glass of champagne. "As my late business partner used to say, you look lower than a fat penguin's balls. I'm guessing all that lowness has something to do with one of them." Lucky tipped his head to Reese and then Helene.

"Reese," Logan readily admitted.

For just a second, Logan had considered lying, but it was hard to get away with lying to an identical twin. Probably something to do with sharing the same quarters and food source for the first nine months of their lives.

Lucky made a sound of agreement. "Is Reese still planning on leaving?"

"She says she is." And since leaving was exactly what she'd done all her adult life, Logan had no doubt she would do it now.

"And you can't change her mind? You must be losing your touch."

The little dig was mandatory between brothers. Logan suspected it was to mask the emotional core of this conversation. If it got too much more emotional, one of them would have to curse or add some crude reference regarding dicks since a ball reference had already been used.

"I tried to convince her that it didn't matter about her juvie record or what had happened in her past, but I don't think I got through." Hell, Logan knew he hadn't. "Of course, it didn't help that Chucky reneged on his deal and that now Vickie is free to do what she wants."

"Yeah, that sucks donkey dicks."

The fact that Lucky had gone to the D-word so soon meant he was feeling a lot of this dark-hearted crap that Logan was feeling. And it was something he didn't want to feel.

"Has the police chief arrested Chucky yet for trying to extort money from Helene?" Lucky asked.

"He would arrest him if he could find him. Vickie and Chucky are nowhere to be found."

That wouldn't last. Those two smelled money the way sharks smelled blood, and they would be drawn right back to the McCord bank accounts.

Logan watched as Helene reached the table where Reese was standing. He couldn't hear what they said to each other, but it was all smiles. And brief. The brief-ness brought on an even more genuine smile from Reese.

"I don't want to hurt her," Logan went on, and that didn't have anything to do with Jimena's cat-shit threat.

"Reese?" Lucky asked.

Logan frowned. "Of course."

"Just checking. Come on. Take a walk with me. I want to show you the new rodeo bull I bought."

It didn't seem like a good time for that, what with the party in full swing, but Lucky led him outside, anyway.

"A lot of changes going on," Lucky said once they were in the backyard. "I've already talked to Riley and Anna about this, but I wanted to get your opinion about Cassie, me and the girls staying on here at the house permanently."

Logan was sure he looked surprised. "I thought that was already a done deal. Why, were you thinking of moving elsewhere?"

"No, we all love it here, but I wanted to make sure it was okay with you. It's your home, after all."

True. Home, in name only. Logan rarely stayed there

anymore. He'd moved to his town loft because it was easier for work purposes, but he'd also done that because after Lucky, Riley and Anna moved away, it just hadn't felt much like home. It was starting to feel more like it now, but his loft wasn't that far from the ranch. Plus, the house was huge so he would always have his suite there. Well, unless Cassie and Lucky had a houseful of kids, that is.

"Riley's okay with it, too," Lucky went on. They continued walking toward the barn and that attached corral. "Claire and he are planning an addition to their house, though, so they can have a playroom for Ethan and a nursery."

So many changes, and while Logan didn't feel left out exactly, he was the oldest. Okay, he did feel a little left out, but that didn't mean he wasn't happy for his siblings.

"Anna gave it her blessing, as well," Lucky said. "If she decides to move back after finishing law school and getting married, she said she wanted to build a house by the springs, anyway."

Logan knew the exact spot. In fact, his kid sister had talked about having a house there since she was in first grade.

"I think it's all great," Logan assured him. "The ranch and the house will be a great place to raise the girls and a baby."

Lucky stopped for a second, laughed. "*A baby.* Now, that's something I'll bet you never thought you'd say when it came to me."

Logan would have liked to say he'd expected it, but it hadn't been anywhere on his radar. Until Cassie came back in his life, Lucky's longest track record with a woman was less than the same amount of time Reese stayed in one place.

Not very long at all.

"Fatherhood will suit you," Logan assured him. "Riley, too. I can't wait to have more nieces or nephews." He already thought of Claire's son, Ethan, as family. Also thought the same way about Mia and Mackenzie.

Logan spotted the bull when they reached the corral. It was a beauty and would no doubt earn them a pretty penny once it was trained. That was yet something else Lucky had added to the ranch—the rodeo bull training program. It was as successful as the cutting horse operation that Riley had started.

All the pieces were falling into place.

"Dad would have loved this," Logan said.

It was something he hadn't intended to say, though. It'd just slipped out, and while it was true, it was also a downer because it was a reminder that their folks weren't here to share any of it.

"They're here," Lucky whispered, seeming to know exactly what Logan had been thinking. He blinked hard as if blinking back tears and then shook it off. "No fat penguin balls today. I'm getting married." He pointed to the trees in the backyard. "Right there." He checked his watch. "In an hour or so."

All in all, it was the perfect way to elope.

"Why don't we go back in?" Lucky suggested. "I can tell some off-color jokes to get some of the crowd heading out. Of course, it might cause others to stay."

"You should make some dick jokes," Logan advised.

"Absolutely. Balls and dicks. My preferred way of going off-color."

They'd reached the porch when the sunroom door opened, and Helene stepped out. She didn't seem surprised to see them. Just the opposite. Of course, with all the windows in the sunroom, she had perhaps been watching them.

"Any chance we can talk?" she asked Logan.

This wasn't the time or the place, but then that applied to all times and places when it came to Helene. It was probably best to talk to her in a public place, though, than have her come to his office. Which she would. It was clear she had something to get off her chest. Probably something to do with the Vickie-Chucky mess.

Lucky waited until Logan gave him the nod before he gave Helene a warning glance and then went inside. Logan appreciated the warning; it was good for his twin to have his back, but it wasn't necessary. Logan no longer felt the punch of emotion, either good or bad, when he looked at Helene.

"Thank you for seeing me," Helene said. "I wanted to let you know that I'll be filing charges against Chucky, after all, since he didn't go through with our bargain. Of course, he'll probably just disappear."

Probably. And that was the best-case scenario in this—that the man would disappear and take Vickie with him.

"I don't like all the gossip it'll create," Helene went on. "I was just starting to restore my reputation, and here it'll come out that I told Chucky where Reese was."

"Are you trying to back out of filing charges against Chucky?"

Her hesitation let him know that she was. "I'll do

it. For you. I know you're still upset with me, and this might help mend the rift between us."

"No, I'm not upset, not anymore. I wish you only the best."

And he meant it. Even more, Helene knew he meant it. But as for that rift, well, Logan figured her idea of rift-mending meant getting back together. That wasn't going to happen.

Unlike him, there was plenty of emotion on her face. He saw the hurt and knew there was nothing that could be done about it. Nothing that he could do, anyway.

"Can we talk about what happened that night?" she asked.

He lifted an eyebrow. "Are we going to discuss clown noses?"

"No. God, no." She shuddered. "All of that was just a fantasy. I couldn't bring myself to ask you to dress up like a clown."

"Then that should have been your cue to break up with me. Because if your boyfriend can't fulfill your fantasies, then he shouldn't be your boyfriend."

Helene nodded, paused, nibbled on her bottom lip. "And now you have someone else in your life to fulfill your fantasies."

"No clown stuff, though," he said to add a light touch. It didn't lighten anything, though, because it basically confirmed to Helene that Reese and he were indeed into some fantasy-fulfilling. Of course, right now the sex was enough of a fantasy.

"You don't feel it's too soon?" she asked.

"For what?" he asked right back.

Helene lifted her shoulder as if the answer were obvious. "To be involved with someone. I mean, I can't even think of being with anyone else yet. After all, we were together for eight years."

She seemed to be implying that this was some kind of rebound relationship between Reese and him. Was that what it was? Helene was right about it being soon, only four months now since the clown incident, but Logan wasn't at all certain that it was *too soon.*

But that did get him thinking.

If it was too soon, then Reese would be the one to get hurt. Maybe that's why she still seemed so hell-bent on leaving. And the problem with that? Logan couldn't even guarantee her that she wouldn't get a broken heart from this.

"No word about Chucky or Vickie?" Helene asked.

It took Logan a second to switch gears and remember that he was still having a conversation with Helene. "Nothing. You?"

"Nothing," she repeated, then paused. "Have you seen Greg?"

Logan shook his head and caught a glimpse of Reese walking past one of the windows. She didn't exactly look out at them, but he figured she'd seen them talking.

"I haven't seen Greg, either," Helene went on, "but I heard you hired Reese's friend to replace him. I suppose she has a lot of office experience?"

"None whatsoever."

Added to that, Jimena had a smart mouth, vile threats and dressed like a call girl. Still, she could handle Crazy Cat, and other than the threats, she hadn't done too much to get on his bad side.

"I see," Helene said, which was probably code for *I can't believe this shit. You hire someone with no expe-*

rience. You sleep with a fry cook, one with a police re-
cord. And you haven't been flossing regularly.

Logan decided to skip the code and go with a direct
question. "Did you give Elrond one of your porcelain
boob bookends?"

Clearly, she hadn't been expecting that question.
"Wh-what?"

"Porcelain boob bookend," he repeated even though
Logan doubted repetition was necessary in this case.
"Because he had a boob identical to the one you gave
me, and he also had a clown suit. I just figured that
wasn't a coincidence."

Her mouth tightened a moment. "I didn't sleep with
him. Not after Greg decided he'd fulfill the fantasy
for me."

There it was again. Fantasies. And clown suits. No
doubt lies, too. Logan was almost positive she wasn't
telling the truth about being with Elrond.

"I didn't sleep with him," Helene repeated, and this
time she had a bite to her tone. "I'm not a whore."

Logan shrugged. "Even if you'd had sex with both
of them, it wouldn't have made you a whore. Just a liar
and a cheater." There was no bitterness in his voice, but
she probably would have preferred it if there had been.
Because it would have meant he was still emotionally
invested in her.

"There you are," Jimena said, opening the back door.
"Cassie and I were talking about litter boxes and cat,
um, droppings, and then I looked up and saw you out
here, with Helene."

Logan scowled at her. "No threat necessary. Helene and
I were just having a friendly chat, but we're done now."

"Good, because the party's wrapping up, and I

thought you'd want to say goodbye to the guests especially since three of them are business associates. One
of which you have a meeting with in two days."

That was code, too, for *get your ass inside before
you hurt Reese's feelings.*

Helene quickly picked up on the code because she
got moving. Jimena would have followed her, but Logan
stopped her by stepping in front of her.

"One question," he said.

"Yes, I have been stockpiling cat shit," Jimena answered right off.

He made sure his scowl deepened. "That wasn't the
question. I want to know if Reese packed to leave."

Jimena suddenly didn't look so smart-assed. "She's
always packed and ready to leave. Now, if you're wanting to know if she *will* go, that I can't say. You should
ask her. Then you should ask her to stay."

He already had. Apparently, he was a lot better with
business deals than he was with Reese.

"By the way, should I bring Crazy Cat back here
since she belongs to Cassie and Lucky?" Jimena asked.

They already had Crazy Dog, five cats, two kids and
another on the way. It seemed cruel to add another fur-
critter, especially one with the worst temperament in
the kitty kingdom. Still…

"Keep that cat at the office as long as you're working for me. But when you leave, part of your clearing-
out duties will be to bring the cat here, understand?"

Jimena nodded, turned, but then as quickly turned
back around. "Is it okay if I have sex with your friend
Jason?"

Logan was about to groan, then say okay, but he rethought that. "Only if Jason agrees." Which he would. Jason liked the call-girl-looking, smart-mouth type.

Jimena gave a fake laugh, shot him the bird and went inside. Just as Reese was coming out.

"Is everything okay?" Reese asked. She had no doubt heard and seen the interaction between Jimena and him, but Logan figured her question had more to do with his earlier interaction with Helene.

"Helene and I were just talking," he explained. "I suppose you could say Jimena and I were just talking, too, but it never quite feels like conversation with her."

"I know what you mean." She stayed back. Again, probably because she'd seen him with Helene and wasn't sure what was going on. Reese looked as if she were debating either fight or flight.

"Helene thinks it's too soon for me to get involved with you," he relayed. "I believe she's wrong."

"And if she's not?"

Because she still wasn't coming closer to him, Logan went to her. He slipped his arm around her waist, brushed a kiss on her forehead. "We don't have to push things between us. There's no timetable. We could continue to see each other, and if it's too soon, then it shouldn't take us long to figure that out."

He figured this was the part where she would just remind him that she wasn't a stayer but rather a leaver. But Reese made a sound that could possibly be of agreement. Good. He was making some progress even if, in the back of his mind, he was wondering if progress was just a mistake.

"I should go back in," she said. "Lucky and Cassie want to say their vows as soon as the guests clear out.

I can help with that. Better yet, Jimena can help with that."

She kissed his cheek. So chaste. The kind of kiss that longtime couples gave each other, but it still packed a wallop. Maybe Reese wasn't capable of giving him chaste kisses.

Logan followed her in, but he didn't get far when he spotted the guest who was coming into the sunroom. Delbert Clark. Since Delbert was no longer doing business with McCord Cattle Brokers, Logan didn't have a clue why he was there. He certainly hadn't been invited.

"I need to talk to you," Delbert said the moment he laid eyes on Logan. But Logan realized Delbert wasn't just looking at him. He was looking at Reese.

Hell. What now? If Delbert was going to demand that he break up with Reese, then it was going to be a very short conversation. Logan didn't usually dig in his heels when it came to repairing a business relationship, but in this case he'd make an exception.

"This isn't a good time," Logan said, stating the obvious.

Delbert glanced around as if seeing the party food and guests for the first time. Clearly, he had something else on his mind. "Sorry. I didn't know, but this can't wait. Can we go somewhere and talk in private?"

Logan wanted to say no, but it was Reese who motioned for him to follow her into the family room. It wasn't exactly private since someone could walk in at any moment, but maybe that meant Delbert would say his piece and leave. But he didn't jump right into anything. He just stood there, sweat popping out on his forehead and the veins bulging on his neck.

"You need to call off your mother," Delbert told Reese.

Reese shook her head when he didn't add more. "I haven't seen my mother in days," she said at the same moment Logan asked, "What are you talking about?"

"I'm talking about your mother screwing me over, that's what, and I want it to stop."

"You think I can control what my mother does?" Reese asked. "What *did* she do?"

Still nothing from Delbert to explain. He didn't start talking until after several huffed breaths and some pacing. "You know she called me and said I should quit doing business with Logan because you're bad news, because you could end up hurting me and my own business."

Reese nodded. "And you did break ties with Logan."

Now Logan huffed and folded his arms over his chest. "I'm guessing Vickie did something else. Something more than just bad-mouthing me and playing on your narrow little mind."

A flash of anger went through Delbert's eyes, but it cooled as quickly as it had come, and he cursed. "She's blackmailing me."

Logan glanced at Reese to see if she had any idea what was going on, but she just shook her head again.

"I had sex with Vickie," Delbert finally said. "I didn't know who she was, but she came on to me when I was in a bar. I made the mistake of leaving that bar with her." He groaned, scrubbed his hand over his face and then looked at Logan. "She said I was to do what she told me to do, or else she'd tell my wife."

"Let me guess—Vickie filmed your one-nighter?" Reese asked.

"Filmed with audio," Delbert explained. "And the images aren't blurry, either. Vickie said she'd give me the video if I severed business ties with Logan and told him I was doing that because of you."

"And Vickie wanted even more after that," Logan finished for him.

"Yeah. She wanted me to contact even more of your business associates and get them to blackball McCord Cattle Brokers. She must have a hard-on for you, Logan, to want to screw you over like that."

"She wants money," Logan corrected. "Vickie figures if she hurts my business enough that I'll pay her off. I won't." He was also guessing that this was Vickie's way of punishing Reese, of showing Reese who was in charge.

And it was working.

The color had drained from Reese's face, and she was probably about to launch into some apologies. "This isn't your fault," Logan told her, not that she would believe him, but he had to try. "But this is *your* fault," Logan said to Delbert.

"I know." Another groan. "I just need you to help me. Maybe Reese can help me get that video."

"Vickie probably made multiple copies and has stashed them in hard-to-find places," Reese said. "This is one of her favorite cons, by the way, and it won't end with these first demands. She'll want money from you and lots of it. And she'll keep wanting money."

"So, how do I stop her?" Delbert asked.

Logan and Reese exchanged glances, and since he figured Delbert was going to need it, he gave him a pat on the arm. And he told Delbert exactly what he was going to have to do to make this mess, and Vickie, go away.

CHAPTER TWENTY-ONE

ONCE AGAIN HER mother had ruined things. Not just for Delbert, either. And Vickie would keep on ruining things because that's what she did. Heck, she'd even ruined Cassie and Lucky's wedding for Reese since Reese hadn't been able to think of much else other than their conversation with Delbert.

Thankfully, Cassie and Lucky hadn't seemed to notice. Hard to notice anyone being distracted, though, when they were clearly so much in love with each other.

The informal wedding itself had gone off without a hitch. The rain had held off. There'd been a cool breeze, and the only talk had been of the happy couple and the life they were building together. Perfect, in fact.

There it was again. *Perfect.* The word that seemed like a pipe dream to Reese. Perfection just wouldn't happen with her mother around and her own past always haunting her.

"We won," Logan said, pulling her out of her thoughts.

For a second, Reese thought she'd missed something he'd said, and maybe she had, because that's when she realized Logan had pulled to a stop not in front of the Bluebonnet Inn but in the parking lot of the McCord building. The rain that had held off all day was now sliding down the windshield.

"We won," she agreed. "But this won't be the last of it."

"It will be if Delbert goes through on filing those charges against your mother."

Yes, and while Delbert had hesitantly agreed to do just that, he might change his mind when he realized this would cost him his marriage. Of course, it would end up costing him that, anyway, because even if he paid and paid and paid, Vickie liked to tear apart people's lives.

"Even if Vickie's locked up, she'll find a way to cause trouble," Reese continued. Mercy, she was pure gloom and doom, and here less than an hour after attending a wedding.

"Tell you what," Logan said. "Let's quit thinking about Vickie right now, and get out of this truck before it starts raining any harder. It'd be nice to get inside and stay put while this storm moves through."

"Does this mean you want me to spend the night here with you?"

"Is that a trick question?" he asked.

"No. We just hadn't discussed it, and I thought with everything going on—"

Logan put an end to what she was saying with a kiss. He managed to rid her of her breath and her doubts in one swoop.

Apparently, she was staying the night.

"Wait here for just a couple of seconds until I get the back door unlocked," he told her, and he hurried out of the truck. There was a small awning just above the door, but he still got wet. Logan didn't hurry to unlock the door, though. Instead, he must have gotten a call because he looked at his phone screen.

Reese got out, too, and ran toward Logan just as he opened the door and got them inside.

"It's Chucky," Logan mouthed, keeping his phone pressed to his ear so he could hear whatever the man was saying.

Of course. There was no way Chucky was just going to slink away from this.

Logan continued listening on the way up the stairs, turning on lights as they climbed, and by the time they made it to the loft, Reese didn't have to ask if it was bad news because she could tell from his face that it was. Logan confirmed that by not saying anything until they were inside.

"You're sure you want to do that?" Logan asked the man, but she couldn't hear Chucky's response.

Several seconds later, Logan hit the end-call button, put his phone back in his pocket. He also poured them drinks and had a long sip before he continued.

"Chucky says if Helene files charges against him that he'll copy old newspaper articles about Spenser O'Malley and plaster them all over town."

Her breath vanished again, but this time it wasn't from one of Logan's kisses. Chucky really knew which wounds to go after so he could hurt her the most. And what with her mother trying to ruin Logan, it pretty much killed what little festive mood she had left from the wedding.

"Spenser." Reese sank down onto the nearest chair. She really didn't want all of that brought out in the open again. Especially since it would be gossiped about.

"I think Helene was having second thoughts about those charges, anyway," Logan commented. "She's worried how it'll look when everyone learns she told Chucky you were here."

"Is that what she said to you when she was talking to you on the porch?" she asked.

"Among other things." He had more of that drink and sat down across from her. "Helene and I are not getting back together. Ever. You don't have to worry about that."

Good. Because she had enough to worry about, and apparently so did Logan.

"What else did Chucky say?" Reese pressed.

Logan took a long, deep breath. Probably not a good sign. "Chucky says he'll start rumors that I could have saved my parents but that I was drunk when I got to the scene of the accident."

The profanity flew out of her mouth before Reese even knew she was going to say it, and she slammed her glass on the coffee table. "That little shit. I want to go after him. I want to rip off his dick and beat him senseless with it."

She was halfway to the door before Logan reached her. He caught onto her arm and whirled her back around. Reese was certain that the anger was visible in every part of her body, but Logan managed to look a lot calmer.

"Dick-ripping?" he questioned. "A little extreme, more like something Jimena would do, but thank you for the offer. I did notice, though, that you didn't get pissed when Chucky threatened to slime you, only when he turned that potential slime on me."

"Because he's going after you because of me." She still didn't have control of her voice. It was too loud, too shrill.

"No, he's going after me because he's greedy and wants money. And he believes this is the fastest way to get it."

That was true, but it didn't help that situation. "So, what do we do?"

He kissed the tip of her nose and stepped away so he could get her drink. "We wait him out. Chucky wants money, and he loses the chance of getting that money if he spills all."

Reese knew that was true, but the idea of waiting sickened her. "This is such a mess. Not just what Chucky is trying to do to us, but what Vickie's trying to do to Delbert." She sighed. "At least Delbert and I did something to get ourselves into hot water. You didn't."

She saw Logan flinch just slightly, and the only reason she caught it was because Reese had her attention nailed to him. It was still a sore subject after all these years, but she hadn't heard any gossip about the accident.

"It's ironic that a vehicle killed both your parents and Spenser," she threw out there. Reese went with a hunch. "You think you should have been able to save them?"

He turned now, avoiding her gaze. "Do you think you should have been able to save Spenser?"

"Of course. In a perfect world, Spenser would have lived, redeemed himself and went off to live a happy life." Reese paused. "I'm sorry. I shouldn't have brought it up."

The words had hardly left her mouth when Logan turned, slid his hand around the back of her neck and dragged her to him.

"I'm tired of talking," he said, and he crushed his mouth to hers.

LOGAN HADN'T INTENDED for the kiss to be foreplay. He'd just wanted to end the discussion, and the most pleasurable and fastest way to do that was just to kiss Reese. Of course, anytime he kissed her was pleasurable, but this particular kiss did double duty.

He didn't want to think about his parents' car accident, Spenser O'Malley, Chucky or anybody else. He only wanted to be with Reese tonight, and if he kept kissing her, that just might happen.

Outside, the storm kicked up, the wind and rain slapping against the windows. Since the back wall of his loft was about 70 percent windows and glass, it seemed as if the storm was right inside. Inside him, too, but Logan put all of that raw emotion into the kiss.

Reese staggered back, and for a couple of really bad moments, Logan thought she was calling a halt to this so they could keep on talking. But she was only catching her breath. Once she'd gulped in some air, she came right back to him, and she kissed him with as much emotion and intensity as he'd kissed her.

Maybe they both had some things to work out tonight, and Logan was thinking the bed was a good place to do that. Of course, that was his hard-on talking again, but for once maybe that idiotic part of him was actually making sense. At least this couldn't complicate things because their lives were already beyond complicated.

Logan pushed that thought aside, too, and pulled her to him. Not that he had to do much pulling. Reese was already in the mode of having her body pressed against his. His hard-on thought that was an excellent notion, too, but there was something in his brain that kept telling him to slow down, to enjoy the moment, because with Reese he never knew how many more moments like this he was going to get.

So, Logan slowed the pace. Since it was already at

frantic, it wasn't easy. Still, he took his time, savoring her taste and the way she felt in his arms. Savoring her.

Man, she fired up every inch of his body, and he'd quit trying to figure out why. It probably didn't make sense to her, either. He wasn't the perfect man for her because she would always be worried about what people thought. About what people would find out to hurt them. But for this moment, it was perfect.

She was perfect.

Logan brushed some kisses on her neck, then lower to the tops of her breasts. It did exactly what he'd intended it to do. It got her hotter. Did the same to him as well, and without breaking those kisses, she started maneuvering them toward the bed.

He didn't resist, but he continued to keep things slow. Tiny steps. Big, long kisses. So that by the time they did tumble onto the mattress, Reese knew that he meant business. A different kind of business since it was usually a frantic grab-and-get when they were with each other.

"You don't have to make it nice for me," she whispered.

"I'm not. This is for me," he whispered back.

Reese stopped a moment, her gaze meeting his. The lights weren't on, but a well-timed lightning bolt let him see her face. She was questioning this. And Logan knew why. For lack of a better word this was intimate, and they weren't just swept up in the moment. They could decide whether to stop or not, but the decision would be made not with hard-ons and arousals but with their heads.

Scary shit.

Logan braced himself for Reese to cut and run, and

she probably thought about doing that. But she didn't. Her mouth came back to his, and she kissed him. Long, slow, deep.

He eased up her loose cotton dress, slipping it off. Her bra, too, so he could lower those kisses to her breasts. She made a silky sound of pleasure, took what he was offering, and she slid her fingers into his hair. He stayed there a moment, pleasuring her. Pleasuring himself, too, before he took the same slow pace to remove her panties.

His hard-on made itself known then. The brainless wonder wanted to dive right in, but Logan fought the urge and did something else he'd been wanting to do. He kissed every inch of Reese. By the time he worked his way back up to her mouth, she was panting. And grabbing at his clothes.

Logan let her grab, and he tried not to wince when she fumbled, and fumbled, and kept on fumbling with the zipper of his jeans. Since he didn't want this to be a hand job, he finally helped her. Got his eyes uncrossed, too.

The condom was an issue since Reese tried to help with that, as well. Obviously, she'd reached her threshold for long and savoring and just wanted him inside her. Logan and his hard-on were all for that, but he still tried to hang on to the moment by entering her slowly.

That lasted a heartbeat.

Reese turned, flipping him on his back, and she got on top of him. The pace was anything but slow. It didn't take her long to find the right rhythm, and since she was clearly hell-bent on finishing this too fast, Logan caught onto her hips to help her.

She looked amazing on top of him. Not like something from a porn movie, more like one of those sensual scenes where everything seemed graceful and choreographed. Of course, that was probably influenced by the fact she was fucking his brains out.

Thanks to some more lightning, Logan was able to see her face when she climaxed. Amazing. Watching her was almost better than having a climax of his own.

Almost.

Logan would have liked to watch a little while longer, but his hard-on had had enough. He caught onto Reese, pulling her down to him, and he let his hard-on finish what it'd started.

LOGAN FIGURED IT was the sound of the storm outside that triggered the storm in his head. The dream came just as real as it always was.

He was on the mental hamster wheel again, going through images so familiar that he didn't need the dream to see them. Just like all those other times, he fought the skid on the road, fought everything inside him that tried to claw its way to the surface.

The fear.

The sickening dread of what he would see as he ran to the tangled wreck.

Tonight was no different. He pulled Claire to the side of the road. Protecting her. And then he was on the hamster wheel again, hurrying back to his parents. Realizing he'd made a mistake by not calling for help the second he'd spotted the wreck.

Just like every other dream, his mother turned and looked at him, the life already leaving her eyes. But she said something. This time, though, it was different. Logan didn't just hear the words in his head; he saw them form on her lips. Barely a whisper. But it was more than loud enough for him to hear.

I love all five of you.

"Logan?" someone said.

Since he was still in the dream, it took him a moment to realize it wasn't his mother calling out his name. It was Reese. She was shaking him, and she sounded very concerned.

Logan forced his eyes open, and just like that, the dream vanished. He hadn't wanted to hold on to those images, anyway, but he wanted to hold on to those words.

"I love all five of you?" Reese questioned.

Obviously, he'd talked in his sleep. "The dream," he managed to say.

"I suspected as much. I didn't think you were talking to me and four other women."

Good. Reese had kept it light. Not quite a joke, but it batted away some of the dark cobwebs.

"One of your parents said that?" she asked.

Logan sat up, nodded. "My mother. But I'm not sure she actually said it. Sometimes, in the dream she doesn't say anything. Sometimes, she says what I want to hear her say."

Reese stayed quiet a moment. "What do you want to hear her say?"

Logan stayed quiet a moment, too. *"It's all right. I forgive you for not saving us."*

He figured Reese was going to be surprised by that, but she didn't seem to be. She made a sound of understanding. "I do that with my Spenser dreams. I rewrite what happened so that it has an ending I can better handle. It doesn't help."

"Then what does help?" And he was serious. Because while Reese was still troubled by what'd happened to Spenser, she wasn't the one having nightmares or migraines.

"Accepting it," she said.

"You're able to do that?"

"Most days." She settled against him. "It's not a perfect solution, but I don't think we ever get perfect when it comes to our past." She groaned softly. "Sorry, that's probably too deep for a postsex chat."

Only if they were trying to make sure the postsex chat didn't mean anything. This conversation meant something. On the surface, they didn't have a lot in common, but beneath the surface, that was a whole different story.

"Jimena said you were always packed and ready to leave," he threw out there.

"I am. Though I can't imagine why she'd tell you that."

"Because I asked her. I figured now that the engagement party was over, you'd be looking to move." Logan adjusted his position so he could look her in the eyes. "Give it at least another week."

Reese certainly didn't jump to agree to that. "And then?"

"And then give it another week after that."

She smiled. Barely there and brief. But it was still a smile. "I'll think about it, but Jimena doesn't believe this will turn out well between us."

No, she didn't. Most people probably felt that way including members of his own family. Thankfully, they hadn't voiced those concerns to his face.

"Get some sleep," she said, brushing a kiss on his cheek.

"You, too." But Logan thought he should add one more thing. "Don't let Jimena put cat shit in my coffee."

Not just a smile this time but also a chuckle. Logan suddenly wasn't sleepy at all and wondered if he could cash in that laugh for another round of sex. But he must have tempted fate with that thought because his phone buzzed.

He checked the time. It was just past midnight. Way too late for someone to be calling him about business so that meant it was some kind of emergency. He got a slam of instant memories. Of another storm. Of the car accident. And Logan grabbed his phone so fast that he nearly dropped it. He didn't even check the screen before answering.

"McCord," the caller said. Definitely not family, but it was a voice that Logan recognized.

Chucky.

"What the hell do you want?" Logan greeted.

"Just thought you should know that I worked out a deal with your lady friend, and I'll be leaving town."

By lady friend, Chucky was no doubt referring to Helene. "She paid you off?" Logan countered, and he put the call on speaker so Reese could hear.

"Just in case you're recording this, let's just say we came to a mutually satisfying agreement." Chucky mispronounced *mutually*.

Yeah, Helene had paid him off.

"Then why call me with all of this?" Logan asked. But as soon as the question left his mouth, he got a really bad feeling about this.

"Because I didn't want to leave without telling you about Vickie." Chucky cleared his throat. "Your lady friend probably doesn't know it, but Vickie broke into her office. Vickie's sneaky like that. Anyway, Vickie found something that she might try to use against your lady friend. Something Vickie can use as blackmail."

Logan dragged in a long breath. "Let's just cut the lady-friend crap and tell me what Vickie found in Helene's office."

"Not Helene," Chucky corrected. "Your other lady friend, the one who works for you now. Jimena."

CHAPTER TWENTY-TWO

JIMENA WAS LATE for their meeting, and Reese figured that was exactly what her friend wanted to be. Because Jimena was avoiding this conversation.

Reese didn't need any special powers to determine that.

When Reese had called Jimena immediately after Chucky's bombshell news, Jimena hadn't been asleep—because she was with Jason—but after Reese had told her it was important that they talk, Jimena had said she'd meet Reese at the Bluebonnet Inn at eight the following morning. That way, they could chat before Jimena had to go to work. Well, Reese was here.

But Jimena wasn't.

It was only ten past eight, which meant Jimena was hardly late enough to start thinking about her friend being hurt and lying in a ditch or something, but Reese had to know what Vickie had found in Jimena's desk.

Of course, this all could turn out to be some kind of con on her mother's part. Maybe on Chucky's part, too. Because maybe there'd been nothing to find, but this could be a way of stirring up Reese. If so, it had worked.

It had worked for Logan, too. He was at the McCord building with a team that was installing a security system. One that would no doubt be top-notch and would prevent future break-ins. It was too bad they didn't have a time machine to go back and undo the break-in her mother had supposedly done.

Reese prayed this didn't end up hurting Jimena in some way.

Her phone rang, and Reese was ready to chew out Jimena for being late, but it wasn't Jimena. It was Helene. Good gravy. She hadn't had enough caffeine yet to deal with Helene. Reese answered, anyway, because she was still worrying about the "Jimena in a ditch" theory, and Helene might know something to dispel that.

"Sorry to bother you so early," Helene greeted, "but I knew you were up because I saw you leave Logan's about an hour ago."

Reese didn't ask how she'd seen that, but Helene did have an office just up the street from the McCord building so it was possible the sighting had been accidental and that Helene wasn't spying on her. From everything Reese had heard about Helene, the woman worked long hours and was often in early enough to have seen Reese leave.

"I was hoping we could meet for coffee and a chat. I called the café," Helene said, "but Bert said this was your day off."

"It is, and I'm kind of busy right now. Besides, I'm not sure we actually have anything to discuss. Unless it's about you not filing those charges against Chucky."

"You heard. Yes, it's true. I'm not filing charges, and he's agreed to leave town."

"You paid him?" Reese asked.

"I'd rather discuss that in person," Helene answered. "I'll tell Logan this, of course, but I also wanted you to know that Delbert called me last night. He said he wasn't going to have charges filed against your mother, either, that he was going to take care of the matter himself."

That meant Delbert was going to pay Vickie off. Reese didn't especially care if a rich, cheating man was willing to pay hush money, but it wouldn't be the last of her mother's demands.

"I know it's hard for you to understand," Helene went on, "but a reputation is a delicate thing, and sometimes it's worth any price. I understand why Delbert's doing what he's doing."

That might have prompted Reese to say something along the lines of wishing them both luck and that there was no need for a chat over coffee, but there was a knock at the door, and when Reese threw it open, Jimena was standing there.

"I have to go," Reese told Helene, and she ended the call before the woman could say another word.

Jimena did something similar to Reese. She started talking before Reese could get out her first question. "I had the hottest night with Logan's friend Jason. Can't wait to tell you all about it."

Reese was well aware that Jimena had left the engagement party with Jason. Was also well aware they'd started groping and kissing each other before they even made it to his truck. Under normal circumstances, Reese would want to hear a few PG-rated details but not now.

"Your date update can wait," Reese told her.

"And so can a few other things."

"No. I need to tell you about Chucky."

"Later. For now, get your grandfather's watch and come with me," Jimena insisted. "We can talk while we walk. And hurry. I have to be at work in an hour. I have an asshole for a boss who'll fire me if I'm late." Jimena chuckled as if this were some kind of joke. Well, the asshole for a boss part was a joke, but the rest of this wasn't.

Reese shook her head. "Where are we walking, and why do I need to bring the watch?" She froze. "Oh, God. Does Vickie know about the watch?"

"If she does, she didn't hear it from me. Just get the watch and come on. I have a surprise for you. And FYI, I'm not going to spill anything juicy until you get it so the longer you fart around, the longer it'll take for you to hear what you want to hear."

Reese doubted that was a bluff, and since she really was anxious to hear what had happened between Chucky, Jimena and Vickie, she hurried to the coffee bag where she'd hidden the watch after wrapping it in foil.

"Is someone going to try to steal the watch?" Reese asked.

Jimena shrugged, and with that as her only explanation—which, of course, was no explanation at all—she started out the door and down the stairs. Reese put the watch in her jeans pocket, grabbed her purse and hurried after her.

"All right, start talking," Reese insisted the moment they were outside. "Did you really pay off Chucky?"

"I did," Jimena readily admitted. "I figured it was time you had one less dickwad in your life. Can't do anything about the mother-dickwad, but you'll never have to see Chucky's boney ass again."

Reese was stunned. "You paid off Chucky? Where did you get the money?"

"From Elrond," Jimena said in a discussing-the-weather kind of tone. "I blackmailed him. Told him I'd give Logan pictures of Helene and him having clown sex."

"But Helene had clown sex with Greg," Reese pointed out.

"Well, she had it with Elrond, too. He let that slip when he was talking to me." Jimena stopped, paused. "Do you have any idea what they do with those big red clown noses?"

Reese huffed. "No, and I don't want to know." She had to lower her voice when she realized this wasn't a conversation she wanted others to hear, and they were passing people on the street as Jimena led her heaven knew where. "Where did Elrond get the money to pay you off?"

"From Helene. He blackmailed her, and he stole my threat. Sheez, the man can't even come up with his own blackmail idea."

Reese's head was hurting now, and she rarely got headaches. "So, let me get this straight. You blackmailed Elrond. He blackmailed Helene, and you gave the money to Chucky to get him to leave? Why didn't you just spend the money on yourself?"

Jimena looked at her as if she'd laid an egg. "I couldn't let Chucky keep pestering you, and besides, it wouldn't have been right to keep dirty money."

It was hard for Reese to fault that logic, especially since it might work. *Might*. And that *might* was only temporary. "Chucky will just be back when he runs out of money."

Jimena smiled. "No, he won't, and here's the kicker. I altered copies of the clown sex photos. I erased El-rond's face and put in Chucky's to make it look as if

Chucky's got his nose where it doesn't belong—if you get my meaning." She winked.

Yes, Reese did get her meaning. "So, you're blackmailing Chucky because if he comes back, you'll give those pictures to his wife."

"Yep. Easy peasy, huh?"

Nothing about this was easy or peasy—whatever the heck that meant. Jimena might need a flowchart to keep up with who was blackmailing whom and why. Plus, there was the other matter that Reese wanted to discuss.

"Chucky called Logan last night, and he said Vickie stole something from your desk," Reese put out there. "Chucky thought it was something she could possibly use to blackmail you."

Now it was Jimena who stopped. "Hmm. Well, I did have both sets of the clown sex pictures in there. Copies, mind you. I have the originals in a password-protected storage cloud."

Sex pictures that wouldn't shed good lights on Helene or Chucky. Her mother could be planning to blackmail both of them.

Again, a flowchart might be needed.

"Are you sure Vickie couldn't have taken something else from your desk?" Reese asked. "Maybe something she could use to hurt you?"

Jimena paused a second, giving that some thought, and shook her head. "There were some other sex pictures of Elrond and me, but if she plans to blackmail me with that, she's barking up the wrong tree. I don't care who sees my sex pictures."

Reese put herself in a con-artist frame of mind to see if she could figure out how this might work for her mother. It didn't take her long to come up with an angle.

"Jason. If Vickie thinks you're trying to have a relationship with Jason, she could hold on to the pictures to try to cause some trouble between you two."

"Oh, you mean because Jason wouldn't go for sleeping with a woman who had sex with the man who had sex with his best friend's ex."

Heck, they needed a flowchart for that, too. "I don't know Jason that well, but it could be an issue for him. He could see being with you as some kind of disloyalty to Logan."

Jimena made a sound of agreement. Followed by a sound of annoyance. And that's when Reese knew that Jimena did indeed have a thing for Jason.

Damn.

Reese wasn't sure how her mother pieced together stuff like this, but Vickie always seemed to be one step ahead of them. And speaking of steps, Jimena quit walking, and she pointed to the sign in the front of the jewelry store.

Watch Repairs.

"I called ahead," Jimena said. "They don't usually open until ten, but we've got an appointment. Don't worry about the cost. I milked a little extra money from Elrond."

It was a wonderful gesture. Not milking money from Elrond—Reese didn't care much for that. But with everything going on, she was surprised, and pleased, that her friend had thought of this.

So, why couldn't Reese make herself go into the shop? She held her ground even when Jimena opened the door and tried to usher her in.

"All right," Jimena finally said. "What's this about?"

Reese shook her head. "I'm not sure I can put it into words."

"This is about Spenser. He broke the watch, and you don't think you deserve to have it fixed because of what happened to him."

All in all, that was an accurate assessment. Was that it? Reese did a quick soul-examining and realized that it might be.

"Of course that's malarkey," Jimena went on. "You love that watch, and it should be fixed so that it's the way it was when your grandfather gave it to you."

Reese did a little more soul-examining and realized Jimena was right. A broken watch wasn't doing service to her grandfather's memory. The brokenness was only a reminder of Spenser, and that was something Reese could do without. Or rather it was something she *wanted* to do without.

They went inside, and the repairman, Jeff Latch-wood, motioned for them to come to the back counter where he was working. Reese knew him from the café. He was a "well-done burger, no cheese, with pickles on the side" kind of guy.

He took the watch from her, holding it with what she thought might be reverence, and he gave it a good examination. "Yep, I can fix it, but I'll have to order a crystal to replace the broken one. It might come in right away, or it could take up to two weeks. I'll give you a call as soon as it's done, and you can come in and pick it up."

Reese's heart sank. Not the feeling she'd hoped to get so soon after all that soul-searching and the revelation of why she did indeed want this fixed.

"While I'm waiting on the crystal," Jeff went on,

"I'll give it a cleaning and make sure nothing else is broken inside."

"Sounds good," Jimena declared, and she got Reese out of there probably before she could change her mind. Which she was about to do.

"Two weeks?" Reese repeated. "I wasn't sure I'd be in town that long."

"Well, now you have to be." And Jimena smiled.

Reese frowned. "Did Logan put you up to this?"

"No." She seemed sincere about that. "Why?"

"Because he asked me to stay."

"Then maybe he's not an asshole, after all." Jimena's gaze flew to the time on her phone screen. She took off. "Shit. Gotta go. I don't want to give Logan a reason to fire me. Bye!"

That sounded as un-right as something could sound coming from Jimena. To the best of Reese's knowledge, Jimena had never cared whether or not she got fired. And she'd never before sprinted toward work even when there was imminent threat of being fired. Reese hoped that didn't mean Jimena had gotten her heart set on keeping this job because Logan would almost certainly hire someone more qualified.

Reese looked back at the jewelry shop, considered returning to say she'd changed her mind, but then she saw Helene walking toward her.

Apparently, Logan's ex wasn't giving up on having that chat with her because Helene waved and called out to her. "I'm so glad we ran into each other. I really do need to talk to you."

Reese got that, which made her believe this wasn't "running into each other" coincidence. Helene had probably tracked her down, and that meant Logan had perhaps told her about Vickie's latest break-in, the one that might or might not involve clown sex pictures of Helene.

"I need to get back to my apartment," Reese said. That was a polite way of saying she really didn't want to talk to her. But Helene was evidently determined to do this because she fell in step alongside Reese.

Because Reese wasn't sure how much the woman knew about Vickie's theft, she just stayed quiet and let Helene take the lead. And Helene jumped right in.

"For the record, I didn't cheat on Logan because I was dissatisfied with the sex," Helene blurted out. "I wasn't satisfied with *me*. Strict upbringing, always following Daddy's rules. Everything I've done in my life was for someone else." She shrugged. "Well, except for having sex with a clown. I did that for me."

"All right," Reese said because she didn't know what else to say. It seemed creepy talking about sex with Logan's ex. Actually, it seemed creepy talking about clown sex, period.

"I hate that I hurt Logan," Helene went on. "If I could go back and undo it, believe me, I would."

Reese did believe her. Those minutes of pleasure—if that was the right word—had cost her a good man. Of course, it had likely been more than mere minutes since Helene had been with both Greg and Elrond.

Helene stayed quiet a second while the Starkley twins walked past them. The twins noticed, though, and judging from the lingering looks they gave Helene and Reese, it would soon be all over town that she and Logan's ex were having a discussion. In the gossip mill, that would turn into a heated discussion. By the end of the day, it would be a catfight on Main Street.

"I'm just going to come out and say this," Helene
continued after dragging in her breath. However, she
didn't just come out and say whatever was on her mind.
She took so many breaths that she sounded asthmatic.
"I want to offer you the chance of a lifetime."

That got Reese's attention, though—as the daughter
of con artists, she was always skeptical of chance-of-a-
lifetime offers. Usually they were meant to screw the
offeree while benefiting the offerer.

"I want to set you up in your own restaurant or bakery," Helene went on. "Your choice. I'll front all the
money, build it to any specs you want. I'll even pay your
employees until you start to turn a profit."

Reese stopped in her tracks so she could look at the
woman to see if she was serious. She was. And because
Reese was the daughter of con artists, she followed this
through to the most obvious question of all—what was
in this for Helene?

And the answer to that was Logan.

"That's very generous of you." Reese started walking again because she figured this conversation wasn't
going to last much longer. "And the only condition…
wait, there are two conditions. One is that the restaurant and or bakery can't be anywhere near Spring Hill.
The second condition you want is for me to agree to
never see Logan again."

Judging from the way Helene suddenly got very interested in studying the cracks on the sidewalk, Reese
was spot-on. "It's a really good offer. It could set you
up for life."

"Yes, it could set me up to be the kind of woman
who accepts bribes," Reese argued. "Not exactly what
I'm going for in life."

Helene stayed quiet a moment. "So, your answer is no?"

"No times a gazillion."

"I see." More of those quiet moments while she looked at anything and anybody but Reese. "I guess this means you're in love with Logan, then."

Reese opened her mouth to answer another "no times a gazillion," but she suddenly found herself studying sidewalk cracks, too. She couldn't be in love with Logan.

Could she?

But then she remembered this chat had zilch to do with love. It was about Helene trying to control a situation she'd lost control of months ago.

"It means I'm not for sale," Reese settled for saying. "When and if I leave Spring Hill, it will be my decision and under my own terms."

Oh, mercy. She'd actually used the *if* word when it came to leaving. In the past, there'd definitely been no ifs involved. And Reese could thank Logan for that.

"Well, I had to try, didn't I?" Helene said.

Now Reese used her "No." And then she added some more. "Do you really think you can win Logan back by getting me out of the picture?"

Helene shrugged. "I suppose you're right. I could just wait this out since I believe this is a rebound relationship for Logan."

The rebound comment felt like a sucker punch, but since it might be doused in truth, Reese stayed quiet. Helene didn't.

"But waiting's not exactly my style, you know?" Helene added.

Reese had to shake her head. She didn't know. Helene had dated Logan for eight years. That was a long time, and it had no doubt included plenty of waiting to see when they were going to the next level.

"Does that mean you're giving up?" Reese asked her, but figured she wouldn't get a straight answer. That's why it surprised her when she did.

"Yes," Helene said. "I think I need to do something drastic with my life to make some changes. I have a bucket list. I think it's time for me to start checking things off. I've always wanted to have a one-night stand. A no-names-allowed kind of thing."

Reese nearly choked on her own breath, and at first she thought this was Helene's way of getting in a dig at her, but the woman didn't give any indication that she'd just summarized Reese's life four months ago.

They finally reached the Bluebonnet Inn, and so that Helene wouldn't follow her in, Reese stopped and turned to her. "I wish you the best."

Helene blinked as if surprised by that. "Logan said pretty much the same thing. I thought he was lying. *Hoped* he was lying, because saying that meant he no longer had feelings for me," she amended.

The look on Helene's face implied she'd said too much. She checked the time on her phone. "I have to run." She turned as if to do that, but then stopped, as well. "You won't mention our chat to Logan, will you?"

"No." Reese didn't have to think about it. Logan didn't need to know that his ex had tried to pay her off.

Helene made a sound as if she didn't quite buy that, but she headed off, anyway. Reese didn't waste any time going into the Bluebonnet Inn and up to her room. She didn't want anyone seeing her watch Helene make her exit because the gossip would spread about that, too.

By the time the story was done, Reese would have been rushing to call Logan to tell him about the encounter.

Reese would call Logan but not about that.

There was still the whole issue of clown sex pictures and how they might be used. The whole question was if Reese would really wait two weeks for the watch to be repaired. And the biggie question...

That whole L-word thought she'd had about Logan.

With that question staring her smack-dab in the face, Reese opened the door to her room and came smack-dab in the face with someone else.

"Reese," her mother purred. "I've been waiting for you."

CHAPTER TWENTY-THREE

LOGAN SMELLED HIS coffee before he sipped it. No cat shit, or if it was in there, it hadn't altered the taste. However, he was concerned that he'd done something to put that pissed-off look on Jimena's face.

"Did another seller cancel business with us?" he asked her.

Jimena shook her head. "No, but you do have a visitor. I told her you were really busy, but she insisted on seeing you. She would have just charged back here, but I'm bigger than she is and threatened to put her in a headlock. That's okay to say that, right?"

"Depends on the visitor. Is it Vickie?"

"Helene."

Logan thought about it a second and decided the headlock threat was still all right. If he could live with the cat-shit threat hanging over his head, then Helene could manage this.

"What does she want?" Logan asked.

Jimena rolled her eyes. "To talk to you privately. And yes, she emphasized the *privately* part."

If this had something to do with the clown-sex photos, then it was possible Helene didn't know they'd been stolen from Jimena's computer. Or maybe she did know and that's why she'd insisted on a private conversation.

"Show Helene in but also call Reese for me and see if

she can come over for lunch." Logan had been swamped all morning with meetings and paperwork, but he really did need to talk to her about these blackmail attempts.

"I'll make sure she comes." Jimena turned to leave, but Logan thought of something else.

He took out the blue boxed ring from his desk. The ring that was supposed to be Helene's. "Could you take this over to the jewelry store and return it?"

"Sure. Is this what I think it is?"

"It is, and yes, I should have returned it months ago, but I kept forgetting. Just ask for Jeff."

"I've met him. Reese and I were there earlier. She's finally getting her grandfather's watch fixed." Jimena leaned in closer as if telling a secret. "Jeff said it'd take two weeks for the repair. Two weeks," she emphasized, and waggled her fingers at him. She had on polka-dotted nail polish. "A smart man would use those two weeks to sweet-talk Reese into staying even longer."

Yes, a smart man would, and Logan would try, but with Vickie breathing down their necks, Reese might just run and then sneak back later to get the watch.

"Logan?" Helene called out from the hall. "I really need to see you."

Jimena's eyes narrowed. "I told her to stay put. Can I headlock her now?"

While the petty part of him might have found that satisfying, there was no need. "Just do that errand for me. I'll answer the phones while you're out." That was something Helene probably wouldn't appreciate, but she'd appreciate a headlock even less.

Jimena glared her way out as Helene slunk her way in, and Helene closed the door behind Jimena as soon as she could.

"You know I can recommend some qualified office help," Helene started.

"No need." Best to get right down to business. "What can I do for you?"

Considering that Helene had been so darn anxious to get in to see him, she still took her time answering. "I came by to say goodbye. I'm leaving town for a while. Hoping to regroup my life."

He nodded. "Good luck with that." The phone rang, and Logan held up his hand in a "wait a sec" gesture and answered it. Delbert.

"Logan, we have to talk," Delbert blurted out.

"Apparently, there's a queue for that. Is this about that personal matter?"

"It is. I gave that woman money to keep quiet, and she wants more."

"Of course she does." Logan didn't want to mention names because even though Helene appeared to be studying some new artwork, she also appeared to be listening in. "There's only one way to fix this. You know what you have to do. Come clean." And with that, Logan hung up and moved on to the second cog in this blackmail wheel.

"Do you want to talk about those photos that Vickie has?" Logan asked.

Helene seemed to release the breath she'd been holding. "You know about those." She sighed, sank down in the chair across from his desk. "She's blackmailing me."

"Of course," Logan repeated. Now he sighed. "There's only one way to fix this—come clean."

She glanced at the phone, probably putting the pieces together. Helene likely didn't know that it was Delbert who'd called, but now she had an inkling that someone else was in the same leaky boat that she was.

"That's hard to do." Her voice was whispery, the sound of a woman of the verge of tears. "I could hurt you and your business."

He lifted his eyebrow. "If anything, people will just feel sorry for me. I hate pity business more than pity sex, but I won't be the one hurt in this."

She conceded that with a soft sound of agreement. "So, how would I go about coming clean?"

Logan had a few suggestions. Helene wasn't going to like them, though. "You could just tell one of the town's bigger gossips that there are sex photos. Or print an apology in the newspaper along with enough details to defuse future threats from Vickie. Or you could record Vickie blackmailing you and use it to have her arrested."

The last one, though, wouldn't stop the threat because Vickie would just continue the blackmail when she got out of jail.

Helene nodded. Stood. Whether she would do any of those things, he didn't know. But this was a case of not his bull, not his bullshit. Logan already had enough of his own he had to shovel.

"Oh," Helene added. "I tried to bribe Reese into leaving town. I figured I should tell you before Reese does."

"She won't tell me," Logan assured her.

"Of course she will." Said like gospel coming from a woman who clearly didn't know squat about Reese.

The phone rang again so Logan motioned for Helene to close the door on her way out. He figured it was Delbert again, calling to whine about the mess of his own making. But it was a different whiner.

Chucky.

"Have you seen Vickie?" the man greeted.

"No. Why? What's going on now?"

"She's gone bat-shit crazy, that's what." Chucky was talking so fast that his words ran together. "She hired some thug to bust my nut, and the only way I got out of it was to pay the guy off."

"Maybe that was her plan along—to have you pay the guy so she could split the profit with him?" Logan suggested.

Judging from the long pause, then the profanity, Chucky hadn't considered that. "Vickie," he growled, and he made the woman's name sound like profanity, too.

"Look, I don't know what you expect me to do—"

"I want to leave the country and start a new life," Chucky readily answered. "I got dreams of owning a beach house in Hawaii."

Logan wasn't sure if he should point out that Hawaii was part of the country. "And you expect me to help you with that?"

"Yes, I do," Chucky verified. "I told you about Vickie taking stuff from Jimena's computer. Well, I took stuff from it, too. Pictures. And I know a lot of other stuff that could ruin you."

Hell. Not another round of this. "Are you blackmailing me?"

Chucky hesitated. "No, of course not." Yeah, he was blackmailing him. "Wouldn't want to say anything in case you're recording this. Let's just say I expect you to help me make my dreams come true because you're a generous person."

"I'm not generous," Logan reminded him. "And neither is Jimena. Do you remember that she can make things difficult between you and your wife?"

"Let her try. My wife will come back to me when I'm richer than you. I'll meet you at your office first thing in the morning to discuss this. I'll see you at 8:00 a.m. sharp. Be there and be prepared to make my Hawaii-house dream come true."

Logan would rather eat Hawaii than pay off this turd.

The moment Chucky ended the call, Logan took out his phone and pressed Reese's number. If Vickie was hiring thugs—even conning ones—to threaten Chucky, she could do the same to Reese, and Logan needed to warn her.

Her phone rang but then went straight to voice mail. Logan left her a message to call him ASAP and then got busy thinking up a plan. He had to do something to put an end to Chucky's and Vickie's threats once and for all.

"How DID YOU get in here?" Reese asked her mother once she got her mouth working. She cursed the jolt of surprise and knew she had let down her guard. Not a good thing to do around Vickie.

"The door was unlocked so I decided to come in and wait for you."

That might be true. Reese had left in a hurry with Jimena so it was possible she'd forgotten to lock up. Just as possible, though, that her mother had picked the lock. Vickie was good at that.

"Well, you can just un-wait," Reese told her. "Because I have nothing to say to you." However, she did have something to do. Reese started checking around the room to make sure her mother hadn't stolen anything.

"I have something to say to you," Vickie answered. "I'm tired of being messed over by life. By you. By everybody."

Reese didn't bother to give her a flat look for the "by you" comment. She just kept checking to make sure everything was there. Things were okay in the kitchen so she went to the small closet.

"You might have heard," Vickie went on, "that I happened to come across some interesting photos and information."

"I heard." Since she didn't have much stuff, it didn't take Reese long to go through the closet, but that's when she saw that her backpack was unzipped. She laid it on the bed so she could go through it.

"You're pretending not to be interested, but I know you want to know what I have."

"Sex pictures that you stole from Jimena's computer." She rummaged through her things and found the chef's knives. It was the only thing that mattered to her now that the watch was at the jeweler's. For the first time, Reese was actually glad it hadn't been in the room for her mother to find.

"And do you know what I can do with those sex pictures?" Vickie asked like a greedy dog over a coveted bone.

Now Reese gave her the flat look. "Blackmail people." She used her Captain Obvious voice.

"Yes," Vickie answered as if it hadn't been so obvious, after all. Clearly, she wanted to play a game here, but Reese wasn't in a playing mood. "I have sex pictures I can use to blackmail that uppity bitch Helene. More sex pictures to blackmail that trashy bitch

Jimena. More sex pictures to blackmail that hound dog Delbert."

Reese continued her flat look. "Is that all?"

Vickie's eyes narrowed. No, this game wasn't going her way, but then Reese saw something she didn't want to see. A gleam in those beady-rat eyes. Her mother had something else.

"I have something else," Vickie verified a split second later. "I got copies of the old newspaper articles about Spenser O'Malley. How do you think your hot cowboy will react when he sees those?"

"Hot cowboy?" someone said from the doorway.

Logan.

Reese wasn't sure she wanted him here for this conversation, but her mother smiled, thinking she was about to drop a bombshell.

"You don't know what Reese did," Vickie said.

"Yes, I do. I read the entire report on Spenser O'Malley. I personally think he got what he deserved, and Reese was in no way to blame for that."

If her mother's eyes narrowed any more, she'd look as if she had straight lines where her eye sockets should be. "Well, the town might not be so forgiving," Vickie spat out.

That was true, but then Reese had never stayed around a town long enough to know how they reacted to news like that.

"Plus, there's Jimena," Vickie went on. "I can mess things up between her and her cowboy lover boy. I can show him those sex pictures of Jimena with another man."

"Please." And Reese didn't say it as a plea, either. "Jimena will probably show Jason the pictures herself. She uses them as foreplay." That was possibly true, anyway.

More eye narrowing from Vickie. Reese wished she had some superglue to squirt on them so they'd stay shut that way.

"Fine. But you're not going to blow off the rest of what I've got." When Vickie opened her eyes again, she didn't look at Reese but rather Logan. "I've heard plenty of stories about the night your folks were killed. Word is you blame yourself."

Everything inside Reese went still, and she thought she might permanently shut her mother's eyes without the use of superglue. A couple of punches might do it.

"You stay away from Logan," Reese warned her. Then she instantly regretted it. Because her mother smiled again, and Reese knew she'd given her exactly what she wanted.

A way for her to manipulate Reese.

"Those stories are old news," Logan explained.

"Yes." Vickie could have won a smugness award with the tone slathered on that one-word response. "But it's another thing to see those stories in print. Think of how painful it would be for your family to read them. Oh, did I mention that I'd be going to the newspaper with all of this?"

Reese wanted to believe the newspaper wouldn't touch it, but they actually had a gossip section under the general label of "What's Going on, Y'all?"

"So, basically you're trying to hurt Logan, Delbert, Helene, Jimena and me?" Reese asked. She didn't have to ask why. "How much?"

Still smiling, her mother stood. "I'm still consider-ing that, but I thought you could talk to all parties involved, and you could find out what they'd like to do to make me go away."

"If I bargain with you," Logan said, "will you give me dirt to put Chucky away? I only want to deal with one of you."

Vickie's smile widened. "Well, of course. I have… things on Chucky, too. I'd be glad to give them to you for, well, let's just say services rendered."

Logan nodded. "I'll meet you later with my answer."

"Wonderful. Just know that if you double-cross me, I have those photos and articles hidden away. They're with a friend, and if I get arrested or if I disappear, the package will be delivered not just to the local newspaper but to everyone in the tricounty area."

With that threat still hanging in the air, Vickie turned and walked out. If Reese had thought it would do any good, she would have gone after her, but her mother's favorite things were steak and desperation. Reese didn't want to give her either. So, she did the only thing she could do even though she knew it would do no good at all.

"God, Logan. I'm so sorry," she said.

Reese could have added a whole lot more to that apology if Logan hadn't kissed her. Not a little peck, either. He really kissed her. When he had robbed her of her breath and seemingly the cartilage in her knee-caps, he pulled back.

And he was smiling.

"I have a plan," Logan announced.

CHAPTER TWENTY-FOUR

6:00 p.m.

LOGAN SUSPECTED THAT some wars had been launched with fewer working parts than this plan, but if it worked, it would solve all their problems. Well, it would solve everything for everyone but Vickie and Chucky.

Of course, there was a big-assed "if" attached to all of this, and it was possible it could blow up in his face. He didn't mind some face-blowing every now and then but not when Reese could be hurt. And his family.

Hell, lots of people could go down if he screwed this up.

That probably explained why his stomach was doing some twisting and turning. But it wasn't all bad. He got that feeling a lot right before he closed a big sale. Maybe it was a good sign now, too.

Logan opened the back door to the Fork and Spoon, and once he made his way into the dining area, he spotted Chucky right away. The weasel had taken the far corner booth, and he was already doing that rat-twitch thing with his face. The twitching eased up just a little when he saw Logan. Probably because Chucky was relieved that he'd actually shown up.

Chucky was perhaps smiling about something else, too. He could see Vickie pacing in front of the gro-

cery store across the street. That wasn't by accident.
The woman was exactly where she was supposed to be,
and she was waiting for Logan to show. Of course, she
hadn't seen Logan go into the café because he'd been
sure to use the back door.

"I made sure Reese wasn't here," Chucky said right
off while Logan was still standing. "Bert said it was
her evening off. I also checked the table and booth to
make sure it wasn't bugged. Now you gotta empty your
pockets just like you said you'd do."

Logan had indeed agreed to that since Chucky was
afraid that Logan would record him saying something to
incriminate himself. But that wasn't Logan's plan at all.
He took out his wallet, phone, the small tape recorder,
the pocketknife and his keys. Chucky didn't pat him
down exactly, but he did motion for him to turn. Logan
had purposely worn a tighter fitting shirt so the man
would be assured that he wasn't wearing a wire, either.

"Okay, no recording anything until we finish the first
part of this," Chucky stated. He glanced out at Vickie
again, who was now checking her watch.

Logan nodded since that was the deal. Chucky and
he would work out blackmail payments from everyone
involved, and then in turn Chucky would spill the dirt
on Vickie.

"You made a smart choice dealing with me instead
of that crazy she-bitch Vickie," Chucky said as Logan
sat across from him.

"Now you empty your pockets," Logan insisted.

That was part of the deal, too, but in hindsight he
wished he hadn't. There was no reason for Chucky to
record this, especially the parts where he was going to
say how much he demanded and the names of the peo-

ple he'd be demanding it from. But Logan wanted to make it look as if he was being thorough.

He should have known, though, that abnormal people might have abnormal pocket contents.

A wallet. Keys. Phone. Handkerchief—well used. Two malted milk balls—unwrapped. A breath mint—unwrapped. Turtle decal stickers. Two wads of what appeared to be lint. Or perhaps fungus. A stick of gum also seemingly coated with fungus/lint.

Chucky checked the time on his phone—6:05. "We don't talk until Vickie's given up on you and leaves," Chucky insisted.

Since that was part of the deal, too, they just waited. Vickie paced while she waited, and she was clearly on edge, her gaze darting to her phone and then all around. A couple of seconds later, she disappeared into the grocery store.

"Why's she going in there?" Chucky asked.

"Who knows? Now that she knows I'm not going to show, she might be buying rat poison or something."

Chucky made a sound of suspicion. "Don't think you can cook up something here with me and then head over there and do more cooking up with her."

"Huh?" That was the best Logan could do with the info Chucky had just given him.

"I don't want you double-crossing me by meeting her after you meet with me. That's why I'll be following you when you leave here, and I'll keep right on following you until I got my money."

Logan simply nodded, though he was slightly impressed that Chucky had thought to take such measures.

Chucky popped the breath mint in his mouth. "All right, now let's get down to business. I want twenty-five

thousand each from Delbert and you. Another twenty-
five from Helene. Another twenty-five from Reese and
ten from Jimena. Now, I'm figuring Reese and Jimena
haven't got that kind of money so you'll have to pony
up for them." He grinned, revealing a piece of lint on
his teeth, probably from the breath mint.

Logan rubbed his forehead and appeared to be dis-
tressed about that amount. One hundred and ten grand.
It was a lot of money, but Logan was betting it wouldn't
buy much more than some sand itself on a Hawaiian
beach. Apparently, Chucky's big ideas weren't so big,
after all, but Logan wasn't going to point that out to him.

"And how did you want the payment?" Logan asked.

Chucky slid the stick of gum closer to Logan, and
that's when he saw the email address written there. "For
my PayPal account. Make sure y'all send it as a gift so
I don't have to pay fees."

In addition to teeny ideas, Chucky was also an idiot
since the account could be traced. Of course, Chucky
was counting on them never turning any of this over to
the authorities or he would release all the crap he was
holding over their heads.

"The money's gotta be in my account no later than
8:00 p.m.," Chucky added.

Again, Logan pretended that would be a problem. It
wasn't. Those kinds of payments could be made in
under a minute.

"Now, to your side of the deal." Logan turned the
tape recorder. "Tell me everything I'll need to have
Vickie arrested and put behind bars for a long, long
time."

Chucky smiled. A second piece of lint was now on
his teeth. He started talking. And he talked and talked

and talked. When he was done, Logan motioned toward the kitchen where Deputy Davy was waiting.

Davy didn't waste a second hurrying out to use his handcuffs on a gob-smacked Chucky.

VICKIE COULD ALMOST feel that money in her hands, but she didn't like this little twist that Logan had added to their arrangement. For one thing, he was late, and that was going to cost him. It would continue to cost him for every minute he kept her waiting.

The second thing she didn't like about this was the meeting place. What the hell was a shitake mushroom, and why would Logan tell her to meet him there? Maybe because that's where he'd planted some kind of bug. Well, this wasn't her first rodeo, and they wouldn't be standing anywhere near the shitake when he arrived.

She meandered her way through the vegetable row and found something that wasn't spelled at all like it sounded. Still, this had to be it. There were no other mushrooms with a name that came close.

Vickie waited some more, glanced around to make sure Logan hadn't hired a stock boy or something to use some long-range recording device. But the only person who appeared to be in the entire store was a clerk and a teenager mopping up a spill in the milk aisle.

6:16.

Yeah, being late was going to cost him.

She pulled out her phone, ready to call Logan and blast him a new one, but then she finally spotted the devil himself. Too bad that he hadn't shown any interest in her because she wouldn't have minded a tumble in his hay.

"Give me your phone," she insisted as he approached her. "And anything else you could use to record this."

He obliged and gave her a small tape recorder. He also showed her the contents of his pockets—keys, a wallet and a pocketknife. That wallet, or rather his bank account, was going to be a whole lot lighter before this was over.

"I'll keep this simple," she said, and Vickie handed him the routing numbers for an offshore bank account. "I don't care how you, Delbert, Helene, Jimena and my daughter divvy it all up, but in the next twenty minutes I want five hundred thousand dollars added to that account. In exchange I'll give you the password for the storage cloud where I'm keeping all the pictures, reports and such."

"Does that include the dirt on Chucky?" he asked.

"No. As soon as you agree to the money, you'll hear all you need to arrest Chucky."

Shit, she would have given him that for free. Anything to make Chucky fry, but it was a nice touch to tie it to their business deal. Except she had her own twist to add to the deal. One that these marks wouldn't know about until, well, until she ran out of money and needed more. Yes, she'd give him the copies of stuff she had in the storage cloud.

But there were three clouds.

Good thing she'd learned all about computers during her last stint in jail.

"So, do we have a deal?" Vickie asked.

Logan nodded.

That was a half-million-dollar kind of nod. So, Vickie decided to help him out a little. She turned on the recorder for Logan and started telling him all the dirty little secrets that she knew about Chucky.

When she was done, Vickie heard the footsteps and saw the chief of police making his way toward her.

"Vickie Stephenson," he said. "You're under arrest."

"What the hell do you think you're doing?" Vickie howled.

Logan smiled. "Double-crossing you." He handed the recorder to the cop. "Thanks, Luke," he told him.

"Anytime, Lucky," the cop answered, and he hauled Vickie away.

REESE HAD NO idea how the rest of the plan was going, but she felt as if she were juggling cats. Everyone was talking at once, and the poor newspaper editor, Marlene Holland, was trying her best to write everything down.

Operation Dirt Sweep was in full swing.

For Marlene, it had to be like Christmas, her birthday and Fourth of July all rolled into one. She'd have enough stories for the newspaper to last for weeks. Maybe months.

"Everybody get quiet for a second," Marlene finally shouted. Surprisingly, everybody did. "All right, now let's do this alphabetically so I'll make sure to get it all down." She looked at Cassie. "That means you go first."

Cassie pushed her way through the others to get to Marlene's desk. The editor's office was the size of a broom closet so it took some doing.

"I'm two months pregnant," Cassie announced. "So yes, that means I got pregnant before getting married and before Lucky and I got custody of our girls."

All in all, it wasn't big news, but it was something Cassie probably would have preferred to spill at a family gathering rather than to the town's biggest blabbermouth. Still, it needed to be said so that it couldn't be used as gossip fodder against her.

Claire was up next, and Riley was right by her side. "I'm pregnant, too, and I was trying to keep it a secret so I wouldn't steal Cassie and Lucky's thunder what with their wedding."

Again, not a big revelation, but judging from the dog-with-a-bone look Marlene gave her, it was still news that Marlene could use.

"Delbert?" Marlene called him up.

Unlike Cassie and Claire, he didn't charge forward. He stayed in the corner. "I slept with her mother." He flung a finger at Reese. "Vickie." Said like venom. "And now she's blackmailing me."

Surprisingly, Delbert had managed to get through that with only mumbled profanity, but no matter how he went with this, it was going to cost him. This way, he would just pay money to his wife in a divorce settlement rather than paying it to Vickie as hush money. Either way would eventually bleed him dry, but Delbert had been the one to cheat, and he wasn't exactly blameless in this.

Reese motioned for him to finish up. It wasn't called Operation Dirt Sweep for nothing.

"I, uh, told Logan I couldn't do business with him," Delbert went on, fessing up to Marlene, "but that's because Vickie told me to say that. I'll keep doing business with Logan if he'll let me, and I'll tell everybody to do the same."

Reese wasn't sure how much clout Delbert would have with those friends after this. Then again, maybe the publicity would actually help.

Helene was up next, and this was where Reese held her breath. Unlike Cassie and Claire, whose secrets would have soon "shown," Helene could have kept hers buried if she'd wanted to keep being blackmailed.

"There are sex pictures of me with two different men," Helene finally said after a long silence. "Greg and another man who worked for Logan."

"Elrond, my ex," Jimena piped up.

Helene gave her a sharp look. "He was only your ex after he was my ex."

It was a valid point, and Jimena shrugged, nodded.

"I also located a man, Chucky," Helene went on, "and told him that Reese was here in town. And I did that with the hopes that he'd pressure her into leaving. I also tried to bribe her to leave. I'm really sorry about that."

Reese hadn't expected the woman to confess that last part since only Helene and Reese knew about it, but maybe Helene had thought it would come back later to bite her in her perfectly shaped butt.

"One final thing," Helene went on, "I paid off Elrond because he was blackmailing me with those sex pictures."

Marlene looked up from her writing. "Is that everything?" she asked when Helene hushed. "Nothing about Logan and you maybe having some ex-sex on the side?"

"No. Logan's choice, not mine. Trust me, I've thrown myself at him enough times, and he's turned me down. That's why I'm leaving town and finding some new adventures."

Reese and she actually shared a smile. She wanted to tell Helene that she was proud of her for doing this, but the words weren't necessary. Helene appeared to be proud of herself.

Jimena went closer to the desk when it was her alphabetical turn. "I blackmailed Elrond because of his clown sex fetish so I could pay off Chucky so he'd leave Reese alone. Do you want to hear about the other men I've had sex with while I've been in town?"

"Of course," Marlene said.

"Even if one of them is someone close to you? As in very close?" Jimena's gaze lingered on Marlene's wedding band.

"No, what you already gave me is fine." Though Marlene did narrow her eyes at Jimena.

Reese knew Jimena hadn't slept with Marlene's husband, Roy. Roy was in his sixties, chewed tobacco and was missing several teeth. Still, it had given the town's biggest gossip a small dose of her own medicine.

It was finally Reese's turn, and she was dreading it. No way could she back down when the others had been so brave, but she suddenly wished Logan was there with her.

And he was.

At that exact moment Logan came through the door, Lucky behind him, and even though there was no room for them, they made room. Lucky went to Cassie, pulling her into his arms, and Logan went to Reese.

"How'd it go?" Reese asked, afraid of the answer.

He gave her a thumbs-up and a kiss. Both were exactly what she needed.

"Is it finished?" Delbert asked. "Did you get Vickie and Chucky?"

Helene asked a variation on the same question except she added, "Are they rotting in jail?"

Logan and Lucky nodded.

"I got Vickie to rat out Chucky," Lucky continued,

"and Logan got Chucky to rat out Vickie. Both have been arrested and will face multiple charges."

That caused some whoops of joy and some hugs throughout the room. Sometimes, like now, having an identical twin brother came in handy. But Logan and she weren't out of the stew pot just yet.

Reese handed the PI's report to Marlene. "I have a police record, and the details are all in there."

Marlene didn't exactly start drooling, but it was close.

"What Reese's not saying is that the charges were trumped up," Logan explained. "Also, she wasn't responsible for Spenser O'Malley's death. He was an abusive dick who got hit by a bus. It was an accident and not her fault."

Reese felt it again. The L-word. Other than Jimena, people didn't usually stick up for her, and here Logan was doing it even though it could cost him plenty.

But his next admission would cost him even more.

That's why Reese knew she wanted to stick up for him. "My mother tried to blackmail Logan by saying she'd have you print gossip about his parents' death. Gossip and rumors," Reese emphasized.

Somehow, Claire, Cassie, Lucky and Riley all worked their way to the desk and joined Reese and Logan in hovering over Marlene.

"I'm sure everyone here wishes they could have saved the McCords," Reese added. "But since it was an accident, no one had control over that. What happened happened, and it's certainly nothing to be gossiped about."

"Understand?" Jimena added.

Despite barely having her face squeezed between

three lethal-looking cowboys and the three determined women with them, Jimena's expression was somehow more fierce than all of theirs combined.

Jimena mumbled something about cat shit in coffee.

And Marlene nodded. "Understood." She glanced down at the all the notes she'd made. "Plus, I have enough here to last me until I retire." She paused. "Why exactly did you tell me all these things?"

"So that Chucky and Vickie can never use any of this to blackmail us," Logan answered, and one by one, they all gave a confirming nod.

The cons had been conned, and when the McCords, Delbert, Jimena, Helene and she all walked out of the newspaper office, they'd be doing it with something they hadn't had when they came in.

A clean dirty slate.

CHAPTER TWENTY-FIVE

LOGAN WASN'T SURE Reese would show. Even though Chucky and Vickie were in jail, the whole town of Spring Hill would soon be talking about the tell-all gossip. That could send Reese running for the hills, but Logan was hoping it would send her running for him.

A lofty wish.

He sipped his Glenlivet, not at the "make me forget this shit" pace he'd had the last time he was in the Purple Cactus hotel bar. Tonight, there was nothing he wanted to forget and plenty that he wanted to remember. His family had stood by him and Reese, and while they had personal motives for what they'd done, Helene and Delbert had come through, too.

His phone dinged, and he saw the new text from Lucky. Anything yet?

As Logan had done with Riley's, Claire's, Della's and Jimena's texts, he answered no. He'd told them all what his plans were for the night. In hindsight, that had been a mistake, since they were collectively texting at a pace greater than that of a teenager. But as corny as it sounded, Logan had wanted their approval.

And he'd gotten it.

Well, he'd gotten it from everyone but Jimena, but Logan was hoping she'd come around if and when Reese came around. And if and when he could put his family's approval to good use.

Logan frowned.

There were a lot of ifs and whens in all of this, and he always liked to deal in sure things. Especially when it was something this important.

He had all the arguments worked out in his head. If Reese said this was a rebound relationship, he could argue that four months was plenty enough time to get over a woman he'd never actually loved. He could admit that to himself now. He'd never been in love with Helene. She'd just been part of that perfect plan he'd had to make that perfect life.

Of course, Reese's other argument would be the effect she could have on his business, and Logan had a comeback for that, too. He could give her data and examples of other storms the McCords had weathered. He had all his ducks and stats lined up. And forgot every single duck and stat when Reese walked in.

Even though his back was to her, thanks to the bar mirror their gazes connected, and she made her way to him. No turtle shirt tonight. She was wearing jeans and a snug red top that he wished he could take off her.

In the privacy of a bedroom, of course.

She slid onto the bar stool next to him. "Jimena dropped me off. If I hadn't agreed to come, I think she would have kidnapped me and brought me here, anyway."

Logan made a mental note to give Jimena a raise. And offer her the job permanently. He didn't like the idea of living with the cat-shit threat, but Jimena's pluses outweighed her minuses.

Most days, anyway.

"How much tequila is it going to take to make you stay?" Logan asked. And he ordered her a shot.

"To stay here tonight or to stay in Spring Hill?" she clarified.

"Both."

Reese shook her head. "Tequila won't do it tonight. If I stay in Spring Hill, it could still hurt your business."

It hadn't taken her long to bring that up. "Business might fall off with the cattle, but Lucky seems to think it'll help with the bull sellers. They tend to prefer selling to someone with a little mud in their past."

Judging from the look she gave him, he hadn't convinced her, so Logan kissed her. He made it French, and even though it still might not have convinced her, he thought maybe he left her with a nice buzz, one not caused by the tequila, either.

"Let's play the word-association game we played the last time we were here," he said when he eased back from her. "I'll start. Family."

Another flat look, but she did respond. "Good."

Logan smiled and wondered if she knew that four months ago that wouldn't have been her answer. She probably would have said, "Shitty."

"Sex?" he continued. And he slid her his room key.

She angled her eyes at him. "Isn't it early for that? We went a couple of rounds with the game last time before I offered you sex."

"True, but you were easing into things." Clearly, though, he needed to do some more easing.

"All right. Here's another word. Watch?" he continued.

"Grandpa." Reese drank more of her tequila. "You do know this game sounds like caveman talk?"

He took out the pocket watch and placed it on the bar next to her shot glass. "Jeff from the jewelry store checked the antiques shop, and they had a crystal that was the right size. He fixed it and gave it to Jimena to give to me."

Reese opened it as if she were handling the queen's jewels. Of course, this was even more valuable to her than an entire treasure trove.

"It's perfect," she said, and he didn't have to see her eyes to know there were tears in them now. Logan hoped those were happy tears and that seeing the watch fixed and whole didn't trigger any memories of the person who'd broken it.

She kissed him.

So, no bad memories, after all.

"Thank you." Reese eyed the watch, the room key. His mouth. His crotch. "You're not about to offer me a white picket fence, are you?"

"We're not really the picket-fence types. Actually, I'm just offering you, well, me. You can take that on whatever terms you want. You can keep having sex with me. Or not. You can keep working at the café…"

"Or not?"

He nodded. "You can take Cassie's offer to open your own bakery. Though I'm kind of hoping that won't be an 'or not.' You could probably get a good deal on that Shirley's Sweets sign."

Ah, that got a smile from her.

"You could put down roots in Spring Hill," he added. "Or not," he mumbled.

She stayed quiet a moment. "You're really offering me just you?"

"Darn tootin'." Of course, he'd never actually used

the term *darn tootin'* before, but he hoped it showed his playful side. "Seems only fitting since I want you to be my…"

Now, here's something Logan had given much thought.

"Lover?" Reese supplied.

"Definitely that, but I'm thinking more. Maybe the right word is *woman*. I want you to be my woman."

"Sounds a little caveman-ish." Reese smiled again. "But I like it. After all, we're not the white-picket-fence type as you pointed out." The smile didn't last long, though. "What I'm about to say is terrifying for me," Reese continued, "but I love you."

Yes, that fell right into the terrifying territory for him, too, and it was something he'd never said to a woman other than his mother.

"I hate you for it," Reese went on before Logan could get his tongue untangled. "In fact, when I first realized it, I called you some really bad names and considered letting Jimena put a voodoo curse on you."

"Minus the voodoo curse, I had the same reaction." He let that hang in the air for several seconds before he eased his gaze to hers. "There are a lot of things that can make my life easier, Reese. You're not one of them."

"Gee, thanks—"

"But there's only one thing that can make my life happier," Logan interrupted. "And that's where you come in."

The smile returned, soft and sweet, and then not so sweet when she kissed him. She slipped the watch into her pocket and eyed the key card. "You really got a room?"

"Yep. Two-sixteen. The room we were in four months

ago." Which suddenly seemed like a lifetime ago. It also suddenly seemed as if it'd been a lifetime since he'd had sex with her, and the stirrings behind his zipper reminded him of that.

The stirrings in his heart did, too.

It was good to have a second opinion from two different parts of his body.

They finished their shots together, got off the bar stools, also together, and Logan picked up the key card. In the same motion, he slid his arm around her waist to get her moving. Not that he had to add one bit of pressure. Reese kissed him all the way to the elevator. Groped him part of the way there. Talked dirty to him for the last few steps.

Then blew his mind on his last step. Not with her mouth or hands but rather with something she said.

"By any chance do you love me?" she asked in the same tone of the most skeptical question that'd ever been asked.

"I thought you'd never bring it up." He flipped over the room key where he'd written, "I love you, Reese." Except there must have been some water or something on the bar, and it now looked more like 'I *blob* you, Reese."

"That's supposed to be *love*," Logan clarified, and he kissed her again just in case she had any doubts about that.

They kissed the rest of the way to the room, which made it sort of difficult to get the door unlocked. It also didn't help that she was already trying to unzip him. Logan let her do that while he kicked the door shut and maneuvered them to the bed.

"What if three months from now, my wanderlust kicks in and I decide to leave town?" Reese asked.

Since she now had her hands in his boxers, it was a little hard for Logan to think. "Then I can go with you. Or you can promise when the wanderlust runs out, that you'll come back to me for another round of regular lust."

Her hand froze, and she looked up at him. Logan decided while she was mildly thunderstruck that he would try to get some even ground here. He shoved down her jeans and panties to her knees and kissed his way to the part of her that he'd just uncovered.

She cursed him, but this time he thought it was because she wasn't pissed off about falling in love with him. "If you're going to do that, let's do it together."

All in all, it wasn't a bad idea. But there was something Logan wanted to do first. No, they weren't the white-picket-fence type, but he wanted Reese to have something to make her understand just how much she meant to him.

He took it from his pocket and slipped it into hers.

"A condom?" she asked.

Logan shook his head. "My father's knife. I want you to hold on to it for safekeeping."

If he'd offered her the world, Reese couldn't have had a better reaction. Her eyes filled with tears, and she kissed the living daylights out of him—which was the way Logan preferred to be kissed, anyway.

"I really do love you, hot cowboy," Reese said.

If she'd offered him the world…wait, that *was* the world. "I really do love you, too, Julia Child."

While Reese blinked back tears and kissed him,

she fumbled with his jeans, and for a moment Logan thought she was trying to turn this into a hand job.

She wasn't.

"For safekeeping," Reese said.

Logan felt around his pocket, and there it was. Her grandfather's watch. A knife and a watch.

Yeah, Reese had given him the world, all right. The only world that Logan wanted, anyway.

* * * * *

Turn the page for the special bonus story,
COWBOY UNDERNEATH IT ALL, by USA TODAY
bestselling author Delores Fossen!

COWBOY
UNDERNEATH IT ALL

CHAPTER ONE

"I GUESS YOU'RE not feeling too good about your girl-friend getting married, huh?" the bartender said to Captain Kane Bullock.

Kane didn't know the bartender's first name, but he was one of the Fletcher boys, probably barely old enough to tend bar. But he should be old enough to know that it was a stupid-ass thing to say.

Of course Kane wasn't feeling "too good" right about now. It felt as if he'd been kicked in the teeth by an eight-legged bull. All because his girlfriend was apparently about to be wed...

And she didn't have plans to say that "I do" to him.

Not that Kane wanted an "I do." He didn't. But he darn sure hadn't expected to come home and find Violet Wright, his flame of more than ten years, wearing another man's engagement ring.

"Heard about you getting out of the Army," Fletcher went on.

"Air Force. I fly fighter jets. *Flew* fighter jets," he corrected.

Kane had to get used to saying that because once his terminal leave was up in a month, he would no longer be a captain, a fighter pilot or on active duty. It was the right thing to do, giving it up, because it was finally time to put down some roots. Also the right thing to move home to the ranch where he'd grown up. The very place where he thought he'd see Violet again. And he had seen her all right. He just hadn't counted on seeing her like this.

"You know for a fact that Violet's marrying a good fella," the bartender went on. "For what it's worth."

Well, it was better than her wedding a bad one, Kane supposed, but hell in a handbasket, it still stung.

Violet could have at least called or emailed to give him a heads-up before he'd gotten back to town. That way he wouldn't have been blindsided ten minutes earlier when he'd literally walked in on her bachelorette party at Calhoun's Pub. All Kane had wanted was a beer after the two-day trip where he'd driven from the base in South Carolina and then here to Spring Hill, Texas.

He'd gotten a lot more than just the beer, though.

After all that driving, Kane had learned of his girlfriend's engagement from Sissy Donovan, the senior-citizen cocktail waitress who had blurted out the news before he'd even been able to sit down at the bar. It wouldn't be long before that same waitress pointed out to Violet that Kane was there. In fact, it was a shocker that she hadn't already done it. Maybe Sissy was the sort who liked to watch a train wreck play out in slow motion. Or perhaps she was just too busy calling every single person she knew to come to the bar for a *showdown*.

"Hate to say it, but my cousin, Charlene, is plenty happy about you and Violet breaking up," the bartender went on. "She'll be calling you real soon to give you a sweet deal. On some cows," he added with a knowing wink.

Yeah, Kane was betting Charlene would be calling, and the sale of cows might be involved, but Charlene would have a lot more than that on her mind. Even when Kane had been with Violet, Charlene had made open plays for him, once even offering him sex when Kane had been at a party with Violet. Despite that, Kane might have to deal with Charlene, along with fending her off, because he did need her livestock.

"Guess you gotta have some time to work through this." The bartender again. Fletcher had been wiping the same spot on the bar—the spot directly in front of Kane—since he'd served him his beer.

Kane decided to keep his response simple, and he gave the guy a look that could have frozen the hottest corners of hell. Fletcher was obviously too young or too stupid to pick up on facial cues because he stayed close.

He ignored the bartender, sipped his Lone Star and watched the goings-on in the mirror above the bar. Normally, it was a pretty good place to take in the action in his small hometown even late on a Wednesday afternoon when there wasn't much to see.

But right now there was plenty in the seeing department.

Kane wished there had been a different scene playing out behind him other than a giggling Violet who hadn't even noticed him. Wished, too, that he could just leave, but if he did now without finishing his beer, it'd be all over town that he was jealous.

Of course, the jealousy would get blown to epic proportions, and by the time the gossips were done, it'd be all around town that he had been crying in his beer. No tears, but he was well past the being pissed-off stage.

Along with maybe being a little hurt.

He'd always thought of Violet as his. Had always counted on her being there when he came home on leave, and not once had she ever asked to carry their relationship to the next level. She certainly hadn't mentioned anything about putting a ring on it. Of course, if she had, it might have sent him running.

The sound of more laughter pulled Kane's attention back to the mirror. Violet and her pals were in a booth in the back corner of the pub, where they were tossing back pink-colored drinks with green paper umbrellas on them. Violet was wearing a bridal veil that sparkled even in the dim lighting. The veil-wearing was a little early, since according to the bartender, the wedding was still three days away.

And the groom was none other than Kane's old high school football buddy, Dax Foreman. Dax was a cowboy, of course.

It wasn't hard to find one of those around Spring Hill, since it was basically a town that'd built up around the sprawling McCord Ranch. But what riled every rileable bone in Kane's body was that Violet had thought this pretty-boy bronco rider was more of a cowboy than Kane was.

Pretty Boy wasn't. No one was.

Kane silently cursed. Yes, he'd been gone for a while, finishing up ten years in the Air Force. And beneath the flight suit he'd worn all those years, he was pure cowboy. Raised on a ranch not far from here. A ranch his parents had sold when Kane had left for the Air Force, but he'd recently rebought it.

Hell, he wasn't just a cowboy, he could be a poster model for one.

He shifted his attention when the front door opened, and a woman hurried in. A brunette in a clingy red dress. The bartender made a sound of appreciation, and

Kane could see why. All those curves and long legs. She stopped, no doubt to give her eyes time to adjust to the lack of light, and she glanced at the back of the room before she looked in Kane's direction.

Crap.

It wasn't a woman. Well, it was, but it was the wrong woman. It was Eliza, Violet's kid sister.

When the hell had she gotten curves like that?

"I've been looking all over for you," Eliza greeted. Except it wasn't much of a greeting. She sounded annoyed or something.

Since he hadn't seen her in ages, Kane didn't think he was the reason for the annoyance. Unless Eliza was miffed because he wasn't the one marrying her sister.

"I tried to call you, but your old number didn't work," she added.

"I had to change providers since the old one didn't have good service here." That didn't explain, though, why Violet hadn't contacted him because he'd only switched two weeks ago. He was betting she'd been engaged longer than that.

Volleying glances between him and the booth with the bridal party, Eliza caught onto his arm, practically dragging him off the bar stool. "We have to talk—now," she said. "I'm so sorry about everything."

Kane didn't put up a fuss about her dragging him, but this was unnecessary. Especially the apology. It wasn't her fault that her sister was getting married.

"I've already heard about Violet," he assured her.

Eliza didn't respond to that other than mumbling the "I'm so sorry" again. She also just kept pulling him, and Kane didn't like the direction they were heading. Right toward the women's bathroom.

"The waitress told me about your sister," he repeated, hoping it would stop her. It didn't. In fact, Eliza didn't stop until she had him inside the ladies' room, and had shut the door.

"I didn't think you were still in the dark, not about that, anyway," she said, as if that explained everything. It didn't explain squat. "No one in this town would have kept that a secret from you."

Well, they hadn't after the fact, but he would have liked a heads-up even if it'd come from the gossip mill.

"Why'd you bring me in here?" Kane asked. "And since when did you start wearing dresses like that?"

All in all, that last one just wasn't a very good question, especially considering everything else that was going on. He followed it up with a comment that wasn't very good, either. "It makes you look like, well, a woman."

She glanced down at her dress. Then gave him a look that was anything but flat. Her left eyebrow lifted. "I *am* a woman. A twenty-eight-year-old one. You're the only man in Spring Hill who hasn't noticed that."

Well, he was sure noticing now.

Eliza had always been a looker, even as a kid. But she'd always been just that. A kid.

Until right this minute.

"You're really twenty-eight?" he asked. That was a year older than the last woman he'd gone out with in South Carolina. Then Kane remembered something really important he should be addressing. "Why are we in the ladies' room?"

"Yes, I'm twenty-eight. Only four years younger than you. And that's the reason we're in here."

Kane did a mental double take. "Say what?"

Eliza huffed. "I lied, all right! That's what I'm sorry about. I heard from Lucky McCord that you were getting out of the Air Force and moving back to try your hand at running the ranch. Most people thought you'd never actually return, since you've owned the place for over a year and had barely stepped foot on it."

"Because I had to finish up my military commitment."

"I know, and I kept telling folks that you'd be home, but I wasn't expecting you until next week."

"I finished up earlier at the base than planned." He stopped. "How'd you find out I was coming home today?" He no longer had family here, and Kane hadn't gotten around to telling Lucky or anyone else the exact day he'd be arriving, since he'd been so busy out-processing from the Air Force.

Another huff from her. Obviously, these were not questions she wanted to hear, but Kane was trying to make sense of it. And it was just the beginning of the things he needed to ask her.

"I went to your place to check on it, and there was an electrician there from San Antonio," she explained. "He said you'd wanted the house checked to make sure everything was working fine because you were moving back today." She huffed. "You know, it wouldn't have killed you to let someone know."

Heck, he never let anyone know that. Kane just showed up. He'd been doing that for years, and no one had complained. Not until now, anyway.

Since he wasn't getting anywhere with this discussion, he moved on to the next questions. "And what does any of this have to do with you lying? Better yet, what lie did you tell?"

"Lies," she corrected. Eliza groaned, squeezed her eyes shut a moment and leaned against the aqua-painted concrete-block wall. "God, I'm so sorry, but I told my sister that you and I had been texting and calling each other. And we do talk, remember?"

Yes, around Christmas Eliza had called to chat. It was June now. And, yes, they had also texted a couple of times since then, but both the calls and the texts had been about business. Kane often hired some of the hands at Eliza's family's ranch to keep the yard and pastures in shape at his own place. Eliza was the business manager there, so Kane went through her to get that done.

But why had Eliza told her sister about his needing the grass cut?

Kane tried to follow that through to some logical conclusion, but he couldn't come up with one. "Why the hell would you do that?"

"Because I could see that Violet was falling for Dax, and I didn't want there to be any obstacles."

He had to throw his hands up in the air. Not a good idea because he raked his fingers across her left breast. Nice breasts, too. Something he wished he hadn't noticed. He wished Eliza hadn't noticed his reaction, either, because a slightly heated look followed her sound of surprise.

Kane quickly got his mind back on the right track. And the right track certainly wasn't noticing or touching her breasts. "I'm not an obstacle. I'm her boyfriend."

Eliza had obviously practiced flat looks over the years because she gave him a good one. "You two saw each other when it was convenient. It was more of a habit than a real relationship, and you know it."

He didn't want to admit it. Even if it was true. "So what? I called Violet just a couple of months ago, and she didn't mention a word about Dax."

"You called her eight months ago," Eliza corrected.

Kane frowned. That was possibly true. Heck, had it really been that long?

"That's about the time she and Dax started dating," Eliza went on. "It wasn't love at first sight exactly, but it happened shortly afterward. And then they got engaged, and they hurried to put this wedding together because they didn't want to wait to get married."

And no one had told him. Of course, he wasn't exactly in the gossip loop since his best friend in Spring Hill, Lucky McCord, didn't spend much time here, either. Lucky was a bull rider on the rodeo circuit and was gone almost as much as Kane was.

"You could have let me know what was going on," Kane pointed out to her.

Eliza nodded. "I started to do that a couple of times, but then the lie kept snowballing. And you know that Violet has always wanted to marry a cowboy."

There weren't enough curse words for his response. "And what in Sam Hill am I—French toast?"

She looked at him, and for a moment he thought she was going to point out the obvious, that he was a fighter pilot. She didn't. "You're someone who hasn't been around very much, and my sister fell in love with another man. I lied to her because I wanted her to have an open path to finding the happiness she deserves."

Kane wished he could dispute at least one part of that. Any part. But, hell, he wanted Violet to be happy, too. He just didn't want her happy with another man. He was so glad he hadn't said that aloud, though, because it made him sound petty and selfish. He wasn't normally either of those things, but the shock and anger were getting the best of him.

And the confusion.

Because his mind was in a whirlwind, it took Kane a moment to pick through the whirl and process something Eliza had said.

"How'd the lie that you told keep snowballing?" he asked.

Eliza opened her mouth, closed it. Groaned. That groan was not a sound he wanted to hear, because Kane knew this had to be bad.

"How?" he pressed. But Eliza didn't get a chance to answer because the bathroom door flew open, and a woman came in.

Violet.

She was still wearing that veil, and she halted in midstep, literally with her foot still in the air. There was just a moment of surprise on her face before she smiled.

And then giggled.

That giggle wasn't something Kane wanted to hear, either. Not just because it sounded drunk, but it also seemed as if Violet was thrilled about something. Since he was in the ladies' room with what had to be a very confused look on his face, Kane couldn't see anything for her to be thrilled about.

Violet hurried to them, gathering them both into her arms, and she kissed them on their cheeks. "Kane, I'm so glad you're here." When Violet pulled back, there were tears in her eyes.

Happy tears, Kane was sure of it. But he couldn't figure out why they were there. He had a really bad feeling, though, that this had something to do with the snowballing.

"I'm in seventh heaven for both of you," Violet went on. "When Eliza told me you two were seeing each other, it just made my life complete. I mean, it was long over between us, and I wanted you to move on. It's nice that you moved on in my sister's direction."

Kane had to shake his head. "Seeing each other?" Kane questioned.

Eliza had mentioned texting but not *seeing*. He figured there were other things she'd left out when Violet's happy tears continued. "I just know you two are going to have the perfect life together."

"Say what?" he growled.

Violet slapped her hand over her mouth as if she'd just blurted out a huge secret. Well, it was a secret to Kane all right. A secret that soon became a whole lot clearer when Eliza put her arms around him.

"Violet, I didn't say that Kane and I were engaged," Eliza pointed out.

Violet winked. "Not yet, anyway. But since you're in love, that's the next step, right?"

The blood rushed to Kane's head. Crap on a cracker. This wasn't snowballing. This was an avalanche.

One that continued.

Violet caught onto both his and Eliza's arms and practically threw them together. "Go ahead, Kane. Kiss the woman you love."

CHAPTER TWO

ELIZA FELT LIKE an idiot. Man, oh man, what had she done?

Kane was no doubt about to ask her the same thing, along with blowing her lies to smithereens, but Violet put a stop to him saying much of anything. He managed a grunt before Violet pushed them together at the exact moment when Eliza was looking up at him. And Kane was looking down at her.

Or rather glaring at her.

Violet finished pushing, and Kane's mouth landed on Eliza's for what had to be the stiffest kiss ever. One of the best kisses ever, too.

Here, all these years she'd fantasized about kissing Kane, and now they were doing exactly that even if it wasn't what Kane wanted to do. Even with that extreme limitation, it certainly lived up to expectations, but it was part of the snowball of lies.

Kane didn't let the scalding kiss go on. After just a few seconds, he pulled back, and his glare got significantly worse.

"Is there something you want to say to your sister?" he asked Eliza.

This was easy. No, she didn't want to admit to the white lie that had turned into a series of whoppers. But she had to fess up. Now that Violet was engaged, maybe it wouldn't even matter.

"She doesn't have to tell me anything," Violet blurted out before Eliza could get her mouth working. "It's just so nice to see both of you happy." She glanced at the stalls, hobbled around a little on her toes. "Now, if you don't mind getting out of here, I have to pee. Like right now," she added when they didn't budge.

Kane volleyed glances at them while Violet continued to hobble around. Just when Eliza was about to confess all, Violet hurried past them and into one of the stalls. Despite there being a door on the stall, Kane bolted out as if someone had scalded him.

"We'll talk when you're finished," Eliza told her sister. She followed Kane into the bar, not near anyone, though, because Kane pulled her to the side.

"When she comes out, you tell her the truth," he demanded just as Eliza gave him another "I'm so sorry."

"The truth," he emphasized. "And don't apologize again. It won't help. The only thing that'll fix this is to tell Violet the way things really are."

"I will." She paused. "But you don't think it could wait until after the wedding? Just hear me out," she added when Kane growled out a no. "It's just for a couple of days, and then I'll tell her the truth when she's back from her honeymoon. I don't want anything to put a damper on her mood."

"And this would?" He cursed, and it seemed to take him a couple of seconds and another round of profanity to find the words he wanted to say. "Why the hell would Violet care if we're together or not?"

Uh-oh.

He was not going to want to hear this, but she'd already told so many lies that she had to go with the truth. "Violet knows I've always had a thing for you. And she was worried about you, that you would take her engagement hard. Worried about me, too, because I broke up with my boyfriend. She thought this would be the perfect fix for both of us."

Kane was staring at her as if she were on fire.

"It's true," she insisted. "You must have known I had a thing for you."

Judging from the next round of profanity, apparently he hadn't known that after all. Well, he certainly knew it now.

"You were a kid. I wasn't," he argued.

"*Was* a kid." That was all she needed to say.

He frowned and glanced at the bathroom again. He was no doubt wishing Violet would hurry so they could have the air clearing that Eliza didn't especially want. Not until after the wedding at least. Then maybe Kane and she could quietly "break up." Violet and her family would know the truth, but maybe she could save a little face without everyone in Spring Hill hearing about it.

"Why did you split with your boyfriend?" he asked.

Kane was probably just killing time with that question, but it threw her. Mainly because she didn't want to tell him the truth but definitely didn't want to lie, either. She'd filled her lie quota for a lifetime.

"I, uh, thought it was for the best," Eliza settled for saying. Since she was going to have to fess up to Violet, there was no need to fully fess up to Kane as well about her ex, Brett.

Judging from the way his mouth went into a flat line, he wasn't buying that vague response. However, before he could press for more that Eliza didn't want to give him, the front door of the bar opened.

And Dax walked in.

As Eliza had done, Dax stopped a moment, his gaze combing over the dimly lit pub, but it didn't take him long to see Kane and her. Dax smiled. Or rather the smile started to form on his mouth, but it froze. Maybe because he remembered that Kane might want to pulverize him. But the smile returned when he saw how close Kane and she were standing.

"So, it's true," Dax said, when he reached them. He pulled Kane into a man hug, hooking his arm around Eliza and squeezing her in those beefy arms of his. Two hugs in one day.

Hugs based on lies.

Dax took Eliza's hand and dropped a set of keys into her palm. "Violet forgot these, and she'll need them to let herself into the house tonight. Violet and I went ahead and moved in together," he added to Kane. "She won't be in any shape to drive, I'm sure, so somebody will need to drop her off."

"I've got that taken care of—" Those were the only words Eliza managed to get in.

"Figured you had. Don't worry. I won't be driving, either. Rico fixed up everything in that department, I'm sure. You remember Rico," Dax said to Kane.

Kane nodded. Of course he remembered him. They'd all gone to school together, and Rico Callahan was a hand at the McCord Ranch, where Dax also worked.

"Listen, Dax." Eliza wiggled out of his grip. "There's something I have to tell you."

"No need. I can see it written all over your face. You're in love." He lifted his shoulder. "But then you've always been a little in love with Kane. That's why you gave that guy from college his marching orders."

Well, so much for her not wanting to fess up about that. Kane stared at her with an "is that true?" expression, but Eliza just sighed and shrugged. Apparently, this was going to be the day for a serious air clearing. But it didn't continue. Violet came out of the bathroom, and she was still in giddy giggle mode because she hurried to her fiancé and kissed him. Dax kissed her right back, and it went on way too long, considering they had an audience.

And one of those audience members was shell-shocked. Maybe Kane was reacting to the kiss or everything that he'd just heard, but his "is that true?" expression turned into "what the hell?" Of course, he'd had that expression a lot since this ordeal had started.

"Sorry," Dax said when Violet and he finally broke the lip-lock. "Every time I see her, I just have to kiss her."

And put his hands on her. Eliza had grown accustomed to seeing them together like this, but she was betting it would take Kane a while to get used to it. If they had a while, that was.

Eliza could see this playing out in three bad ways. Violet would be so upset when she learned the truth that it would spoil the wedding. Scenario two was that Kane would just leave town and never come back. Scenario number three was that once everyone heard about the lies, she would be branded the town's liar, along with people calling her pathetic.

The last one was pretty much the best of those choices.

"I was just about to tell Kane that I was worried,"

Dax said to Violet. "I wasn't sure how he'd take us getting engaged. But I can tell he's fine with it."

No, he wasn't, but Kane stayed mum. And he glared at Eliza again, giving her a not-so-subtle clue to start explaining.

"So, what did you want to talk to me about?" Violet asked her, but her sister continued talking before Eliza could answer. Violet snapped her fingers as if remembering something. "The family dinner. Did you get a chance to tell Kane about that?"

Eliza shook her head, and once more Violet continued without giving her a chance to speak. Her sister was clearly past the giddy stage now. "We're having a family dinner tomorrow night, and we want you there."

It must have taken Kane a moment to realize Violet was talking to him because his scowl morphed to a blank stare before he shook his head. "I can't—"

"I won't take no for an answer," Violet interrupted, and she plopped a sisterly kiss on Kane's cheek. "Be there at seven. I might have recovered from the bachelorette party by then."

Just when Eliza didn't think there could be any other complications to this mess, one more walked in.

Charlene Fletcher.

Even though Charlene was a rancher, she was dressed like one of the exotic dancers at the strip joint just outside town. Low-cut dress, nail-me-now heels and a hungry smile that she aimed at Kane. Since Charlene didn't seem surprised to see him there, that meant her cousin, the bartender, Frankie, had likely called her to let her know.

"Kane," Charlene said, her voice a seductive growl.

"I'm here to seal the deal on those cows you're buying from me."

"Cows, my butt," Eliza mumbled a little louder than she'd intended.

Charlene was going to love the fact that Kane was now unattached. And she'd love even more that Eliza would be dubbed the town liar. There was a history between Charlene and her. Also between Violet and Charlene. Simply put, the woman had tried to bed every single man that Eliza and her sister had ever dated. Eliza had considered going out with a slimeball just so Charlene would eventually get a dose of that slimeball, too.

Charlene sauntered closer and touched her index finger to Kane's chest. "Maybe you have some time right now." It wasn't a question, and Charlene slid a cool glance at Violet. "Since I'm sure Violet and Dax have plenty of things to do. Eliza, as well," she added like an afterthought.

"Eliza does indeed have things to do," Violet piped up. "Now that her honey's back in town, I suspect she'll be plenty busy."

Charlene pulled back her shoulders as if she'd just snapped to attention. "What honey?"

Violet smiled, slipped her arm around Kane. "This guy. Eliza and he are, well—" she lowered her voice to a whisper "—hot to trot for each other. Isn't it wonderful?"

Clearly, Charlene didn't think it was wonderful at all. Her mouth squeezed together as if she'd sucked a basket of lemons. "Since when?" Charlene snapped.

Now, this would have been a really good time to come clean since it might cost Kane the sale of those cows, but Eliza let the old rivalry kick in, and she didn't say a word. Neither did Kane. There wasn't an old rivalry between Charlene and him, but maybe he wanted a break from a barracuda like her while he got his footing.

"For months now," Violet answered. "I'm surprised you hadn't heard."

There was a reason for that. Eliza had asked that the lie stay limited to family and Dax. Of course, now that Kane was back, no way would Violet keep quiet, and the couple rumor would catch fire. Then the big news that the couple part wasn't real after all would soon follow that fire.

Violet giggled. "Everybody who knows is thrilled for them."

Not everybody. The look Charlene gave Eliza was sharp enough to cut galvanized steel.

"I'll be in touch with you," Kane said to the woman. "About a business deal I want to discuss with you."

"Yes, I'll be in touch," Charlene repeated, her voice as sharp as the look she was still giving Eliza. The look lingered a moment before Charlene finally left to head to the bar.

"Somebody's got her nose out of joint," Violet remarked. "And she'll dislocate her hips if she keeps swinging that way." That resulted in another of her sister's giggles.

"Violet, get back over here," Misty Reagan, the bridesmaid, called out. "You're missing your own party, and you'll have plenty of time to fool around with Dax on the honeymoon."

"Sorry, but Eliza and I need to go." Violet looked at Kane. "This is just stop one. Eliza hired us a limo, and we're hitting some bars in San Antonio."

Violet kissed Dax. "You and Kane have fun at your bachelor party. Keep him away from strippers," she added to Kane with a wink.

Kane was still shaking his head, but Dax took hold of his arm. "Come on. Let's head over to the party. We can do some catching up along the way, and you can tell me all about how you fell for Violet's kid sister."

CHAPTER THREE

KANE WAS A bona fide liar now. One with a serious hangover that was likely punishment for the lying.

He located the biggest mug he could find in his kitchen and filled it to the brim with coffee. The coffee was stale, a package he'd bought over a year ago when he'd come home on leave, but stale would have to do. He needed the caffeine hit to try to ease the throbbing in his head. Or maybe that would only make him more alert and aware of the throbbing. If so, he'd have to risk it.

Cursing the headache and his decision to attend Dax's bachelor party, Kane took his coffee to the front door so he could go outside and start surveying the land. Something he'd intended to do the day before, but he'd gotten distracted.

And blindsided.

Damn Eliza and her lies. And now she'd made him a part of those lies as well, since Kane hadn't set Dax or the other partygoers straight. Worse, he wasn't sure he wanted to set Dax straight. The guy was happier than Kane had ever seen him, and it would have taken a special kind of cow dung to stomp on that happiness. No, if there was stomping to be done, it needed to come from Eliza.

Kane stepped onto the front porch. And damn near killed himself when he tripped over something.

Or rather someone.

Speak of the devil. It was Eliza.

Amid all his cursing and his spilled coffee, she shrieked like a banshee and scrambled to get to her feet. She was still wearing that smoking-hot red dress and heels from last night, and judging from her position and appearance, she'd slept on his porch.

"What the heck are you doing out here?" Kane was so sorry he'd spoken in such a loud voice because it roared through his already aching head.

It must have roared through Eliza's, too, because she winced, took his coffee and gulped some down. "I had the limo driver drop me off…" She checked her watch but had to move her arm several times while she tried to focus. "About two hours ago."

He checked her watch as well, and by his calculations, that meant she'd gotten here at four in the morning. Not exactly a normal visiting hour.

"I knocked on the door," she added, "but when you didn't answer, I decided to sit out here and wait. I must have fallen asleep." Eliza handed him back his coffee. "I need to wash up, and then we'll talk. Or rather I'll grovel while you talk. I want to hear all about Dax's reaction when you told him the truth about us."

Kane was actually glad that she stumbled off toward the bathroom so he'd have a moment to figure out what he was going to say. A moment to get more coffee, too, and since it appeared that Eliza needed it as badly as he did, he poured her a cup and put on another pot.

Eliza didn't take long with the washing up, though he did hear the shower going for a couple of minutes.

When she came out, he was ready to get that conversation started and do some groveling of his own.

But someone sucked all the air from the room, maybe from the entire planet.

Yes, Eliza was definitely a twenty-eight-year-old woman. A hot one. Of course, he had noticed that in the pub, but he was noticing it again.

The ends of her hair were damp and clung to the tops of that dress she'd put back on. Her face was practically glowing despite the fact she'd washed off her makeup. How could someone look that amazing with a hangover?

"Thanks." She took the coffee from him and gulped down more. "The limo driver will be here soon. No way did I want to walk home in these heels so I told him to come back for me." The gulping lasted a few seconds, and then she seemed to do a double take after seeing the look on his face. "What?"

It would have been a good time for him to say something. Anything. A good time, too, for him to have a different expression, one that didn't cause Eliza to smile. Because right now he was clearly gawking at her, and she was clearly pleased about that. Probably because it confirmed that he knew she was a woman and not his ex-girlfriend's kid sister.

"Yes," she said, her smile still in place. Heck, her mouth was hot, as well.

Kane quickly tried to fix his expression, but he doubted there was a way to take the heat from his eyes. Eliza went to him, and in those heels she was only a couple of inches shorter than he was. Just the right height for her to lean in and brush a kiss on his cheek.

"Thanks for that, too." Her breath was warm, smelled like coffee and felt like something he wanted more of on his face. "It soothes my ego a little after everything that went on in Calhoun's Pub." She paused. "I hope this didn't screw over your deal with Charlene."

He also hoped that, but you never knew with Charlene. She wanted him in her bed, and the deal might have hinged on her thinking that could happen. It wouldn't. Ever. Charlene wasn't his type.

Apparently at the moment, though, Eliza was. Because his body was still reacting to her.

"I hope this didn't screw up a lot of things for you," Eliza added.

Kane considered getting into that, but since he was still trying to wrap his mind around his thoughts, he needed more coffee. Needed to put some distance between Eliza and this heat that she was generating in his body. He took his coffee and the frenzy she was creating behind his jeans' zipper to the back porch. She followed him, but she kept a safe distance while he looked over the ranch.

There was plenty to see.

He owned about three hundred acres, not big by Texas standards, but most of it was fenced and ready for him to bring in the livestock he wanted to raise. There was a pond just in the distance, two barns and a corral. Not perfect, not by a long shot, but everything looked a lot better than he'd thought it would.

"I had someone come over and check the fences and such," Eliza told him.

Ah, that explained why things weren't falling apart. "Thanks."

"Well, I didn't do it totally out of the goodness of my heart. One of the hands, Simon Jenkins, has a sick daughter who's been in and out of the hospital, and he needed the extra money. I'll bill you."

Good. He thanked her again, and part of that thanks was because she'd obviously kept an eye on the place for him even when he hadn't specifically asked her to do it.

Kane drank more coffee, and once he could feel the cobwebs starting to clear out, he figured it was time to confess to what had gone on when he'd talked to Dax.

"If you're looking for horses," Eliza went on before he could say anything, "my father's selling a lot of his. He's cutting back on work, and that means there'll be a shortage for the McCord Ranch. Logan McCord would rather buy local when it comes to horses."

That was good to hear. Logan was Lucky's twin brother, and Kane preferred to do business with someone he knew. Too bad he couldn't get the cows from Logan as well, but the McCords ran a brokerage business, which meant they dealt in bulk. To start out, Kane only wanted the fifty head of cows that Charlene was to sell him. Horses were a different matter. Even for a place the size of the McCord Ranch, Logan would only need a dozen or so horses at most in any given year. Kane could easily supply that once he had the ranch up and running.

"So, why is your father cutting back?" Kane asked. "He's, what…only in his midfifties, since your folks had Violet and you when they were young?"

Eliza suddenly got very interested in staring down into her coffee cup. "I think he's just ready for a change."

Kane thought there might be more to it than that. Or not. He was certainly in the "ready for a change" mode, and that's why he'd gotten out of the Air Force and returned home to his cowboy roots.

"How'd Dax take the news of me lying about us?" she asked.

She was still staring at her coffee so Kane put his fingers beneath her chin, lifting it so that they could make eye contact. Kane was ready to admit that he'd chickened out, that Dax still believed they were a couple. But he felt that punch of heat again.

Maybe it was the hangover or that red dress. Maybe it was the fact that Eliza suddenly looked good enough to taste.

And that's what he did.

Kane leaned in and kissed her. Not a peck on the cheek like the one she'd given him earlier or the hesitant kiss in the ladies' room at the pub. No. This was a real kiss, and even though he felt some hesitancy—or maybe that was shock—in Eliza's stiff muscles, it didn't take long for her to give in. She relaxed, made a silky sound of pleasure and kissed him right back.

All in all, that was not a good thing.

He was still battling the cloudy head and the fire she was creating, and kissing her was a confirmation of a couple of things he already knew. One, Eliza was indeed a woman. And two, he was damn attracted to her.

Kane went with blaming it on the dress again, but that was just a reminder that she would probably look even better out of that dress. Especially since the kiss had moved past the mere hot stage.

And speaking of hot, they were both still juggling their coffees as they tried to get closer to each other. Kane remembered that when he sloshed more of it on himself, and it was a good cue for him to either toss the coffee or take a moment to consider what the hell he was doing.

He pulled back, dragging in a much-needed breath. Eliza did the same, and she stared at him, repeating the "what the heck?" expression with her bunched-up forehead. Since her face was flushed from the kiss, it somewhat diminished that question because "what the heck" was pretty darn clear. They'd kissed each other's lights out.

"It was a test," he said. That was more or less the truth. He had wanted to know if he could pull off what he was about to suggest. But it was also shallower than that. He'd really just wanted to kiss her.

"I didn't tell Dax," he admitted. "I let him keep on believing the two of us are together because it didn't feel right to tell him something like that when he was gushing about the woman he loves." Then Kane picked through his cluttered thoughts and remembered there was a second component to this.

Violet.

Heck.

"How did your sister react when you told her the truth?" he blurted out.

Because obviously when Dax and Violet compared notes of the conversations they'd had with Eliza and him, then Dax was going to know Kane had joined the "liar, liar, pants on fire" club.

Eliza's attention went back to her coffee. The way she was staring at it, it held the secrets of the universe. "By the time I got Violet alone, she was already drunk. I told her, but there's no way she'll remember anything I said. When I had the limo driver take her home, she didn't even remember there'd been a bachelorette party."

So, their secret was safe, even though *safe* wasn't exactly the right word for it. More like a festering pile of falsehoods that would soon catch up with them. After all, they were in Spring Hill, where secrets had a very short shelf life. Usually much less than the two days until the wedding. Of course, if anyone had just seen him kissing Eliza, then the lies wouldn't have looked so much like a festering pile as much as the scalding hot truth.

"Are you mad I didn't tell Violet before she got drunk?" Eliza asked. She was nibbling on her bottom lip now, her nerves showing, but it was a flashing neon sign to Kane's libido that he wanted to be nibbling on her lip, too.

"No. In fact I think it's for the best."

Since she was giving him the same kind of stunned look he'd given her the night before, Kane figured he needed to add something to that.

"It's best *for the time being*," he amended. "Until after the wedding. And then we don't have to spill the whole truth. We can just let everyone believe that we gave this romance thing a whirl and then broke up."

She stayed quiet a moment. "But what about your cow deal with Charlene?" she asked.

It was a better question than the one he figured was on her mind: "But what about that kiss?" It was certainly on his mind.

Kane shrugged. "I doubt she'll sell them to anyone else before the wedding day. After that, you and I can split." And then he could dodge Charlene's advances.

Eliza looked up at him, did a few more moments of lip nibbling. "What if we do give this romance thing a whirl?"

Since the heat was still zinging between them, it was

certainly timely. And hard to answer. In some ways, she was still forbidden fruit.

Which didn't help the mental argument he was having with himself.

Because forbidden fruit suddenly seemed like the exact kind of *thing* that he wanted. Especially right now. At this very moment.

Kane didn't think he could explain away another kiss by calling it a test. After all, there were only so many tests a man needed before he got an erection. Which he was working on just by looking at Eliza.

His silence must have dragged on too long because Eliza did some dragging of her own. She caught onto the front of his shirt, gathering up the fabric in her fist, and she yanked him to her.

And she kissed him.

There it was again. That kick of pleasure. That taste. Yeah, this whole forbidden-fruit thing was making him nuts.

Blindly groping behind him, Kane located the window ledge, where he put his coffee so that it would free up his hands to get her closer to him. Unfortunately, her cup was still in the way, and since he wanted to save his groping skills for Eliza, he tossed her cup into the backyard. She took full advantage of that and used her free hands to make that whole getting-closer thing happen.

Her breasts against his chest.

Her other parts against his. And they were the right parts, too.

The kiss went on and on, just the way he liked his kisses, especially when paired with all that body-to-body contact. It went on so long that Kane was ready to drag her back into the kitchen. But he held on to the small thread of reason that was trying to fight through the lust and the haze.

The thread that told him he really needed to rethink this.

And that's why he stepped back.

She stared at him, her face flushed, her breathing way too fast, and even though Kane didn't say a word, Eliza seemed to understand what was going on in his head.

"You think if we have sex, it'll mean something," she said. "Something more than just sex."

Bingo. Sex with Eliza would come with strings. Whopping big ones. They'd have to live in this small town, just a few miles from each other, and even casual sex might not stay so casual. Not in her mind, anyway. He'd managed a relationship like that with Violet, but Kane didn't think he could pull it off with Eliza.

"Maybe you're right," she admitted.

That didn't help. He was hoping she would come up with an argument that would convince Kane that they could do this. Of course, his erection was cheering for that particular option.

"But maybe you're wrong," Eliza added.

Yeah. There it was. The argument he'd been waiting for. It was a weak one. No doubt about it, but it was something his erection wanted to hear. It was his brain that was having some trouble with it.

"The limo's here," she said.

Kane hadn't heard a thing, but then his heartbeat was pounding in his ears. He went to the side of the porch so he could see the front yard and sure enough, the limo was sitting there with the engine running. And the limo driver wasn't the only person out there. He saw Lucky

McCord riding up on a horse. Lucky had another sad-
dled horse that he was leading by the reins.

Eliza stared at him, and Kane was pretty sure she
was waiting for him to respond to the "maybe you're
wrong." He didn't, because he wasn't sure what to say.
But then Eliza didn't say anything, either. She gave
him a sneaky little smile and hauled him back to her
for another kiss.

Mercy, this one was just as hot as the others, and
after a few seconds, Kane was about to ditch his argument to halt this and send the limo driver and Lucky
on their way.

But Eliza stepped back. "Maybe you're wrong," she
repeated.

With that smile still on her face, she strolled away.
She stopped, though, when Lucky got off his horse, and
she made a detour over to him. Kane couldn't hear what
they said, but Lucky flashed his panty-dropping smile,
Eliza laughed, and she kissed Lucky on the cheek. She
gave Kane a wave before she got into the limo, and it
drove away.

"So, it's true," Lucky greeted.

His friend didn't need to explain what he meant.
Lucky was grinning in that guy sort of way because he
was certain that Kane had just finished off a night of
sex with Eliza. But Kane wasn't thinking of sex right
now. Well, not sex between Eliza and him, anyway.

"Please tell me that you didn't sleep with Eliza,"
Kane growled. It wasn't a friendly tone for his best
friend.

Lucky's grin turned into a chuckle. "No. Eliza falls
into the kid-sister category for me."

Kane instantly regretted the growl because Lucky

had seen right through it. Actually, what Lucky had seen was the reaction of a jealous man.

"I thought she fell into that category for me, too," Kane admitted after he cursed.

Now Lucky laughed. "Yeah, right. You sure could have fooled me, because I always thought you were fighting to keep your hands off her."

Kane frowned and was about to say "no way," but heck, maybe Lucky was right. Still, Kane had a beef with his friend. "Why didn't you tell me Violet was getting married?"

"I haven't been in town much. Logan," he said as if that explained it.

And it did. Lucky didn't always see eye to eye with his twin brother, mainly because Logan was always trying to suck him back into the family business. Kane couldn't understand why Lucky was so mule-headed about not doing that, but that wasn't his rodeo, wasn't his bulls. He had his own bulls and bullshit to worry about.

"One of the ranch hands filled me in on Violet, Eliza and you this morning," Lucky added.

So, that meant it was already all over town. Not that Kane had expected anything after Charlene and the others had seen Eliza and him at the pub.

"Of course, Eliza always had the hots for you," Lucky went on. "Any fool could have seen that."

Kane hadn't, and that put him several notches beneath the fool level. Sheez. He was learning crap about himself that he wasn't sure he'd wanted to learn.

"Guess you two finally gave up fighting it and got together after all," Lucky added.

That only deepened Kane's frown. "We're not together. Eliza told her sister we were so that Violet wouldn't feel bad about being with Dax."

Lucky just stared at him and glanced at Kane's shirt. "Spilled coffee. One cup in the yard, another on the windowsill that's about to fall off. Plus, Eliza looked as if she'd just been kissed by a guy who hadn't had a morning shave. You, my friend, have stubble."

"Hell. When did you become Sherlock Holmes?"

"A three-year-old could have figured this out. So, you want to tell me what's really going on between Eliza and you?"

"No." Because Kane didn't know what was going on. Didn't want to analyze it, either. "Why are you here, anyway? Don't get me wrong. I'm glad to see you, but it's early."

Lucky shrugged. "I just got back this morning from a rodeo. Thought I'd ride out and check your fences so they'd be ready when you get those Angus you want to buy. I brought an extra horse in case you wanted to do that with me."

Kane had already cursed enough for the morning, but he wanted to add some bad words aimed at himself. "Thanks. I would like to check the fences. And thanks for keeping an eye on the place while I've been gone."

Another shrug. "Eliza does more than I do. I have a theory that she takes care of this place because it's her way of taking care of you. Nonsexually, of course. Although it appears she's working on the sexual part now that you're home to stay."

"How the hell did we go from fences back to sex?" Kane snarled.

Lucky jabbed him with his elbow. "It always goes

back to sex. If you're thinking you can resist Eliza, then you're not thinking straight."

That was probably true, but Kane didn't want to discuss Eliza and sex in the same sentence. Especially after that stubble-irritating kiss they'd just shared.

"Eliza and I can come clean after the wedding," Kane explained. "After that, I'll have time to get my footing. And it's not as if I don't have things to do. I'll be so busy rebuilding this ranch that I won't have time to even think about Eliza."

As if on cue, both horses whinnied.

Lucky grinned. "You can lie to yourself. Lie to me. Heck, you can even lie to Eliza. But horses know bullshit when they smell it."

CHAPTER FOUR

THERE WERE A bunch of hungover people at the dinner table, and Eliza was one of them. The other three were Dax, Violet and Kane. The only people without the obvious signs of overindulgence were her mom and dad.

In hindsight, it had been a really bad idea to plan a family dinner the night after her sister's bachelorette party. Especially when that party hadn't ended until the wee hours of the morning.

And especially since there was a secret dangling over her head.

The relationship ruse.

Because of it, she had to be on her best behavior and not let anything slip. Kane was on the same high alert while seated right next to her at the dinner table. But they were the sole ones who knew that the long, lingering looks he kept giving her were as fake as the smiles Eliza kept doling out. She was happy for her sister and Dax, but once they were married and off on their honeymoon, there'd be no looks from Kane. No kisses on his porch.

That wouldn't stop her from having dirty thoughts about him, but apparently he was not going to take her up on her suggestion that it might not be so wrong for them to do more kissing. Which, of course, was an offer that would lead to sex.

"It's good to see you all so happy," her dad said. He'd "dressed up" for the occasion and was wearing what he called his Sunday jeans. If he owned dress pants, Eliza had never seen him wear them. Even for the wedding, he'd likely have on jeans and a suit coat.

Eliza pasted on another smile, which made her face hurt. Judging from the wincing that Kane did, he was in the same boat. Maybe that's the reason he hadn't taken her up on her offer to make their relationship a real one. Or called her. Or given her any indication whatsoever if that porch kiss had meant anything.

Her mother wasn't smiling, but she was watching them in that way that only a suspicious mother could manage. It was hard to tell what was going on in her mind, especially recently, but it was possible her mom was picking up on whatever nonverbal cues Kane and she were giving off. Cues that hinted they weren't the happy couple they were pretending to be.

"Heard you'll be buying some cows from Charlene Fletcher," her father said to Kane.

"Maybe. She's waffling so the deal might not happen."

This was the first Eliza was hearing of it, so that meant it hadn't hit the gossip mill yet. Nor was it a surprise. Charlene was using those cows as leverage to get Kane into bed.

"You might want to talk to Logan," her father suggested.

Kane nodded. "Already did, a couple of hours ago. He doesn't have any small herds right now, but he'll keep a lookout. I'm just anxious to get started."

Judging from the way her mother covered up a small

cough, she might have thought Kane was referring to more than just cows.

"Is there something you want to tell us?" her mother asked.

Eliza hoped that question wasn't directed at her. But no such luck. Her mother was looking right at her.

"No, nothing," Eliza said. It was an easy answer. The less she said, the less she'd have to lie. Or risk exacerbating the stabbing pain in her head.

Her mother flexed her eyebrows. "Well, you didn't come home until after six this morning. Violet got to Dax's around four because he texted me to let me know she'd made it in all right."

Since Eliza lived in a cottage just about thirty yards from her parents' house, it wouldn't have been hard for her mother to notice the limo dropping her off. Which meant her mother might be fishing for some kind of admission that Eliza had spent the night with Kane. Her mom wouldn't see that as fodder for a shotgun engagement, but she might be asking Kane's intentions.

"She was with me," Kane volunteered.

"I see," her mother said. Her father pretended to be oblivious to the conversation. He probably didn't want to know that his grown daughters did such things.

"You stayed the night?" Violet asked her. She attempted a smile, winced again.

"A few hours this morning," Eliza corrected.

And the room fell silent. Then something happened that Eliza certainly wasn't expecting. Tears filled her mother's eyes.

"They're happy tears, I promise," her mother quickly assured her. "It's just when you broke up with Brett, I thought maybe you were chasing a dream that wasn't meant for you."

Oh, God. Her mother hadn't just said that, had she?

Yes, she had, and she just kept on going.

"I mean, I felt responsible because I thought maybe you were in the 'seize the day' frame of mind because you realized life was short. And I knew you'd always had a crush on Kane, but I had no idea it would ever work out between you. I can see now, though, that you were right to break up with the wrong man so you could go after what you really wanted."

Eliza mentally repeated that "oh, God."

Her mother didn't seem to notice what had to be a shell-shocked look on Eliza's face. Maybe because her happy tears had clouded her eyes. Maybe also because everyone had finished eating, and she stood to start clearing the table. Eliza stood, too, to help, but Kane stepped in front of her.

"We need to, uh, talk," he whispered.

It seemed like a good time for another "oh, God."

"I'll be back to help you in just a minute," Eliza told her mother.

"Take your time," Dax insisted. He winked at Kane and her. "I'll do the dishes."

Dax probably thought Kane was carting her off to a kissing session, but Eliza figured that was the last thing on his mind right now. Not with the juicy little detail her mother had just tossed out there. Since she didn't want her family to hear this, Eliza took the lead and motioned for Kane to follow her to the front porch.

"You broke up with your boyfriend to be with me?" Kane asked the moment they were outside. "And what was all that 'seize the day' stuff about? Why would your mother feel responsible for any of this?"

Figuring she'd need it, Eliza took a deep breath and decided how much of this she should tell him. Since there'd already been too many lies, she went with the whole truth.

"Yes," she admitted. Judging from his flat look, he wanted slightly more than that. "I ended things with my old boyfriend because I thought I'd give it one last shot to be with you."

Obviously, he still wanted more because he made a circling motion for her to continue.

She sank down onto the porch swing and hoped she could get through this without tears. They wouldn't be of the happy variety, either. Not with the emotions still raw and too close to the surface.

"My mother has breast cancer," she explained. "She's had the surgery and the treatments. That's why she's so thin."

He shook his head, cursed softly. "I noticed the weight loss, but since I hadn't heard anything about her being sick, I just thought she'd been on a diet."

"She didn't want anyone in town to know. I'm not sure why. But she's going for her treatments in San Antonio."

Kane sat down beside her. "Will she be all right?"

"Her odds are good. The treatment seems to be working." She swallowed hard, trying to ease the lump in her throat. Eliza wanted to add more, but she needed a minute to compose herself.

"I'm sorry," he said, slipping his hand over hers.

Eliza appreciated that more than he would ever know. She'd been through an emotional wringer with her mom's health, but Kane had a way of easing the pain with just a simple touch.

"Seize the day," he repeated. "I get it now. Is that also the reason for Dax and Violet's hasty wedding?"

Eliza nodded. "We both just realized how short life can be. And Violet really does love Dax, and he loves her."

Kane nodded. "Yeah, I can see that. But it was a gamble for you to break up with your boyfriend. You guys had been together for—"

"I didn't love him," she interrupted. "I wanted more."

There. She'd said what she wanted to say. Almost. But she should have just admitted that "more" was "Kane." Or maybe it wasn't necessary. When Kane looked at her, she could see that he got it.

He cursed. Groaned. Scrubbed his hand over his face.

Eliza decided to give him an out. "Look, I don't expect anything from you. I broke up with Brett knowing full well that nothing might ever happen between us. I just didn't want to go on, well, settling. So, no pressure on your part."

Kane cursed again. "I kissed you. That's pressure."

She supposed in a way it was, so Eliza went with a second out. "We got caught up in the moment, in a hangover haze."

He nodded as if giving that some thought. If he truly wanted an out, she'd just handed him one, and it was right there for the taking—

Or not.

Because Kane cursed again, turned to her, pulled her into his arms and kissed her.

Eliza wasn't sure who was more shocked because

both of them made sounds of surprise. Sounds that got trapped in the kiss. Actually her hand got trapped, too, between Kane's chest and her breasts, but Eliza didn't move it. Instead, she turned her palm to his chest and inched in even closer so that it would make it easier to deepen the kiss.

And deepen it he did.

Oh, my. He was so good at this.

Despite the heart-tugging conversation they'd just had, all of that hurt vanished. Kane was apparently the cure for plenty of things. Not the cure for the tug below her belly, though.

That only got worse.

He slid his hand around the back of her neck, pulling her even closer. Not that he had to put up much of an effort to do that because Eliza wanted to be closer. And somehow, the fingers on her trapped hand worked their way into the gaps between the buttonholes of his shirt. Finger foreplay. It didn't have nearly the effect that the scalding kiss did, but touching his bare skin took her from the tug stage to needing much, much more.

And Kane gave her more.

He kept on kissing her, kept on moving against her until she was certain the planet had spun out of the galaxy. When he pulled back, he left her with that raging fire that was mixed with the dreamy feel of pleasure.

"You want to do something stupid?" he asked.

It took her a moment to get her vocal cords working. "If it involves more of this."

"It does. Do you want to go back to my place and see just how stupid we can get?"

CHAPTER FIVE

YEAH, THIS DEFINITELY fell into the stupid category. And the sad part about it? Kane had plenty of time to change his mind in the minutes that followed his offer to Eliza.

Minutes that didn't do anything to dull the stupidity.

Of course, Eliza was only adding to it.

After they said a hasty goodbye to her parents and Dax and Violet, they hurried out of there while trying not to look as if they were hurrying. But Kane doubted they were fooling anyone.

Eliza didn't help with any attempt to rethink this plan. That's because she started kissing him the moment they got into his truck. He had to hand it to her. It was hard to get a seat belt to stretch that far, but she somehow managed it, along with landing some of those kisses in the very spots that made him forget all about rethinking and stupidity.

There was a definite urgency to her kissing, and speed seemed to matter here. It was as if they were suddenly starved for each other. Strange, since Kane hadn't felt himself burning for her until he'd seen her the night before at the pub.

That was partly true, anyway.

Deep down, he'd always been attracted to Eliza. Kane knew that now. But that attraction was no longer anywhere near the "deep down" area. It was right there, burning him alive.

Kane was extremely thankful that there wasn't any traffic on the farm road that led from Eliza's house to his. Also thankful that it was pretty much a straight line. Hard to turn corners when Eliza had moved on from kissing his neck to his chest. He wanted to tell her to stop and wait until they got in, but hell, he'd entered that urgency zone, too.

Somehow, Kane managed to pull into his driveway and bring the truck to a stop. He turned off the engine but didn't get out. That's because the fire was a frenzy now, and there was no way he'd be able to walk to the house. Not now that he was as hard as stone. Nope. The only way to fix this was to take hold of Eliza and kiss her exactly the way she'd been kissing him.

Everywhere.

Of course, he had to get control of her hands first because she was trying her damndest to unzip him. He wanted that, a few minutes from now, but first he had to get her in the house.

Or not.

Despite the kissing/wrestling match that was going on, he failed at the zipper mission. Eliza was able to pull it down and get her hand inside his boxers.

Oh, man.

Kane no longer cared about getting in the house. Nope. Sound reasoning vanished. He also knew Eliza was going to put a quick end to this if she continued with all that maddening touching she was doing.

He turned her, laying her back on the seat. She was wearing a loose cotton dress, and he shoved it up. No finesse. None. But they were past that point, because in addition to trying to give him a hand job, she was trying to get out of her panties. She banged her elbow against the dash. Cursed.

Then banged her arm against his face.

There'd be bruises, possibly even a concussion, since Kane did his own share of banging. And not of the sexual variety, either. He bashed his head against the steering wheel when he tried to take out a condom from his wallet.

By the time he finally managed that, Eliza's panties were off, and it was obvious she didn't want to wait another second. Neither did he, but in the back of his mind, Kane thought he might like to savor this a bit.

"We can take our time with the second round," Eliza murmured, making him wonder if he'd said that aloud or if they were just on the same page.

They were certainly on the same page when it came to the actual sex. Kane hadn't had sex in a vehicle since high school, and despite the logistics, he managed to get Eliza in just the right place so he could get the condom on and push inside her.

Hell, yeah. It was right.

Everything was suddenly right.

Kane couldn't think too much beyond the "fire hot" stage, but this seemed past the point of just plain pleasure. It was, well, special.

He didn't know how Eliza maneuvered her body like that, but she got her legs around him. Got him to pick up the pace that would almost certainly be the opposite of taking the time to savor it. Like their drive over, everything was frantic.

Kane went faster, harder, deeper.

He braced himself for the onslaught of the climax.

It came all right. He did. She did. And Kane knew he'd just made a huge mistake that he was sure to regret.

Well, he'd regret it later.

Right now Kane wanted to get Eliza inside for that second round.

IT WAS POSSIBLE that Eliza could no longer move any part of her body.

She was too slack to test that theory, though. The only thing she wanted to do right now was stay in Kane's bed, snuggled up against him. Exactly where she'd spent most of the night.

Well, most of the night excluding the time in the truck. And on the living-room sofa. They'd finally made it to the bed after midnight.

Like their kiss in the pub and on the porch, Eliza had fantasized about being with Kane this way. And now it had finally happened. Also like that kiss, the hype of this experience lived up to the fantasy.

Of course, in her fantasies Kane and she went on to live the perfect life while having lots more sex. And even though that would be jumping the gun to think they could actually have a future together, this was a start. Now that they knew they were good in bed—and in his truck—then maybe that "good" would extend to other areas.

That rosy outlook lasted just a short while before the doubts began to creep into her head. Kane probably had casual sex like this all the time. He might intend to keep having casual sex. And maybe that's what she wanted, as well.

As long as that casual sex was with her.

She winced even though she'd only thought that and

not said it aloud. It was a dumb thing to think. And, heck, she might not even want more than just this. Eliza was hanging on to that resolve until Kane shifted, pulled her even closer and dropped a kiss on her mouth.

Mercy, she was in so much trouble.

"What kind of trouble?" he asked.

The sound of Kane's voice jarred her. The realization of what she'd done did some jarring, as well. She'd actually said that trouble part aloud. Great. Now she would have to explain something she didn't want to explain.

"I'm just thinking," she settled for saying.

"Thinking too much," he mumbled back, and he checked the clock on the nightstand. "Especially thinking too much, since it's barely seven in the morning."

Good. He was going to let this slide. Or not. Just when she thought she was in the clear, he opened one eye, peeked out at her and then groaned softly when he touched his lips to her bunched-up forehead.

"Is this about Violet?" he asked.

Eliza was certain her forehead bunched up even more than it already had, because her sister was the last thing on her mind. "Uh, no. Should it be?"

He groaned, kissed her again and adjusted the pillow so that he was looking down at her. "No. But I thought it might bother you that I'd been with your sister. In fact, I wasn't sure you'd be able to get past that."

"Oh, I'm long past that." She paused. "Are you?"

No groan this time, just a long breath, and he gave the pillow another adjustment so that he was looking up at the ceiling. He tucked his hands behind his head. "I am. You shouldn't have to ask after what just happened."

That sounded…promising. For a few moments anyway. But Eliza could tell from Kane's next long breath that it wasn't going to be promising for long.

"I have no idea where this is going," he said. "Still don't. And that means this wasn't fair to you. I shouldn't have started this."

Good grief. That sounded like a goodbye. Eliza wanted to ask if he was about to dump her, but her throat didn't cooperate. Kane must have taken her silence as a cue for him to continue.

"I'm sorry for not thinking this through," he said. "But I'm not really sorry for what just happened between us." He paused. "Are you?"

She couldn't answer this fast enough. "Not a chance."

He gave her a lazy smile. A kiss. And she thought maybe the kiss had the potential to turn into another round of lovemaking. But the ringing sound stopped any chance of that. Or at least delayed it.

Kane fumbled around on the nightstand, located his phone, but he cursed when he looked at the screen. She cursed, too, when she saw the name of the caller.

Charlene.

He didn't take the call, and it went to voice mail. Kane played the message and put it on Speaker so that she could hear.

"Kane," Charlene said in her message. "Call me about those cows. I'm pretty sure we can work out a deal now."

He shrugged. "Guess she had a change of heart."

Maybe. But Eliza suddenly had a bad feeling about that. The bad feeling went up a notch when there was a knock at the door. It was a little too early for visitors.

"That'd better not be Charlene," Kane grumbled.

He threw back the covers, got up and started to dress.

Eliza did the same, but Kane finished ahead of her and went to the door. Whoever was visiting was persistent about the knocking, and the knocking got louder and louder with each passing second.

"How could you?" someone asked. And it was a voice that Eliza immediately recognized.

Violet.

Her sister repeated her question and then shifted her gaze to Eliza. "I remember everything you told me when I was drunk. You and Kane have been lying to me, to everyone, and it has to stop right now."

CHAPTER SIX

"HELL." AND SINCE Kane didn't know what else to say, he just repeated it a couple more times.

Violet was clearly upset, and judging from her red eyes, she'd been crying. The moment she stepped inside, fresh tears came, but even then she managed to give both Eliza and him a stern look.

"Why?" Violet asked. That question was for him. "Why would you even do something like this?" She directed that one to her sister.

Eliza shook her head, and Kane figured it wouldn't be long before she had tears in her eyes, too. "I thought... Well, I thought I was doing the right thing by lying to you," Eliza said. "I didn't want anything to get in the way of you being with Dax."

Violet threw her hands in the air. "And you thought telling me you were in love with Kane would help?"

Kane had figured the L word had been thrown around when Eliza had first told Violet about their budding relationship. Their fake budding relationship, that was. But he hadn't known that it could possibly be true. Eliza could be in love with him. Or maybe she thought that she was. He certainly hadn't helped matters in that department by spending the night with her.

"I'm sorry," Eliza said to Violet. "I honestly believed I was doing the right thing."

"Well, you weren't," Violet snapped. Her gaze slashed to Kane. "And how long have you known about the lies?"

"He didn't know," Eliza jumped to say.

She was obviously trying to defend him, but Kane wasn't going to let her take all of this on her shoulders. "I found out the day I got home. Eliza told me when we were at the pub."

That sent Violet's hands up in the air again. "And you didn't put a stop to it then and there?" But she didn't give him a chance to answer. "You should have told me. Not while I was drunk, either," she quickly added to Eliza.

Eliza gently took hold of her sister's arm and led her to the sofa. Judging from her stiff posture, the last thing Violet wanted to do was sit down, but she did when Eliza sat.

"Kane didn't have any part in this. Not before the fact," Eliza explained. "He wanted to tell the truth while you were at your bachelorette party, but I talked him out of it."

Again, she was defending him, and it was certainly something Kane didn't deserve. "I had plenty of chances to tell Dax that night, and I didn't," he admitted.

"Well, he knows now, and he's not any happier about this than I am," Violet informed them. "Neither are Mom and Dad."

Eliza groaned. "Mercy. They know?"

"Of course. I couldn't let them go on believing this sham of a relationship. Heck, I think Mom was ready to start picking out your china pattern. She believed it was serious between you two."

Kane didn't know if it was serious or not. In fact, he

wasn't sure where he stood with Eliza now that the cat was out of the bag. More to the point, he didn't know where he *wanted* to stand with her.

Obviously, Kane owed several people apologies. Eliza's parents, Dax, Violet and anyone else who was upset by this. One person who didn't fall into that upset category was Charlene, and Kane thought maybe now he knew the reason for Charlene's phone call.

"Just how many people did you tell about this?" Kane asked Violet.

"It's early, so not that many. But I did tell Dax's sister, Veronica."

Hell's Texas bells. It was all over town by now, and yes, Veronica would have definitely called Charlene. Heck, it was possible that every single person in Spring Hill already knew.

"Mom and Dad want to see you right away," Violet added to Eliza.

He could have sworn that the color bleached from Eliza's face. "Did Mom get really upset?"

Kane knew the reason for the color loss and Eliza's frantic tone. He doubted this would set back her recovery, but it wasn't a good thing for her mother to have an emotional upheaval.

"Mom's not any happier about this than I am," Violet answered. She glanced at Kane, then Eliza. Specifically, at their clothes.

Which were a little askew in places.

The right strap of Eliza's dress was dangling off her shoulder, and Kane realized his jeans were unzipped. He fixed that. Eliza smoothed her hand through her hair. Added to the fact that it was early morning and they were together, Violet must have put her anger aside long enough to figure out what had gone on.

Violet huffed. "This is all part of the sham," she declared. "You were going to show up home looking like this so Mom and Dad would think Kane and you were lovers."

Kane wasn't sure if he should confirm that Eliza and he had achieved the label of lovers. Not through a ruse, either. But through good old-fashioned sex. But it didn't feel right coming from him, and if Eliza planned on saying anything, she didn't get a chance to do that before Violet continued.

"Well, a fake night with Kane won't work because Mom and Dad know." Violet stood. "Let's go."

Violet didn't wait for Eliza to agree before she headed for the door. Eliza followed her but looked back at Kane.

"I'll call you as soon as I've talked to my parents," Eliza said.

Kane hated to try to guess what she was thinking, but there was enough doom and gloom in her voice for him to know that she was dreading this. Maybe even regretting it. Not just the lies that'd started this, but regretting, too, that the lies had led to sex.

Just when Kane thought his morning couldn't get any worse, Violet threw open the door, and he spotted a visitor walking up the steps of his porch.

Charlene.

"I heard," she said. Barracudas didn't smile, but if they did, it would be the very smile that Charlene flashed him. She dismissed Eliza and Violet with a cool glance.

"It's early for a visit," Kane pointed out.

"Yes. Good thing they're leaving." She spared another glance at Eliza and Violet as they got into Violet's car.

Before Kane could point out that he'd meant that comment for her, Charlene hooked her arm around his waist.

"Come on," Charlene said. "Let's iron out the final details on the sale of those cows."

COWS. SPECIFICALLY, HOLSTEINS, the black-and-white ones. That's what Eliza was seeing now as she looked in the mirror.

Violet probably hadn't been thinking about Holsteins when she'd chosen the maid of honor's and bridesmaid's dresses. Black with white sashes that were clumps of satin swirls meant to resemble flowers. The clumps flowed down the front and back of the dress, giving the appearance of random spots. Added to that were the white gardenia corsages pinned just above the left breast.

Misty Reagan, the bridesmaid, stood next to Eliza as they eyed themselves in the full-length mirror of the dressing room at the church. "Is it my imagination," Misty said, "or do we look like two strays from Bill McClemore's herd?"

"It's your imagination," Eliza lied. But she figured it wouldn't be long before someone confirmed Misty's observation. Maybe even Bill McClemore himself, since he did indeed raise Holsteins.

Misty frowned, adjusted the satin clumps. It didn't help, and her gaze met Eliza's in the mirror.

"Oh, honey." She pulled Eliza into her arms for a hug that was no doubt squishing the spots. "I'm so sorry."

Eliza realized she must have looked pretty down to

generate that kind of response from Misty. It was hard to keep a smile on her face after what'd happened between Kane and her the day before. Also, hard to smile when she was about to walk out in front of everyone in town.

Everyone who knew she was a liar.

This story was certainly the juiciest morsel of gossip this town had heard in a long time. The dresses might help with that, though. Certainly, they were ugly enough to generate some kind of buzz.

"Is, uh, Kane coming?" Misty asked.

Eliza cleared her throat, tried to sound stronger than she felt. "No. He thought it would be best if he stayed away, just so the focus would be on Dax and Violet."

At least that's what he'd said when Eliza had called him after the chat she'd had with her folks yesterday. Eliza had made the same offer to Violet, suggesting that she stay away as well, but her sister would have no part of that. It was just something they would have to put behind them.

Since Brett and Dax were friends, Brett would almost certainly be at the wedding, perhaps hoping for a reconciliation with Eliza that stood no chance of happening. Even if she didn't have a future with Kane, she wasn't going back to a man she was certain she could never love. Of course, every man but Kane fell into that category.

"Oh, honey," Misty repeated, and she gave Eliza another hug. She whipped out a Kleenex from her bra. "Don't cry or your mascara will run. Besides, nobody will say anything mean to you. Not to your face, anyway."

She was right. The gossip would go on behind hands,

but Eliza knew what everyone had to be thinking. They wouldn't see this as her attempt to clear her sister's path to happiness. She would just look pathetic in their eyes.

"Plus, it's possible Kane isn't staying away just because this would be a sticky situation. His cows are being delivered today, so I'm sure he's busy with that."

Eliza hadn't heard about the cow delivery. But then she'd avoided just about everyone, so she was out of the immediate gossip loop.

"He got the cows from Charlene?" Eliza asked.

Misty wasn't a fool, and she no doubt quickly connected the dots. "I think so, but don't read anything into that. Maybe Kane just made her a good offer."

Yeah, or else Charlene now believed that Kane was hers for the taking. Kane wouldn't go along with that. At least, Eliza didn't think he would, but maybe being part of the lying scandal had sent him into another woman's arms.

Charlene's arms would have been open and waiting.

There was a light knock at the door, and just like that, Eliza's heart went into overdrive. Maybe Kane had come after all… But it was her mother. Not that she didn't want to see her. She did. But it was still a little hard for Eliza to face her.

"I'm going to run to the little girls' room," Misty said. She must have sensed that Eliza's mother wanted a moment alone with her. Since the bathroom was just one wall away, though, she'd likely be able to hear everything, anyway.

Her mother smiled as if Eliza were a vision instead of a pathetic liar in a cow dress. "You look beautiful. Well, except for those eyes. You haven't been crying, have you?"

"Happy tears." It was another lie. Sheez. They were just rolling off her tongue these days.

"Good. I'm glad you're happy." She put her hands on Eliza's shoulders. "But I wanted you to know that you don't have to be happy with Brett."

No lie needed here. "I won't be. It doesn't matter how many things Violet invites him to, I won't be getting back together with him."

"I see." She paused. "And what about Kane?"

Since they probably only had a couple of minutes before the ceremony started, Eliza considered another quick lie. One to assure her mother that all would be well with or without Kane. But that lie wasn't rolling off her tongue. It was just sort of stuck there in her throat.

"I know," her mother whispered. She brushed a kiss on her cheek. "I recognize the signs of a woman in love. But then you've always been a little in love with Kane, haven't you?"

"Always," she admitted. "And it's always been more than just a little."

Her mother nodded. "That's the way I was with your father."

Yes, Eliza had heard all about love at first sight; her parents had been in the fourth grade. The love had stayed strong for all these thirty-five years.

"But you never had to let people believe you were in a fake relationship," Eliza reminded her. "A relationship that turned real. For one night, anyway. I upset Dad and you—"

"You surprised us," her mother interrupted. "That's all. You don't have to walk on eggshells around me, Eliza. And you don't have to shelter me from anything.

I really am doing better, and none of this affected me as much as you seem to think it has."

Eliza searched her mom's eyes to make sure that wasn't BS. It wasn't. That was something at least. "You certainly seemed…affected yesterday morning when I got home from Kane's."

"I was upset because Violet was upset, but it didn't last. As you see."

Yes, she could see. And Eliza couldn't blame her folks for being shocked that she would do something like that. She'd shocked Kane, too. And herself.

Her mother dropped another kiss on her cheek and checked the time. "I want to look in on your sister before we all walk down the aisle. Misty, you can come on out, since it's time for Eliza and you to get in your places, anyway." Her mother winked because she hadn't raised her voice at all, but Misty had clearly heard her. She practically bolted out of the bathroom.

"Those dresses are certainly interesting," her mother muttered before she left.

Misty frowned, made another attempt to fix the dress. Eliza didn't bother to tell her that it wasn't fix-able. This was just one of those garments that a brides-maid had to endure.

"It's time for us to start lining up," Misty said, glancing up at the wall clock.

Yep. Eliza dug down deep, searching for some steel and resolve. She didn't find much because she was al-ready tapped out, but she wouldn't let her sister down.

With Misty leading the way, they went into the cor-ridor they would use to enter the church. The double doors leading down the aisle were closed, but from the glass windows on top, Eliza got a peek at the guests.

With the exception of the ones reserved for her parents in the front row, there wasn't an empty seat in the place.

The groomsmen came up the hall. Dax's brother, Patrick, and his cousin Jake. An usher, Paul, who was another cousin, was there as well, waiting to accompany her mother since her father would be walking Violet down the aisle. The three dodged her gaze, which meant they didn't know what to say about all the gossip that was floating around. Good. She preferred the silence.

The door to the bride's dressing room was still closed, and since her parents weren't in the hall yet, that meant they were still inside with Violet. Eliza considered popping in there as well, but before she could play around with that idea, the main doors to the church flew open.

And in walked Kane.

Eliza's heart did a little flip-flop. Until she saw his expression. His face was rock hard, and if anyone had doubted he was a cowboy, there was no way to doubt it now. His jeans were worn and snug in all the right places. Ditto for his blue shirt. He pulled off his black cowboy hat when he spotted her and strode toward her, his boots thudding on the wooden floor.

"Uh, you're not here to try to stop the wedding, are you?" Patrick asked.

Kane frowned as if that were an insult. "No. I'm here to set some things straight."

That sounded a little unsettling because maybe he was there to let everyone know his side of the lie pact. But if he planned on saying anything else, he didn't do it. Kane went to her, hauled her into his arms and kissed her.

He smelled like cows.

But beneath that, she caught Kane's own scent, too. A scent that stirred every part of her body. Just the way she liked her parts to feel.

Oh, the kiss was so dreamy, and like his scent, it created a flurry of emotions inside her. Heat, yes. Most of all, though, Eliza felt relief. Kane was there, kissing her, and everything was right with the world.

"Is that part of the fake stuff?" Patrick again. "Because we know the two of you were lying about being together."

Kane ignored that and just kept on kissing her as if trying to convince her of something. But she didn't need convincing of anything right now.

Or maybe she did.

She pulled back, met his gaze and tried to figure out if this was some kind of test on his part. Maybe he was trying to figure out if the attraction was real.

It was.

Because he went back in for another kiss. One that caused her knees to give way. Good thing Kane's arm was around her waist or else she would have slid straight to the floor like a tipped-over cow. He didn't stop this second kiss until Violet and her parents came out into the hall. Judging from the way Violet's mouth dropped open, she was surprised at the display of affection. Her mother, not so much. Eliza and she shared a smile. Her father scowled. It was a mandatory reaction, since it probably wasn't fun for him to see any man kissing his baby girl.

"What's going on here?" her father growled.

Eliza opened her mouth to answer, but Kane beat

her to it. "It's true. This all started out as a lie, but it's damn sure not a lie now."

"Don't curse in the church," her mother scolded, but she was still fighting back a smile.

"Sorry," Kane quickly said. "But I hope you heard the part about this not being a lie." He turned to her. "It's not a lie, is it?"

"No." Eliza answered as fast as she could, and she shook her head so there'd be no misunderstanding.

The doors behind them opened, and that's when Eliza realized Kane and she had more of an audience than just the wedding party and her folks. Most of the guests had left their seats and were right there, listening. Good. It meant she could clear this up once and for all.

She pulled Kane back to her. "Everything I feel for you is the real deal."

He smiled. First a happy smile, but it turned a little naughty. It was a naughtiness she recognized, since she'd been on the receiving end of it during their marathon night of sex. He clearly wanted a repeat of that night. And he would get it, after the wedding.

"Yeah, definitely the real deal," he agreed. "I'm thinking this could be the start of something…" His gaze drifted down to her face. Then to her dress. "…really, really interesting."

Eliza had no trouble agreeing to that, either. And it didn't have anything to do with the fact that she was dressed like a cow or that Kane smelled like one.

"Are you staying for the wedding?" Violet asked at the same moment her father asked, "Kane, exactly what are your intentions with my daughter?"

Kane smiled again. "Yes," he said to Violet before

looking at her father. "And as for my intentions, well, they're the best kind when it comes to Eliza."

Eliza figured that meant she was in for all sorts of good things ahead, and she got a sneak peek at one of those things when Kane hauled her back to him and kissed her.

* * * * *

Don't miss LANDON, part of USA TODAY bestselling author Delores Fossen's miniseries THE LAWMEN OF SILVER CREEK RANCH, *when it goes on sale from Harlequin Intrigue next month. And be sure to look for her brand-new HQN Books trilogy,* A WRANGLER'S CREEK NOVEL, *coming in 2017!*

  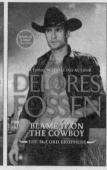

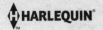

HARLEQUIN®

INTRIGUE
EDGE-OF-YOUR-SEAT INTRIGUE, FEARLESS ROMANCE.

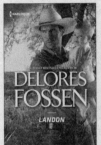

Save $1.00
on the purchase of
LANDON
by *USA TODAY* bestselling author
DELORES FOSSEN,
available October 18, 2016,
or on any other Harlequin® Intrigue book.

Available wherever books are sold, including most bookstores, supermarkets, drugstores and discount stores.

- ✂

Save $1.00
on the purchase of any Harlequin Intrigue book.

Coupon valid until January 31, 2017. Redeemable at participating outlets in the U.S. and Canada only. Not redeemable at Barnes & Noble stores.
Limit one coupon per customer.

52614239

5 65373 00076 2   (8100)0 12214

® and ™ are trademarks owned and used by the trademark owner and/or its licensee.

© 2016 Harlequin Enterprises Limited

HICOUP01016

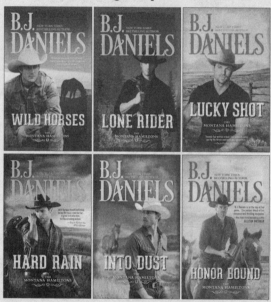